THE LILAC BUS

Also published in Large Print
from G. K. Hall by Maeve Binchy:

Circle of Friends
Firefly Summer
Echoes
Light a Penny Candle

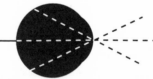

**This Large Print Book carries the
Seal of Approval of N.A.V.H.**

THE LILAC BUS: STORIES

Maeve Binchy

WITHDRAWN

G.K.HALL &CO.
Boston, Massachusetts
1992

Published in Large Print by arrangement with
Delacorte Press.

Dublin 4 was first published in Ireland by Ward River Press; and
in Great Britain in 1983 by Century Hutchinson Ltd.
The Lilac Bus was first published in 1984 in Ireland by Ward
River Press; and in Great Britain in 1986 by Century Hutchinson Ltd.

G. K. Hall Large Print Book Series.

Printed on acid free paper in the United States of America.

Set in 16 pt. Plantin.

Library of Congress Cataloging-in-Publication Data

Binchy, Maeve.
  The lilac bus : stories / Maeve Binchy.
     p. cm. — (G.K. Hall large print book series)
    ISBN 0-8161-5383-3 (alk. paper). — ISBN 0-8161-5384-1
  (pbk. : alk. paper)
    1. Large type books. I. Title.
  [PR6052.I7728L6 1992]
  823'.914—dc20   92-17122

For my dear Gordon, with all my love

CONTENTS

THE LILAC BUS

DUBLIN 4

THE LILAC BUS

NANCY

Nancy was early, but then she always was, and she didn't like being seen there too soon. It looked as if you had nothing else to do if you arrived far too early for the bus home. The others all arrived rushing and panting and afraid they'd miss it, because if they missed it then they really did. Tom turned the key in the ignition at 6:45 and swung the Lilac Bus out into the road. That way he had them all home before ten o'clock and that was his promise. No point in going home for a weekend if you aren't in the pub by ten, that was his philosophy. It wasn't Nancy's, but she was compulsively early for everything. It was just her way. She went into a shop that sold magazines and cards. She knew a lot of the cards by heart from studying them on a Friday. There was the big one with tears falling down it: "Sorry I missed your birthday." They had the country papers in this shop, too, but Nancy never bought one. There'd be a paper at home and she could catch up on everything then.

She examined her new perm in the big round mirror that was not meant so much as a mirror as a deterrent to shoplifting. It was set high on the wall and at a funny angle, or she hoped it was.

3

Otherwise the perm looked very odd indeed. She stared up at her reflection anxiously. Surely she didn't look like some small worried animal with fuzzy hair and huge terrified eyes. That's what she saw in the mirror, but of course that's not what people down at her own level would see? After all, everyone looked silly from this point of view. She patted her head and had another pang about the perm. It looked to her dangerously like those old-fashioned perms that people like her mother got in Rathdoon. The summer perm and the Christmas perm. Frizz, fuzz . . . tight curls growing out into what looked like flashes of lightning or electric shocks as the weeks went by. The girls in the salon assured her that she was mad to think this. She had got a modern perm, one of the newest on the market. Think what she'd have paid if she had to pay for it! Nancy had smiled grimly. Paid for it! At that price! Nancy Morris wouldn't have paid half that price or a quarter of that price for a perm. Nancy Morris had crossed Dublin to go to a salon where she heard they needed people to practice on. *Models* was the expression, but Nancy was more realistic. They needed heads with hair and smart people like Nancy found out which were the big salons with lots of trainees and on what nights their classes and demonstrations were. She had only paid for two visits to a hairdresser since she came to Dublin six years ago. That wasn't bad going, she smiled proudly. Still, it was done now, this perm, no point in peering up at herself and worrying. Better go across and

4

get on the bus. Surely some of the others would be there by now, and it was well after half-past six.

Tom was sitting there reading an evening paper. He looked up and smiled. "Evening, Miss Mouse," he said pleasantly and lifted her big suitcase up onto the roof rack with one easy movement. She got in crossly. She *hated* him calling her Miss Mouse, but it was her own fault. When she had rung to ask for a place in his minibus she had given her name as Miss Morris. Well, she was used to being formal on the phone—that was what her job was about, for heaven's sake. How was she to know that she should have said her first name and that he genuinely misheard the Morris bit. But it was very galling that he still refused to call her Nancy, even though he always called old Mrs. Hickey Judy and she could have been his mother.

"It's light for such a big case," he said pleasantly. Nancy just nodded. She didn't feel like telling him it was her only suitcase and she had no intention of going out and spending over a fiver on some kind of nylon holdall like the others had. And anyway she needed a big case: there were always things to take back to Dublin, like potatoes and whatever vegetables there were, and anything else that turned up. There was the time that her mother's friend, Mrs. Casey, was getting rid of her curtains: Nancy brought them back and they were lovely in the flat.

She sat down in one of the middle seats,

5

straightened her skirt under her so that it wouldn't crease and took out her glucose sweets. They had jars of them in the hospital, and they always told her to help herself. She didn't eat them normally but it was nice on a bus journey to have something; the others often bought barley sugar or toffees, but what was the point of spending money on sweets when they were there for the asking? She unfolded a newspaper that one of the patients had left behind in the waiting room. She got a lot of her reading material this way—people waiting for the specialists were inclined to be forgetful about papers and magazines, and there was rarely an evening she didn't have something to read. And it was nice to have a variety, she told herself. It was like a surprise. Mairead didn't understand. Nancy's brow darkened when she thought of Mairead. All that had to be sorted out. It had been so unexpected and so unfair.

She held up the newspaper so that Tom would think she was reading and she went over it all again. Mairead coming in on Wednesday and walking around restlessly picking things up and putting them down. You didn't have to be a genius to know there was something on her mind. Nancy thought she was going to ask about the television again. They had a perfectly good black and white set, which was a bit snowstormish now and then but usually got a terrific reception. What on earth was the point of paying out a fortune renting a color set? And even a video: Mairead had once mentioned this as if they were some kind of

6

millionaires. She had looked up from the telly, which was admittedly having one of its bad nights and you had to guess a lot from the soundtrack; but Mairead had wanted to talk about something much bigger.

"I've been thinking all week at work how to say this, Nancy, and I can't think of any proper way, so I'll just say it straight out. I want to share the flat with someone else, and I am going to have to ask you to leave. In your own time, of course, I'm not throwing you out on the road . . ." She had given a little nervous laugh, but Nancy had been too astounded to join in. "You see," Mairead had gone on, "it was never permanent. It was just to see what we thought. . . . That was the arrangement. That was what we said. . . ." Her voice had trailed away guiltily.

"But we've been sharing for three years," Nancy said.

"I know," Mairead said miserably.

"So why? Don't I pay the rent in time always and the electricity? And I contribute to the food from home and I got curtains for the hall windows and—"

"Of course, Nancy, nobody's saying you didn't."

"So why?"

"It's just . . . no, there's no reason, can't we do it nice and easily now, without quarrels and questions? Can't you just find another place and we'll still meet now and then, go to the pictures, you come over here one evening, me go to your place?

7

Come on, Nancy, that's the grown-up way to do things."

Nancy had burned with rage. Mairead, who worked in a flower shop, telling her what was the grown-up way to do things. Mairead, who hadn't got one honor in her Leaving Certificate, ordering Nancy out of her flat. *Her* flat. True, she had found it, and when she needed someone to share the rent her aunt, Mrs. Casey, the friend of Nancy's mother, had suggested Nancy. Where had Mairead got these notions and more important, why? Who did she want to share with?

The worst thing was that Mairead didn't seem to know or care, she just said she would like a change. At this point Nancy had turned off the flickering telly and had settled in for what she thought was going to be a heart-to-heart where Mairead would tell her all about some star-crossed love. But no. Mairead was busy looking at the calendar. Would we say just over a month, like the middle of October? That would surely give her time to find somewhere.

"But who will I share with?" Nancy had wailed.

Mairead had shrugged. She didn't know, maybe Nancy could get a bed-sit on her own. She didn't do much cooking or entertaining, a bed-sit might be just as good. But they cost a *fortune!* Mairead had shrugged again as if it didn't concern her.

The following morning Nancy was having her tea in the kitchen—she never bothered with a breakfast since there was always food in the hospital, and what was the point of being a receptionist for all these doctors unless you got some perks like a canteen and glucose sweets? Mairead rushed in late as usual and Nancy asked her had she forgiven her.

"Forgive you, Nancy? What for? What in heaven's name for?"

"Well, I must have done something, otherwise you wouldn't be asking me to leave our flat."

"It's *my* flat and don't be such a clown. We're not married to each other, Nancy. You came in here to share my rent, now that bit's over. Right? Yes. That's all there is to it." She was gulping down a bowl of cornflakes and trying to pull on her boots at the same time. Mairead loved these boots; they horrified Nancy—they had cost a week's salary. For a pair of boots.

"What'll I tell them in Rathdoon?" Nancy asked solemnly. Mairead was startled.

"About what?" she had asked, bewildered.

"About us breaking up?"

"Who would want to know? Who even knows we share a flat?"

"Everyone: your mother, my mother, your aunt—Mrs. Casey—everyone."

"Well, what do you mean what will you tell them?" Mairead was genuinely surprised.

"But your mother, what will she think? What will I tell her?"

Mairead had lost her temper suddenly. Nancy still felt a shock just thinking about it.

"My mother is a normal woman; she's like everyone else's mother, including your mother. She

9

doesn't think anything. She wants to know that I'm not pregnant and I'm not on drugs and I'm still going to Mass. That's all any mother wants to know in the name of God, those same three things. In India mothers want to know that or Russia or wherever, and it may not be Mass for them but it's something. People's mothers don't give two flying damns about their daughters sharing flats with people and whether they get on well or whether, as in our case, they drive each other up the wall. They just want to be told the essentials."

"We don't drive each other up the wall," Nancy had said quietly.

"No, well, irritate each other. What's the difference? Why bother your head explaining and telling and reporting back? People aren't bloody interested."

"Do I irritate you?"

"Yes."

"How?"

"Oh Nancy, *please.*" Mairead was stricken. "We agreed last night to be grown up and not to have pointless rows and recriminations. We agreed. Now look what you're starting. Of course people irritate each other. I probably drive you mad. Listen, I must go."

Nancy had a terrible day: she had looked at the prices of flats and bed-sitters and they were sky-high. The further out you went they came down a bit, of course, but she had to be within cycling distance of the hospital. There was no way she

10

was going to spend her hard-earned money on bus fares. She had thought, too, about what Mairead had said. She couldn't think why she was irritating. She didn't smoke, she never invited rowdy people in like Mairead often did, people who brought a bottle of wine each and then went out for chicken and chips. She didn't play records loud—she didn't have any records. She did everything to help. Often she cut special offers out of the paper and collected vouchers for foods or detergents. She suggested often to Mairead that it would be cheaper to come home every weekend to Rathdoon, because people spend a fortune at weekends in Dublin and you could live free at home. How had she been so irritating?

Even this very morning she had asked Mairead if it was definite, and Mairead had nodded wordlessly. Nancy had offered to let Mairead have the weekend to consider her decision, but in a low, soft voice, unlike her harangue of the previous morning, Mairead had said there would be no considering and she realized that Nancy would be cooperative and start looking for another place straightaway.

She looked up at the sound of voices. Dee Burke had arrived; she wore her college scarf even though she had left UCD two years previously, and she carried a canvas grip, which she threw up on the roof herself. Tom was laughing at her.

"You'll be a discus champion yet," he said.

"No, it's to show you that women are genuinely

11

liberated, that's all—besides, there's nothing in it except a couple of pairs of knickers and some law books I'm meant to be studying."

Nancy was amazed that Dee, who was Dr. Burke's daughter and lived in a big house covered with creeper, could talk about knickers to Tom Fitzgerald in such a relaxed way. It didn't even sound rude the way she said it. Dee was a law unto herself, though, and always had been. You'd think she'd have her own car, but she said that she wasn't earning much as a solicitor's apprentice. Still, Nancy would have thought that this minibus would have been beneath the Burkes. They were people of such standing in Rathdoon, they must find it strange that their daughter traveled with anyone and everyone. Dee never seemed to notice. She was friendly with everyone; with that tinker of a fellow, Kev Kennedy, that you'd try to cross the road to avoid; with desperate Mikey Burns and his dirty jokes. Dee was specially nice to Nancy; she came and sat beside her and asked, as she often did, about Nancy's work.

It was quite extraordinary the way Dee remembered the names of the doctors she worked for, and knew that one was an eye specialist, one an orthopedic surgeon and one an ear, nose, and throat man. She knew there was Mr. Barry and Mr. White and Mr. Charles. Even Nancy's mother wouldn't know that, and as for Mairead, she could hardly remember the names of her own bosses, let alone Nancy's.

But then Dee was nice and she had great breed-

12

ing. People like that were courteous, Nancy always thought, and they had the manners to be interested in other people.

Rupert Green arrived next. He was wearing a very smart jacket.

"Merciful God, Rupert, is that Italian? Is that the real thing?" Dee asked, feeling the sleeve as Rupert got in.

"Yes, it is actually." Rupert's pale face flushed with pleasure. "How did you know?"

"Aren't I worn out looking at them in magazines? It's gorgeous."

"Yes, it's a second, or a discontinued line or something, but a friend got it for me anyway." Rupert was very pleased that it had caused such a stir.

"Well, they'd need to be a second or something, otherwise your father would have to sell his practice to buy it," Dee laughed. Rupert's father was the solicitor, and it was through Mr. Green she had got her apprenticeship in Dublin. Nancy looked at them enviously. It must be great to have such an easy way of going on. It was like a kind of shorthand in professional families, she noticed, they could all talk to each other at the drop of a hat. She felt a twinge of annoyance that her father, long dead, had been a postman and not a lawyer. The annoyance was followed by a stronger twinge of guilt. Her father had worked long and hard and had been pleased to see them all do well at their books and get secretarial or clerical jobs.

Rupert went to the back seat and almost on cue

Mrs. Hickey arrived. Suntanned even in winter, she looked healthy and strong and as if she might be any age. Nancy knew she must be in her late fifties, but that was only by questioning people and piecing it all together. Judy Hickey worked in some kind of mad place that sold herbal cures and grain and nuts, and she even grew some of the things herself, which was why she came home every weekend to harvest them and bring them back to this shop in Dublin. Nancy had never been to the shop; Dee told her it was marvelous, that everyone should go and see it just for the experience of it, but Nancy took her position as receptionist to three of Dublin's leading consultants very seriously. It wouldn't do for her to be seen going in and out of some quack's shop, would it?

Judy went to sit beside Rupert in the back and Mikey Burns had begun to squeeze himself into the front seat. Laughing and rubbing his hands, he told them a joke about hairy tennis balls. Everyone smiled and Mikey seemed to be able to settle down now that he had told at least one dirty story. He looked out eagerly.

"Will I be lucky and get the beautiful Celia beside me or do I get Mr. Kennedy? Oh dear, just your luck Mikey, here comes Mr. Kennedy."

Kev sneaked into the bus looking over his shoulder as if he expected a guard to lay a hand on him and say "Just a minute," like they do in films. Nancy thought she had never seen anyone who looked so furtive. If you spoke to Kev Ken-

14

nedy he jumped a foot in the air, and he never said much in reply, so he wasn't spoken to much.

Lastly, Celia came. Big and sort of handsome in a way, though Nancy didn't admire those kind of looks. She often wore tight belts; as she wore them when she was nursing, she had probably got used to them. They made her figure very obvious. Not sexy, but it certainly divided it for all to see: a jutting-out top half in front and a big jutting-out bottom half at the back. Nancy would have thought she might have been wiser to wear something more floppy.

Celia sat in beside Tom: the last person always sat beside the driver. It was only twenty to seven and they set off with five minutes in hand.

"I have you very well trained," Tom laughed as he nosed the minibus out into the Friday evening traffic.

"Indeed you have. No wee-wees until we're across the Shannon," said Mikey, looking around for approval, and since he didn't hear any he said it again. This time a few people smiled back at him.

Nancy told Dee all about Mr. Charles and Mr. White and Mr. Barry and how they saw their private patients on certain days of the week and how she kept their appointment books and shuffled people around and how patients were often very grateful to her and gave her little presents at Christmas. Dee wanted to know were they well thought of, the doctors, and whether people

15

praised them. Nancy tried to dredge examples but couldn't. She was more on the administrative side, she kept insisting. Dee wanted to know whether she met them socially, and Nancy had laughed to think such a thing was possible. That was the joy of being a doctor's daughter, you didn't think class distinctions existed anymore. No, of course she didn't get involved in their home lives. Mr. Barry had a Canadian wife and two children, Mr. White's wife was a teacher and they had four children, and Mr. Charles and his wife had no children. Yes, she sometimes spoke to their wives on the phone; they all seemed very nice, they all remembered her name. "Hallo Miss Morris," they would say.

Dee fell asleep when Nancy was explaining about the hospital switchboard, which was very awkward, and how they had been looking for a separate switchboard for the consultants for ages, but maybe things would get better with the new set-up in the phone headquarters. Nancy was a bit embarrassed at that. Maybe she had been rabbiting on, possibly she did irritate people by talking too much about little things; sometimes her own mother got up and went to bed in the middle of one of their conversations. Mairead might be right. But no, that couldn't be, Dee had been positively pressing her for details of her working life, she had asked question after question. No, Nancy couldn't blame herself for being boring. Not this time. She sighed and looked at the fields flying by.

Soon she nodded off too. Behind her Judy Hickey and Rupert Green were talking about someone they knew who had gone to an ashram in India and everyone had to wear yellow or saffron. In front of her Kev Kennedy was half-listening as Mikey Burns explained a card trick with a glass of water. Mikey said that it was better if you saw it done but you could still grasp the point if you concentrated.

In front of them Tom was saying something to Celia; she was nodding and agreeing with it, whatever it was. It was very comfortable and warm, and even if she did lean over a bit in sleep and slump on top of Dee, well, it didn't matter. She wouldn't have let herself doze if she were beside one of the men. Or indeed beside Judy Hickey: there was something very odd about her.

Nancy was asleep.

Her mother was still at the kitchen table when she got in. She was writing a letter to her daughter in America.

"There you are," she said.

"All in one piece," said Nancy.

It wasn't much of a greeting between mother and daughter, when the whole country had been crossed. But they had never been a demonstrative family. No hugging and kissing, no linking arms.

"How was the journey?" her mother asked.

"Oh, the same. I had a bit of a sleep, so I have a crick in my neck." Nancy rubbed it thoughtfully.

"It's great to be able to sleep on that road, with maniacs screeching past you in all directions."

"Oh, it's not that bad." Nancy looked around. "Well, what's been happening?"

Her mother was poor at handing out news. Nancy would have liked her to get up, wet a pot of tea and come back full of detail and information. She wanted to hear the week's events and who had been home, who had been heard from, who had revealed what. But somehow it was never like that.

"Whatever happens? Nothing's been happening—weren't you here until Sunday night?" Her mother went back to the letter, sighing, "Do you never write to Deirdre at all? Wouldn't it be a Christian thing to write to your own sister in America and tell her what's going on? She loves to hear little things, you know."

"So do I, but you can never remember anything to tell me!" Nancy cried in complaint.

"Ah, will you stop that nonsense? Aren't you here the whole time? You only go up to Dublin for a couple of days in the week. Poor Deirdre's on the other side of the Atlantic Ocean."

"Poor Deirdre has a husband and three children and a freezer and an icebox and a sprinkler in her garden. Poor Deirdre indeed."

"Couldn't you have all that yourself if you wanted to? Stop grudging things to your sister. Have some bit of niceness in you."

"I've plenty of niceness." Nancy felt her lip tremble.

18

"Well, stop giving out about Deirdre then, and go on, take a sheet of paper and put it in with mine. It'll save you getting a stamp and everything."

Her mother shoved a writing pad across the table. Nancy hadn't even sat down yet. The big suitcase with the hard corners was in the middle of the floor. She felt this was a shabby welcome home, but she was also a practical person. If she scribbled off a page to Deirdre now, well, it would save her having to do it some other time, and it would please her mother, who might go and bring out some soda bread and apple tart if she was in a good humor. Nancy wrote a few lines hoping that Deirdre and Sean and Shane and April and Erin were all well, and saying she'd love to come over and see them all but the fares were desperate and it was much easier for them to come over this way because of the pound and the dollar. She told Deirdre about Mr. White's new car, and Mr. Charles going to Russia on his holidays and Mr. Barry's wife having a new handbag that was made from the skin of a baby crocodile and had cost what you wouldn't believe. She added that it was nice to get back to Rathdoon at weekends because . . . She paused at this point. It was nice to get back to Rathdoon because . . . She looked at her mother sitting at the table, frowning over the letter writing. No, that wasn't why she came home. Her mother was only mildly pleased, and if she weren't here there was the television or Mrs. Casey or the bingo or half a dozen other things. Sometimes on

19

the long summer evenings, Nancy had come home and found the house empty and her mother out at ten o'clock. She didn't come home for the dance like Celia did, or Kev or Mikey on the bus. She had not got what you'd call friends in Rathdoon.

She finished the letter, "It's nice to get back at the weekends because the Lilac Bus is really very good value and you'd spend a small fortune in Dublin over the weekend without even noticing it."

Her mother was packing up for bed. No tea, no apple tart.

"I think I'll just make myself a sandwich," Nancy said.

"Did you have no tea? Aren't you very disorganized for a high-up receptionist?" said her mother, who went to bed without a word of goodnight.

It was a bright sunny September Saturday. The tourists were mainly gone, but there were always a few golfers around. Nancy wandered up the street with no plan. She could have bought a newspaper and gone to the hotel to have coffee, but apart from the money altogether she wouldn't do that. It was being uppity going in there sitting as if you were the type. No. She saw Celia's mother washing the step of the pub. She looked older, her face was lined like that Gypsy-looking Judy Hickey's. She called out a greeting, but Celia's mother didn't hear, she kept scrubbing.

20

Nancy wondered was Celia still in bed or was she helping to clean up inside. Celia worked weekends in the pub, that's why she came home. Her mother must have made it worth her while, because it was a hard job to stand on your feet all weekend there after having stood on your feet as a nurse all week. But you'd never know the time of day with Celia, she was so tight with information or anything at all. It was odd to see her talking away to Tom on the bus last night; usually she looked out the window with a moon face. Not like Dee, who was so full of life and so interested in everything. Nancy often wished that things were different, and that she could call on Dee at the weekend, or go off somewhere with her. But she wouldn't dream of going up to the Burkes. Not in a million years would she call on the house. The surgery was a different matter, that was the way things were.

She passed Judy Hickey's cottage and saw signs of great activity out in the back. Big packing boxes were laid all around, and Judy was wearing old trousers and had her hair tied up in a scarf. The house itself was shabby and needed a coat of paint but the garden was immaculate. It was odd that so many people watered and weeded and kept the birds off for Mrs. Hickey, Nancy thought; she wasn't the kind of woman that you'd think people would like at all. She only went to Mass one Sunday in four, if that. She never spoke of her husband and children. They had gone away years ago when the young lad was only a baby; Nancy could hardly remember the time there were children in that house. Anyway, up and away with the father and the two children and not a word out of the mother. She never got the court to give them back to her; people had said there must be some fine secrets there that they didn't want to come out, otherwise she would surely have gone to law. And for years her working in this shop, which sold things gurus used out in the East and things that must be disapproved of, ginseng and all that. Still, Judy Hickey seemed to have more friends than a few. Even now there were two of Kev Kennedy's brothers helping her, and last week Mikey Burns was there with his shovel. Young Rupert would probably have been in the team, but his father was very sick and that's why he had been coming home every weekend.

Nancy sighed and passed on. A half-thought that she might help, too, had come in one side of her mind but flashed quickly out the other. Why should she dig and get dirty in Judy Hickey's garden for nothing? She had better things to do. When she got back home and there was a note on the kitchen table, she wondered what better things she meant. Her mother had scribbled that Mrs. Casey had called to take her for a spin. Mrs. Casey had learned to drive late in life and had a dangerous-looking old car, which was the joy of her heart. It had brightened life for many people, including Nancy's mother; indeed there was talk of a few of them coming the whole way to Dublin in it. The plan had been that Mrs. Casey

22

and Mrs. Morris would stay at the flat. After all Mrs. Casey was Mairead's aunt. Now there would be no flat and no Mairead. Nancy's heart lurched at the memory of it all.

And nothing for the lunch and no mention of when the spin would be over, and nothing much in the press or in the little fridge, nothing you could eat. Nancy put on two potatoes to boil and went across to Kennedy's shop.

"Can I have two small rashers, please?"

"Two pounds is it?" Kev Kennedy's father didn't listen much to people: he was always listening to the radio in the shop.

"No, just two single ones."

"Huh," he said, picking two out and weighing them.

"You see, my mother hasn't done the shopping yet, so I don't know what she wants."

"You can't go far wrong on two slices of bacon," Mr. Kennedy agreed, morosely wrapping them in greaseproof paper and putting them in a bag. "She'll never accuse you of getting the family into debt over that."

She heard a laugh and to her annoyance noticed that Tom Fitzgerald was in the shop. For some reason she didn't like him hearing her being made fun of like that.

"Oh, Miss Mouse is a great one to live dangerously," he said.

Nancy managed a smile and went out.

The afternoon seemed long. There was nothing on the radio, and nothing to read. She washed

23

her two blouses and put them out on the line. She remembered with great annoyance that nobody, not even her mother, had remarked on her perm. What was the point of getting one if people didn't notice? Paying good money for one of the newest perms. Well, paying money if she had had to: fortunately she hadn't. At six she heard the banging of car doors and voices.

"Oh, there you are, Nancy." Her mother always seemed surprised to see her. "Mrs. Casey and I've been for a great drive altogether."

"Hallo, Mrs. Casey. That's nice," Nancy said grumpily.

"Did you get us any supper?" Her mother looked expectant.

"No. Well, you didn't say. There wasn't anything there." Nancy was confused.

"Oh, come on, Maura, she's only joking. Surely you've something made for your mother, Nancy?"

Nancy hated Mrs. Casey's arch voice treating her as if she was a slow-minded five-year-old.

"No, why should I have? There was no food there. I presumed my mam was getting something."

There was a silence.

"And there was nothing for lunch either," she said in an aggrieved tone. "I had to go over to Kennedy's to get rashers."

"Well, we'll have rashers for our supper." Mrs. Morris brightened up.

"I've eaten them," Nancy said.

"All of them?" Mrs. Casey was disbelieving.

"I only got two," she said.

There was another silence.

"Right," Mrs. Casey said, "that settles it. I wanted your mother to come back with me but she said no, that you'd probably have the tea made for us all and she didn't want to disappoint you. I said it was far from likely, judging from what I'd heard. But she had to come back, nothing would do her." She was halfway back to the door. "Come on, Maura, leave the young people be. . . . They have better things to do than getting tea for the likes of us." Nancy looked at her mother, whose face was set in a hard line of disappointment and shame.

"Enjoy your evening then, Nance," she said. And they were gone. The car was starting with a series of jumps and leaps.

What could Mrs. Casey have heard? What did she mean? The only person she could have heard anything from was Mairead, or Mairead's mother. What could they have been saying—that Nancy was irritating? Was that it?

She didn't want to be in when they came back, but where could she go? She had arranged no lift to the dance: she would as soon be hanged as to go out on the straight road and hitch all the way to the night entertainment—which she wouldn't enjoy anyway. She supposed she could always go to Ryan's pub. She'd be bound to know people and it was her own hometown and she was twenty-

25

five years of age so she could do what she liked. She put on one of her freshly cleaned blouses, which she ironed with great care. She decided the perm was an undoubted success and gave herself a spray of the perfume she had bought her mother last Christmas and set out.

It wasn't bad in Ryan's; some of the golfing people were buying big rounds, shouting at each other from the counter: What did you want with the vodka, Brian; Did you want water with the Power's, Derek? Celia was behind the counter helping her mother.

"You don't usually come in here," Celia said.

"It's a free country and I'm over twenty-one," Nancy said snappishly.

"Oh Jesus, take it easy," Celia had said. "It's too early for the fights."

There was a phone in a booth and she saw Dee Burke making a call; their phone must be out of order at home. Nancy waved but Dee didn't see her. Biddy Brady, who had been two classes below Nancy at school, had got engaged and she was celebrating with a group of the girls. The ring was being passed around and admired. She waved Nancy over to the group, and rather than sit on her own she went.

"We're putting a sum into the kitty each and then the drinks keep coming and we pay for it until the money runs out," said one girl helpfully.

"Oh, I don't think I'll be here all that long," Nancy said hastily, and noticed a few odd looks being exchanged.

26

She waved at Mikey Burns, who was carrying two drinks over to a corner.

"Have you any pub jokes?" Nancy asked, hoping he might stop and entertain them for a moment.

"Not tonight, Nancy," he said, and didn't even pause. Mikey! Who would do anything for an audience! He was heading for the corner; a woman with her head down sat there; it looked like Billy Burns' wife.

Billy was Mikey's brother, the one that got the looks and the brains and the luck, people said.

There was a bit of commotion behind the bar and Celia's mother seemed to be shouting at her. It was hushed up, but Celia looked very anxious. One of the Kennedy brothers had stepped in behind the bar to help wash glasses.

Nancy felt a bit dizzy. She had drunk two gins and orange, which she had bought for herself, and two as part of Biddy Brady's celebration. She had had nothing to eat since lunchtime. She decided to get some fresh air and some chips in that order. She could always come back. She sat on the wall near the chip shop and ate them slowly. You could see the whole town from here: the Burkes' house with all that lovely creeper cut away from the windows so neatly. She thought she saw Dee leaning out a window smoking, but it was darkish, she couldn't be certain. Then there was the Fitzgeralds' drapery, Tom's family's business. His two brothers and their wives worked there, as well as his father. They had a craft shop now attached to it, and they made up Irish tweeds into skirts for the visitors. Mrs. Casey lived about a mile out, so she couldn't glare at her windows and imagine her mother eating lamb chops and looking at television, counting the days with Mrs. Casey until the *Late Late Show* came back from its summer break. When they had been planning the Dublin trip they had wanted Mairead and Nancy to get them tickets for the show, and Mairead had actually written and found out what the chances were. Nancy had thought it was madness of the first order.

It was chilly and the last chip was gone. She walked back to Ryan's and thought she would go in the side entrance and visit the Ladies' on the way. She nearly fell over Mrs. Ryan, who was sitting on the step.

"Oh, it's *Miss* Morris," the woman said with a very snide little laugh.

"Good night, Mrs. Ryan," said Nancy a bit nervously.

"Oh, Miss Morris, Miss Mean Morris. Mean as all get-out, they say about you."

She didn't sound drunk. Her voice was steady and cold.

"Who says that about me?" Nancy was equally cold.

"Everyone. Every single person who ever speaks your name. Poor Biddy Brady's crowd of girls, just to mention a few. You sat down and took a couple of spirits off them and walked off. That's class, Miss Morris, strong men have wanted to be able to do that and they're not."

"Why do you call me Miss Morris?"

"Because that's what you call yourself, that's what you think you are. And by God that's the way you're going to stay. No man would take you on, Miss Morris, a mean woman is worse than a nag and a slut put together . . . ."

"I'll be off, I think, Mrs. Ryan."

"Oh, I would, Miss Morris; those little girls in there have had a few drinks now and if you haven't come back to put a couple of fivers into their kitty, I think you'd be far better to be off."

"Put *what* into their kitty?" Nancy was stunned.

"Oh, be off, Miss Morris, I beg of you."

But her blood was up now. She pushed past the woman and went into the smoke and heat.

"Sorry, Biddy," she said loudly, "I went home for change. I hadn't my money with me. Can I put this into the kitty and I'm having a gin and orange when the round comes."

They looked at her in disbelief and with some guilt. Those who had been loudest against her were abashed.

"A large gin and orange for Nancy," they called; and Celia, who was working alone with only Bart Kennedy to help her, raised her eyebrows. Nancy Morris ordering large ones.

"They cost a fair whack nowadays, Nancy," she said.

"Oh, for Christ's sake, will you give me a drink,

29

not a sermon," Nancy said, and the others all laughed.

They were singing "By The River of Babylon, where I sat down," but Nancy was only mouthing the words.

Mean, Mean, Mean. That was what Mairead thought, what she told her mother and her aunt, why she wanted her out of the flat; that's what Mrs. Casey thought, that's what her mother had felt tonight, that's what the Kennedys' father had been jeering at in the shop. That's what Celia meant now, talking about the price of a drink. That is what Mrs. Ryan, who must have gone stone mad tonight, meant, sitting on the floor of her own public house in the side entrance.

Mean.

But she wasn't mean: she was careful, she was sensible, she was not going to throw away her money. She was going to spend it on what she wanted. Which was . . . which was . . . Well, she didn't know yet. It certainly wasn't clothes, or a holiday, or a car. And it wasn't on dear things to furnish rented accommodation, and it wasn't on going to dances or discos or to hotels with fancy prices. And it wasn't on smart hairdressers or Italian shoes or fillet steaks or a stereo radio with headphones.

They had linked arms now and they were singing "Sailing" and swaying from side to side. Mrs. Ryan had come back and was singing with the best; in fact, she was standing up in the middle of the circle and playing the Rod Stewart role with somebody's golf club as a microphone.

Celia was pulling pints still; she looked at her mother with neither embarrassment nor pride—it was just as if she were another customer. Tom Fitzgerald was talking to her over the bar. They were very thick, those two. Tears came down Nancy's face at Mrs. Ryan's words. A mean woman. She wasn't at all mean. But if people *thought* she was, then she must be. Mustn't she?

Deirdre had once said she was a bit tight with money, but she had thought that was Deirdre being all-American and accusing people face to face of things. Her brother in Cork had once said that she must own massive property up in Dublin now, what with her earning a good salary and paying hardly a penny out a week except her rent and the Lilac Bus. She had said nonsense, that it cost a packet to live in Dublin. He had pointed out that she had a bicycle and she got a three-course meal in the hospital at midday, and what else did she spend it on? The conversation had ended fairly unsatisfactorily, she had thought. Now she realized that he was saying she was mean. Mean.

Suppose people *really* thought she was mean? Should she explain that it wasn't meanness, and she was only making sure she didn't throw money away? No, somehow it was one of those things that you couldn't explain. It was either there, the belief, or it wasn't there. And so, unfair as it was, she was now going to have to go overboard the other way.

Tomorrow she would suggest to her mother that she take them both to a nice Sunday lunch in the hotel as a treat. It was too late to do anything about Mairead, there was no promising to be more generous or to spend more or whatever it was people wanted. And maybe she could get some posters of Ireland and send them to Deirdre's children. Happy birthday Shane or April or Erin from your auntie Nancy in the Emerald Isle. And to the silent brother in Cork, some book about fishing and a pressing invitation to visit her when next he came up for the Spring Show.

It must work: look at Biddy Brady's party, they were delighted with her. But why shouldn't they be, she had put ten whole pounds into their bowl on the table. But it seemed to please them a lot and they were raising their glasses a bit crookedly and saying Nancy Whiskey and things to her that they'd never have said otherwise.

There was no sign of Mrs. Ryan; she had gone out again after her party piece. Nancy would like to have thanked her. Because now she had a lot of problems licked. And the great thing, the really great thing was this: it needn't cost a lot of money. In fact, if she was very careful, it need cost hardly anything. She could take a lot of those glucose sweets and put them in a box, say, that could be a present for her mother one week. And she could give as presents those paperweights that she got from the drug companies—sometimes you could hardly see the name of the medicine they were advertising. And wasn't it just as well she had told nobody about the rise in her wages. She had negotiated it herself quietly, so no one need ever know about that at all.

DEE

They often had a drink on a Friday night in the pub beside the office. Dee would only stay for half an hour. The Lilac Bus wouldn't wait, she knew that. She knew, too, that a lot of people in the practice were surprised that she went home every weekend. It was so far, and there was so much to do in Dublin. Wasn't she very dutiful? Oh no, she had denied, no. It was selfishness: she went home because it was peaceful, there were no distractions, she could study at home. But the law books that crossed Ireland in her canvas bag came back again unopened as often as not. Dee Burke spent much of her weekends sitting at her bedroom window and staring out at Rathdoon. Until it was time to go back to Dublin again on Sunday evening.

And of course, her parents were pleased. She could get off the bus at the corner and walk up to the golf club, waving cheerily as the Lilac Bus went on into town. For every Friday night in human memory Dr. and Mrs. Burke were at the golf club, and if there was a birth or a death or something untoward in between, people knew to phone the club and the doctor would take the call.

34

They had been surprised at the beginning of the summer when she began to come home so regularly. Surprised but glad. It was great to have company around the house, and Dee was always the liveliest of the family. They would jump up with pleasure when she put her face around the door on a Friday night to join them and whoever else in the club bar. Her father would get her a toasted sandwich and put his arm around her shoulder if she stood beside him at the bar counter. Her mother would smile over from the table. They were so delighted to have Dee home again. Sometimes her stomach rose and fell at their innocence and their kind welcome. What did people do when they didn't have the Burkes to go back to, Dee wondered? Went mad maybe? Went to discos? Got sense? Pulled themselves together? Oh, who knew what other people did? Who cared?

Tom Fitzgerald was quite handsome; she had never thought of it until tonight when he was laughing at her for flinging her own bag up on the roof rack. He had a lovely grin. He was an odd fellow—you could never get a straight answer out of him on anything. She knew nothing about him, nothing at all, and she had grown up fifty yards from him and his brothers. She didn't even know what he did for a living. She had asked her mother once.

"Don't you travel across the country sitting beside him? Why don't you ask him yourself?" her mother had said, not unreasonably.

"Oh, he's not the kind you could ask," Dee had said.

"Well then, you'll have to remain ignorant." Her mother had laughed. "At this stage of my life I'm not going to go into the drapery and ask personal questions to the Fitzgeralds about what occupation their son follows."

Nancy Morris was sitting in the bus, first as usual. She looked different somehow. Was it a new blouse or her hair? Dee wasn't sure—she wouldn't ask in case Nancy would start bewailing the cost of everything, as she usually did. Yet, she was getting a fine big salary, so Sam had told her. Far more than any of the receptionists or clerks were getting in the solicitors' office. Maybe I won't sit beside her tonight, Dee resolved, but she knew she would. Who else knew Sam, who else could tell her about Sam Barry and his daily life except Nancy? Imagine being able to travel home with Sam's receptionist every weekend. It was like having a bit of Sam with her. It took a lot of the loneliness away just to be able to talk about him. Even very indirectly, even if it meant talking about Mr. Boring White and Mr. Boring Charles as well. Because Nancy must never, never know that it was only Mr. Sam Barry that she was interested in.

Nancy would talk forever: she explained the routine and the kind of problems the consultants had, not being able to get beds quickly enough in the hospital, and all the complications of the Voluntary Health Insurance and the forms and people not understanding them. But she knew

36

nothing about their lives outside the hospital. Nothing except what they told her and what the nurses told her, and that was little.

"Do their wives ever ring them at work?" Dee asked. It was like probing a sore tooth; she knew she shouldn't ask.

"Oh yes, sometimes they do." Nancy was maddening.

"And what do they say?"

"They're all very nice, they call me by my name."

That surprised Dee: Nancy was so unforthcoming and businesslike, you couldn't imagine anyone chatting to her.

"Oh yes, 'Hallo Miss Morris,' they say. All of them: Mrs. White, Mrs. Charles, Mrs. Barry."

So that's what she meant by calling her by her name!

"And has Mrs. Barry much of a Canadian accent?"

"Gosh, Dee, you do have a great memory for them all. No wonder you're so brainy and going to be a solicitor. Imagine you remembering she was a Canadian. No, not much of an accent, but you'd know she was from over there. American sounding."

Imagine my remembering she was Canadian? Imagine my being able to forget it! *She doesn't know many people here; she's far from home; its not as if she grew up here and has her own circle of friends; she needs time to make a life for herself; we have to wait until things settle down.*

Dee could never understand the logic of that. If they were going to wait until Candy Barry settled into Irish life, they were building up more and more trouble for themselves. Why didn't they settle her back into Canadian life, she wanted to know? Before she had become isolated from her roots there. Why? Because of the children of course, the two little Barrys, small clones of their father, five and seven. He wasn't going to let those go four and a half thousand miles away and see them once a year on a visit.

But what about the children that he and Dee would have together? That would be different. Wonderful but different. You didn't parcel away your two lovely sons because you were going to have a new family with somebody else. No indeed. Dee was immature to suggest it.

Sam used that word as a great insult. He said it had nothing to do with age. People younger than Dee could be mature and people much older than both of them would never achieve it. She didn't like the word, it seemed to mean whatever he wanted it to mean. Like when you're playing poker and the two is wild, the two can be any card you want it to be.

She didn't know why she asked Nancy about his work. She never learned anything new, but it was like seeing a photograph of some scene that you knew well; it was always interesting to see it again from another angle. The only bit she shouldn't have asked was about their wives ringing up. That had made her uneasy now.

38

Sam said that Candy never called him at work and yet Nancy Morris said she did. Nancy probably wanted to show off about how well she knew them all. Boasting. She was in the middle of some complicated diatribe about the telephone system now. Dee felt her eyes closing. She slept and dreamed that she was getting her parchment from the Chief Justice and Sam was there congratulating her, and a photographer from the *Evening Press* had the three of them lined up and was writing their names down in his notebook.

Dee often dreamed that Sam was part of her life: she felt that this must signify that she was not guilty about him and that everything they had together was aboveboard and out in the open. Not too much out in the open, of course, but not hole-in-the-corner either. For example, her flatmate Aideen knew all about Sam, and met him when he called. And Sam's friend Tom knew too: he used to go out to meals with them sometimes. So it wasn't as furtive as you might think. Sam had wanted to know why her parents didn't cop on, but Dee had said it would never cross their minds, and anyway she was softening them up for the future by insisting she had no romantic interests yet but would certainly fall for somebody highly unsuitable when the time came. Dee had pealed with laughter over this, and Sam had looked sad. She had stopped laughing suddenly and he had been very quiet.

"The future mightn't be perfect," he said. "Not for us: you shouldn't hope too much, you know."

"The future's not going to be perfect for most people," she had said cheerfully. "But they have to keep hoping, otherwise what's the point of anything?"

That had seemed to cheer him a little, but he had been quieter than usual.

Dee wasn't sure why she came home so often now. Aideen couldn't understand it either.

"Sure, if you're down there, he'll never see you. Can't he ring you here, if he has a free minute?"

True. But he was having less and less free minutes. Candy's parents were over from Toronto. They had to be shown around. One of the little blond boys had fallen off a bicycle and opened his forehead; he had to be visited in hospital, and looked after when he got home.

There was the family holiday on the Shannon, on the cruiser, and the hurried phone calls from coin boxes when he was meant to be buying drinks or going to the Gents'.

Recently, there were times that weren't explained at all, but they were times that seemed to have no minutes in them all the same. It was easier in Rathdoon, he *couldn't* ring her there, even if he wanted to. Her father would recognize his name, the phone was in the hall, it would be hopeless. Perhaps that's why she went, because anything was better than sitting in a place where he could ring and didn't.

Aideen said she should fight harder for him, force him to leave that Candy. He had been so keen on Dee at the start that he would have done

40

anything for her; now she had let him believe that he could have it both ways. But Dee thought she might want it both ways too. She didn't want a huge scandal, and having to leave her apprenticeship and end up half-qualified, half-married, half-home-wrecker and half-disgraced. Aideen said that was nonsense and that Dee's parents had been able to accept that her brother was living with a girl, so why couldn't they accept what she planned to do? Dee thought there was a lot of difference between Fergal living with his girlfriend when everyone knew that they would get married soon anyway, and her making off with a well-known Dublin consultant and forcing him to abandon his wife and two little boys. It was a matter of degree. Aideen had said that was nonsense, it was all Sin and it was all Not Respectable. So why not do it?

Why not? It wasn't really up to her anymore: Sam was not nearly so ardent. In fact, once or twice he had made excuses that seemed just like the things he had said to Candy on the phone a year ago. "Sorry love, I tried, but it's useless, there's this meeting, it's the only time they can get all the people together. I pulled out last time. I can't be seen to do it again." Very familiar. Frighteningly familiar. But was he making excuses to his young mistress so that he could be with his middle-aged Canadian wife? Or was there another young mistress? Someone even younger than twenty-three? Someone who didn't sigh and groan when he canceled an arrangement? Someone who never suggested that Candy be sent back to Toronto?

Dee was remarkably calm about the possibility of a rival. She couldn't take it seriously. He really *was* a busy man, by anyone's standards; he worked long hours and there were still more people straining to see him. He had barely time for one relationship, not to mention two. To think of three would be ridiculous. Nobody could juggle that many romances and promises and endearments in the air. Nobody.

She was glad when they stopped, just for the chance to stretch her legs. Tom gave them ten minutes and not a minute more in the pub beside the garage where he filled up the Lilac Bus. The men usually had a half-pint each and sometimes Dee bought Nancy a gin and orange and Celia a bottle of Guinness. She would have a little brandy herself if her stomach felt cold and nervous. But tonight she felt all right. Sam was away on his conference.

He had rung her from the airport to say goodbye. He had said he loved her and that he'd see her on Monday night, late, when he got back from London. He'd tell Candy the conference went on until Tuesday. That was fine, it was ages since he had been able to stay a full night, she would make sure that there'd be no confrontation and scenes. Just like it had been in the beginning.

They were settling back in the bus. Poor Mikey Burns, the bank porter, who was so nice apart from all his lavatory jokes, said that he felt much better now that he'd shaken hands with the wife's best friend. He said it twice in case people hadn't got it. Kev Kennedy still hadn't.

"You're not married, Mikey," he had said.

Mikey looked defeated.

Dee said she mustn't sleep too much on the bus, it gave her a cramp in her shoulders, and Nancy said there was a great way of getting rid of tension in the neck: you had to hang your head down as if it were a great weight and then roll it around. Judy Hickey joined in the conversation unexpectedly and said that this was one of the principles of yoga and seemed greatly in agreement. Dee thought Nancy was put out by this, as if she didn't want to join up with yoga over anything.

He would be in London now, staying in that big posh hotel near the American Embassy where she had once spent a weekend with him as Mrs. Barry. It had been so racy, and she kept thinking she'd meet someone from home, as if anyone from Rathdoon would ever go inside a place like that. He had said there would be a reception at 8:30 and they would all wear name badges. It would have begun now. She felt an urge to talk about him again. This would be her last chance since she wouldn't be able to mention him at home.

"I expect they go away a lot on conferences, professional sorts of things," she said to Nancy.

"Sometimes." Nancy was vague. "Not often. Of course they've all had their holidays in August, and you've no idea how hard it is to fix appointments; people don't understand that doctors, specialists, have to have holidays like anyone else. More than anyone else," she added righteously.

Dee wasn't going to go down that martyr road; she wanted to hear about Mr. Barry being invited to this very prestigious gathering in London. She wanted to hear what he said when he got the invitation, and she wanted to hear Nancy say that he was coming back on Tuesday, so she could hug that to herself like a little secret.

"Yes, but didn't you say one of them was off to a conference this weekend?" she said.

"No." Nancy was puzzled. "No, definitely not."

"Maybe they'd go and not tell you?" Dee's heart had started to move in a very unacceptable rhythm.

"I don't think so." Nancy was lofty. "But anyway, it wouldn't be this weekend, because I know where they're all going, as it happens. It's a big do. Mr. and Mrs. Barry—she's a Canadian, you know—well, they're having their tenth wedding anniversary party tomorrow, and it's going to be a big barbecue. Mr. Barry asked me to pray especially that it wouldn't rain."

She didn't hear anything else for the rest of the journey home. But she must have managed to nod or smile or something because she certainly didn't notice Nancy looking at her puzzled or anything. She felt as if somebody had opened her throat just under the gold horseshoe he had bought her as a pendant that time in London, and poured in a jug of iced water. The water was freezing up again. Why? That was all she wanted to know.

44

Why the elaborate lies? Filled with such detail, about the name badges, the names of Americans and French and Germans that he was going to meet? Did these people exist at all, or had he picked names out of a phone book or out of literature? Why? If he and his wife had such a good marriage that they were gloating publicly with a big babyish barbecue over the whole thing . . . then why did he need Dee as well?

She went over it all, from the very start, when they had met at a party on the day of a Rugby International. It had been a big lunch where people had been invited to prematch snacks, and most people had such a good time they had stayed on and watched the match on telly instead. Dee had felt guilty about their tickets and all the young disappointed hopefuls who could have used them and Sam had gathered up half a dozen and run out on the road and given them to the first crowd of passersby he saw. They had looked through the window and laughed at the waving kids and the eager way they had run toward Lansdowne Road. She and Sam had laughed a lot that afternoon, Candy was at the other end of the room talking about recipes. When they were leaving, Sam had said, "I must see you again," and she had laughed a peal of delight, and told him it was pure Hollywood.

"I am pure Hollywood," Sam had said, and somehow it had sounded endearing and nice. She had given him work and home numbers and he had called the next day. He had pursued her, yes, that wasn't too strong a word for it. *Pursued.* She had said she didn't want to get involved with a married man, and he said that he knew it was more pure Hollywood and pure corn and pure things-that-married-men-said, but actually his marriage was empty and a great mistake and something he should never have done, but he had been in Canada and lonely and far from home; and that, apart from Dee altogether, he and Candy would undoubtedly drift their separate ways when the children were old enough to understand, and that he would be very gentle and careful, and that he would love her always. Now, why would someone do that? If you loved one person and thought they were smashing and lovely and fresh, why would you then have big parties and hand-holding and a lot of bullshit with another person? What was the point? Or suppose you loved the other person and enjoyed being married to her for ten years and adored the two little boys and everything, then why would you tell lies about being fresh and lovely and tell tall tales about conferences in London with name badges to someone else? It was beyond understanding, and Dee felt that something in her head was about to break with the effort of understanding. She bent forward a little. Tom's eyes in the mirror caught the movement.

"Are you okay, Dee?" he called.

"Sure," she muttered.

"Right, coming to your corner in five minutes," he said. He must have thought she was carsick.

46

"We're never home already?" She was genuinely shocked. She thought they were seventy miles from Rathdoon. "You should try driving Concorde," she said, managing a sort of joke for him.

"Sure, that would be child's play after the Lilac Bus." Tom grinned back at her.

She wondered should she go straight home and not get off at the golf club. But that would be worse, back to an empty house on her own. No, better join in and be with people who would talk and laugh and be pleased to see her.

She opened her bag and got out a mirror before she went in. Unbelievably she was not too bad, her face tanned from all those weekends at home, her hair straight and shoulder length—Sam said it was like an advertisement for shampoo, which was high praise. Her eyes normal looking, not wild. No, she wouldn't frighten her parents and their friends. In she would go, and when they asked her what she'd have, she'd say she had a stomach upset and could she have a brandy and port. Someone told her once that this was a great drink and it cured every ill. Or most ills anyway.

They were delighted to see her as always, but they were bursting with news. They couldn't wait for the drink to be in her hand so that they could drink a toast. They had had a phone call from Fergal— what do you think, he and Kate had bought the ring, they were getting married just before Christmas, wasn't it marvelous? And Kate's parents had been on the phone, too, and they had all said wasn't it wonderful the way things turned out, and maybe young people nowadays were much wiser than their parents and didn't rush into things. Dee Burke raised her glass of port and brandy and drank the health of her brother Fergal and her new sister-in-law-to-be, Kate, and she wondered with her mother what they both would wear to the wedding. And the drink went down through that channel where there had been iced water before, and it sort of burned it with a fiery anesthetic, and she began to think that whoever said it cured all ills might have had a point.

But it didn't bring sleep. And she had to move gently if she moved at all. The big old house was full of creaks and bumps. If you went to the lavatory during the night, you woke the whole house. It was considered courteous to arrange your functions so that you didn't have to. Her parents talked on long downstairs. They had been married for thirty years, she realized. They never made much of anniversaries and when her mother was fifty last year it had been very politely ignored. No showy barbecues for them, no public displays.

But that didn't matter. What was she going to do? Was she going to pretend that she knew nothing, let him lie on about London? No, that would be living out a total dishonesty. But then wasn't he prepared to do that with her? Some of the time. And with Candy some of the time. He didn't have this high regard for total honesty. How had he not known that Nancy would prattle about it? She had told him that she traveled home on the same mini-

48

bus every weekend as his receptionist. But Sam didn't know that she talked to Nancy about the consultants, and Sam would never believe for one moment that Nancy would mention something as trivial as his party to someone who was not meant to know him. Would she ring him at home and confront him? What earthly good would that do? None.

She would try to be calm and wait until daylight. What was that thing you were meant to do to your neck and shoulders? She tried what she remembered of the instructions but it just made her feel worse.

An hour later she understood what insomnia was about. She had never understood why people didn't just turn on the light and read if they couldn't go to sleep.

Another hour later she laughed mirthlessly to herself about her lack of sleeping pills. There she was, a doctor's daughter, and another doctor's lover and she hadn't one little Mogadon to call her own. A bit after that she started to cry and she cried until she fell asleep at twenty to eight just as her mother was creaking down the stairs to put on the coffee.

She woke after one o'clock: her mother was standing by the bed.

"Is your tummy better?"

Dee had forgotten the so-called gastric attack to excuse the ports and brandy.

"I think so," she said, bewildered.

49

"If you're well enough, can you do me a favor? We've had another phone call from Fergal." Her mother paused expectantly.

"The wedding's off?" Dee said, rubbing her eyes.

"No, stupid, but they're coming this evening, about six o'clock. Can you run me into town, I'll want to get things." "Into town" meant the big town seventeen miles away. "Downtown" meant Rathdoon itself.

"What do we want to go into town for?"

"You can't get anything nice here, anything different."

"Mummy, in the name of God, isn't it only Fergal? Why do we want anything *nice*, anything *different* for Fergal?"

"But it's Kate as well."

"But hasn't he been living with Kate for a year? Are you losing your marbles or something, what would she want anything nice and different for? Can't we go to Kennedy's and get some ham or lamb or whatever we'd be having anyway?"

"Well, if you don't want to drive me, you need only say so. I'm sure your father won't mind giving me a quick spin into town." Her mother was huffy now and annoyed.

"It's not a quick spin, you know it, it's seventeen miles. It's a bad road, it's jam packed with shoppers on a Saturday in there, we'll never get a parking place, the whole thing will take three hours."

"Well, don't *you* worry about it, Madam: you're so busy you can sleep on into the broad daylight—

50

I see what a demanding life *you* have. No, your father may be able to give up his one game of golf a week to take me."

Dee got out of bed, and picked up a dressing gown.

"I'll have a bath and I'll take you now, but I want you to know that there's a grave danger you're going mad. Next week you'll be going into town to get something nice and unusual for me."

"If you were bringing home a fiancé I'd be glad to," her mother said. "And by the way, do you never wear pajamas or a nightdress or anything? Isn't it very peculiar to wear nothing at all in bed?"

"It's very peculiar, Mummy—I'd say I'd be locked up if anyone knew."

"Oh, there's nothing like a smart aleck, nothing as lovely as your own daughter turning into a smart aleck," said her mother and went downstairs happily to make a list.

Mrs. Burke bought a new tablecloth and six napkins to match. Dee cast her eyes to heaven so often her mother asked her not to come into the next shop to be making a show of her. She was moved on three times by guards, hot harassed men who could never have dreamed that this is what it would be like when they joined the force. She saw a woman slap her three-year-old hard on the legs until he roared in fright and his father thought she had gone too far and gave the woman a hard shove. Marriage! Dee thought. Family life. If a

Martian were looking at us, he would think we must be insane to run toward it like a crowd of lemmings. And it's all we want, everywhere: romantic books, *Dallas* on the telly, everyone we know. Nobody seems to learn any lessons on the way.

Her mother came out weighed down with parcels just as a guard was coming at her again; she dragged the parcels and her mother into the car with one movement.

"You're becoming very rough, Dee, very ill-mannered," her mother said, annoyed and flustered.

"It's all this naked sleeping," Dee said, smiling up at the guard. "That's the cause of it, I'm certain."

Halfway home Dee realized what had happened. That stupid Nancy had got the weekend wrong. That was it. Hadn't Sam said he'd be tied up with the family *next* weekend. Imagine believing the daylight from Nancy Morris. She really was going mad, it wasn't just a joke she made to her mother, of course that was it. Nancy was fussing and filling in her appointment book and complaining about the cost of living and she hadn't heard.

The relief was immense: it was the joy of getting an exam, it was like going to confession, not that there had been much of that lately—it was like passing your driving test.

She laughed happily and her mother looked at her in alarm.

"Mummy, I was just thinking of the day I passed my driving test," she began.

"Well, I don't know whether you'd pass it if you had it to do again," her mother said. "You've been hitting those potholes at a great rate; your father wouldn't like his car to be belted about like that."

"No, I was just thinking of the lovely feeling when the man said I passed. Would you like me to teach you to drive, Mummy, seriously?"

"I would not," her mother said. "And what's more I don't think I'll ever sit in a car with you again. Will you look at the *road*, Dee!"

"It's an open invitation. One lesson on a Saturday, one on a Sunday—you could drive us all to Fergal's wedding."

She felt light-headed and happy. If she had seen stupid Miss Mouse, as Tom called her, she would have mown her down.

When Fergal and Kate arrived, Dee thought they both looked slightly touched. They were a revolting mixture of overtalkativeness and utter wordlessness. They explained at tedious length how they had become mature in the last few months and both of them had developed this sense of their immaturity and lack of responsibility at exactly the same time. They wanted to make their commitment now in front of everyone, rather than shillyshallying any longer. Doctor Burke, who looked as if he wouldn't have minded if they never married, nodded and grunted appreciatively. Kate's mother gasped and pounced on every word, and reminded them of every detail of John's wedding five years before—every detail, that is, except the one that his bride was four months pregnant. Dee switched off for a little and thought of Sam in London. He had said there would be papers all of Saturday afternoon, but that he was going to skip the official dinner. Together they had looked at an English newspaper and circled plays or shows he might see. She wondered was it a nice warm night in London as it was here. Then it hit her like a tennis ball coming suddenly into her stomach. He had asked Nancy Morris to pray for a fine weekend for the barbecue. *This* weekend.

She wasn't able to eat the meringues that her mother had filled so carefully with a coffee-flavored cream to impress Fergal and Kate. She asked to be excused for a few minutes because she had remembered there was something she had to give Celia Ryan down in the pub.

"Won't it do later?" her mother had asked.

"No, she wants it now." Dee was standing up.

"Will I come down with you and have a pint?" She shooed Fergal away. "What a thought, after all this lovely meal Mummy's got for you. No, I'll be back in a few minutes."

"What does Celia want at this time of night?" her father asked mildly. "Won't she be pulling pints and trying to help that poor mother of hers to cope?"

"See you," Dee called.

She ran up to her room for her handbag and swung down the road.

"Can you give me a pound of change for the phone, Celia?" she asked.

"God, you're a great customer; if we had more like you we could open a singing lounge and have a cabaret on the profits," Celia laughed.

"Piss off, Celia. I'll have a brandy in a minute, I just want to make a call to Dublin."

Celia's level glance never changed, she never inquired whether the Burke phone was out of order, she just gave her the money.

"Could I get a call back in that box?" Dee wanted to know.

"Yes. I'll give you the number, but I don't put it up—I don't want other people to know."

"You're a pal," Dee said.

"Barry residence," said the Canadian voice she hadn't heard since the one and only time she met its owner at that rugby party, which was only a year and a half ago but felt like a lifetime.

"May I speak to Mr. Sam Barry, please."

"Well, it's a little awkward just at this very minute. Who is this, please?"

"It's Miss Morris, his receptionist."

"Oh, Miss Morris, I didn't recognize your voice. I am sorry. Sam is just getting the barbecue going, it's a very delicate moment." There was a little laugh. "Once the thing has taken we can all relax. Can I ask him to call you, Miss Morris? I assume it's urgent?"

"I'm afraid it is, Mrs. Barry." She sounded apologetic. "It's just a short message, but I should speak to him. It won't take a moment."

"Well, listen, I know he says that you are a rock of stability in a changing world. I'll have him call you."

"In the next half hour, if he could." Dee gave the number that Celia had written down.

"Rathdoon, what a pretty name!" Mrs. Barry was determined to be charming to the rock of stability. Or else she was so happy about the anniversary barbecue, she was at peace with the world. Dee didn't wait to find out.

"Very pretty. 'Bye, Mrs. Barry." She hung up; she was shaking. She sat on a stool at the bar. Celia made it a large brandy but charged only for a small one. Dee made a move to protest.

"Nonsense, you're always buying me drinks."

"Thanks." She held the glass with both hands. Celia must have noticed the shake.

"They tell me your Fergal's engaged," Celia said.

"Lord, that didn't take long." Dee grinned.

"Oh, it's stale news, I heard last night when I came off the bus."

"So did I: the parents are over the moon."

"Well, they don't have to pay for the wedding." Celia laughed.

"Celia, stop that, you sound like Nancy Morris."

The phone rang. Celia refilled her glass wordlessly and Dee slipped into the booth.

"Hallo," she said.

"A call for you," exchange said.

"Miss Morris?" Sam asked.

"No, Miss Burke," Dee said.

"What?"

"Miss Burke speaking, can I help you?"

He wasn't sure. "I'm sorry, I was asked to ring a Miss Morris at this number . . ."

"No, you weren't, you were asked to come in from the barbecue and talk to your mistress, Miss Dee Burke. That was the message I gave your wife."

"Dee. Dee." He was horrified. There was actual fear in his voice.

"Oh, she was very nice about it, she got a pencil from her purse and wrote down the number. She said Rathdoon sounded a pretty place."

"Dee, what are you doing?" His voice was a whisper.

"I'm at home for the weekend, like I told you I would be. The question is, what are *you* doing? Did they cancel the conference? Let's see, you were leaving the airport about four thirty—gosh, did they tell you at London airport or did you have to get into town?"

"Dee, I can explain exactly what happened, but not here and now; what did you really say to Candy?"

"Oh, just that, and she really did say that Rathdoon sounded pretty—ask her."

"You didn't . . . but why?"

"Because I felt it was all so confusing, all this business of lies and saying one thing and everyone knowing it wasn't true. Everyone. I thought it would be easier not having to pretend so much."

"But—"

"I mean she knows, Candy does, that you'll be spending Monday night with me, and so now you don't have to lie to her about that, and I know that you and Candy are having a marvelous tenth anniversary barbecue and that Mr. Charles is there and Mr. White and all your friends and they were all watching you start up the fire. She told me all that, so there's no more pretending: it will be much easier from now on."

"You didn't, Dee. You didn't really say those things to Candy."

Her voice was very hard now. Very hard. "You'll have to find out now, won't you?"

"But she said it was Miss Morris on the phone."

"Oh, I told her to say that." Dee sounded as if she were explaining things to a child. "Much simpler for your guests; I mean, I don't know what you want to tell other people, but we'll talk about it all on Monday, won't we?"

"Dee, please don't go, you've got to explain."

"I have explained."

"I'll ring you back."

"Ring all you like, this is a pub."

"Where are you going now?"

"I see the real Miss Morris over here in a corner. I think I'll buy her a gin and orange and tell her all about us. That will make it easier for me to ring you at work; you see, I couldn't before because she knew me, but now with all this new honesty . . ."

"What new honesty?"

"What Candy and I have been talking about."

"You're a bitch, you told Candy nothing; this is a game, some vicious little game."

"Hush hush, don't let them hear you."

"Where will you be tomorrow?"

"I'll see you on Monday night, as arranged: come any time, straight from work if you like, now that there's no need to hide things anymore."

"I beg *you*, tell me what you told Candy."

"No, *you* must ask Candy that."

"But if you told her nothing then . . ."

"That's right, you'll have walked yourself into it."

"Dee."

"Monday."

"I'm not going to be blackmailed into coming around to you on Monday."

"Suit yourself. I'll be at home then, if I don't get called away or anything." She hung up.

"If he rings again, Celia, will you say you never heard of me and I haven't been in all night?"

"Sure," said Celia.

She went back to the house. Fergal was explaining that there came a time in your life when you couldn't play anymore—you had to face up to things.

"Jesus Mary and Joseph, Fergal, you should have been a philosopher!" Dee said admiringly.

"Did you have a drink with Celia Ryan?"

59

"I had two large brandies, Mother dear," Dee said.

"How much was that?" Fergal, the man saving for a mortgage, was interested now in the cost of fun.

"I don't know; I only paid for one small one, when I come to think of it." There were sudden tears in her eyes.

"Dee, why don't you and I go for a walk for a bit and let the wedding talk go on to a crescendo here?" Dr. Burke had his blackthorn stick in his hand.

They walked in silence. Down past the chip shop and over the bridge and on to the fork in the road.

It was only coming back that there was any chat.

"I'll be all right, Dad," she said.

"Sure, I know you will—aren't you a great big girl and won't you be a solicitor one day, a fierce terror making them all shake in the district court?"

"Maybe."

"Of course you will, and all this other stuff will sort itself out."

"Do you know about him?" She was genuinely surprised.

"This is Ireland, child. I'm a doctor, he's a doctor—well, a sort of one; when they get to that level it's hard to know."

"How did you hear?"

"Somebody saw you and thought I should know, I think, a long time ago."

"It's over now."

"It may be, for a while—"

"Oh no, it is, tonight."

"Why so suddenly?"

"He's a liar and nothing else; he lied to her and to me. Why do people do that?"

"Because they see themselves as having lost out and they want some of everything, and society doesn't let us have that, so we have to tell lies. And in a funny way the secrecy keeps it all going and makes it more exciting at the start."

"You know what it's like all right; I don't know how you could."

"Oh, the same way as your fellow does."

"*Daddy.* No, not you. I don't believe it."

"Oh, years and years ago. You were only a toddler."

"Did Mummy know?"

"I don't think so. I hope not. But she never said, anyway."

"And what happened to the girl?"

"Oh she's fine; she hated me for a bit, that was the worst part—if she had been just a little bit understanding. Just a small bit."

"But why should she?" Dee was indignant.

"Why, because she was young and lovely like you are, and she had the world before her; and I had made my way and it was nice but a bit—you know . . . a bit samey."

"She should have shook your hand like a chap and said, 'No hard feelings, Johnny Burke, you'll be a treasured memory.'" Dee was scathing.

"Something like that." Her father laughed.

61

"Maybe she should have." Dee linked arms with her father companionably. "Because you're a much nicer man than Sam Barry will ever be. I think he deserves a bit of roasting, actually."

"Ah well, roast away," her father said good-naturedly. "You've never listened to me up to now—there's no reason why you should now."

Dee sat in her room and looked down at the town. She thought she saw Nancy Morris sitting on the wall near the chip shop, but decided that it couldn't be. Nancy . . . pay for a whole portion of chips . . . ridiculous.

MIKEY

Mikey always said that you couldn't come across a nicer crowd of girls than the ones who worked in the bank. The men were grand fellows, too, but they were often busy with their careers, and they wouldn't have all that time to talk. And one of the men, a young buck who'd be some kind of a high manager before he was thirty, had taken it upon himself to say to Mikey that it would be appreciated if he watched his sense of humor, since the bank ladies had found it rather coarse on occasions. Mikey had been very embarrassed and had said nothing all day. So silent was he that the nice Anna Kelly, who was pure gold, asked him if he felt all right. He had told her what the young buck said, and Anna Kelly had said that banks were stuffy old places and maybe the buck had a point: jokes were fine with friends, but God, the bank—it wouldn't know how to laugh if you were tickling its funny bone for a year.

So he understood now and he never uttered a pleasantry within the bank walls again. If he met them on the street that was different; he could pass a remark or make a joke like anyone then, because they were all on neutral ground. And he used to tell the girls about his family in Rathdoon

—well, about the family that Billy and Mary had, really. The twins with the red hair and the freckles, and then Gretta with the pigtails and the baby, a big roll of butter with a laugh you could hear half a mile away. He told Anna Kelly that sometimes on the summer evenings when it would be very bright the twins wouldn't have gone to bed, and they'd be sitting at their window waiting till the Lilac Bus turned into the street and Uncle Mikey would get off. They collected stamps and badges, any kind of badges; and he had them all on the lookout for anything of that order so as he never went home empty-handed.

He was the only one of the bank porters who came from the country. The rest were all Dubliners: they used to laugh at him and say there'd have to be an official inquiry as to how he got the job. But they were a very good-natured lot, and there was great chat all day as they manned the doors, or wheeled the big boxes on trolleys where and when more money was needed or had to be put away. They delivered letters and documents up and down the street. They knew a lot of the customers by name and they got great Christmas presents altogether.

The Lilac Bus had started just when Mikey had needed it. His father was getting senile now, and it was hard on poor Billy and Mary to have the whole business of looking after him. But it would have been a long way to come back without Tom Fitzgerald and the little minibus that dropped you

64

at the door. Imagine having to get yourself to the town by a crowded train, packed on a Friday night and maybe not a seat, and then after that try to organize the seventeen miles home. It would take all day and all night and you'd be exhausted.

His old father was pleased to see him sometimes, but other times the old man didn't seem to know who he was. Mikey would take his turn spooning the food, and combing the matted hair. He would play the Sousa marches his father liked on the record player, and put the dirty clothes in the big buckets of Dettol and water out in the back. Mary, who was Billy's wife and a sort of a saint, said that there was no problem to it if you thought of it all as children's nappies. Into a bucket of disinfectant for a while, throw that out, into a bucket of water awhile and throw that out and then wash them. Weren't they lucky to have space out the back and a tap and a drain and all. It would be desperate altogether for people who lived in a flat, say.

And the nurse came twice a week and she was very good too. She even said once to Mikey that he needn't come back *every* weekend, it was above the call of duty. But Mikey had said he couldn't leave it all to Billy and Mary, it wasn't fair. But they'd be getting the house: what would Mikey be getting? the nurse had pointed out. Mikey said that sort of thing didn't come into it. And anyway, wasn't it a grand thing to come back to your own place.

The twins told Mikey that there was never any fighting when he came home, and Mikey was surprised.

"Why would there be fighting in this house?" he asked.

The twins shrugged. Phil and Paddy were afraid of being disloyal.

"Sure, you couldn't be fighting with your poor old grandfather, he would never harm the hair of your heads," Mikey said.

The twins agreed and the matter was dropped.

They loved Mikey around the house and he had a fund of jokes for them. Not risky ones, of course, but ones they could tell anyone. Gretta even wrote them down sometimes so that she'd remember them to tell them in class. Mikey never told the same one twice; they told him he should be on the television telling them one after another with a studio audience. Mikey loved the notion of it. He had once hoped that he might be asked to do a turn for the bank's revue, but nobody had suggested it, and when he had whispered it to that nice Anna Kelly, she said she had heard that you had to be a member of the union to be invited, that only members of the IBOA were allowed to perform. He had been pleased to know that, because otherwise he would have felt they were passing him over.

He had his doubts about the Lilac Bus when

he arrived the very first Friday. Tom Fitzgerald had asked them to be sure not to wave any money at him, because the legalities of the whole thing were what you might call a gray area. He did have the proper insurance and everything, and the Lilac Bus had a passenger service vehicle license, but there was no point in courting disaster. Let them all give him the money when they were home in Rathdoon, where it would be nice and calm. None of them had understood the ins and outs of it, but they all agreed. Mikey wondered if people like Dr. Burke's daughter and Mr. Green's son, Rupert, would fancy sharing a journey home with Mikey Burns, the bank porter and the son of poor Joey Burns, who before he lost his wits had been a great man for standing waiting till Ryan's pub opened and nothing much else. But Dee and Rupert were the salt of the earth, it turned out. There wasn't an ounce of snobbery between the pair of them. And Mrs. Hickey, she was a lady, too, but she always seemed pleased to see him. Nancy Morris was the same as she always had been since she was a schoolgirl, awkward and self-conscious. Nothing would get her out of that, she'd be an old maid yet. Celia Ryan was another fish altogether: it was a mystery she hadn't married someone by now. She always looked as if her mind was far away, yet she was thought to be a powerful nurse. He knew a man who'd been in Celia's ward, and he couldn't speak highly enough of her. He said she was like a legend in the hospital.

Nowadays he enjoyed the journey home, after he had got over his shyness of the first few runs. He would tell them a joke or two; they weren't a great audience, not like Gretta and Phil and Paddy, but they did smile and laugh a little, and didn't it cheer them up?

Sometimes he sat beside Celia and he would tell her tales of the world of banking. He told her of all the new machines, and the days of bank inspections, and how the tourists would drive you mad, and how in the summer you'd have a line half a mile long of Spanish and French students all wanting to change about £1 each of their foreign money. Celia didn't tell many tales of the hospital, but she often gave him helpful advice about his own father, all in a low voice so that the others didn't hear her talking about incontinence pads and Velcro fastenings for clothes.

But tonight it was the young Kennedy fellow sitting beside him. There was something seriously wrong with that boy. His brothers Bart and Eddie were the nicest fellows you could meet in a day's walk, but whatever had happened to young Kev he looked as if he had seen the Day of Judgment. You only had to address a civil word to him to have him leap out of his skin. Try to tell him a good story and he'd miss the point altogether. Mikey thought he'd teach him a few tricks that might be of use to him, to be able to do a trick in a pub. But the young fellow looked at him with the two eyes staring out of his head and didn't take in a word of it. In the end Mikey let him be, staring out the window as if the goblins were going to leap out of the hedges and climb into the bus after him.

Mikey nodded off. It was easy to sleep in the bus. The two girls behind him were already asleep, dreaming of fellows probably. Mikey dreamed that his father was well and strong again and had opened some kind of import and export agency in Rathdoon and that he, Mikey, was the manager and that he was able to give grand summer jobs to Phil and Paddy and Gretta, delivering letters to people up and down the street. He often dreamed of the children. But he never saw a wife for himself in the dream. Mikey Burns had missed the boat as far as wives were concerned. Too nervous and eejity at the time he should have been looking for one, and now at forty-five he wasn't the kind of forty-five-year-old that would be in the race at all. Better not make a fool of yourself going to dances or picking up fast-knowing women in pubs and being made to look thick altogether.

When they crossed the river and were really in the West they paused for the ten-minute comfort stop, and the half-pint to open the throat a bit. Celia came up to him quietly and put an envelope into his hand.

"That's for the bedsores: it's all written on it, keep him moving as much as you can."

"Aw, Celia, you're terribly good. Can I pay for this?"

"Are you mad, Mikey? Do you think I paid for

69

it? Dublin Health Authority would like you to have it as a little gift." They laughed. She was very nice.

What a pity he hadn't found a grand girl like Celia when he was young and promising looking. After all, he had a grand well-paid job now, he'd be able to make a home for anyone. The reason he didn't really have one wasn't money, it was lack of interest. He couldn't be buying a place and furnishing it and getting tables and chairs in it all for himself. The room he rented was grand and comfortable and he denied himself nothing. He had a grand big telly and he had bought himself a mirror to fix to the front of the wardrobe—that way he'd go out properly dressed. Beside the bed he had a lovely radio, which was a lamp and a clock and an alarm all in one. When he went out to people's houses, and the Dublin fellows often invited him up to their places, he was always able to bring a big box of chocolates, a fancy one with a ribbon on it. He was able to give a good account of himself.

But when he'd been a young lad, who were they, except the sons of poor Joey Burns and his mother had taken in washing and cleaned people's floors? It hadn't held Billy back: Billy strutted around Rathdoon as if he owned it, as if he were as good as any other citizen of the place. And wasn't he right? Look where he was now, he had all kinds of business interests, he employed five people in Rathdoon. He had the take-away shop; nobody believed there was a need for it until it appeared.

Half the families in the place ate Billy's chicken and chips on a Saturday night, and they had fried fish, too, and hamburgers. They sold cans of lemonade, and stayed open late to get the crowds going home from Ryan's, and Billy had put up two huge mesh litter bins at his own expense and everyone was delighted with him.

And he had an insurance business as well. Not a big one, but anyone who wanted cover went through him—it could all be filled in quickly, in the house. And he had some kind of a connection with a fellow who came to do tarmacadaming. If you wanted the front of a place all smartened up, then Billy would get other people with their places facing the same way to agree and the man with the machine and the tar would come and it was cheaper for everyone, and the place looked a king to what it looked before. A whole section of the main street looked really smart now, and Billy had got a tree planted in a tub and it was like something you'd see in a film. Billy had the brains and Billy never ran away the way Mikey ran off up to Dublin after his mother had died. Billy had stayed to marry Mary Moran, who was way beyond anyone they'd ever have thought about. Or that Mikey would have thought about.

He was looking forward to being home tonight. He had a computer game for the twins' birthday. It was several cuts above the Space Invaders they had tried out once, and it could be plugged into any kind of television; he had been playing it on his own television all week, but the shop assistant

71

said it would work as well on a smaller set. The twins had their birthday on Monday and he was going to give them the game on Sunday afternoon. He would set up the room with the curtains pulled and pretend they were going to watch something on the television, and then would come the surprise. He had got a smart red girl's handbag for Gretta, even though it wasn't her birthday, because he didn't want her to be left out, and a yellow rabbit for the baby in case it might have feelings of discontent in its pram.

Mary would never let him near his father on the Friday night; she'd have a supper warm for him, or if it had been a busy day she'd run across the road to the family take-away and get him fish and chips as soon as she saw the Lilac Bus pull up. She used to thank him so much for coming back to help with his father, and she'd tell him funny things about the children and what they had done during the week. They were back at school now, so there would be tales of what devilment Phil had got up to and the threatening messages that came home about him from the Brothers.

Mikey was the second to get out. They would leave Dr. Burke's daughter up at the golf club entrance; her parents were always there of a Friday night and she'd go and join them. Then when it came to the end of the street, the first drop was Mikey. He would take down Nancy Morris's huge suitcase, which weighed as light as a feather, and leave it inside the bus because she and Kev Kennedy would be next out, and Kev had nothing with him ever except a parcel that he kept under his seat.

Mikey advised them all to be good and if they couldn't they should be clever and if they couldn't be clever then they should buy a pram. He laughed happily and closed the door behind him.

There was no light in the kitchen and no meal on the table. There was no sign of Mary and no note either. He didn't mind not seeing Billy—his brother was usually up at the take-away or in Ryan's doing some deal with someone. But Mary?

He looked in the other rooms. His father was asleep, mouth open, wheelchair near the bed; on the chair was a large chamber pot, optimistic since the old man was never able to time things so accurately.

There was a smell of disinfectant mixed with better smells. Mary had big bunches of flowers around the room. She always said that she thought it cheered the old man up, and sometimes she had seen him stretch out and touch the flowers gently. He snored lightly. There was a night-light, and a Sacred Heart lamp as well.

Then Mikey went up the stairs quietly. The twins had bunk beds; their toys and clothes and books were all around. Phil slept in a ball with his fists clenched; Paddy was more peaceful, lying on his side. Gretta looked funny with her long straight hair brushed out. He remembered her with plaits for as long as she had been old enough to force her hair into them. She had a smile as if she were dreaming. She was a thin little thing, gawky and plain-looking, but she had a smile that would tear the heart out of you. Even when she was asleep.

The door of Billy and Mary's bedroom was open: they weren't there. The baby, round and soft like a cream bun, lay in its cot near the bed. There was a lovely white lacy bedspread, and on the wall there was a picture of Our Lady in a field of flowers. It had a blue lamp lighting under it. It was called "Queen of the May." Mary told Mikey once that the day she and Billy got engaged he had won a competition at a carnival where you had to throw rings over things and he had chosen that picture for her because she liked it so much.

Mikey put his small bag in his own room, which was neat as anything. She always had a bright clean pillowslip on the top, as if he was the highest quality coming for the weekend. Sometimes Mikey's mind went back to what the house had looked like in his mother's day, when they hadn't any such style or time for it.

It was puzzling, but maybe she had gone to get him fish and chips. He waited downstairs and listened to the news on the television. Eventually he began to get worried. They never left the children all alone in the house, even though they were perfectly safe, but it was just the way they were. His anxiety increased. He walked across to the take-away and to his surprise there was Mary serving. There were four people waiting for their order and only one of the young girls who worked there was behind the counter. They were working flat out.

"Mikey! Lord, is it that time already?" She was pleased but flustered to see him.

"Will I get behind there and give you a hand?" He knew the way—he had done it with them a few Saturday nights during the summer when they had been very busy. And the prices were on the wall.

"Oh, Mikey, would you?" She was very grateful.

He hung up his jacket and took an apron from a drawer. In a few moments they had the crowd thinned, and Mary was able to draw breath again. She spoke first to the girl who worked there.

"Treasa, would you take off your apron like a good child and run up to Ryan's. Tell them that we're short-staffed tonight and we'll be closing early. Tell them if they want anything, to come down in the next half hour for it otherwise they'll be disappointed."

"Who will I tell, ma'am?" The child seemed worried.

"That's a point—not much use telling poor Mrs. Ryan these days. Let me see, if there's anyone behind the bar helping, like Bart Kennedy, anyone like that, someone who looks in charge."

"Celia's home: she was on the bus, she'll probably have got behind the counter by now," Mikey said.

"That's it, tell Celia."

Treasa skipped off up the road, pleased to be out of the heat.

"Where's everyone?" Mikey looked around.

"Oh, there's been a lot happening, I'll tell you all when we get back. Keep a brave face on it for half an hour more and then it will be done." A trickle of people came in, and Mikey served them, and just as Mary had guessed would happen, a great influx came from Ryan's pub. They were full of good-natured abuse about it being against the law of the land to close the chipper before the pub. Mary had laughed good-naturedly and said wasn't she going above and beyond the call of duty to let them know now, rather than have them going home with stomachs full of beer and nothing to soak it up.

She didn't want a portion for herself, so Mikey wrapped up his own choice, and when they had drained the fat, scrubbed the tops and swept up anything that could be swept up into black plastic bags which were tied with little wires at the top, they crossed the street and went home.

Mary heated a plate under the hot-water tap, got out the tomato sauce and some bread and butter.

"Will I wet you tea or would you like a drop of anything?"

They got a bottle of Guinness each and sat down.

"Billy's gone. Gone for good."

He stared at her, fork halfway to his mouth.

"He went this day before lunch, he'll not be back. Ever."

"Ah, no, Mary. That's not possible."

She took a sip of her drink and made a face.

"I never like the first sip, but it tastes grand after that." She smiled a weak little smile.

Mikey swallowed and said, "It was just a bit of a row, that's all. People have rows, they get patched up."

"No, there was no row, there was no difference of opinion even."

Mikey remembered the way the twins had said there was no fighting when he was around the place.

"But just a bit of a barney now and then, these things sort themselves out, really they do." He was pleading now.

"No, I'll tell you it from start to finish—there was no row. Back there early on in the summer we did have rows all right: he was very touchy, I thought, bite the head off you as soon as look at you, but he said that's the way I was too. The children even noticed us."

"So what happened?"

"Well, I don't know, honestly. But anyway we had a great summer; as you know, business was booming. He used to be tired, but he was never cross anymore, and what with the baby getting to be so grand—you know they're like devils for the first few weeks—anyway we hadn't a worry under the sun." She stopped and looked away beyond him.

Mikey was silent.

"Eat up your fish and chips, Mikey. You can eat and listen."

"I can't."

She lifted the plate from him and put it into the oven very low down. "You'll eat it later then. Today was when it all happened, and if I hadn't come back I wouldn't have known: I wouldn't have known at this moment. I wouldn't have known until the end of next week. The whole of Rathdoon would have known before me."

"Known what, for God's sake?"

"He's gone off with Eileen Walsh, you know the one we said was too good to be working in a chipper. Well, she was far too good, she was only biding her time to go off with the owner of the chipper. That was the little plan. Could you beat it?" The voice was steady but the eyes were over-bright.

"But it's only a fancy, isn't it? It's a bit of madness. I mean, where would they go, and what would they do? And how could he leave you and the baby and the whole family?"

"He's in love with her. That's the word: *in love.* Isn't it marvelous? He was never *in* love with me; he loved me, of course, but that was different apparently."

Mikey stood up, but he didn't know what to do so he sat down again. Mary went on with the story.

"I was meant to be going into the town. There's always a lift in on Fridays and I had a list of things

78

we needed for the take-away, not things we get from the suppliers, but stupid things, big ashtrays for example and a couple of tins of bright red paint—we were going to paint the windows to match the geraniums, can you believe? But to go on with what happened: You know old Mrs. Casey, who's only just learned to drive. Well, she was giving me the lift and as soon as we were out on the road beyond the golf club, didn't the engine splutter and make these desperate sounds.

"Ah, well, I said to myself, there's my day in town gone for its tea. But she's such a nice woman, Mrs. Casey, you couldn't offend her. I told her it was a blessing in disguise and I could get the things next week and maybe I'd go home and make an apple tart since Mikey'd be coming back on the bus tonight."

A big lump came up in Mikey's throat.

"And I said to her to sit tight, I'd walk back and tell the Brennans in the garage to go out for her."

Mary took another sip.

"It was a gorgeous day, and I picked wildflowers from the hedges, and when I came in, there was Billy at the table with a whole load of papers all around him. I was delighted because he was meant to have been gone for the day. So I said wasn't this grand and we'd have a bit of lunch the two of us—something we hadn't done in years—and I saw that there was 'Dear Mary' on one piece of paper and on another and only two or three lines on each. And I *still* didn't know any-

79

thing was wrong, so I said, 'Are you writing me love letters at my age?' as a kind of joke. You see, I thought he was just back unexpectedly and was writing me a note to explain that he'd been in."

"Oh, Mary, isn't this terrible," said Mikey, believing it for the first time since the saga had started.

"This is the awful bit: he started to cry, he started to cry like a child. Well, I nearly dropped dead—Billy Burns crying. I ran to him to try to put my arms around him and he pushed me away. And he was sobbing like a baby that's getting teeth, so I said to him to hush it down or his father would hear. I'd left the baby next door, but your father would have been having a doze and it would have frightened the daylight out of him like it was doing to me." She paused for a moment.

"Then he said about Eileen, and her expecting and all."

There was a silence and the clock ticked and the soft snoring sound of the old man could be heard from the back room.

"He said he couldn't face me, and he was leaving a letter. And I said that he didn't have to go now, not at once, that surely he could stay and we could talk about what was to be done. But he said there'd been too much talking and that was it, now he was going." Mikey put out his big hand and patted Mary's arm hopelessly.

"There was a lot of this and that—but funny, no fight, no shouts or me saying he was a bastard or him saying he couldn't bear me anymore, that I was an old nag or anything."

"Well, no one could think that," Mikey cried loyally.

"No, he said I'd been the best wife and mother in the world, and that he couldn't tell me how sorry he was, he was just heartbroken, he said. All the papers were to show me that the chip shop is in my name, and the thousand pounds in the building society is for me, and the name of a solicitor who'd be able to find him, who'd pass letters on."

"And where does he think he's going?"

"To England. Where else?"

"How will he earn a living for himself and this floozy?"

"She's not a floozy—Eileen a floozy? Billy would earn a living on the planet Mars, don't worry about that."

Mikey was struck dumb.

"But the thing that upset him most was his father, your father."

"Billy never gives much time to poor old Dad."

"No, but he thought it wasn't just for me to be left with him—to have to look after an old man who isn't my own father. I said that Da was the least of the problems, what I wanted to know was how he could leave me, his wife, his friend for years and years, for fourteen years married, and a year before that mad about each other. That's when he explained all this *in love* business."

"What did you do?"

"What could I do? His mind was made up, he was leaving. He had a list of things he wanted me to do. There was a special sum of money left in one envelope that was for me to have driving lessons. I was to find out who taught Mrs. Casey: whoever taught her could teach the devil himself. He was leaving the van. I was to ask Bart Kennedy to give me a hand and pay him a proper wage. I was to decide whether he should write to the children or not and what I should tell them, if anything. He thought I should say he had gone away for a bit and then they'd grow used to it."

Mary stood up to get another bottle of stout.

"He had been packing his things, too, it nearly broke my heart to see his good shirts stuffed in all creased, and he had forgotten all his shoes. I asked him to say good-bye to your father—he's been very clear the past couple of days, knows all of us—but no, he wouldn't. I said he might never see him again and he said that he'd never see any of us again. That's when I got a bit frightened about it all. I knew there's never any changing his mind. So I decided I'd let him go, without screaming and roaring and begging."

"You let him walk out—"

"No, I said I'd go out and let him finish at his ease. I said he needn't bother about the letter now, he'd said it all, that I'd go out and get more flowers and things and keep out of his way for an hour or two until he left. That he could leave all the insurance papers where they could be found, and the solicitor who would pass on the messages to him if there was anything we hadn't thought of. He was *so* relieved: you should have seen his face— you see, he was afraid there'd be this big scene. He said that maybe I'd be glad of the change, too, and I said, oh no, I wouldn't, I would miss him every day of the year and so would his children, and on the days when his father was clear his father would miss him too. I wasn't going to give him the nice comfortable feeling that he was doing us any favors. And out I went. I crept along the back way and he finished his packing and his leaving things out on the table, and your one came along in her car and he put the boxes and cases in and she kissed him just standing at our door and they drove off.

"When I came in it was all in neat piles on the table and a piece of paper saying 'Thank you very much, Mary. All the best, Billy.' So now you know everything, everything that's to be known."

"Isn't he a callous bastard, isn't he the biggest, most selfish—"

"That won't bring him back."

"I'll bring him back, I'll get him back. He's not going to desert you, there's ways of bringing him back."

"Not if he doesn't want to come back! Will you have your fish and chips now? They'll go all hard otherwise."

He hardly slept all night; it was only when the dawn came that he fell off, and it wasn't long after that that the twins were in the room followed by Gretta carrying a cup of tea. That was always their excuse to wake him: it was called bringing him his tea in bed. Most of it was in the saucer and some of it was on the stairs, but it was still an excuse. They were full of plans for the day. They'd come down and wait while he was feeding Grandpa and changing him. They accepted that routine as part of life, like sunsets or having to wash your hands before meals. They wanted to show him a new game that had arrived in Brophy's shop. It was a huge thing like a Space Invaders but it cost twenty pence a time and they could only have three goes altogether, unless of course Uncle Mikey wanted an extra game. And Mammy had said they could go on a picnic in the afternoon because since Daddy was gone to Dublin for a bit there'd be no work to be done around the house and no one coming in about insurance who had to have tea. And hadn't he better get up now in case all the good went out of the day.

Mikey felt the day was very heavy on his hands, that things kept happening as if he were outside looking in at all the things that were happening instead of being part of them. He saw himself feeding his father slowly with a spoon, he saw himself cutting crusts off the sandwiches for the picnic, and climbing for the blackberries. It was like playing a part in a play.

He was glad when it was evening and the children went to bed; they went easily because he had promised them the most monstrous surprise of their lives tomorrow. Something that he absolutely guaranteed they would never expect. He assured Gretta that it was something she could share, too, and that there was a small non-birthday present for her as well.

"I don't know what I'd have done without you, and that's the truth," Mary said. "The day just flew by for me." He was glad it had. He had arranged for two girls to help Treasa in the chip shop.

"Will Eileen not be in again?" Treasa complained. Her tone was guileless, she didn't know.

"No, she won't, she's gone off somewhere; we'll get you these two young ones you've had in there before on bank holidays and high summer," he said firmly. "Mrs. Billy and I are going to be down in Ryan's for a bit, so you'll know to send one of them down there if there's any problem, but a big bright girl like you, Treasa, you'll manage it. Don't you know it all like the back of your hand?"

Treasa was delighted with him.

"Oh, go on, Mr. Mikey, you and your Dublin chat," she said.

"Are we going off down to Ryan's?" he asked her.

He was going to make a joke and say something about stepping out together or hitting the high spots, but he felt it would have been the wrong thing to do. She looked up at him, pleased and surprised that he seemed so eager.

"I'm not much company for you."

"I think we should go out though, don't you? From the start like. No hiding away in corners, no crawling out when people think you've got two heads. Be out there from the word 'go.' After all, *you* haven't done anything."

"I've failed to hold on to my husband, that's a great crime around these parts."

"Oh, I don't think so; aren't they all stuck into television every night here? I think you'd have to do far more than that to be a disgrace."

"I hate you to be involved in it, Mikey, you've been nothing but kindness itself, every weekend as nice as anything and look what happens to you: caught up in all the scandal, all the gossip."

"There won't *be* scandal and gossip, and that's up to you to make sure of." He heard his own voice in his ears. He thought it sounded very confident, very sure. Mary must have thought so too.

"You're a great help to me making all these decisions, I'm like one of those things in films that just walk about not knowing what they're at."

"Zombies," he said.

"Imagine you knowing that," Mary said.

"I see a lot of films," Mikey said. "What else have I to do?"

Ryan's was crowded. He put Mary in a corner and went up to the counter. Celia was going full strength and Bart Kennedy was giving her a hand. Mikey remembered his brother's instructions about paying Bart a proper wage and bile against Billy rose in his throat. To be able to calculate like that, to plan for her desertion, to deceive her so long.

86

"It's not like you to be short of a word, Mikey Burns." Celia was standing in front of him. She must have asked him his order and he hadn't heard.

"I'm sorry." He had to force his sense of outrage down before he could speak.

"Are you all right?" Celia's voice was concerned.

Mikey shook himself. *He* was full of brave words to his sister-in-law about how *she* was to behave, now he must do the same for himself. He could speak again, but he hadn't the heart for jokes.

He gave his order and carried the pint and the glass of Snowball across to Mary. As he was passing young Biddy Brady's engagement party, Nancy Morris of all people put her hand out as if to stop him. Wanted him to come and tell them some funny stories. He always thought she was such a superior-acting kind of a one, always looking in on herself and never having time for other people. Well, well.

"Not now, Nancy," he had said, and he saw her face turning away embarrassed. He hadn't meant to be so short with her, but honestly, *now* of all times.

"Here we are," he said.

She had her head down looking at the floor.

"Look up, Mary Burns, look up and smile."

She looked up and gave a watery smile.

"That's marvelous but it isn't a patch on your daughter's." She gave one of Gretta's sudden grins, the kind of grin that split a face in half; they both laughed.

"That's better," said Mikey. "Now, let's see what we'll do."

They got out a writing pad and made out a list of things she had to do this week. Ring suppliers—their names were all on some kinds of bits of paper on various spikes around the office. Billy Burns hadn't kept any books that would gladden the heart of a taxman, but at least there was some method in his ways. They wrote out a kind of notice that she could give to anyone who called about insurance: "Mr. Burns' policies are all being dealt with by the following office . . ." followed by the name of the solicitor. She would give these to anyone with a laughing explanation that unfortunately as a mere woman she was never kept informed of the Master's doings. It seemed fairly sure that he hadn't absconded with other people's money, so his Book had been passed on or sold to some other agent by now. The solicitors would know. They listed the people they could call on to work in the take-away, and how much they should be paid. He went for two further pints and two further Snowballs, and by that time they had covered every eventuality and worn themselves out.

"I'll sleep tonight, I'm that exhausted," Mary said, letting out that she hadn't slept the previous night.

"I'll sleep too: I'm less frightened," Mikey said.

She looked at him gratefully. "You're very very good to me, but there's one thing you haven't mentioned at all."

"What's that?"

"What about you? Will you still be coming home on the bus at weekends?"

"I'll get off the Lilac Bus before ten every Friday, with the help of God," he said.

"You're very different tonight, you're not always cracking jokes and making games out of things people say. I find it much easier to talk to you, but hard to believe it *is* you, do you know what I mean?"

"I think so," he said.

"Like I want to ask you do you want to come home to Rathdoon even more than at weekends, but I don't know how to put it. If I say, will you come back altogether, it looks as if I want you to come back and look after us all and take it all on, and that's not it. And then, if I don't ask you, you might get the notion you're not welcome."

"I've thought all that out too," Mikey Burns said.

"And what did you arrive at?" She leaned over the glass with its rim of froth. She couldn't wait to hear.

"You're still hoping in your heart he'll come back. That it's only a bit of summer madness. That it'll be all forgotten by the end of the month."

"I'd like it, but I don't think it's going to happen," she said simply.

"So, suppose I came home and settled myself in and Billy Boy came over the hill one fine day, where would that leave us all?"

"As we were, wouldn't it?" She looked at him inquiringly.

"No. I'd have to run away again, there wouldn't be room for us all in the one nest."

"So are you not coming back to us. I always thought you had a great soft spot for us altogether." She sounded sad.

"I'll come back for good if he isn't back for Christmas. That's the best way. That's the way to do it." He looked proud of his deductions.

"It's your home," she said gently. "You were always as welcome in it as the sun coming in the windows."

"You say that because you're like that. My brother Billy didn't say it, did he, when he was leaving. He told you to get Bart Kennedy and pay him a proper wage."

"He did say it but I didn't repeat it. I didn't want to be making you think you had to do anything." She looked troubled now.

"What did he say?"

"He said . . . ah, it doesn't matter what he said. He made it clear he thought of the place as your house too."

"I want to hear it."

"Why? What does it matter? We know he hardly

knows what he's doing: he's half mad these days, he couldn't string words together."

"Well, I'd like to know anyway, please," he said simply but firmly. This wasn't the giggling, jokey man of last weekend.

"He said something like: 'Mikey's not likely to settle down anywhere with anyone at his age, and he's very good to the old man, and the children love him. Maybe if he could find something for himself around here, he'd be in the place. Sure, the house is half his anyway, he has a right to it.' It was something along those lines."

She didn't look at him, and he looked hard at the beermat, which had a puzzle on it.

"Full of charm, my little brother, isn't he?"

"That's what he is: your little brother, don't ever forget that."

"Would it suit you, Mary, if I were to be about the place?"

"Would it suit me? Wouldn't I love it, isn't it what I always wanted? There's always been a living for us all in that take-away alone, you've seen the takings, and if we were working in it together . . ."

"Well then, I'll come back at Christmas, that's the best. I might even get myself made redundant up at the bank, and have a lump sum. Those fellows up in the bank, the porters, are fierce organized, you'd never know what kind of a deal they'd get for me."

"Wouldn't it be dull for you, after Dublin?"

"No, don't I come home for nearly half the week as it is?"

"And maybe finding yourself a girl?" She was hesitant.

"I think brother Billy was right on that one, the time is past."

He smiled an ordinary smile, not a screwed-up one.

Rupert Green passed the table. "Did you see Judy Hickey at all?" he asked.

"No, I'm afraid we were talking, I didn't notice," Mary said.

"She could be around the corner behind the pillar there." Mikey pointed. Biddy Brady's party had linked arms and were singing "Sailing," and Celia's mother was arriving with a golf club as if she were about to brain them, but as they all watched horrified it turned out that she had no such intention: she was about to join in the singing, and was in fact calling for one voice only, her own.

"I've met everyone from the Lilac Bus except the one I set out to meet," grumbled Rupert. "Dee Burke was just flying out the door, Miss Morris looks as if she's had a skinful, Kev is cowering in a corner, and the rest of the cast is at the counter canoodling."

"If she comes in, what'll I tell her?"

"Oh, I'll find her, I have to tell her something extraordinary."

Mary and Mikey looked politely interested. He was gone.

"It's probably about some toadstool or mush-room; they're always talking about herbs and elderflowers and things," Mikey said. Mary laughed and tucked her bag under her arm.

"Won't you want another man?" he said suddenly. "I mean, you're still young. Won't living with a brother-in-law cramp your style?"

"No," she said. "No, I won't. I mean, even if I could have one and I can't. But I think I'm through with all that sort of thing. I think I just want a bit of peace and for the children to be able to grow up happily enough and for me to have a place here, you know, just like you said, not running away. That will do me."

He remembered the dream that he had on the bus: the dream where there had been no wife but he was in charge of the children, sending them on little messages up and down the street. He realized now there had been no Billy in the dream either. Some of the details were different, of course, but the central part was the same. He would be safe at home with them all. And there would be no demands made on him as a man. He could be just himself and he'd be as welcome as the sun that came in the windows.

JUDY

There had been four customers in the shop that afternoon. Judy had been taking note recently and writing it down in a little book. After lunch two students came in and spent almost half an hour reading books on herbalism and the art of home-made wines. An elderly man bought a copper bracelet for his arthritis and said that when the savages who came into his house and robbed him blind were leaving, they pulled his copper armband off in case it had been valuable. A woman with a tight, hard face bought some Evening Primrose oil and asked could you dilute it with ordinary vegetable oil or baby lotion to make it go further.

It was a matter of weeks now before they had to close. Judy's heart was heavy as she walked toward the Lilac Bus. She was tired, too, and not in form for a long drive to the West. She had been tempted to opt out. To go back to her little flat and have a long, long bath listening to some nice music on the radio. Then to put on her caftan and her soft little slippers and lie there until the aches in her limbs and the buildup of a headache behind her eyes was gone. Fine advertisement I am for a health shop. . . . She smiled to herself as she strode on toward the bus. Aching and creaking and bankrupt. No wonder people live such unhealthy lives if they see what good living leads to!

She hoped that Mikey Burns wouldn't be too loud tonight with his schoolboy jokes. He was a decent poor fellow but he was hard to take at any length. The trouble was that if you made no response to him he thought you hadn't heard and said it all again, and if you did manage a laugh he got encouraged and told you a few more.

She arrived just at the same time as Rupert: that was good, they could sit together in the back seat. It looked a bit standoffish if you were to keep a seat for anyone, but she really couldn't bear to be nudged by Mikey the whole way to Rathdoon, or even worse, to hear that solemn tedious little Nancy Morris telling her how to get free soap by buying toothpaste on a Wednesday or some such harebrained scheme.

He was a good boy, Rupert. Yes, that was exactly how she would describe him if anyone asked her. Good. He was an only child of parents who were middle-aged when he was a toddler and who were old now that he was a man of twenty-five. His mother was sixty-seven and his father was seventy this year. But Rupert said there were no celebrations; his father was bedridden now and was failing by the week. Rupert said it was harder and harder each time he came home because he had this vision of his father as a hardy man with views of his own on everything, and then when he got into the big bedroom on a Friday night it was the same shock, the same readjustment—a paper-thin man with a head like a skull, with nothing alive except the big restless eyes.

Judy had known Rupert since he was a baby and yet she had only got to know him since the bus. He had always been a polite child. "Good morning, Mrs. Hickey. Do you have anything for my pressed-flower collection?" Protestants were like that, she had always thought in her good-natured generalizations: pressed flowers, politeness, neat haircuts, remembering people's names. Mrs. Green was so proud of her Rupert, she used to find excuses to walk him down the town. The Greens had been married for twenty years when Rupert was born. Celia Ryan's mother in the pub had whispered that she gave Mrs. Green a novena to St. Anne that had never been known to fail, but because of her religion she had delayed using it. The moment she had said it, Catholic or no Catholic, St. Anne had intervened and there you were, there was Rupert.

Judy told him that one night on the Lilac Bus and he laughed till the tears came down his face. "You'd better tell me about St. Anne and what class of a saint she is. I suppose I should be thanking her that I'm here, or speaking sharply to her when times are bad."

Judy often smiled at Rupert's quaint ways. He was wonderful company and the same age as her own son, Andrew, miles away in the sun of California. But she could never talk to Andrew like she talked to Rupert—in fact, she could never talk to Andrew at all over the years. That was the legal agreement.

Judy wondered, would you recognize your own child?

Suppose she went to San Francisco now and walked through Union Square, would she immediately know Andrew and Jessica? Suppose they passed her by? They would be grown man and woman—imagine, twenty-five and twenty-three. But if she didn't know them and they didn't know her, what was all the point of giving birth and holding a child inside you for all that time? And suppose they did recognize her, that something like an instinct made them stop and look at this fifty-year-old woman standing in the sunshine. . . . What would they do? Would they cry "Momma, Momma" and run to her arms like a Hollywood film? Or would they be embarrassed and wish she hadn't turned up? They might have their own idea of a momma back in Ireland. A momma who was just not suitable. That's what Jack said he would tell them. Their mother hadn't been able to look after them—no other details. And when they were old enough to hear details and understand them, they would be given Judy's address to write to and she could send them an explanation if she felt able to. She never felt able to because they never wrote. For years and years she had been rehearsing it and trying out new phrases, like practicing for a job interview or a school essay.

Little by little she realized they were eighteen, nineteen, twenty. Well old enough to ask about an unsuitable mother. Well old enough to be told. But no request ever came.

She didn't even write to Jack's brother after a while. Jack's kind big brother, who had given them all a home on the West Coast of America, but who had always tried to patch up the split. He had told her nothing in his letters except to assure her that the children were settling in to their school and that all was for the best.

This evening she wondered about them both, Andrew and Jessica—golden Californians now. Were they married? Very probably. Californians married younger, divorced sooner. Was she a grandmother? Very possibly. His name might be Hank or Bud or Junior. Or were those all old names? Why did she think it was a grandson, it might be a girl, a little girl in a sunhat like Jessica had been the day they took her away. She had a Californian clock in her mind always, ever since they left twenty years ago. She never paused and said, "I wonder what time it is out there," she always knew. It was coming up to a quarter to eleven in the morning for them. It was always that when she came around the corner to the Lilac Bus. And she didn't know if they were married or single, working in universities or as domestics. She didn't know if they were happy or wretched, she didn't even know if they were alive or dead.

She slipped neatly in beside Rupert on the backseat, passing young Dee Burke, who had been looking so troubled for the last Lord knows when, it was amazing she hadn't cracked up. Past the odd young Nancy Morris. What a cuckoo in the nest that little one was—her mother was a grand little woman altogether, and Deirdre who had gone to the States was very nice, whenever she came back, full of chat. The brother in Cork was a nice lively fellow too. What had come over Nancy to make her so prissy or whatever it was she had become?

Rupert was wearing a new jacket that obviously thrilled him to the core. It just looked like an ordinary teddy-boy jacket to Judy, but then she was the first to admit she knew nothing about smart clothes. Dee Burke had gone into ecstasies over it and Rupert had flushed with pleasure.

"It's a birthday present," he whispered as the bus started. "I'll tell you all about it later."

She didn't want to hear all about it on the bus, not while her hip was aching and her head was throbbing, and that young Morris girl might well pretend not to be listening but was only two feet away from them. She felt old tonight. She was years older than everyone on the bus except Mikey Burns, and she was a good few years beyond him too. She was twenty years older than the young couple who had set up the health shop and who would be dismantling it within six weeks unless there was a miracle and they discovered the Elixir of Youth and bottled it in expensive but appealing packaging. Surely she was past all this rattling backwards and forwards across the country. Surely she should have some peace and settle down, in one place or the other.

She rooted in her big bag and gave Rupert a small parcel. "It's green tea," she said. "Just a little, to see if you like it."

His eyes lit up. "This is what you make the mint tea, the proper mint tea with?" he said.

"Yes, a handful of fresh mint, a little sugar in a glass, and you make the tea separately in a silver pot, if you have one, and then pour it on the mint leaves."

Rupert was very pleased. "I'd been making it with tea bags since we came back from Morocco, and it tasted really terrible, but out there it was like heaven. Oh, I *am* grateful to you, Judy."

"It's only a little," she said warningly.

"Look on it as a sample. If we like it we'll come in and buy kilos of the stuff and make your shop do a roaring trade."

"It would need it." She told him about the kind of trade they were doing. He was reassuring, it was the same everywhere.

He worked in an estate agency. Things were very slow. Houses that would have leaped off the books weren't moving at all. And there were shops closing down all over the place. But these things went in phases, he said. Things had to get better soon, the kind of people who knew about these things were confident, that's what you had to remember. Judy said wryly that the kind of people who knew about such things could probably still afford to be confident, they had so many irons in the fire. It was the rest of the world that was the problem.

They felt like old friends, the way they talked. She asked him to come and advise for a bit at the cutting of the elderflower, and to help choose some of the dried rosemary and lemon balm for the little herb pillows she was making. Rupert said that for the Christmas trade she should make dozens of those and sell them herself to big shops in Grafton Street—they would make great Christmas gifts. Fine, Judy said, but what about her own shop, the shop she worked in? That's the one she wanted to help, not big stores, which would make money anyway.

He told her about a politician's wife who had come into the auctioneer's and inquired politely about the location of her husband's new flat. Somehow they all knew that this flat was not a joint undertaking and that the wife was trying to find out. Everyone in the place had copped on and they all became vaguer and more unhelpful by the minute. Eventually the woman had stormed out in a rage. They had drafted an immensely tactful letter to the politician pointing out that his nest had not been revealed but was in danger of coming under siege.

"Poor, stupid woman," said Judy. "She should have let him install a harem in there if it kept him happy."

"You wouldn't have let him do that, you'd have too much spirit," Rupert said admiringly.

"I don't know. I let a man walk away with my

two babies twenty years ago. That wasn't showing much spirit, was it?" Judy said.

Rupert gasped. Never had Judy Hickey mentioned the amazing happening that the whole town knew about in garbled versions. He had asked his mother, who had said that nobody knew the whole ins and outs of it, and that Rupert's father, who had been the local solicitor then also, had been very annoyed because nobody consulted him, and he was the obvious person to have been brought in on it. But there had been something about a Garda charge and a lot of conversation and a solicitor from Dublin coming down for Jack Hickey and then documents being drawn up and Jack and the two children going to America and never coming back.

"But people must know *why*," Rupert had insisted.

His mother said there were more explanations than there were days in the year.

She had been only six years married and twenty now without her man and her children, but she always kept the name Hickey. It was in case the children ever came back, people said. There was a while when she used to go into the town seventeen miles away and ask at the tourist office if you could get the lists of American tourists, or just those with children. There was a while she would go up to the bus tours that sometimes came through Rathdoon and scan the seats for nine-year-old boys with seven-year-old sisters. But all that was long in the past. If it was

102

so long in the past, why had she mentioned them now?

"Are they on your mind then?" Rupert asked gently. She replied as naturally as if she was in the habit of talking about them. She spoke with no more intensity than she had talked of the mint tea.

"They are and they aren't. We'd probably have nothing to say to each other at this stage."

"What kind of work does he do now? He's not retired, is he?"

Who? Andrew? He's only your age. I *hope* he hasn't retired yet." She looked amused.

"No, I meant your husband. I didn't know whether your children were boys or girls." Rupert felt as if he had put his foot in it.

"Boy and girl, Andrew and Jessica. Andrew and Jessica."

"Nice names," he said foolishly.

"Yes they are nice names aren't they? We spent ages choosing them. No, I've absolutely no idea whether Jack Hickey is working or whether he is lying in a gutter being moved on by big American cops with sticks. And I don't know if he ever worked in California or whether he lived off his brother. I never cared. Honestly, I never gave him a thought. It sounds like someone protesting, I know it does, but it's funny: I have great trouble remembering what he looked like then and I never until this moment wondered how he's aged. Possibly got fatter. His elder brother, Charlie, was a lovely man;

he was fat, and there was a family picture I remember, and the parents were fat."

Rupert was silent for a moment. Such obvious indifference was chilling. You could understand hate or bitterness even. You could forgive a slow fire of rage and resentment. But she talked about him just as you would about some minor celebrity who had been in the news one time. Is he dead or alive? Who knows, who remembers? On to another topic.

"And do the children, well . . . do Andrew and Jessica keep in touch even a little bit?"

"No. That was the agreement."

If he was ever to know, it would be now. He inclined his head slightly to see if anyone else was listening. But no, Dee was fast asleep with her head at an awkward angle, and that awful Morris girl was asleep too. The others were too far ahead to hear.

"That was a harsh sort of agreement," he said tentatively.

"Oh, they thought they were justified. People used to think it was quite justifiable to hang a sheep stealer, don't forget."

"Is that what you did?" he asked, smiling. "Steal a sheep?"

"Would that it had been so simple. No, no, I thought you knew, I thought your father might have told you. No, I was a dope peddler. That's even worse than anything, isn't it?"

She looked like a mischievous girl the way she said it. He felt she couldn't be serious.

"No, what was it about really?" He laughed.

"I told you. I was the local drugs person." She spoke without pride or shame. Just as if she was saying what her name was before she was married. Rupert had never been so startled. "You do surprise me," he said, hoping he was managing to keep the shock out of his voice. "But that was *years* ago."

"It was the sixties. I suppose it is years ago, but your lot aren't the first to know about drugs, you know—the sixties had their own scene."

"But wasn't that only in America and England? Not like now."

"Of course it was here, too, not in huge housing estates, and not kids and not heroin. But with brightish, youngish things, at dances, and people who just left college who had been abroad, and it was all very silly, and to this day I think perfectly harmless."

"Hash, was it?"

"Oh yes, marijuana, pot, a few amphetamines, a bit of LSD."

"You had acid? *You* had acid?" He was half-admiring, half-shocked.

"Rupert, what I had was everything that was going, that wasn't the point. The point was that I was supplying it, and I got caught."

"Why on earth were you doing that?"

"Out of boredom in a way, I suppose. And the money was nice, not huge but nice. And there was a lot of fun too; you met great people—not deadwood people like Jack Hickey. I was very stupid really. I deserved all that happened. I often think that." She had paused to muse. Rupert mused with her for a bit. Then he spoke again:

"Were you doing it for long? Before you were caught?"

"About eighteen months. I was at a party and we all smoked something, Lord knows what it was called. I thought it was great, Jack had said nothing at the time, but when we got home he roared and shouted, and said that if this ever happened again, and what he'd do and what he wouldn't do."

"Had he refused it, then?"

"Ah, you didn't know our Jack, not at all, he had passed the poor little cigarette with the best, but he had kept his mouth closed and only pretended to inhale. He was sober and furious. Oh, there was a barney that went on all week, then the ultimatum: if I ever touched it again —curtains, he'd take the children off to America, I'd never see them again, no court in the land.

You could write it out yourself as a script and it would be right, it would be what he said." Rupert listened, fascinated. Judy's soft voice went on.

"Well, Jack was dealing with the livestock. It wasn't like a farm, you know, the house then, it was like a ranch: there were only livestock—no milking, no hens, no crops, just beasts in the field—buy them, graze them, sell them. We had poor old Nanny, she had been my nanny in the days of old decency and she minded Andrew and

106

Jessica. I used to go here and there, gathering material for a book on the wild flowers of the West. Gathering bad company more likely. Anyway, because I had my little car and because I went here and there, what could be more natural than I go to Dublin or to London—as I did twice to get some stuff for people. Others suggested it; I took it up like a flash."

"It's like a story out of a book," Rupert breathed admiringly.

"A horror story then. I remember it as if it were yesterday: acting on information received, warrant, deeply embarrassed, Mr. Hickey, a person of such importance as yourself, absolutely sure there's nothing in it, but have to apply the same laws to the high as to the low, and if we could get it all over as quickly as possible wouldn't that be for the best? Dear, dear, heavens above, what have we here, in *Mrs.* Hickey's car, and *Mrs.* Hickey's briefcase in the bedroom. And hidden away behind *Mrs.* Hickey's books. Well, he was at a loss for words, and perhaps Mr. Hickey could come up with some explanation?"

She was like an actress, Rupert thought suddenly. He could see the sergeant or the superintendent or whoever it was. She could do a one-woman show, the way she was telling the story; and it was without gesture or emphasis, since it was being told in a low voice not to wake the others as the minibus sped through the evening.

"It took forever. And there were people down

from Dublin and there was a TD, someone I didn't even know Jack knew. And Jack said that the whole place was becoming too much for him anyway and he had been thinking about selling it for a while, but if there was this scandal then people would know he was doing it under a cloud and the price of the place would drop right down. They were all businessmen, even the guards, they could understand that.

"Then the documents. Jack was going to take the children to his brother unless I signed a sworn statement that I agreed I was an unfit person to act as their mother any longer. The sergeant could charge me, as soon as Jack had the place sold, his plans made and was off to California with the babies. He begged me to think of the children."

"He did that and yet took them away from you?" Rupert was confused.

"Yes, you see, his point was that I was a drugs criminal, that wasn't a good start for any child: they'd be better without me. A deal had been done; kind, wise people had seen extenuating circumstances; it was up to me to make the most of them."

She looked out the window for a while.

"I didn't think it would be forever. I was frightened, I was sure it would all die down. I said yes. He sold the place—well, he sold it to that gangster, remember, who conned everyone and went off with a packet. Then the Liquidator or whatever sold it to the nuns and they made it into the conference center. So now you know the story of the Big House and all the bad people who lived there until the present day." He hadn't realized that she was once mistress of the big Doon House where she now lived in the gate lodge. Today the house had priests, nuns, and laypeople coming to do retreats, have discussions. And sometimes there were ordinary conferences that weren't religious at all: that's how the community made the costs of the place. But it was usually a very quiet type of conference where the delegates weren't expecting much of a night life. Rathdoon could offer Ryan's Pub and Billy Burns' chicken and chips; people usually expected more if they came a long way to a conference.

"I had to leave Doon House within a month. But he tricked me in one way. Even with the slightest hint of a drugs offense in those days you couldn't get into the States. They wouldn't give me a visa. And in order to make the distance as great as possible between poor Andrew and Jessica over there and their mad mother over here, Jack arranged that I be charged with a minor offense: possession. It was a nothing, even here, and compared to what I could have been charged with, which was dealing, it was ludicrously light. But then the deal had been done, don't forget. And even being charged with possession kept me out of the States."

There was another silence.

"Wasn't that a bad trick to play on you?" Rupert

"Yes. Yes. I suppose he thought like the people who burned people in the Inquisition . . . that they were doing the right thing. You know, rooting out evil."

"It was very drastic, even for the sixties, wasn't it?"

"Will you stop saying the sixties as if it was the stone age. *You* were born in the sixties, don't forget."

"I don't remember much about them." Rupert grinned.

"No. Well, I suppose you'd call it drastic; Jack would have called it effective. He was a great man for getting the job done." She spoke with scorn. "That's all he cared about. 'That's done,' he'd say proudly. It was the same coping with me. But Rupert, did you not know all this before? I mean, I don't want to make out that the whole town talks of me morning, noon, and night, but I would have thought that you must have heard some drift of it?"

"No, never. I knew that the children had gone away with their father and I think I asked why but I was never told."

"That's because you're so nicely brought up! They're too well bred in your house, they'd never talk of other people's business."

"I think my mother'd be glad to if she knew about it. And it's not only us. I once asked Celia why you didn't have your children, and she said there was some desperate row years ago when judges were even worse than they are today.

110

That's all, nobody knows about the . . . er . . . the smoke and things."

"I don't know whether to be pleased or disappointed." Judy laughed. "I always thought people believed I was up to no good with all the herbal remedies, bordering on the witch doctor nearly."

"I'm afraid people think that's very worthy, we'll have to make your image more villainous for you," Rupert said.

"Oh, for ages the unfortunate guards used to come and inspect my herb garden. I had a map of it for them in the end, and told them they must come in whenever they liked and that I would explain anything that looked a bit amiss. Then by the time I went to Dublin, they'd more or less written me off as a dangerous drugs pusher."

"You mean you're in the clear at last, after twenty years?"

"I don't know: sometimes I see the imprint of heavy boots round the camomile beds. Eternal vigilance."

"Do you hate Jack Hickey for it?"

"No, I said to you I never think of him. But you'd probably find that hard to believe, especially when I think of the children a lot, and to all intents and purposes I don't know them at all. They're strangers to me."

"Yes." Rupert obviously did find it hard to understand.

"It's the same with your mother, you know. Even though she doesn't let on, she thinks of you every day up in Dublin, she is aware of you in a way that it's hard to explain."

"Oh, I don't think so."

"I know it, I asked her once, just to know whether I was odd. She said that when you were away at school it was the same and at university and then when you went into the company. She says that often in her day she pauses and wonders what Rupert's doing now."

"Heavens," he said.

"Not for long, just for a second, you know, not brooding. But I expect you don't pause and wonder what she's doing."

"No, well I think of them a lot, of course, and since Father's been so badly and everything. I *do* think of them, of course," he said somewhat defensively.

"Stop getting upset, I was only using you as an example. Even if Andrew and Jessica had lived with me until they were grown up they might still be away and not thinking about me anymore. It's the way things happen."

"You're dead easy to talk to, I wish I could talk to my mother like I talk to you. She's much older, of course," he added tactfully.

"She is indeed, she could nearly be *my* mother, too, but that's not the point. . . . You can never talk to your own mother, it's a law of nature."

She smiled and looked out the window, and when that Nancy Morris started talking sense for once about how to relax neck muscles, she joined in. She was afraid that young Rupert Green had too much of the Meaning of Life and the Wronged Woman's viewpoint. She decided to let him snuggle back into his expensive Italian jacket and dream whatever his dreams were.

She always got on better with young people. Someone once said she should have been a teacher, but she said no, that would have been putting herself on the other side of the desk from them. But she had many more young friends than people her own age. Bart Kennedy, for example. She could talk to Bart till the cows came home, and she only exchanged the time of day with his father. Kev Kennedy up there in the front of the bus, he was another story: it was very hard going having a chat with Kev. He'd remind you of a young lad who'd been posted at a doorway to give a warning when the master was approaching. And she liked Celia and Dee, she thought, looking around the bus. And young Tom Fitzgerald, he was a great lad. You couldn't like Nancy Morris, but she wasn't young anyway. Despite her years she was an old woman and always had been.

The young people of Rathdoon had always been a great help to her with the things she grew in the small bit of land that Jack Hickey had given her twenty long years ago. She was *different* from other people, they told her: she didn't pass judgment on them all, she didn't tell them they should be married, or settled down, or more provident or less drinky. And even though they may have thought she was half cracked they came and helped her dig and pick and dry and pack.

113

helped her dig and pick and dry and pack.

She never found the house lonely, no more than the flat in Dublin. Not after all this time. She liked her own company, she ate meals at odd times, she would listen to music at midnight if she liked. In the flat she wore padded earphones and thought she must look like some aging raver if anyone could see her, but it was a house with many bedsits and flats and you couldn't wake civil servants and people who worked in big office blocks by playing your music through their walls. She did not feel the need of headphones in the lonely little lodge that was all Jack Hickey gave her from the big house. There was nobody near enough to hear, and the birds seemed to like hearing concertos and symphonies. They came and sat on the fence to listen more carefully.

The first time Tom had dropped her there he said he'd wait till she turned on the light. She had been pleased. He had enough nature in him to make sure that she got in safely. But then he was like all the youngsters she knew nowadays, far more natural and a lot more decency in them than the bombasts of her time. Like young Chris and Karen, who ran the health shop. They cared so much about it, they never wanted to be rich, to find a good line in anything that would be a snazzy seller and move quickly. They knew none of the jargon of the middle-aged businessman, and because they *were* idealistic and simple about things they were going to go to the wall. Her heart was ifornia somewhere Jessica and her husband, if she had one, were starting a health shop. Suppose they were in difficulties, wouldn't it be great if some kind older person were to help?

Judy only had a life interest in her gate lodge, she couldn't sell it even if she wanted to. She only rented her bedsitter in Dublin, she had no savings. Once she had saved the fare to America and kept the post office book thumbed and touched so often, it was almost illegible. She had it always in her handbag and would finger it as if it were the ticket to the States. But not now. And she would love so dearly to be able to contribute to Chris and Karen and their dream. Because it was her dream, that shop too. They could make her a director or some such nonsense. If only she had a small lump sum and a regular little subsidy for them instead of taking a small wage from their very sparse little till.

She told Rupert not to waste his weekend coming up to help her in the garden. He had come home to be with his parents and he might as well stay in Dublin if he didn't spend his time with his dying father and give his mother some lift by being in the house all weekend. She was very firm about this, even when he said he'd like the work and the exercise. There'd be plenty of time for all that later. Let him not waste the last months or weeks of his father's life digging and hoeing in a stranger's garden.

"You're not a stranger, Judy, you're a friend,"

Rupert had said. She had been pleased at that too.

It was a bright, sunny September Saturday. The place seemed to be full of activity. You got weekends when that happened, when Rathdoon seemed to hum with excitement, and you got other weekends when not even a tornado coming down Patrick Street would shake them up. She saw Nancy Morris prowling up and down as if she were looking for lost treasure, Kev Kennedy was in and out of his father's shop with a face on him that made it clear the Mafia had put out a contract on him that morning. Every time you stepped out on the road there was someone driving into town that would nearly mow you down. Mrs. Casey's ramshackle car with Nancy Morris's mother in it, Mikey Burns going around the place with a set face on him, either doing messages or taking his brother Billy's children blackberrying. He was preoccupied to a degree she had never known. She saw Celia, too, during the day, driving a car with the intent look of someone in a rally. Tom Fitzgerald came in for a couple of hours to help in the garden, saying that since he hadn't had one single cross word from any member of his family or their spouses he felt things were too good to be true and he wouldn't risk staying in their company one more minute in case the whole thing would fall apart. She saw Dee Burke driving her mother to town, her face empty and sad, her mother talking away without seeing any emptiness at all beside her. Imagine anyone thinking the country was quiet. Some weekend she must ask Karen and Chris to come and stay—some bank holiday, if they were still in business.

Red Kennedy come in to help his brother Bart. "Would these make a lot in Dublin?" he asked, looking at the little boxes of seeds.

Judy reflected. "Not a lot. In a way, we're just the wrong size. If it were a one-woman operation selling them at the side of the road, yes, there's a living; otherwise it should really be huge nurseries and big chain stores and all that. Still, we struggle on."

But it underlined to her the fruitlessness of it all, and the waste of effort not just from her but from decent young fellows like Bart and Red, like Mikey last week and Tom Fitzgerald's nephews when they were home from school. Was it really fair asking them to help in such a doomed business venture? They never did it for money, there wasn't any, but even in terms of their enthusiasm was it wrong to take so much of that as well? She thought of Chris and Karen in Dublin, anxious and also anxious on *her* behalf. They felt they owed her a place and a living because she had been so solidly supportive of them. How she wished that there had been a letter from a firm of American solicitors saying that the late James Jonathan Hickey of San Francisco, California, had left her a legacy and that her two children were going to fly over and deliver it personally. She often had fantasies about the children arriving, but this was

117

the first time she had thought about the money. Yes, she'd even take a legacy from Jack, even if the children didn't deliver it. Anything to help Chris and Karen.

Soon she called a halt to the work. Judy's great success was that she stopped her helpers before they got tired.

There were huge glasses of her elderflower wine, which some said was better and reached you more powerfully than anything that was pulled as a pint down in Ryan's. They sat on a wall in the sun and drank it, and the Kennedys went home.

It was dark in the small house and she felt well when she had washed the earth off. She lay out on her window seat with her hands behind her head.

"You look like a cat," Rupert said as he came in. The door was never closed in summer, never locked in winter.

"That's good. Cats are very relaxed," Judy said.

"Are you relaxed?" he wanted to know.

"Not in my head. My head is worrying about inessential things like money. I never worried about money before."

"I suppose it was always easy to get it before."

"Yes, well, in the old days I told you how I got it, but since then I haven't needed it much. Now I'd like to keep the shop open, that's all."

Rupert sat down on a rocking chair that squeaked. He got up immediately and went for the oil.

She thanked him, but said his mother had a rocking chair, he should be sitting on that.

"There's nothing to say; I had to escape for a little bit," he pleaded.

"Only a little," Judy said.

"It's just that he tried to talk. He asks are there many houses on the market and things." Rupert had a face full of pain.

"But isn't that good? He's well enough, alert enough to know. Kind enough to care."

"Mother says that he really likes having me home. But it's nothing. Nothing at all."

"Only if you make it nothing for them." Judy lost her sympathy. She stood up and stretched. "Listen to me, Rupert Green, not one more minute of your father's time am I taking. I'm going for a walk in Jack Hickey's woods." He looked hurt.

"Please, boy, please. Think of all those years when you'll say, if only I could have just sat there and talked about any old thing. And for your mother, please. I'll meet you and you can buy me a pint of that synthetic stuff they call chilled wine down in Ryan's." He brightened up.

"Will you? That would be nice."

"When he's asleep, when he's had some return from you."

"I'm not *that* bad."

"No, but he was nearly fifty years of age when you arrived in his life and he had to be woken up with your teething and your screaming and then you didn't come into his office: he couldn't

119

put Green and Son. It's Green and MacMahon. Go on, sit with him, talk about anything. It doesn't matter if it seems formal and meaningless, you're there, you're trying . . . that's all that matters."

"And what time will we go to Ryan's?" He was eager.

"Rupert! Will you give over! This is not a date. Ryan's is not a cocktail lounge, it's the only bar in Rathdoon. I'll be down there when I feel like it and you come when your father's well asleep and you've had a bit of time with your mother."

"Around nine or so?" he said, desperate to be specific.

"Around nine or so," she said resignedly.

She put on her boots. It was a long time since she had walked the woods. The three nuns who ran the ecumenical conferences and the diocesan seminars in the big house knew vaguely that Mrs. Hickey in the gate lodge had once lived in the big house. They were always polite to her and encouraged her to wander around if she ever felt like it. They were possibly relieved that the wildish looking woman in the Gypsy-style headscarves didn't take them up too often on their offer. She never went anywhere near the house, but she had told them it was nice to be able to feel free to walk under those old trees and pick flowers. Sometimes she would leave a great bunch of bluebells at their door, wrapped up in damp leaves. She never rang or asked to be entertained in the parlor. It was an ideal relationship.

120

Today she walked more purposefully. She didn't just stroll, following a whim or a line of young saplings. No, today she knew where she was heading.

It was still there in among the ivy-covered trees. Wild now, but hidden from the most determined searchers because of that old fallen tree. It looked as if there was nothing beyond. She eased herself over the tree and stood once more in her own little marijuana grove. She saw the cannabis plants that she had begun twenty-two years ago, many dead, many seeded and wasted. Some living though, some needing only a little attention.

It wouldn't take her long to find a proper outlet in Dublin. It must be done well away from the shop; Chris and Karen must never know.

She felt as strongly about this as her husband had felt that Andrew and Jessica must never know.

She felt the old quickening under her heart. It would be exciting to be back in the business again after all these years.

KEV

Kev thought he'd never get away from the Pelican. The Pelican was in one of those good moods, very rarely seen of late, where he'd ramble on about people known only to himself. There was a cast of thousands in the Pelican's stories and the same people never appeared twice. Kev listened attentively because if you miss the bit where your man came in one day and your other man was already in there and your old fellow came out the other door then you lost the whole grasp of it, and the Pelican might easily snap some kind of a question at you to make sure you were on the ball.

Kev was only afraid of the Pelican; he was *terrified* of some of the others. But even though the Pelican was not the highest in the terror stakes, Kev would have let the Lilac Bus go to Rathdoon without him rather than risk insulting this man whose big hooked nose was the cause of his name. You didn't mess with the Pelican. Kev didn't know much, but he knew that much.

Fortunately, the Pelican was hailed by someone more interesting and Kev was released; he sprinted around the corner. The bus was almost full. But he wasn't the last. Mikey Burns was rubbing his hands: oh please, may he not have any quiz games tonight. Mikey was perfectly nice when he quietened down, but all this "I say I say I say" like one of those comics on a music hall show on telly. He was no *good* at it, that was what was so hopeless; he always laughed in the wrong place. It would have been nice to sit beside Celia; that's what he liked best: she'd address about five civil sentences to him and then she'd leave him to his own thoughts, as she looked out the window. Or Rupert, he was a quiet fellow, too, and not toffee-nosed or anything. Kev's brothers, Bart and Red, were always surprised that he didn't seem to know Mrs. Hickey better. They were mad about her. In fact, his da was always saying that they'd go over to her place and dig her witch's brews in the garden and her lavender and her forget-me-nots, and they wouldn't dig their own potatoes, like men. Mrs. Hickey was nice enough, but she had a disconcerting way of looking right through you when she was talking, as if she didn't want any small talk. Neither did Kev, of course, want any small talk, but he didn't want that dark intense face with those X-ray eyes looking at him either. He always got the feeling that she saw just a little bit too much.

Kev worked in security—well, not real security, with helmets and coshes and alsatians and vans with no hand signals. More like being a porter really or a commissionaire, but it was called security. When anyone phoned down to the front desk to ask if a letter had been delivered by hand or if a visitor had arrived Kev answered the phone with the words, "Hallo. Security?"

Once he had got a phone call from his father asking him to bring down boxes of some new potato chips that had been advertised on the television and the place was going mad looking for it. Kev's father had been so entertained by Kev calling himself security that he had threatened to telephone every day just for the sheer pleasure of it. Kev had told him anxiously that they had been told to keep personal calls down to the minimum. But he shouldn't have worried; his father wasn't going to waste good money on hearing the same joke over and over.

Bart and Red didn't know what he came home for every weekend. It wasn't that they didn't want to see him, they were just as happy that he was back as not. But why *every* weekend? That was what would fox you. He didn't even go to the dance on a Saturday night. And he didn't have a crowd to drink with in Ryan's; he'd go in and out for a couple, but he wouldn't have a session there. The Kennedys had little or no conversation with their da, who had a cigarette in his mouth and the radio on full blast from morning to night. It was unlikely to be for company.

Kev knew that he was a bit of a mystery to them. And to Tom Fitzgerald, who had explained that the bus only made a profit if he could be sure of his seven passengers on a Friday. That's why he could do it so cheaply. You agreed to come on the bus every Friday for ten weeks, or if you couldn't you'd send someone in your place—not to Rathdoon, of course, but part of the way, or as far as the big town seventeen miles from home. Or if you could find nobody you still paid for your seat. That way it was half the cost of any other bus going that route, and what's more, it brought you to the door. Kev was getting out of the bus before ten o'clock and saying good night to Nancy Morris, who only lived across the street. He was home in Rathdoon safe. He would take a big breath of air and let it all out in a long sigh of relief. Tom often looked at him puzzled, and his father would nod welcomingly over the radio and tell him it was just coming up to the news. A mug of tea might be handed to him and a slice of shop cake cut. They had never known any other kind of cake, Kev and his brothers. Their mother had died long ago and even Bart, who could remember her, never knew her when she was well enough to make bread or cakes. When the news was over his father might ask had it been a hard week and were there any savages with crowbars in. He said there were more cases of violence in Dublin than there were in Chicago and he would never set his foot in the city again without an armed guard. Kev had tried to argue with him in the beginning, but now, he didn't bother. Anyway, nowadays he was beginning to think his father was right.

Nobody at work knew where Kev went at weekends: they all thought that he was some kind of lay monk or something and that he went to do good works but part of the goodness was that you didn't talk about it. The kind old Mr. Daly, one of the nicest people Kev had ever met, would shake his head in its uniform cap, full of admiration.

"I don't know why they give out about the younger generation," old Mr. Daly would say, "I really don't. There's that young Kev who works with us in the front hall, and he's off giving soup to winos and praying in front of the Blessed Sacrament, and teaching illiterates to read. Gone out of here like a bow from an arrow at six o'clock and we never hear hair nor hide of him until Monday morning."

Kev had never told one word of this fabrication to Mr. Daly or to anyone else. But having heard it, and seen that it was accepted, he let it pass. After all, if anyone came nosing around and asking questions, wasn't it better that old Mr. Daly and John and the others thought he was with the Simon Community or the Legion of Mary rather than knowing he caught a lilac-colored minibus as regularly as clockwork and sped out of Dublin and all its danger every Friday night.

Just suppose for one sickening minute that Daff or Crutch Casey or the Pelican came around, upset over something—well, there was nothing they could be told. Nobody knew where Kev went at weekends.

He had always had this secrecy, even when he was a young fellow. He remembered Bart telling a total

126

stranger in the shop that their mother was dead, that she had died in the hospital after two months and a week. Kev would never have given that information to a woman who had come in to buy bars of chocolate and ice cream for the children in the car. No matter how nice she had been, no matter how much she had praised the three young lads serving in the shop because their father was out getting the shed at the back built to hold the gas cylinders and the briquettes. Kev would have told her nothing and put his arm in his mouth, which was a great way to stop having a conversation. But Bart and Red would tell anyone anything. . . . Bart even told about the time when Kev was seventeen and he had tried to get Deirdre Morris, who was the much nicer sister of Nancy, to come into a field with him and swore it was to show her a nest of small birds.

Deirdre Morris had thrown back her head laughing, pushed him over so that he fell in the mud and had gone home laughing. "A nest of small birds's—is that what they call it nowadays?" Kev was shocked. To admit to such a lustful thing, and even worse, to admit to such a defeat. But no, Bart thought it was a scream; and that time that Deirdre had come back from America, married, with a baby called Shane, Bart was still able to laugh over it with her. And Red was the same, a demon dancer and he'd tell half the country their business, and about how they should have got an agency for tarmacadaming the place but his da hadn't moved quick enough and Billy

Burns had got it first. Kev told nothing. But then Kev had much more to hide.

Celia arrived just after him and the doors were closed. They were off. Around the corner and through the open door of the pub he could see the Pelican holding a pint in one hand and a rolled-up newspaper in the other. A rolled paper was a great thing for making a point, for emphasizing something. That was the Pelican's style. Emphasizing things.

Mikey was unfortunately in top form tonight: tricks with matches and a glass, have them rolling in the aisles in a pub. Didn't poor Mikey realize that it was only drunks that suddenly started doing match tricks in a pub, or lonely people, or madmen. Not ordinary people, unless they were all in a group of friends, and if you had a group of friends, why would you need to do tricks anyway? He was explaining how to weight the matchbox; Kev looked out the window and saw the housing estates outside Dublin flashing by. Old Mr. Daly said to him that any day now Kev would find himself a young woman and they'd save for a house in a place like that and there'd be no knowing him ever after. People like Mr. Daly and Mikey knew nothing about the real world. There was Mikey going on about how you weighted the matchbox deliberately with a twopenny piece in it and it always fell over on the side you'd put the coin in, so you could bet someone that it would always fall on the side you said. Kev had looked at him vacantly.

"I bet you Bart or Red Eddie would love a trick like that," Mikey muttered. Kev knew they would. They had the time and the peace of mind to enjoy it.

Kev never told Mikey that he was a porter, too, in a way. Well, security really, but it was the same field. He never told any of them where he worked, except that it was in the big new block. You could be doing anything there, literally anything. They had civil servants and they had travel agencies, and airlines and small companies with only two people in them; they had a board in the hall with a list a mile long of the organizations who were tenants of the building. Kev just said he worked there; when anyone asked him what he did, he said this and that. It was safer. One morning he was standing there in his uniform and he saw Dee Burke coming. She was going with some papers to a solicitor on the fifth floor. Mr. Daly phoned up and announced her, and Kev had sorted furiously on the floor for something so she didn't see him. Later he wondered why. It couldn't matter whether Dee Burke knew that he worked at the front desk of the big new office block. She hardly thought when she went to buy her cigarettes at the Kennedy shop that their youngest son was the chairman of some company up in Dublin. He didn't even want her to think he was in a clerical job. Why hide then? Wiser. Like not walking on cracks in the road. No reason, but it just *seemed* the right thing to do.

Of course, in a way it was all this secrecy that

had him where he was. If he had been a different type he'd never have got into this mess at all.

It began on his birthday, he was twenty-one. It was an ordinary working day. His father had sent him a ten-pound note in a card with a pink cat on it. Bart and Red Eddie had said that there would be great drink in Ryan's next Friday on account of it. Nobody else knew. He hadn't told Mr. Daly in case the old man might get a cake and embarrass him; he didn't tell anyone back up in the house where he had a room. They kept to themselves a lot and if they heard him saying he was twenty-one they'd feel they had to do something for him. He didn't tell anyone up at the pigeons either. In the lofts they didn't have time for birthdays and such things. So that day nobody in Dublin knew that Kevin, youngest son of Mr. Michael Kennedy, shop proprietor, and the late Mrs. Mary Rose Kennedy of Rathdoon had now reached twenty-one. He thought of it a lot all morning and somehow it began to seem over-important to him. Other people had records played for them on radio programs, other people who were twenty-one had cards, lots of them, not just one. Dee Burke had a party in a hotel—he remembered hearing about it just a couple of months back; Bart and Red had been invited and Bart said he couldn't get into a monkey suit, but Red the demon dancer had hired one and had a great time. And even his own brothers had bits of celebration. Bart and all his pals had a barbecue down by the river; those were before every Tom,

Dick, and Harry were having barbecues. They roasted a bit of beef and ate it between doorsteps of bread and it was gorgeous, and there'd been great singing and goings-on. And when Red was twenty-one two years back, there had been a crowd of them who had all come to the house for a few drinks and a cake, then they'd got into a truck and driven off to the dance. But nothing at all for Kev.

It got on his mind. He made an excuse to Mr. Daly and said that he wanted to go out the back for half an hour. He didn't feel well. Mr. Daly was so concerned that he immediately felt ashamed. Those were the days before he had been a regular disappearer at weekends, before Mr. Daly had assumed that he was an unsung and uncanonized saint.

He sat out in the loading area, as it was called, a place where vans could come with deliveries of paper, or messengers on those big motor bikes with speaking handlebars could leave their machines. He took out a cigarette and thought about other fellows his age and wondered why he had been so anxious to get away and why he had ever thought it would be any better. Four men were loading a van efficiently. A fifth was standing leaning on a crutch and staring around him idly. Into the van were going sanitary fittings, hand basins, lavatories, small water heaters. Without haste but with commendable speed they loaded.

Kev dragged his cigarette. They must be getting new fitments somewhere upstairs, that looked like a big contract. Wait. He hadn't seen any of them come through security, and everyone had to come to the front desk. Even if they went straight out the door again and were sent around to the loading bay. The rules said desk first.

His eyes took on the merest flicker of interest, but it was enough to alert the man with the bent leg leaning so casually on the crutch.

"Not wearing a cap, didn't notice him," he said out of the corner of his mouth.

A big man with a beak-shaped nose paused momentarily and then slid from the human chain that was stacking the fitments. He strolled over to Kevin, whose stomach knotted in fright. He realized like a shower of cold rain coming down his gullet that this was a Job, these were five men taking fitments *out* of the new building, fitments that would turn up again in houses all over the city. He swallowed hard.

The Pelican walked slowly: he didn't look a bit furtive, nor did he look worried.

"Can I have a smoke?" he asked casually. Behind him the loading continued regular as clockwork, innocent as anything.

"Yes, um." Kev handed him the packet.

"What are you doing with yourself here?" The Pelican's eyes narrowed.

The question was perfectly polite. It could have been a gentle inquiry of any fellow lounger on a summer morning. He might even have added something like "on this fine day." But he hadn't. The Pelican and all of them were waiting to know what Kevin would say and Kevin knew that what he said now was probably going to be the most important question he ever answered in his life.

"It's my twenty-first birthday," he said. "And I got annoyed sitting inside there in security and nobody knowing, so I thought I'd come out here and have a bit of a smoke, anyway, to celebrate."

There was absolutely no doubt that what he said was true. You didn't need a lie detector or the experience of years with truth drugs to know that Kev Kennedy had given a perfectly accurate account of why he was there, and something about him made the Pelican believe that there was going to be no trouble here.

"Well, when we're finished here maybe we'll buy a drink at your lunch hour. A fellow shouldn't be twenty-one and have nobody know."

"That's what I think," Kev said eagerly, averting his eyes from the biggest and most barefaced theft from the building where he was meant to be part of security. It seemed to be winding up now, the convoy were closing the doors and getting into the van.

"So, what is it? One o'clock?" The Pelican's nose was like a scythe, so large and menacing did it appear, and his eyes were like two slits.

"It's a bit difficult at lunchtime, you see, I only get forty-five minutes and I suppose you'll be moving on out of the area." Kev's face was innocent.

"But where would you like your birthday drink then, and when?" There was no area for argument in the proposal, only a small margin of latitude for the time and place.

"Well, wherever you like, of course, and at about six. Is that all right?"

Kev was eager. The Pelican nodded. He named a city-center pub.

"We'll give you a drink each, and as you no doubt saw there's five of us, so that's five drinks."

"Oh, God, that would be great altogether," Kev said. "Are there five of you? I didn't notice."

The Pelican nodded approvingly. He swung his way back to the van and in beside the driver, who looked like a champion wrestler.

"Six o'clock," he called cheerfully out the window.

It wasn't discovered until four-thirty. A lot of offices on the sixth floor weren't occupied yet. Some people just assumed that the bathrooms were being refitted, and sighing, had gone to other floors. It was only when one of the secretaries said she was getting dropped arches and told Mr. Daly that it was an extraordinary thing to think that brand-new cloakrooms should be redone within three months, that any kind of alarm was raised. The broad-daylightness of it all staggered them. The guards were called, the confusion was enormous. Kev had difficulty in getting away by six. He was ninety percent sure that they wouldn't be there. They could be walking into a trap for all they knew. How were they to know that they were dealing with Kev Kennedy who never told anybody anything? They might have assumed he would have plainclothes guards drinking pints of shandy all around the pub. But just in case. And just in case they came back and dealt with him. After all, they knew where he worked, he knew nothing about them.

They were all there.

"There was a bit of commotion at work, I got delayed," he said.

"Ah, you would all right," said the Pelican generously. He was introduced to Daff and John, and Ned and Crutch Casey.

"What's your real name?" he asked the man with the twisted leg.

"Crutch," the man said, surprised to be asked.

They each bought him a pint and they raised their glasses solemnly and said Happy Birthday at each round. By the fourth round he was feeling very wretched. He had never drunk more than three pints in Ryan's and never more than two anywhere else. Ryan's led you to be daring because even if you fell down you got home on all fours without too much difficulty.

Daff was the man like a wrestler. Kev wondered why he was called that, but he decided it might not be wise. Daff bought the last drink and handed Kev an envelope.

"We were sorry to see a culchie all on his own with no one to wish him a happy birthday, so that's a small present from Pelican, Crutch, John, Ned

135

and me." He smiled as if he were a foolish, generous uncle dying for the nephew to open the electric train set and begin to call out with excitement.

Kev politely opened the envelope and saw a bundle of blue twenty-pound notes. The room went backwards and forwards and began to move slowly around to the left. He steadied himself on the bar stool.

"I couldn't take this, sure you don't know me at all."

"And you don't know us." Daff beamed.

"Which is as it should be," the Pelican said approvingly.

"But I'd not know you, without . . . without this, you know."

He looked at the envelope as if it contained explosives. There were at least six notes, maybe more. He didn't want to count them.

"Ah, but this is better, this *marks* the day for all of us. Why don't we meet here every week around this time, and if you've that invested properly then you could buy us a drink, and slowly we could sort of *get* to know each other."

Kev's mouth felt full of lemon juice.

"Well, I'd love to . . . sort of keep in touch with you all but honestly, this is too much. Like, I mean, I'd feel bad."

"Not at all, you wouldn't." The Pelican smiled and they were gone.

Every Tuesday since he had met them; sometimes it was just a drink. Sometimes it was more. Once

136

it had been a driving job. He would never forget it to his dying day. They went into a new block of flats and carefully unrolled the brand-new stair carpet. They had heard that the fitting men were coming that afternoon so they had anticipated the visit by removing every scrap of it. The timing had been of the essence on that one. The expensive wool carpet had arrived that morning; there was only a four-hour period when it could be removed, and that meant watching the flats very carefully in case any untoward inquiries were made. It was all completely successful, of course, like all their enterprises seemed to be. Kev had taken a day off work for the carpet heist, but the carpet heist had taken years off his life. He felt as if he had been put down on the street and the whole crowd coming out of Moran Park had walked over him. He couldn't understand how they remained so untouched. Crutch Casey told of horses that had fallen at the last fence. Ned and John were more dog people, they talked of evil-minded and corrupt greyhounds who *knew* how to slow down, through some instinct. The Pelican told long tales full of people that nobody knew, and Daff seemed to say nothing much, but he was as relaxed as a man coming out after a swim about to light his pipe on the beach on a sunny day.

They never told him he *had* to join in, and they didn't ask him so much that he felt he should run away to America to escape them. Often he didn't have to do anything except what they called "re-sorting." That might mean wrapping a whole load of Waterford glass, which arrived from a hotel before it got time to get out of its boxes, into different kind of containers. Each glass to be held carefully and sorted according to type, wrapped in purple tissue paper in gift boxes of six. He became quite an authority on the various designs, or suites as they were called, and decided that the Colleen Suite was his favorite; and that when he got married he would have two dozen Colleen brandy glasses and use them around the house as ordinary everyday glasses, or in the bathroom for his toothbrush. Then he remembered what he was doing and the fantasy would disappear. He would look around the garage and keep parceling in the nice anonymous gift boxes. He never knew where they went, and what happened to them. He never asked. Not once. That's why they liked him, that's why they trusted him utterly. From that very first day in the loading area they thought he was one of their own, and it was too late now to tell them that he wasn't. The longer it went on, the more ludicrous it would be trying to get out.

On calmer days Kev asked himself what was so terrible. They never took from individuals, they didn't do people's houses and flats. It was companies who had to replace miles of red wool carpet, boxes of prestigious glassware, rooms full of sanitary fittings. They never did over old women, young couples; they never carried a weapon, not even a cosh. In many ways they weren't bad fellows at all. Of course, they never actually went out to work in a normal way, and they did lie to

138

people, with their clipboards and their air of being perfectly legitimate. And people did get into trouble after they'd visited places, like poor old Mr. Daly, who'd been hauled in by everyone and though it was never said, the thought had been in the air that he might be getting too old for the job. And they stole. They stole things almost every week and by no standards could that be a thing that Kev Kennedy from Rathdoon wanted to be in. Or worse, caught in. It was unthinkable. They still talked about that young fellow who was a cousin of the Fitzgeralds and worked in their shop for a bit; he was given three years for doing a post office in Cork. The whole of Rathdoon had buzzed with it for months and Mrs. Fitzgerald, Tom's mother, had said she hoped everyone realized that he wasn't a first cousin, he was a very far out one, and they had tried to give him a start and look at the thanks they got. Could you imagine what old Da would have to go through? And all Red's hopes of getting some gorgeous wife would go for their tea, and poor Bart was so decent and helpful, wouldn't it be a shame on him forever?

But how did you get out? He couldn't live in a city that contained the Pelican and Daff and Crutch Casey if they thought he had ratted on them. There was no point trying to pretend that he had left town or anything. They knew everything: it was their business to know things, to know when deliveries were expected, when watchmen went for their coffee, when regular porters were on holidays, when managers were young and nervous, when shops were too busy to notice their furniture being loaded into private vans. They knew where Kev lived and worked; he wouldn't dream of lying to them.

But he got out of weekend work. That's when they did some of their bigger jobs, and he wanted to be well away from it. He told them vaguely that he had to go out of town. He had been going home that very first weekend after they met him and so it had seemed a natural continuation, not a new pattern of behavior. He didn't say it was Rathdoon, he didn't say it was home, but they knew he wasn't lying when he was saying that he went out of town for weekends. Crutch Casey had said good night to him one Sunday night outside the house where he had a room, and Kev knew that it was just a routine inspection. He had been cleared now; even the Pelican, whom he had met by accident just on the corner, knew that he was leaving Dublin for the weekend—he didn't even bother to check.

But how could he get out of working for them midweek? Some of the jobs were getting bigger and Kev was getting tenser. Once or twice Daff had asked him not to be so jumpy—that he was like some actor playing a nervous crook in an old black-and-white B movie. It was fine for Daff, who didn't have a nerve in his body. Simply fine for him. Others didn't find it so easy. The very sight of a guard was enough to weaken Kev's legs, even the shadow of anyone fairly big was enough to make him jump. Oddly enough it hadn't made him feel guilty about religion. He went to Mass, and at Christmas and Easter to communion; he knew that God knew that there wasn't much sin involved. No grievous bodily harm or anything. But he had never been much of a one for talking to God individually like you were meant to: he didn't feel like putting the question personally. And there was nobody else, really, *but* God, when all was said and done, because everyone else would have a very strong view one way or the other, and mainly the other. Like get out of that gang at a rate of knots, Kev Kennedy, and stop acting the eejit.

Mikey's poor, kind face was there a few inches from him. Mikey Burns, who'd be the kind of bank porter that would get shot in a raid—certainly not like Kev, the kind of security man who had become best buddies with the gang that had ripped off all the fittings from the place where he worked. Mikey Burns, sleeping with a little smile, dreaming about something—jokes with glasses of water and coins maybe—and there was he, Kev, who had driven getaway vans and done watch duty and helped to reparcel stolen goods. Kev felt alien as he looked out at the darkening countryside. Lonely and guilty as hell.

His father told him after the news that Red had notions about a farmer's daughter and was going to bring her to tea during the weekend no less, and they were all to keep their shoes on, talk nicely and put butter on a plate and the milk in a jug. He said that he thought Bart might as well join the Franciscans and put on sandals and carry a begging bowl for all the good he was ever going to do with his life and his share of the business. When he wasn't digging up Mrs. Hickey's fox-gloves and hemlocks, or whatever it was she grew, he was helping Mrs. Ryan in the pub to stand on her own two shaky legs and serving the customers from behind the bar and not a penny piece was he getting from either of them. He was surprised that Bart hadn't gone into Fitzgerald's shop and said that if they'd like someone to stand there and serve for a few days a week without wages he'd be happy to do it. Kev didn't know what to say to this. He nibbled a slice of cake and thought about the difference between people. There was Daff, who had a nice big open face like Bart, organizing the transfer of twenty microwave ovens from one warehouse to another by a deceptively simple scheme that involved Ned, who was the most forgettable of them all, going up with a sheaf of papers, an air of be-wilderment, and an instruction that they were apparently to go back to have something checked. And there was Bart Kennedy, who had a big open face like Daff, digging Judy Hickey's garden for her and helping Celia's mother to stay upright in Ryan's. God what different worlds he moved in; Kev thought with a shudder at the danger of it all. "Are you not going down to the pub?" his father asked.

"No, I'm tired after the week and the long journey. I'll just go up and lie on my bed," he said.

His father shook his head: "I really wish I knew what brings you home, you do so little when you arrive, and you've lost your interest in football entirely. You could have been a good footballer if you'd put your mind to it."

"No, I was never any good. You only say that because you wanted a son a county footballer. I'm no good."

"Well, what *does* bring you back here? What are you running from . . . ?" He hadn't finished, but Kev's cup was in pieces on the floor and his face was snow-white.

"Running, what do you mean?"

"I mean, is it the violence up there or the dirt, or those blackguards roaming in tribes or what? Haven't you good wages, and you're always very generous giving me the few quid here . . . but a young man of your age, you should be up to all kinds of devilment and diversions, shouldn't you?"

"I don't know, Da, I don't think I was ever much good at anything, football, devilment, anything." He sounded very glum.

"Haven't you got a fine job up in one of the finest buildings in the land, and you earn your own living, which is more than those two boyos there—oh, they're a great pair I have on my hands. One a sort of Martin de Porres, going around the place giving half his cloak to everyone he meets; one a dandy who has the bright red hair nearly

143

combed off his scalp and the mirrors nearly cracked in bits staring into them. You're the best of them, Kev, don't be running yourself down."

Kev Kennedy went up to bed without a word, and he lay there as the sounds of Rathdoon, which were not very loud, went past his window, a small window over the shop, which looked out on the main street.

Red's girl was coming the very next day it turned out, so they all had to do a spring clean on the back room. There were to be cups instead of mugs, a clean cloth was spread and bread was cut on a tray and then put onto a plate to avoid all the crumbs. They took ham and tomatoes and a bottle of salad cream from the shop, and Red hard-boiled three eggs.

"This is a feast—she'll marry you immediately," Bart said when he saw Red looking speculatively at some of the frozen cakes in the cold-food section.

"Quit laughing and keep looking around the room to see what it would look like to a new eye." Red had it bad this time. Her name was Majella and she was an only child. She was used to much greater style than the three Kennedy brothers and their father could provide, even if they had been trying seriously. But none of them except Red was making much of an effort: their father wanted to be in his shop, Bart wanted to get over to Judy Hickey, and Kev wanted to go off down by the river, where he felt nice and quiet and miles from all that was happening at this very moment to microwave ovens in a warehouse in Dublin.

Majella was arriving at five o'clock. Her father would give her a lift, but he wouldn't call in; it was much too early for that yet. They did a deal, the brothers. Bart and Kev agreed to wear proper ties and jackets and have polished shoes. Red agreed to go over to Judy Hickey's and put in two hours because she needed it this weekend particularly and because it would keep him calm. There would be no bad language, eating with fingers, and picking of teeth, but in return Red would not embarrass them by giving moon-faced sick-calf impersonations, nor would he ask them to delight Majella with stories of their exotic lives. When the bell rang to say that somebody had come into the shop, they would go in order of seniority. Da first, then Bart, then Kev, then Da and so on. Red was not to abandon them to talk to Majella on their own.

She was a lovely big girl with no nonsense in her, and by the time they had sat her down she was like part of the family. She said they must be great fellows altogether to have the butter on the plate and the milk not in a bottle but in a jug. Whenever she went over to her cousin's place they were all putting their dirty knives into the butter at once; they needed a woman to civilize them. Red began to look like a sick calf when she talked of the civilizing influence of a woman, and he had to be kicked until he dropped it again. Majella said she was going to do the washing up and they could all dry, and seeing out of the corner of her eye that the dishcloths were not all they might be she called to Red to bring a new packet out of the shop.

"Isn't it paradise to be here!" she said with a big smile at them all. "Who could want anything better than a shop right off your own living room?"

They had dried up in no time; the big room looked better somehow than it had done for years. Majella said that maybe she and Red might go for a bit of a tour around Rathdoon now and get out of everyone's way. By half past six she had a blushing, delighted Red firmly by the arm and was linking him on her own little lap of honor around the community she had decided to join.

"Oh, there's no escape there, that knot will be tied, poor Red." Bart laughed good-naturedly about the fate that could well be happening to his brother.

"Will you stop that nonsense: poor Red, my hat! Wouldn't a girl have to be half mad or have the courage of a lion to marry any one of the three of you." His father sounded very pessimistic indeed.

"Would you say she *is* mad?" Kev asked interestedly. "She was a very nice class of a girl, I thought."

"Of course she's nice, she's far too good for him. The thing is, will she realize it in time?" Bart and Kev exchanged glances. Their father seemed to be torn between the delight of having the lovely,

146

laughing Majella around the place and the strictly honest course of action, which was to warn the girl that his son was a bad bargain.

"Let her work it out for herself maybe?" Bart suggested and his father looked relieved.

Bart had a lot of sense, Kev realized, suddenly. He wasn't just a do-gooder and a big innocent. But he was the other side of the tracks now, he wasn't in the Underworld like Kev was, there could be no talking to him about the problem.

"Would you fancy an early pint down in Ryan's before the mob gets in there?" Bart said to him. Kev was pleased.

"That'd be the way to do it," he said sagely. Their father had gone back to the shop and was twiddling the dial for the news.

They walked down the road. It was quiet—most people were in at their tea; the sound of the half-past six news that their father was listening to back in the shop came from several windows. Down they walked, past Billy Burns' chip shop. Billy wasn't there today, just Mikey and that bright little Treasa who worked there. No sign of the new girl Eileen—well, she had always looked too good to spend her day lifting pieces of cod or wings of chicken out of a deep fryer in Rathdoon. They came to the bridge. Bart leaned over and looked at the river. They used to race sticks under the bridge here when they were kids, and there were always so many arguments about whose stick had won, Bart invented a system of tying different colored threads onto each one. It seemed very long ago.

"What's eating you?" Bart asked.

"I don't know what you mean?"

"I'm not the world's brainiest man, but I'm not blind either. Tell me, Kev, can't you? It can't be any worse when you've told me. It might even be a bit better. Like, I'm not going to be saying, aren't you an eejit, or blame you or anything, but there's something terribly wrong up in Dublin, isn't there?"

"Yes," Kev said.

"Before Red fell so much in love that he can't think of anything else, he and I were going to go up there one day on the excursion and try and sort it out, whatever it was."

Kev gulped with gratitude at the thought of his two brothers taking on a heavy gang like Daff, the Pelican, Crutch Casey, and their team.

"What did *you* think the problems might be?" he asked nervously, fishing to see had Bart any notion of how bad things were or was he still in a world like the playground of the infants' school.

"I thought it might be a girl you got into trouble, but it's going on too long for that. I thought it might be a debt—you know, poker or the horses—but you don't seem to have any interest in either."

Bart's big innocent face looked puzzled. Kev drew a long breath. Well, it seemed that Bart could take on that much anyway. What about the next step? Could Bart listen to the story that had begun on his twenty-first birthday a year and a half ago, or would he run for the guards? Kev didn't know. Bart was shaping a stick and tying a bit of string around it.

"Here," he said to Kev, "let this be yours: I'll beat you any day with my one." They threw the sticks over the side and rushed across to see them coming through. Kev's stick was in front.

"Would you beat that?" Bart seemed surprised. "I've been up here practicing and I thought I had the shape of stick that ran best with the flow."

Kev began to tell him; in fact, once started it tumbled out of him: a mixture of names and commodities, Crutch Caseys and Microwaves, Daffs and cut glass, Pelicans and Axminster carpet. Kev had no starring role the way he told it, his only stroke of genius had been to go home every weekend on the Lilac Bus to avoid even more major crime in the city at weekends. He was in now and there was no getting out. Bart must know that; they'd all seen the films, they knew the plot. If Kev said to Daff that he'd had enough, thank you, he couldn't answer for the consequences but he knew it'd be awful. He didn't think they'd beat him up: they never used violence, he said almost pleadingly to Bart. But they would punish him. They'd send the guards around to his house or to work, or they'd send a note to Mr. Daly accusing Kev of giving the tip-off about the cloakroom fittings that time. It was a nightmare: he was in it forever.

He hardly dared to look at Bart during some

149

of the confession, and once or twice he gave the odd glance and got the feeling that Bart was half smiling. Maybe he didn't understand the hugeness of it all. Once he was almost certain he got a smile and Bart had hastily put his hand over his face.

"So now, you see I'm caught entirely," he ended.

"I don't think so," Bart said slowly.

"But it's not *like* here, Bart. You don't know, they're different from us. They're not our type of people."

"But they must have thought you were their kind of person, otherwise they wouldn't have pulled you in," Bart said.

"But I *told* you how that happened. I'm not a thief by nature, I'm fairly happy to work for my wages. Not very, but fairly. I'm not any good as a criminal."

"No, I don't mean their type as a thief; you're secretive like they are. That's what they liked about you—you're not a blabber about who you know, what you do. That'll make them think you won't blab about them."

"Well, I don't—haven't until now, that is."

"So that's how you get out if you want to. Tell them you're in with another lot now. No hard feelings, handshakes, pints all around, and that's it."

"Bart, you haven't any idea—"

"But you see, you keep up this hard-man image with them, except once or twice when you've had a fit of the shivers. You never try to talk them out of it, or discuss what they do with the stuff. They probably think you're a silent pro and someone has made you a better offer."

"They wouldn't have such a high regard for me as that."

"They must have a very high regard for you if they let you in on all their jobs. No, leave them as you joined them, with no chat, no explanations except the one they are owed. That you've got a new scene."

Bart talking about scenes, Bart saying that these gangsters are owed an explanation—it was like the end of the world.

"I don't think I'd be able to go through with it."

"You were able to join them; that was harder."

"And should I give them back the money?"

"Give them *what?*"

"My share, I mean, if I'm not staying on, like?"

"Your share . . . you have it still?"

"Of course I do, I didn't spend any of it, in case . . . you know . . . the guards and everything and a court case and I'd have to give it all back."

"Where is it?"

"It's upstairs in the room."

"In Dublin?"

"No, here, back at the house. Under the bed."

"You're not serious."

"But what else would I do with it, Bart? I carry it with me home and back each weekend in a parcel with my clothes."

151

"How much is it all? Your share?"

"I'm afraid it's about four thousand, two hundred pounds," Kev said with his eyes cast down.

Eventually he raised his glance and Bart was smiling at him with pride.

"Isn't that the direct intervention of God?" Bart said to him. Kev would never have seen it like that; however confused his relationship with God was and however nonpersonal it had become, he couldn't imagine that the Almighty was delighted with such a sum of stolen money arriving under a bed in Rathdoon.

"This solves all our problems," Bart said. "When Romeo back there went courting Majella, the only fly in the ointment was would we have enough to build on a bit at the back. We were afraid it would get a bit crowded with us all on top of each other, and we saw the very thing we wanted, a kind of ready-made extension that they dig foundations for and then sort of plant on top of. Do you follow?"

Kev nodded nervously.

"But Red and I were afraid you were in some kind of financial trouble and we'd better not get ourselves too far into a loan. But here you are, a millionaire. Now we can go ahead, and if you'd like to contribute a bit . . ."

"Yes, well, of course I would, but don't you think if I'm getting out of their gang I should *offer* them the share back?"

"What kind of criminal are you at all?" roared Bart. "Won't they know immediately you're a ninny if you start a caper like that. You've got to consider that your wages, your share of the deal. Now you're meant to be going on to a bigger one, you eejit; you're not meant to be giving them conscience money."

"No."

"And there's no way you can give it to the carpet people or the lavatory makers or the microwave people—"

"I wasn't in on the microwave—that's this weekend."

"See?" Bart felt this proved some point. "So what are you going to do with it—wouldn't building up the family home be as good as anything?"

Kev was astonished. No blame, no lecture, no accusation. Sheer hard practical advice, as if he knew the kind of people that Daff and the Pelican were. Because when you thought of it, that was *exactly* the way to go about it. And then he need never see them again.

"I'll give it all to you tonight, Bart," he said eagerly. "Where will we say we got it? Like if anyone asks?"

"You'll keep some of it, put it in the post office, but we'll say nothing to anyone, like you've been doing all your life. We'll get in touch with those people about the extension on Monday. What could be more natural than that country eejits like us would have money in a paper bag under the bed, they'll only be delighted—no VAT, nothing."

153

Kev was stunned. Saint Bart, in the black economy.

"Thanks to your very generous donation, we'll be able to get the bigger extension, and there'll be plenty of room if Majella produces a brood of Kennedys."

A stone fell off the bridge and into the water and Kev Kennedy didn't jump at all, and his eyes didn't widen with anxiety.

RUPERT

He bought a packet of mints because Judy Hickey had told him last week that he reeked of garlic, and much as she loved good herby smells she didn't want to sit cooped up beside a porous sponge of garlic for three hours on a small minibus. Funny, Judy: if he had met her in Dublin, he would never have suspected that she came from home. She wasn't a Rathdoon sort of person. He had told her that once and she had retorted that neither was he—a thin, pale, artistic young Protestant: what could be more unlikely?

But she was wrong. There were handfuls of Protestants in every town in the West; they were as much part of the place as the mountains and the phone boxes and the small beautiful churches with hardly any attendance standing dwarfed by the newer Catholic churches, which were bursting at the seams. No use explaining that to Judy, trying to tell her that she was much more unusual, dark and Gypsylike, living in a small gate lodge at the end of the drive from Doon House, growing herbs and working all week in a health-food shop in Dublin. In another time she'd have been burned as a witch without any discussion, he had once told her. Judy had said gloomily

155

that the way the country was going it could happen yet, so he shouldn't joke about it.

He smelled of garlic because he had eaten a very good lunch. He always did on a Friday; that was because he wouldn't be back again until late on Sunday night when it was the wrong time to have a meal. So Friday lunchtime was the only opportunity they could get to have anything approaching a relaxed weekend meal before he went back to Rathdoon for the weekend. Of course there was the rest of the week, but it wasn't quite the same, as there was work next day, and anyway there *was* something about a weekend that gave you more time—more anticipation. He hated not having his weekends in Dublin. He hated going home on the Lilac Bus.

Rupert had never had an argument with his father in his whole life. And he could remember only three differences of opinion with his mother. Those went back to the time he was away at school and she had written three times to the headmaster to receive assurances that the beds were aired. He knew nobody else in the world who had such a relationship with their parents. Everyone else fought and forgave and loved or hated and stormed and railed or became fiercely protective. Nobody had this polite courteous distance based entirely on gratitude and duty. Nobody else who felt such irritation couldn't express it.

They didn't really need him, that was his whole point, and he wished them well, but he didn't need them either. So why should the pretense be kept up? It made it so much harder on all of them. Not only on Rupert—but maybe it was a little harder on him, he felt—after all, their lives were ending. His hadn't really begun and couldn't begin as things were.

There hadn't even been a row when Rupert had decided to give up his law studies. He had been apprenticed to a firm in Dublin, begun his lectures with the Incorporated Law Society and at the same time read for a degree in Trinity. It wasn't a superhuman load—a lot of people did it easily—but Rupert never took to it. Not any of it. The bit he liked best, oddly, was the office. He was quite happy doing the clerical work, the part that Dee Burke, who worked there now, said she hated. Rupert had made few friends in Trinity, which surprised him; he thought it would be like school, which had been fine. But it was very different and he felt totally outside it all.

He had come home the weekend he knew he had failed his First Law with a heavy heart. He hadn't tried to excuse himself, he just apologized as if to a kind stranger, and his father accepted the apology as if it had been given by a kind stranger. They had sat one on either side of the table while his mother looked left and right at whoever was speaking.

Rupert said it was a great waste of his father's money and a disgrace to him in his profession. His father had brushed these things aside: heavens no, people often failed their first examination, there was no cause for alarm, some of the greatest lawyers claimed that they had never been showy scholars. No need for any regrets, it should all be written off as part of sowing wild oats, part of getting your freedom. Next year it would be more serious, head in book, down to it, wasn't that right?

On into the night Rupert had talked, saying that he wasn't cut out for it. It wasn't what he wanted. He didn't believe he would love it when he was in his father's office: he didn't love the office he was apprenticed to in Dublin, he only liked the more mechanical parts. He couldn't get interested in the theory of the law or the way it was administered. He was so sorry it had turned out like this, but wasn't it better that they should know now rather than discover later. They agreed logically that it was. They asked him what *did* he want. He didn't know; he had been so sure that he would like Trinity, and like studying law, he had never given it much thought before. He liked thinking about the way people lived and their houses and all that. But wasn't it going to be very hard to try to get accepted to study architecture? his father wondered. He didn't mean study it; he didn't know, Rupert said desperately. He would get a job, that's what he'd do. His parents didn't understand this: they thought you had to have a degree to get a job, the kind of job Rupert would want. When he found the position as a junior in the estate agent's, they said they were pleased if that's what he wanted. They didn't sound displeased, they sounded remote as they always had been.

His father was remote when he told Rupert that the time had come to get someone else into the office and that if Rupert was absolutely sure that he didn't intend to come into the profession he was going to offer a position to David Mac-Mahon's son. Rupert assured him it would be fine, and got only a minor start when he realized that young MacMahon would have to be offered a partnership and the name of the office would be repainted to read Green and MacMahon. Once or twice they had asked him whether he had thought of coming back to Rathdoon and setting up his own little auctioneering business. There must be plenty of sites being sold and garages and people liked to keep things local. "It might be no harm to get in before Billy Burns sets one up, he's started everything else in the town," his mother had said, but firmly and politely he had assured them that this was not going to happen. He left them in no doubt that his plans involved staying in Dublin. This had happened on the day his mother had said that she wondered whether they should put a new roof on the house or not. Sometimes she felt that the one she had would do for their time and wasn't that all it would be needed for . . .? Rupert had answered her levelly as if she had been asking no deeper question or making no last desperate plea. He talked of roofs and the value they added to houses and gave the pros and cons as he knew them, bringing himself no more into their plans than if he had been asked by a passing tourist.

His mother asked a bit coyly once or twice if he met any nice girls in Dublin. She didn't ask that anymore. He must have given her some fairly firm answers, because he was only twenty-five, an age when you might be assumed to be still meeting girls. If people didn't know that you never met girls, you only met Jimmy.

Rupert's throat tightened just thinking of Jimmy. They had met for lunch this Friday; it had now become a bit of a ritual. Jimmy had no classes on a Friday afternoon: they had found the boys didn't study too well and had given them games or art or music. So Jimmy could jump into his little car and drive off to meet him. Rupert had noticed with an alarm mixed with pleasure that Dublin was becoming very slap-happy on Friday afternoons anyway, and not just in schools. At the office they did very little business and people seemed to be leaving for home—even if it was just the suburbs—earlier and earlier. If the noise in a nearby pub was anything to go by, those particular workers of the world weren't going to do much to change it when they got back to their desks—if they got back. Still, it was nice for Rupert. He could take a long lunch hour with no questions asked. They had found a restaurant that both of them liked (not easy, as they had such arguments about food), and it was a very happy couple of hours.

Jimmy insisted that he go home every weekend; it was even Jimmy who found the Lilac Bus for him. Jimmy said it was a pity that they couldn't have weekends, but it wouldn't be forever, and since the old man had always been so undemanding, wouldn't it only be right to go back to him now in his last few months? And it must be desperate on his mother waiting all week for him: of course he had to go. Jimmy wouldn't even let him pretend he had flu, not even for one weekend. He was very definite about it.

Jimmy was definite about everything; it was part of his charm. He never wondered about anything or deliberated or weighed things up. And if as it turned out sometimes he was utterly wrong, then he was equally definite about that.

"I was all wrong about the man who invented those cats' eyes for the road at night. I was thinking about somebody totally different. I couldn't have been more wrong." Then he would go ahead with the new view. But he had never changed his view about Rupert going home at weekends; that was an absolute.

Jimmy didn't have any home to go off to on a Friday. Jimmy's home was right there in Dublin. He was the youngest of six, and his two sisters and three brothers had gone exactly the way their father wanted, which was into the newspaper vendor business. Some had pitches on good corners, others had roofs over their heads and sold ice

161

creams and birthday cards as well. But Jimmy's father was in the habit of saying gloomily, "There's always one arty-farty cuckoo in the nest, one who won't listen to reason." Jimmy had been a bit of a pet when he was a youngster: they all encouraged him at his books, and then to university and into teaching in a very posh school. They made jokes about him being gay, but it was never said straight out whether they believed he was or not. Anyone overeducated, as they regarded him, would have had the same abuse, the accusations of being limp-wristed, the mockery of his clothes, the vain search for an earring and the camp cliches from the television: "Ooh Jimmy, you are awful."

But he went there every Wednesday evening. They all called in on the small crowded house; they talked about rivals and which magazine would be seized by the censor as soon as somebody in authority had a look at it. They talked of how the dailies were doing and how there was no point in taking this magazine because it wouldn't survive to a second issue. They told each other how they had long narrow sticks and beat the hands off any kid stealing a comic. Jimmy would join in by asking questions. He always brought a cake, a big creamy one from the nice delicatessen where they often went. His family would have a communal coronary arrest if they knew how much the cake cost. His mother used to say it was a nice piece of cake even though the smallest bit soggy just in the middle. Jimmy would

162

scoop up the bit where the Cointreau or Calvados had concentrated and eat it with a spoon. His brothers said it was a very fair cake, and reminded them of children's trifle.

It would be so easy to have a family like Jimmy's. They asked so little of him; they were so complete in themselves. If Jimmy were to disappear from their lives forever, he would be spoken of affectionately, but if Rupert were to forgo just one weekend going home on the Lilac Bus it would be a national crisis for the Green family. Sometimes he thought that this was very unfair, but Jimmy would have none of it.

"You're a difficult, sensitive plant, Roopo," he'd say. "Even if you had my family, you'd feel threatened and anguished—it's the way things are."

Rupert would laugh. "Don't call me Roopo, it sounds like some exotic bird in the zoo."

"That's what you *are:* like a dark, brooding exotic bird that finds almost every climate too difficult for it!"

He had met Jimmy one great lucky day in the office. There was a picture of what they called a "charming unconverted cottage" in the window. It was a bit far out, too, not in the more fashionable direction and it could not be described as trendy, even by the most optimistic of those who wrote the descriptions.

Jimmy came in, a slight figure in an anorak, wearing tinted glasses. He had blond hair that fell over his forehead and he looked a bit vulnerable.

Rupert didn't know why he moved over at once to him even though Miss Kennedy was nearer. He didn't feel any attraction to him at that stage— he just wanted to see that he got a fair deal. He had been studying the picture of the cottage, and had an eager smile on his face.

Rupert had told him the good and the bad: the bad being the roof and the distance and awful boulders of rocks in what had been loosely called the garden. He told him the good, which was that it was fairly cheap, that it was nice and private, and that if you had any money now or later there was another building attached to it that was a sort of an outhouse but that could easily be made into another small dwelling. Jimmy listened with growing interest and asked to see it as soon as possible. Rupert drove him out there, and without anything being said they knew they were planning their future as they stood in the wild overgrown rocky ground around the little house and climbed the walls of the outhouse to find that the roof there was perfect.

"It's not handy for where you work," Rupert pointed out, as Jimmy had said where he taught.

"I don't want to live handy to where I work, I want to live miles away. I want to have my own life, away from the eyes of the school."

Rupert felt an unreasonable sense of exclusion.

"And will you share it, do you think? That is, if you take it," he had asked.

"I might," Jimmy had said levelly. "I have no plans yet."

He bought the house. He had been saving with a building society for four years and he was considered reliable. The estate agency was pleased with Rupert: they had had the cottage on their books for rather too long. When all the negotiations were over, Rupert felt very lonely. This small, smiling Jimmy was going to be off now, living his own life in the windswept place. He would build that wall that they had discussed as a shelter, he would do up the second part of the house, paint it white, paint a door bright red maybe, grow some geraniums and get a suitable tenant. It would pay his mortgage. And Rupert would hear no more of it. Or of him.

He phoned on the Friday.

"Rupert, will you help me? I've lost all the fire for the place. I can't *see* it anymore; what it's like; what's going to be so great about it. Will you come out and remind me?"

"Yes," Rupert said slowly. "Yes, that's what I'd love to do."

He sat in a kind of trance all that Friday; if people spoke to him he only heard them vaguely. It was all so clear now: the confusions, the guilt, the hope that it would all settle down and sort itself out and that one day a woman would come along who would make him forget all this short-term stuff—which frightened him rather than making him satisfied. But all the time knowing there would be no woman, and not really wanting a woman. But had he read the signs right? Suppose

Jimmy was just a charming fellow with nothing on his mind but a good cheery chat with that nice fellow from the estate agent's? Suppose Jimmy said he had a fiancée or some married lady that he wanted to meet in secret. He drove out, noting that it would take him half an hour from door to door should he ever need to go that way again. Jimmy was standing at the gate. Waiting.

He knew it was going to be all right.

And it had been more than all right for three years now. They had done the two little houses up with such love that now they really *did* merit a glowing description on an auctioneer's books. But they would never be for sale. They were separate enough to pretend that they were two dwellings if it were ever needed. But it never was. When Jimmy invited his family out to see the place, they all thanked him and said they must get around to it, but they never arrived. Rupert didn't press his elderly parents to come to Dublin, and just showed them pictures of his part of the house and of the garden. They made it all into a giant rockery and knew as much about alpines and rock plants as anyone for miles around. They had a big kitchen with a sink and work area on each side so that they could both cook if they wanted to. Every penny they had went into their little place. They had friends soon, people who came to dinner and admired or offered advice but mainly admired. It was ideal and they were so happy.

That's why he hated leaving it at weekends. It was on Saturdays that they used to be most peaceful there, often shopping and cooking a meal—not only for Martin and Geoff or other gay friends but for the nice young married couple who lived nearby and who kept an eye on their garden that time they went to Morocco. These were people to relax with. These and one or two people in the estate agency didn't have to have any pretenses arranged for them. It was only in Jimmy's school and Rupert's hometown that the acting was essential.

Jimmy said it was so ludicrous in the 1980s not to be able to say that he was gay. And he would have at once if it were remotely possible. But no, apparently the boys' parents would think he had designs on them: they would think he was looking at them speculatively.

"I don't want any of those horrible ink-covered filthy ignorant kids," Jimmy would wail. "I want you, Rupert, my beautiful dark Rupert that I love."

And Rupert would fill up with pleasure and pride that Jimmy could be so natural and open and say all that to him. He tried to say spontaneous things, too, but they came out with greater difficulty. He was a bit buttoned up, as Judy Hickey had once said to him. He wondered often if Judy knew that he was gay. Probably. But it never had been the right time to tell her or to invite her out to see the rock plants and alpines that she loved.

Of course, he could tell Judy Hickey: after all, she was a scandal herself in some way, wasn't she?

167

There had been some really murky business years ago. She would be pleased to know there was another Great Secret in Rathdoon. But he could never tell Judy that one of the real reasons he hated so much leaving every Friday for these empty weekends was that he was so afraid Jimmy would find someone else. Or maybe even had found someone else.

At lunch this very Friday he had asked Jimmy what he could do all day Saturday, and there had been so satisfactory answer. Martin and Geoff were having people in for drinks—he would go to that in the evening. He'd mark exercise books, he'd try to fix up the hi-fi, which had never been satisfactory. It was all very vague. Suppose, suppose, Jimmy had begun to like somebody else? His heart was cold inside, like the unexpected bit you find when you take a loaf out of the freezer and it hasn't properly thawed. He could never tell anyone that fear. Not anyone in the whole world.

It was easy to talk to Judy. She told him about her little herb pillows; he told her all the fuss over the politician with the love nest. They both laughed at that and for some reason that he couldn't quite see, it brought her into talking about her own past. He was astounded at her story, a young wife and mother dealing in drugs all those years ago. And the husband doing deals with the law as if he were part of the Wild West. Imagine her not seeing the children, but imagine even more her getting supplies of LSD for the huntin', shootin', fishin' set! And hash! Jimmy would go wild when he heard. He could have listened forever, but suddenly she decided she was boring him and launched into chat with that half-mad Nancy Morris. She had also said that his mother thought about him every day. That couldn't be so. Mother thought about Father, and the house, and the vegetable garden and the hens, but mainly Father and how she was afraid that young Mr. MacMahon didn't have the respect due to the senior partner and founder of the firm. Mother hardly showed any interest in Rupert's life in Dublin, which was, of course, a relief, but it did mean that it was most unlikely that Mother would think about him every day. Surely Judy was being fanciful? She probably hoped no matter what she said her lost children thought of her every day. That was it.

Their house was small and white with clematis growing up over the porch. Jimmy thought that a Protestant solicitor's family would live in a manor house, heavy with creeper and inspiring awe among the peasantry. Rupert had said that only two houses had proper creeper. One was Dr. Burke's, which was beautifully kept, and one was the old vicarage, which was so neglected it now looked like a huge stone covered with ivy. They had a service each Sunday in Rathdoon in the beautiful church, but had no vicar, no rector; he came out from the big town seventeen miles away and had Matins in Rathdoon, and another, later Matins another fifteen miles down the road. Jimmy was fascinated, but Rupert had never asked Jimmy home to meet the family. Jimmy had asked him to his house many a time. Rupert had gone once and felt awkward, even though nobody else had, and they had all buttonholed him about the price of property.

His mother was waiting just inside the door. That always annoyed him, too, and he got annoyed with himself over the very annoyance. Why shouldn't she wait to stop him ringing or knocking and disturbing his father's sleep? But it always made him think she had been standing waiting for his shadow to fall through the glass panels. He said good night with a much lighter tone than he felt, and braced himself. The soft leather of the magnificent jacket touched the back of his neck. It was Jimmy's birthday present to him. A few days early, but Jimmy said it would cheer him up for the weekend. Dee Burke had been right, they did cost a fortune. Again the niggling worry: how had Jimmy been able to spend that much money, even if it was a second? Put these doubts away, Rupert, he told himself firmly. Jimmy is good and true. Why pour vinegar onto it all with your stupid suspicions. Jimmy is at home tonight marking books and looking at television; Jimmy is not in a bar in town cruising someone. Why destroy *everything?*

"He's very well, very clear," his mother whispered delightedly.

"What?"

"Your father. He's very clear. He's awake; he asked several times what time would the Lilac Bus

170

be in. Every time he heard anything change gear on the corner, he said, 'Is that the bus?'"

Rupert put his carrier bag down on the hall floor. "That's great, Mother, that's really great," he said with heavy heart and went up the little stairs slowly to see the man with the head like a skull and the skin like plastic wrap. The man he had never been able to talk to in his life.

It was a sunny Saturday, but his father's room was darkened and the dim light hurt his eyes. His mother was bottling fruit downstairs. Jimmy said Catholics never bottled fruit or preserved eggs—it was something their religion didn't go along with. Jimmy had told him more lies about Roman Catholicism than he ever believed anyone could invent. He had always been brought up carefully to respect it at a distance by his parents, and even though they thought it definitely held the people back, they were impressed by the piety and the crowds going to Mass. His parents had gone to Galway to see the Pope. Jimmy said that his parents had made a small fortune the week-end the Pope arrived, since the whole of Dublin wanted to buy every newspaper twice in case they missed anything.

Back at home in the cottage, Jimmy would be drinking freshly brewed coffee and reading the *Irish Times*. Then he might go out to the garden and do some transplanting. September was the month to move the evergreens if you wanted to change the plan a bit. But no, Jimmy would wait for him to come back for that. Maybe he would

171

be puzzling over the hi-fi. Please may he not be driving into town just because he's bored; please may he meet nobody at lunch over a drink and smoked salmon sandwich.

"You're very good to come down every week-end," his mother said suddenly, as if she could read the homesickness for his real place written all over his eyes. "Your father really does like talking to you. Do you notice that? Can you see it?"

Jimmy had begged him not to cross the whole of Ireland and then have a row. How could Jimmy understand that there were *never* rows, and there never would be. Well, a coldness then Jimmy would say. If you are going to go to all that trouble, it's silly to mess up your weekend: if you're making the gesture, make it properly.

"I think he *does* seem to like talking," Rupert said. "It doesn't tire him too much, does it?"

"No, he plans all week what he's going to say to you. Sometimes he asks me to write it down, or just headings. I want to talk to Rupert about this, he'll say, and I write it down. Often he forgets what it was he was going to say about it, but it's there at the time."

Rupert nodded glumly.

"Like he was going to ask you about those flats you sell in blocks; he was very interested in how they work out the leasehold. He said that there was never any of that in the conveyancing he had to do. But all he asked me to write down was 'Block of Flats,' you see, and then he couldn't re-

172

member last week what it was he wanted to say about them."

"I see," Rupert said, trying to sound more sympathetic than he was afraid he might appear.

"But this week, he seems very much brighter and more aware, doesn't he?" She was pleading.

"Yes, much more. Oh, indeed. He was talking about this house here and what we would say if we had it on an auctioneer's books. I was giving him funny descriptions and he smiled a bit at it."

Rupert's mother was pleased. "Good, he hasn't smiled a lot. That's nice."

"Why don't you have a bit of time off, Mother, when I'm here. Why can't you go into town, maybe, you'd like that. I can keep an eye on Father and be here if he wants anything."

"No no, I want you to enjoy yourself," she said.

"But really, Mother, I mean, I'm not doing anything anyway." He shrugged. "I might as well look after Father and let you have a few hours to yourself." He meant it generously, but he knew it had come out all wrong.

"But you're home for the weekend," she cried. "I wouldn't want to miss that by going off to the town. I can do that any day: Mrs. Morris or young Mary Burns, Billy's wife, would sit with him. No, I want to get value out of your being here."

"Sure. Of course," he said, appalled at his own insensitivity. Jimmy would never in a million years have said anything like that. Jimmy would have brought life and laughter into the house the moment he got back. Jimmy. Oh Jimmy.

They had lunch, the kind of lunch that only his mother could serve: endless preparation and toasting of bread and cutting of crusts and spreading of cheese and slicing of tomatoes. And yet it was nothing—it managed to be both stodgy and insubstantial. If only she would let him cook. But then, he had never asked her. Perhaps it might be giving something away to say that he could have made them a light and delicious lunch in a quarter the time. It was his own fault, like everything.

His father struggled all afternoon. And Rupert struggled back.

Sometimes his mother was there, sewing. She was always making little things for her sister, who was married to a vicar and who always needed things for parish sales. His father would struggle and concentrate. His efforts to please meant that he could even be rerouted back to his own old days as a solicitor coming first to the town, when things were different and better. There was a time when his father had been happy to ramble through the times gone by. But not now: it was as if he was determined to show a guest in his eyes that he *was* interested in whatever kind of strange thing the guest did for a living. All afternoon Rupert's soul was crying out, "It's all *right*, Father. Look, can't you rest? I have an okay life and I wish you and Mother well, but why do we go through all this meaningless chat. There is nothing to say anymore."

The sun was almost going down when he could bear it no more; he said he had promised Judy

Hickey he would do something for her and he had better dash over to her.

"A brave woman, Judy Hickey—she held her head high in this place for two decades," his father said in a surprisingly strong voice.

"Yes, well, why not?" Rupert was defensive. "She got a harsh punishment."

"She took it, and she didn't run away and hide. She stepped down from being lady of the manor and lived in the gate lodge."

"And lost her children," Rupert's mother added. "That was the worst bit."

"Yes, well, I won't be long." He felt he could breathe again when he was out in the air; he left the square and went off toward the gate lodge of the big Doon House.

Judy was lying curled up like a cat. She wasn't pleased to see him—in fact, she nearly sent him back straightaway. She was like Jimmy really, but without the persuasive charm: Jimmy made it seem reasonable; Judy made it seem like a duty.

But she meant it: she got up and stretched and said she was going to go out and walk in her husband's wood. Jack Hickey's wood she called it. She said he should talk about anything, anything to show his father that he was trying too.

But what could he say? He couldn't tell him that his heart was tearing with the barbed wire of jealousy in case his male lover might have been unfaithful. Then, *nobody* could tell a father that about a lover of any sex. But Rupert was worse off: he couldn't talk about his life, about the beautiful gentians that he and Jimmy had planted and how the willow gentian had burst into a whole pool of dark-blue flowers last July and they had taken photographs of each other admiring it. He found it hard to talk about the garden without mentioning Jimmy because the two were twined together, like the house, like cooking, like holidays and reading and laughing and the things people did, for heaven's sake.

Annoyed with Judy for being short with him, he walked home. He passed the Kennedys' shop and saw a big handsome girl being ushered in. The redheaded Kennedy boy, Eddie, was looking at her with a foolish grin: they must be courting. She was very attractive; how simple life would have been if only he had been born to court a big handsome girl who would bring life and laughter into his quiet house.

Suddenly he thought of Jimmy in the house. Jimmy pausing at the door to touch the clematis and cup it in his hands with admiration. Jimmy saying to Rupert's mother that she should sit down and put her feet up and let her big ugly son and himself make the meal for a change. Jimmy telling Rupert's father tales of the boys' school where he taught, and the fees and the extras and the awful school concerts. Jimmy walking casually down the road with him to Ryan's for a drink before dinner while the carbonade was in the oven. Jimmy would lighten their house better than any strapping girl from a well-to-do farm outside town.

"I was just thinking," he said to his mother when she let him in the door again as if she had been hovering. "Could I bring a friend home next weekend?"

After that it was easy. His mother said she was glad that she had got good notice, because she would clear out the guest room. It had been something she had meant to do for a long time, but never had the heart somehow. His father said that it would be very interesting to meet someone who taught in that school, because he had known a lot of people in his time who had been there and they were all united in never having a good word to say for it but having done extremely well as a result of being there.

Then a sudden shock. Suppose Jimmy didn't want to come?

"I hope he'll be able to make it; I didn't think of asking him," he stammered.

"Why don't you ring him?" his mother suggested. His mother, who made trunk calls as one might try to get in touch with another planet—cautiously and without much hope of success.

"God, isn't that lovely to hear you?" Jimmy said.

"I'm ringing from home," said Rupert.

"Well, I hope so. I did think sometimes you went off to exotic places without me, but I decided to trust you." Jimmy's laugh was warm. Rupert swallowed.

"It's lovely here this weekend and I was wondering . . . I was wondering . . ."

"Yes?"

"I was wondering if you'd like to come down next week and stay, you know?"

"I'd love to."

There was a pause.

"You would? You would, Jimmy?"

"Sure, I thought you'd never ask," Jimmy said.

CELIA

Her friend Emer used to call it the Dancing Bus. All over Dublin people got on buses on Friday night to go home to great distances in the country. It had been a revolution, they said—hicks choosing to go home because it was more fun there than in Dublin they had the advantages of a bit of freedom in the city during the week and not losing touch with the home place either.

Celia laughed at the thought of her bus being a Sweetheart Special. She told Emer when they had cups of tea in the day room about the cast that turned up at a quarter to seven every week. Emer had sighed in envy. It sounded great, a nice spin across to the west, a weekend with no washing and housecleaning and trying to tell the three teenagers that there wasn't enough money for anything and trying to tell her husband who had been out of work for three years that there was plenty of money for everything. Emer had a sister married in the town that was seventeen miles from Rathdoon. Wouldn't it be lovely to go off there once in a while? Oh Lord, she'd love it.

And so that's what happened. Celia had to work one in every four weekends. So she gave her place on the bus to Emer. It had suited them all, and

Emer said her family in Dublin were so grateful to see her back on a Sunday night that they never complained about anything, they just made her a coffee and said they'd missed her. Of course, Celia did go to the dances at one time, and they were great altogether: you got a first-rate band to come to a place where the people drove in for miles and there would always be a big crowd. She used to dance with Kev Kennedy's brother, Red, sometimes, but she much preferred Bart, the eldest of that family. He was so solid and reliable. You never quite knew what he was thinking, but he was always there. In fact, you never had to *ask* him to help, he seemed to know when it was necessary and turn up. Emer said he sounded a very suitable sort of man indeed, but Celia thought not. She said he wasn't interested in settling down and she wasn't going to set her sights on another one who was a permanent bachelor. She'd had enough trouble getting over the first. Emer had sighed supportively and wondered why as a married woman she was trying to encourage others to join the club. It certainly wasn't what it was cracked up to be, and in many ways it wasn't much good at all.

But Celia only laughed at her. Emer was thirty-eight and sounded tough and cynical, but deep down she would die for that handsome, whining husband of hers and those tall, rangy kids, who got bigger and needed more clothes every time you looked at them. Celia wasn't going to be put off love and marriage by any of Emer's protests;

it was what she wanted. Not urgently, not immediately, not at any price, but she wanted it sometime. Despite what she had seen of it in her own family.

She could hardly remember a day at home when there hadn't been some kind of a row. A lot of them were in public, too, because if the whole of Rathdoon was coming into the pub from eleven o'clock in the morning on, then they would have to be aware of the shouts and the disagreements and the sight of Mr. or Mrs. Ryan coming flushed with anger from the back room into the bar and serving a pint, only to disappear again and fight the point further. Celia had often heard that children grew anxious and withdrawn when their parents fought in the home. But that's not what happened to the Ryans. They grew up and went away, that was all. As soon as they were able to get out, out they got. Her eldest sister had joined a band of Australian nuns who had come to Ireland looking for vocations. Looking for very young vocations, since Celia's sister had only been sixteen. But the offer of further education had been attractive as well. She wrote home from time to time, incomprehensible letters of places and things that were never explained. Then the boys had gone too. Harry to Detroit and Dan to Cowley in England. They wrote rarely, hard sorts of letters with a kind of graspingness they never had as youngsters—how a bar in Ireland must be a gold mine now. Harry had read in Detroit that Ireland was booming since the Common Market, and Dan had been told in Cowley that having a publican's license in the west of Ireland was like having a license to print money. These letters hurt Celia: there was much more than a hint, there was a direct statement that Celia and her mother were doing very nicely out of the family business, thank you. When she saw how things really were she felt she should laugh, but before she laughed she should weep.

Five years ago when her father died, people said that at least one blessing was that Kate Ryan had always been more or less running the business single-handed and so there'd be no doubt at all that she'd be able to carry on. It wasn't like some establishments where the wife had always been in the background. No, poor Kate had been managing on her own while the husband drank down at one end of the bar with his own little circle.

And poor Kate had carried on for a good bit. In the summer she'd hire a young fellow to wash glasses, and there was always Bart Kennedy to give a hand if things got very busy. No, she was fine. There was no shortage of customers, and mercifully drink wasn't the kind of thing that came and went in fashions—people always loved drink. Apart from the first week of Lent, the custom was always steady and at weekends it was roaring. There was no opposition, and you'd never get another license for a place as small as this. Rathdoon was unusual in that it had only one pub; other places might have had three. There had been talk once that Billy Burns was thinking of applying for a license; he had been interested in buying a place about twenty miles away and asking to transfer that license to Rathdoon, but nothing had come of it.

Celia had been thinking about Billy Burns during the day for some reason. She had woken with that silly tune on her mind, "Where have you been all the day, Billy Boy, Billy Boy?" and she thought it fitted Mikey's brother down to the ground. Mikey was such an innocent old eejit, and there was something a bit too smart about Billy. Nothing to do with his setting up another pub or not. In fact, if he did, that might be a solution to a lot of their problems. If her mother's pub went downhill due to legitimate competition, that would be an honorable way out. If her mother drank Ryan's into the ground, that was a less honorable way altogether.

But you couldn't say anything even vaguely like this to Celia's mother. Other people were hitting it a bit hard these days, other people were making fools of themselves and running up debts: there were men in Rathdoon who had big pores in their noses and red and blue veins in their cheeks from drink; there were women in Rathdoon who went into the big town seventeen miles away to do the shopping, but Kate Ryan could tell you that it was little shopping they did except half a dozen half-bottles hidden under the teatowels or whatever they bought as an excuse. Half bottles were easier to hide and they were easier to dispose of. Kate

Ryan could tell you of those who came in at night for "Just one drink, Mrs. Ryan," and she had seen them topping it up from their handbags. They didn't want to be seen ordering more than the one. But Celia's mother would have no tales of a woman who didn't even have to hide it because she had it there on her own shelves, and she was surrounded by it as her way of earning a living for twelve hours a day.

It had been such a shock the first time she saw her mother drunk. Mam had been the one who didn't and Da had been the one who did. It was like left and right and black and white. To hear those slurred words, to have to cope with an inarticulate argument—Celia had been quite flustered and not at all the calm Nurse Ryan that could cope with anything on her corridor. The next day her mother had made great excuses, frightening excuses. It was food poisoning: she had eaten some of that chicken paste out of a jar; she was going to write to the manufacturers and enclose the label. Not only had it made her sick several times during the night, but it had also affected her mind in some way. She couldn't remember clearly, she couldn't piece everything together. When Celia said agreeably enough that the chicken paste might well have been bad but it was probably the drink that made her forget the night before, she flew into a rage, one of those real rows like there used to be when Da was alive. It was *not* drink. Could Celia kindly tell her what

184

drink she was referring to? Had Celia seen her mother sitting down to have a drink even once last night? Celia shrugged. She thought it might have been just this one time. Let it pass.

Three weeks later she came home for the weekend, and her mother was mixing up the gin and the vodka, forgetting to take the money from people and letting the pints overflow while she went to deal with someone else. It was then that Celia decided she had better book herself onto the Lilac Bus and come home every weekend that she could. This had been going on for a year now and her mother was getting worse and worse. And the really bad thing was that she wouldn't admit it, not for one moment. Not even to herself.

In the hospital Celia had seen dozens—more than dozens, probably hundreds—of people who were trying to help people who wouldn't help themselves. There had been endless conversations about old men who wouldn't go into sheltered accommodation and had set fire to their kitchens three times and old women who had broken their hips over and over because they wouldn't ask anyone to help them across a street. There were shriveled anorexics who wouldn't eat, there were ashen-faced coronary patients who had insisted on doing overtime in stress-filled jobs and eating huge meals filled with cholesterol. There were women worn out with the fourteenth pregnancy, there were the mothers of the schoolchildren who had overdosed, there were the wives of the men whose livers had packed up despite a hundred arguments that alcohol was poisoning them slowly to certain death. Always she had sounded sympathetic, always she had appeared to understand. But inside there was a bit of her that said that they couldn't have tried hard enough. If Celia had a daughter who was desperately unhappy at school and who had lost four stone in weight, she wouldn't hang around—she'd try to cope with it. If she had a father who couldn't cope, she'd have him to live with her. Only now was she beginning to realize that it was not to be so simple. People had minds of their own. And her mother's mind was like a hermetically sealed box in the vault of a bank.

Emer had been in high good humor: she had won a hundred pounds on the hospital draw. Each week they all had to buy a ticket for the building fund. It cost fifty pence, and they *had* to buy it—there wasn't any choice. Three hundred fifty pences added up to £150 and every second week the prize was £50 and every other one it was £100. It kept people interested and that small weekly contribution to the building fund was assured. Even if you were going to be on holidays you had to give someone else your sub. The winning ticket was announced on a Friday afternoon by number and you went to Wages to collect the prize. Emer was going to say nothing about it at home. Not one word. They would never hear. They would want jeans, they'd want a holiday, they'd think you could go on a holiday for a hundred quid. They'd want to go to McDonald's every night for a month, they'd want a video. Her husband would say it should go into the building society, it should be saved in case he never worked again. No, much better to keep it for herself. She and Celia would have a night out next week. Celia had laughed at her affectionately. "Sure," she had said. "People do what they want in the end, isn't that what you always say?"

She knew that what Emer would want despite all the protestations of independence and keeping the money to herself was totally different. She would want to arrive home this Friday night bursting with the news. She would want to send out for chicken and chips and plan endless treats which would indeed include jeans and a bit saved to please her anxious husband and a promise to look into the economics of a down payment on a video. That's what Emer would want and that's what she would do in the end. They both knew it.

And if Celia had a husband and kids she hoped that's what she would want too. Otherwise what was the point of the whole thing?

She was tired. It had been a long day. In other hospitals they worked twelve-hour shifts: eight in the morning till eight at night. Celia thought she'd be ready to strangle some of the patients, most of the visitors, and all of the staff if they had to have that routine. It had been quite enough to have eight hours today. A young woman had become desperately upset because at visiting time her brother, a priest, had said that he was saying a special Mass for her in their house. He had thought she would be pleased; she had thought that this meant it was the end. Then her husband told the priest that he had a neck to come in and upset the wife and there was a row of such proportions that everyone in the ward stopped talking to their own visitors and began to listen. Celia had been called. She pulled the curtains around the bed, she organized some light sedation, she explained in a crisp cool voice that the woman's diagnosis had been entirely optimistic, that nothing was being hidden from her or from anyone. She said that since priests had the power to say the Mass, what could be more natural than he would say one in the family home as a thanksgiving for her recovery so far and a hope that it would continue?

She also said with a particularly pointed look at the priest that it was a pity some people couldn't explain things sensibly without using voices laden with doom and ritual, and have some sensitivity about people's association of having Masses said with being very ill indeed. Then with a reprimanding glance at the husband she said that the whole point of a visiting hour was for the patient to be made more comfortable and happy and not to be plunged into the middle of a huge family row, with accusations being hurled for the whole ward to hear. They were all younger than her except the priest, and he was probably under thirty. They took it very well and nodded their apologies to her and to each other. She drew the curtains open again and busied herself around the ward until she was sure they were all properly calm again. When the priest and the husband had gone she sat with the woman and held her hand and told her not to be an eejit: priests would want to say a Mass in a house at the drop of a hat. And after all, it was their life. If they didn't believe it was important, who did? It was only the rest of the world, Celia explained, who thought that Masses and God were only brought in when all else had failed. For priests they were there all the time. She hit the right note exactly and the woman was laughing by the time she left the ward.

Would that it were going to be so easy at home. Last weekend Bart Kennedy had let slip that he had been there several nights during the week as well as the weekends. She was alarmed. She and Bart never spoke of the reason for his being there. He never said that her mother was drunk, he would say she needed a bit of a hand. He never said that her mother had insulted one of the customers, he would say there had been a bit of a barney but it was probably all sorted out now. She had asked him to take wages for himself, and he had laughed and said not at all. He was only helping out and how could he go and sign on if he was getting a regular salary? He assured her that he took the odd pint for himself and offered one to a friend occasionally, but it was peanuts and

189

couldn't go on. Emer wondered had he perhaps any hopes of marrying into the establishment, but Celia said that was nonsense—Bart wasn't the type. Nothing funny about him, mind you, but just one that would never marry. Don't forget, Celia knew all about those: she had served her time for five years on a hopeless cause. She could spot them a mile off now.

But enough: she wasn't going to think of that fellow anymore. That was all behind her and at least the humiliations weren't known in Rathdoon. It was to another town that she had followed him hopefully at weekends, thinking that there was much more to it than there was, being there, being available; eventually, because it seemed the one thing he was sure he wanted, she had slept with him. That was what he had called it but there was no sleeping involved: it was guilt for fear of discovery, and not very much pleasure for either of them. She hadn't lost him because she had been too easy to get; she hadn't lost him at all, because he was never hers to lose; he had no intention of disturbing the very even pattern of his life by a wife and house and children. No, no, no, he would stay on with his parents while they lived and maybe with a sister later. There would always be girls—girls now and later women—who would believe that they had the secret and the key to unlock his independence. No, Celia could write a book on the Irish bachelor if she wanted to, but she hadn't time: she *had* to sort it out this weekend, otherwise she'd better leave the hospital and come home. It wasn't fair on everyone else in Rathdoon.

She was glad that Kev Kennedy was a little bit ahead of her. That meant that he would sit beside Mikey. Tonight she was not in the mood for Mikey's jokes; some evenings she could take a few and then turn to her own thoughts, but there was too much on her mind, and Mikey was so easily hurt. It was good not to have this battle between offending him or going mad herself. She slipped easily in beside Tom, the driver. He leaned over her and slammed the door shut.

"It's only twenty to seven. I have you all very well trained," he said, and they all laughed with him as the bus went out into the traffic and headed for home.

Tom was a fine companion. He always answered agreeably and gave long answers if he was in the mood to chat and short ones if he wasn't. The silences were companionable. He never talked to the people behind because it distracted him, and he liked the person sitting beside him to tell him if it was all clear on the left as they nosed onto main roads from side roads. Much nicer than the rest of the Fitzgeralds up in the craft shop, but then it was silly to expect families to be the same. Look at Billy Burns: he'd buy and sell Mikey a dozen times before breakfast. Nancy Morris—there was something wrong with her, Celia thought. She had a very fixed look, a look that really was fixed on nothing. Celia had seen it in hospital sometimes. Nancy was as different from that laughing Deirdre, her sister in America, as she was different from a Martian. And there was poor Kev, Bart's young brother behind her there in the bus. And possibly she was different from her own brothers and sister. At the thought of her own family, her brow darkened. Why would none of them do a thing to help? How had it happened? She *could* write them a round robin: "Dear Maire and Harry and Dan, Sorry to have to tell you, but Mam is hitting the bottle worse than ever Dad did. What will we do? Looking forward to hearing by return from New South Wales; Cowley, Oxfordshire; and Detroit, Michigan, Your loving sister, Celia, Dublin." That was the point: Dublin. It was only up the road as far as they were concerned, and she wasn't married, that was even more the point, wasn't it? If she had been a wife then none of them would have expected her to abandon that and look after her mother, no matter how near she was. But being a nurse, an angel of mercy, helping the sick and earning her living . . . that would be written off.

What's more, they wouldn't understand, any of them. Maire would write from Woolowogga or wherever she had gone on a course—she was always going to ludicrous places on courses—and she would say it was blessed to give and blessed to help. Great. Harry would write from Detroit and say she must do what she thought was best, as she was the one on the ground. He would add something about it being a nice tidy living for her, and probably put in a really sensitive bit about not wanting his share out of the family business yet. Dan would write, he might even ring from England: he'd encourage her like mad to go home, he'd say that nursing wasn't a *real* career or anything, and that it was all for the best. His bit of tact might be to hope that now she was known as the landlady of a pub in all but name, perhaps Celia might get a few offers of marriage. She was only twenty-six, why had they written her off in three countries? She was their baby sister; she remembered them as big and strong and great fun, but in their letters and their rare appearances they were selfish and they were strangers. And they thought of her as an old maid.

"Do your family drive you mad?" she asked Tom as they had just overtaken a huge dangerous-looking lorry that seemed about to shed everything it had on everything that was near it.

"Oh, yes, of course they do," Tom said. "I mean, that *is* what drives people mad actually, families. It's not strangers in the street or the bomb or the economy, it's always their relations."

"Or love, I suppose, or lack of it?" Celia was impersonal, interested in talking about ideas. So was Tom. That's why they found their chats easy and never found their long silences threatening.

"Yes, love, but love usually involves some idea of family: you love someone, you want her to be

193

your wife; she won't, you go mad. That's family. You hate your wife, you don't love her anymore, you wish she'd fly off on the next space shuttle. That's family."

Celia laughed. "God, you'd be great in one of those family counseling places with psychiatrists and all."

"I'm always surprised they never asked me in on one," said Tom, and they didn't speak for another fifty miles.

She was glad to get out and stretch. She had heard of other buses where they got stuck into a pub like this one for a real session and maybe it would be an hour and a half before people got back on the road. But Tom Fitzgerald ruled his Lilac Bus very firmly, it was time to visit the Ladies' and a very quick drink. There really wasn't even time for a coffee, because they always took such ages to make it in pubs, and indeed in Ryan's of Rathdoon they wouldn't make it at all.

"What'll you have, Celia?" Dee had a knack of getting to the counter quickest and an even better knack of getting served. Celia had a bottle of Guinness and a few words. Dee had never changed, not since she was a schoolgirl bursting with pride at her new uniform and coming into the bar to show it off to the Ryans. She had been everywhere to show it off, and everyone had given her a lemonade, or a bar of chocolate or even half a crown. Nobody had anything but good wishes for the doctor's daughter off to her posh convent boarding school. Dr. Burke was part of every life and death in Rathdoon; nobody would have a jealous thought about his children and what they had. Who would deserve it more?

She slipped Mikey some ointment that they used up in the hospital to ease bedsores. She didn't want to let Dee see her in case it was thought that she might be trying to improve on the doctor, but Dee would probably never think that in a million years. She was a grand girl with a very infectious laugh, and, of course, she had the patience of Job that she could talk to Nancy Morris so animatedly about Nancy's boring job and her endless tales of Mr. This the consultant and Mr. That the consultant. How did Dee put up with it and even look interested and remember their bloody names? The ten minutes were up and they were back in the dark comfort again.

She saw that Tom had tapes in the van; she had never noticed them before.

"Is that a player as well as a wireless?" she asked with interest when they were on the road again.

"Yes, do you wonder I have to guard this vehicle with my life? All I own is tied up in her." He laughed.

"You don't play any, while we're driving?"

"No. I thought about it: everyone would have a different taste and I wouldn't want to inflict my choice on all of you."

"Oh, it would have to be yours, would it?" Celia threw back her head of thick brown hair, laughing

195

at him. "Where's the democratic bit then? Why couldn't everybody choose their own, even bring one each week?"

"Because if I had to hear any more of the Nashville sound than I already hear by accident in my life, I think I'd drive off the road and into the deepest bog that would close over us," he said.

"Let's have no music then," Celia said agreeably, and they drove on, thinking their own thoughts. Celia was wondering what time she would catch her mother at the most receptive. There must be *some* moments in the day when the unfortunate woman was not suffering from a hangover or withdrawal or had got stuck into it again. There must be a time—late morning maybe—when she could ask Bart to man the place. Not that anyone came in much on a Saturday until it was well into lunchtime. She could always put *closed* on the door—Father Reilly put closed on the presbytery, for heaven's sake, when he simply had to have an hour to himself, or maybe it was for some poor devil that couldn't be disturbed. That was it, no more drawing on poor Bart. Anyway, he liked to work with Judy Hickey during the daytime when she was home for the weekend. She could put *closed* on the door for an hour or two, but apart from chaining her mother by both wrists and ankles, how was she going to get her to stay and listen to the very unwelcome view that she was now incapable of managing her own pub and must get herself into an alcoholic unit before it was too late? It was gone beyond false promises now, and assurances and little games. Celia had been present when a surgeon told a forty-two-year-old man last month that he had terminal cancer and had less than two months to live. This is what it felt like again. That sense of dread and half hoping the world would end before you had to say it. Of course, it had turned out very oddly in the hospital; they had thought the shock might be intense and that was why Celia was there as part of a backup. But he had been very quiet, the man, and said, "Is that a fact?" They had stood dumbfounded, Celia, the great surgeon, and the anesthetist. Then the man had said, "And I never went to America. Imagine, in my whole life I never saw America. Isn't it ridiculous in this day and age." He had said that several times before he died; it seemed to disturb him more than death itself and leaving his wife and three young children.

Suppose her mother were to say something equally unexpected—like that she had been wondering was this what was wrong with her, and she would like to go at once as a voluntary patient to some kind of place that would dry her out. Stop thinking like Alice in Wonderland, Celia told herself sternly. You're a grown-up, it's no use shutting your eyes, wishing things would happen.

"There's a lot of rags tied to a bush coming up now. I think it's a holy well or a wishing tree or something," Tom said suddenly. "Maybe we should all get out and tie our shirts to it," Celia said. They passed it, and indeed there were ribbons and what looked like holy pictures pinned onto it.

"I never saw that before, and all the times we must have driven past it," Celia said, looking back over her shoulder. She thought she saw Dee Burke crying, her face was working in that sort of way a child's does to keep off the sobs. But Nancy Morris was yammering on as usual, so there couldn't be anything really wrong.

"I never saw it before. Maybe it's a new saint; you know the way they get crossed off, like St. Philomena, maybe one got put on."

"Why *did* St. Philomena get crossed off, I wonder?" asked Celia.

"I don't know, maybe they found her out." Tom grinned. "I know my sister Phil was very annoyed indeed at the time, she felt it was an attack of some sort."

"Oh yes, Phil, that would be her name. How is Phil, by the way? I haven't seen her for a while."

"She's fine," Tom said shortly.

Celia went back to the tree for conversation. "Are they pagan or are they religious, I wonder?" she said.

"A mixture, I think." He was still short.

Celia thought about the tree. Wouldn't it be great to go there and pray to some saint who had a special interest in drunken mothers, leave an offering or whatever they left and then go home and discover that it had worked. Bart Kennedy would be serving behind the bar and her mother would

198

be sitting with a packed suitcase and face full of optimism.

"See you during the weekend," Tom said with a friendly smile.

She nodded. He had been a bit moody tonight, she thought. She didn't mind their stops and starts normally, in fact she liked it. But tonight she had wanted to talk. Actually, what she had really wanted was Emer. You could say anything to Emer and you knew she would think about it, but she wouldn't bring it out again on every occasion and ask you how you felt about it. Emer would give you advice but not be annoyed if you didn't take it. "Everyone does what they want to in the end," she would say. She wasn't as specific when it came to knowing how to convince someone else to do the right thing—or the best thing. Celia had long discussions with her over this. Did you wire the jaws of fat kids who were compulsive eaters? Did you have medical cards for smokers and only those who were certified as having good, strong lungs and no trace of emphysema would be allowed to buy a packet—they'd have to show the card first. That would save life, wouldn't it? Celia might suggest. Emer would shrug. Temporarily only: the child with the wired jaw would wait eagerly until the contraption was removed; the smoker would get the cigarettes somehow or smoke butts. But then why were drugs banned? Why not just sell heroin by the kilo in Quinnsworth and be done with it. Those who wanted to kill themselves would and there would be no drugs racket and pushers and people having to turn to prostitution or theft for it.

Emer said that drugs were different: they were poison, they killed. You wouldn't sell arsenic or strychnine, would you?

What about alcohol? That killed, they had seen enough rotted livers to know that; they could see the slow death around them. Emer said that if Celia felt as strongly as that she shouldn't own a pub, and she should have a temperance banner. Then they would both have a bottle of Guinness and talk about something else. But she was such a comfort; no wonder that her handsome husband and her three giant children were always waiting so eagerly for her to come home from work. And she wasn't a superwoman either. There were bad times and low times in Emer's life as well as in everyone else's. That's why she was so good to talk to.

"Good night." She nodded, and added, "Thanks for getting us here." She didn't want to be curt with Tom just because he hadn't been like Emer! That would be unfair.

"Best to the West, as Mikey would say," Tom laughed.

"Don't encourage him—he has enough catch-phrases already." She went in the door and knew from the loud greeting that her mother called across the bar that it was going to be a long hard hour and a half. She put her bag in the kitchen, she hung up her jacket and came out quietly to stand beside Bart Kennedy, who patted her on the arm as she wordlessly began to pull the pints.

Her mother shouted for two hours when the pub eventually closed. She sat at one of the tables and hurled abuse as Celia methodically emptied the ashtrays and wiped the surfaces. She would *not* be patronized in her own pub, she cried; she would not have Celia coming off the bus and taking over as if she owned the place. Celia did *not* own the place, and in fact, the place would never be hers. She hoped that Celia knew this. She had made a will with that nice young Mr. MacMahon in Mr. Green's office, and she had said that after her death the pub should be sold and the money divided equally in four and shared out between Maire and Harry and Dan and Celia. So now. Celia said nothing. She washed the glasses under hot water first, then under cold, then turned them upside down to drain on a plastic grid: that way the air got at them from all angles and dried them without smears.

Her mother had a brandy bottle on the table beside her. Celia made no attempt to touch it. She just moved past her and locked the door. The place was now ready for the next day. She gulped a bit at the thought of the conversation she was going to have in the morning, when the closed sign would appear on Ryan's door for the first time since her father's funeral.

"Aren't you going to have the common manners to say good night, Miss High and Mighty?" her mother called.

"Good night Mam," said Celia as she wearily went up the narrow stairs to the small white bedroom with the iron bed. She lay awake for a while. Long enough to hear her mother stumbling up the stairs and hitting off the chest of drawers on the landing. She must have known it was there: it had been there for thirty-eight years, all her married life.

It was very sunny, too sunny. Celia woke with a jump. The curtains had been pulled back, and there was her mother, with a cup of tea.

"I thought you might like this, after your week's work, and you must have stayed up late last night doing the glasses." The voice was steady enough and the hand wasn't shaking as it passed the teacup and saucer.

Celia sat up and rubbed her eyes. "You were with me when I washed the glasses," she said.

"I know, I know, of course." Her mother was flustered, she hadn't remembered. "Yes, well, naturally, but thanks for . . . um . . . organizing it all the same."

There was no smell of drink, but Celia realized that she must have had a cure, maybe a vodka. That's why she was able to cope. She had smartened herself up, too, combed her hair and worn a dress with a white collar. Apart from her eyes, which looked terrible, Mrs. Ryan didn't cut too bad a figure at all.

This might be the time. Celia swung her legs out of the bed, and took a great swig of the tea.

"Thanks, Mam. Listen, I wanted to say something to you. I've been trying to get a good time—"

"I have a kettle on downstairs; I'll come back up to you when I have a minute."

She was gone. There was no kettle on. Celia got up and dressed quickly. She decided against jeans and put on a skirt and blouse and a big wide belt. It made her look more authoritative, more nurselike in a way. There was no sign of her mother in the kitchen. Where could she have gone? There was a sound of scrubbing out the side entrance, and there was Mrs. Ryan on hands and knees with bucket and scrubbing brush, working away.

"I was noticing this last night: it's in a very bad way, we mustn't let the place go to rack and ruin around us." She was sweating and puffing. Celia let her at it. She went back into the kitchen and made more tea. Eventually her mother had to come back in.

"There, that's much better," she said.

"Good," said Celia.

"I saw that Nancy Morris, a proper little madam, that one. 'Hallo, Mrs. Ryan' if it suits her, and wouldn't give you the time of day if it didn't. I pretended I didn't hear her. She has her mother scalded, coming home every weekend."

"I'm sure," Celia said. Mrs. Ryan's jaw dropped.

"Oh, not like you. I mean, it's grand that you come home, and you're such a help."

"I'm glad you think so this morning. It was a different tune last night," Celia said.

"Oh, you wouldn't need to mind me on a Friday night, the place gets so crowded and they're coming at you from all sides. I probably sounded a bit impatient, but didn't I thank you for doing the glasses, didn't I bring you a cup of tea in bed?" She was pleading now, almost like a child.

Celia took the bucket and the brush away from her gently and closed the door behind her. She lulled her to the table with soft talk. She didn't want the woman to bolt from the room.

"Of course you brought me a cup of tea in bed, and I *know* that deep down somewhere you are grateful to me for coming back and helping out, but that's not the point, Mam, not the point at all. You don't remember anything about last night, not from about nine o'clock on, that's what I'd say."

"What are you talking about?"

"You were well gone when I arrived—that was before ten. You fought with a man and said he'd only given you a fiver, not a ten. You told young Biddy Brady that you didn't want a whole crowd of her girlfriends cluttering up the pub tomorrow— fortunately, Bart got us out of that one. You spilled a whole bottle of lime juice and you wouldn't let anyone wipe it up, so the counter was sticky all night. You couldn't find the tin of potato crisps and you told a group who had come here for the golfing that you didn't give a damn whether you found them or not, because they smelled to you like a child's fart. Yes, Mam, that's what you said."

Her mother looked up at her across the table. She showed no signs of getting up to run away. She looked at Celia quite calmly.

"I don't know why you are saying all this," she said.

"Because it happened, Mam." Celia begged her. "Believe me, it all happened, and more and much more other nights."

"Why would you make this up?"

"I didn't. It was like that; it will be like that again tonight, Mam, you're not able to cope. You've had a drink already today, I can see. I'm only telling you for your own good."

"Don't be ridiculous, Celia." She was about to stand up. Celia reached out and held her there. Hard by the wrist.

"I haven't written to the others yet: I didn't want to alarm them, I thought it might pass. I thought it was only weekends, when you were under a bit of pressure. Mam, you have to accept it and *do* something about it."

"Others?"

"Maura, Harry, Dan."

"You're going to write all over the world with these tales?"

"Not if you can help yourself first. Mam, you're drinking far too much, you can't control it. What you're going to have to do is—"

"I'm going to have to do nothing, thank you very much indeed. I may have had one too many sometimes, and all right, I'll watch that. Now, will that satisfy you? Is the interrogation over? Can we get on with the day?"

"Please, Mam, listen. Anyone will tell you—will I get Bart in here to tell you what it's been like? Mrs. Casey was saying, Billy Burns was saying, they were all saying . . . it's getting too much for you here. . . ."

"You were always prudish about drink, Celia, even when your father was alive. You didn't realize that in a bar you have to be sociable and drink with the customers and be pleasant. You're not cut out for a pub, the way we were, the way I am. You're too solemn, too sticky for people. That's always been your mistake."

There was no point in putting *Closed* on the door; she wouldn't talk. The most she would admit was a drop too much on some occasions. She denied all the scenes, she remembered none of the conversations.

People started drifting in around lunchtime. Celia watched her mother accept a small whiskey from Dr. Burke, who had come in to get some drink to celebrate his son's engagement. Celia wished that Dee's father would lean over the counter to her mother and say "Mrs. Ryan, your eyes are all bloodshot and there are big lines under them; for your health's sake you must give up drink." She wished that Father O'Reilly would come down

206

from the presbytery on a home visit and tell her that for the good of her soul she must go and have some treatment and then take the pledge. But doctors and priests didn't interfere enough these days maybe.

The phone box was way at the end of the bar, quiet and discreet. No wonder half of Rathdoon made their calls from there rather than beside the eager ears of the post office people.

Emer was just getting the lunch. They had all been to the pictures last night on her winnings and tonight they might go again. Videos had gone through the roof: even the kids realized that a video was out of the question.

"What will I do with her?" Celia asked.

"She doesn't admit it to herself?"

"No. I gave her chapter and verse—what she said, what she spilled and broke, who she insulted. Not a word does she believe."

"And you can't get support troops in."

"Not really. Bart will be too polite and anyone else would be embarrassed."

"I suppose you'll have to wait."

"I can't wait anymore, and neither can she. It's terrible. There *must* be some way. How do people come to see things? Is there no way of hurrying it up?"

"Well, I did hear of a man who signed himself in for treatment the moment he saw himself on a video of his daughter's wedding. He had no idea that he was so bad until—"

"That's it. Thanks, Emer."

"What? You're going to turn a video on your mother in Rathdoon? Have sense."

"I'll tell you about it on Monday." Celia was gone.

Mrs. Fitzgerald invited her in. Yes, Tom was here. They were having a pot of coffee—would Celia join them? She felt they had been having a chat, that she shouldn't interrupt. She said she'd only be a minute. Yes, he did have a small cassette recorder, and yes, a blank tape . . . or a tape that she could record over. What was it—something from the radio? No, okay, it didn't matter. Look, it was easy to work. No, he didn't mind being without it until they were on the bus again. He was puzzled, but he didn't ask any more. She took it back to the pub.

There was so much clutter under the pub counter that the small tape recorder passed unnoticed.

Celia used it judiciously, half an hour on one side and half an hour on the other.

She even moved it out in her hand to be closer to her mother when the solo singing began and Mrs. Ryan was screaming a tuneless, racy version of a song that she hardly knew. She let it play for the insults to Bart Kennedy and for the bad language.

At one stage Tom Fitzgerald came into the bar; he saw his recorder and said, "Is that fair?"

"You have your standards, I'll have mine," she snapped, and then much more wearily:

208

"She doesn't know, you see, she really doesn't know."

"She's not going to like it," he said.

"No."

"When will you . . . ?"

"Tomorrow morning, I'd say."

"I'll come in around lunch and pick up the pieces." He smiled. He had a very, very nice smile.

Her mother sat stonily through the first few minutes. She railed with anger at the arguments and the bad language. Then she decided it was a fake, and when she heard her maudlin conversation about what a great man her husband had been, tears of shame came into her eyes.

She folded her hands on her lap and sat like some timid employee waiting to be fired.

Out of the little tape recorder came the voice of Mrs. Ryan as it called on Biddy Brady's engagement party to shut up and let *her* sing. Tears fell from her closed eyes as the voice came out in its drunken, tuneless wail. Celia started to turn it off.

"Leave it," her mother said.

There was a long silence.

"Yes," said Mrs. Ryan, "I see."

"If you wanted to, we could say you had pneumonia or that you were off to see Dan in Cowley. That would sort of cover it up."

"There'd be no point in covering it up. I mean, it's only more lies, isn't it? Might as well say what it is." Her face was bleak.

"Sure, you're halfway there, Mam, if that's the way you think—you're nearly better," said Celia, leaning across the small, dark tape recorder to hold her mother's hand.

TOM

He remembered the day he painted the Lilac Bus. It had been sort of dirty beige before, and there was an exhilaration about pointing the spray can at it and seeing it change before his eyes. His mother had been appalled. It looked so vulgar and called attention to itself. That was about the worst crime in her book—attracting attention. The good went by unnoticed and understated; the bad were flashy and loud and painted their vans this silly mauve color. Tom's father just shrugged. What could you expect? he asked his wife in a tone that meant the one thing he really didn't expect was an answer. Tom's father hardly ever spoke *to* Tom anymore: he spoke about him, in his hearing.

"I suppose that boy believes that money grows on trees . . . that boy thinks we should have the itinerants living in our garden . . . that boy feels that work is beneath him." Sometimes Tom answered; sometimes he let it pass. It didn't really matter which he did. His father's mind was fixed anyway: that boy was a waster, a left-wing long-haired layabout. A purple minibus was only what you'd expect.

It wasn't what Tom expected. He just decided one day on a whim, one day when the washing didn't seem to be making the van look any better. And he *loved* it now that it was lilac-colored: it had much more personality and more life. That was when he decided to go into the transport business. It wasn't *exactly* legal, of course, but suppose they did have an accident: an insurance company would have a hard time proving that he wasn't driving seven friends home for the weekend. No money was ever seen to change hands in Dublin. He didn't stand at the door selling tickets as the bigger bus people did. They were the same people all the time, give or take one or two a month. It wasn't a moneyspinner or anything; he paid for his petrol and cigarettes out of it, that was all. But it did mean he could smoke as much as he liked and he could come home every weekend to Rathdoon, which was what he wanted to do. The Lilac Bus had made all this possible.

Tom knew all about his passengers' lives in Rathdoon, but very little about what they did in Dublin. He had thought of finding out where they all lived and dropping them home rather than leaving them in the city center at ten o'clock on a Sunday night, but something told him that they might prefer the anonymity of the city to be kept absolute; they mightn't want the others to see their digs or their rooming houses or their set-up. More than once Tom had noticed a small, fair-haired fellow in tinted glasses in a car parked near where the bus began and ended its weekend run. He would wave eagerly to Rupert Green. Now, Rupert very clearly might not want that known. It was only because Tom had X-ray eyes that he had noticed the car. And his eyes had sometimes caught Dee Burke slipping into a big car and the arms of an older man. The older man had never been mentioned by Dee or by anyone in Rathdoon, so it was safe to assume that he was a secret older man, not a legit one. No amount of watching or guessing could tell him what young Kev Kennedy was so afraid of. It hadn't always been that way: he used to be a very nice young fellow, and the only one of that family to get up from the kitchen table and leave their father and their slices of bread and ham and the radio on from Good morning to Close down. But for the past year or so he was in bits.

Celia lived in a nurses' house. Six of them shared a place, which was apparently highly successful. They had two television sets, a washing machine, and an ironing board always in position in the back room. Celia had said there was never a cross word exchanged in that house—it was an ideal way to live until they married and had homes of their own. Nancy Morris shared a flat with that nice, bouncy Mairead Hely; how Mairead stuck it was a mystery. He had met her one night at a party and she told him that Nancy's newest trick was to watch out for food tastings in supermarkets and rush in before they closed and have paper cups of soup or bits of cheese on toothpicks and

213

then to come home triumphantly to the flat and say "I've had my supper." That night, and it was about three months back, Mairead had said that she was gathering up her courage to ask Nancy to leave, but she couldn't have gathered it yet. Poor Mikey was so nice, Tom would have driven him home willingly, but he just laughed and walked to a bus stop with the never-failing sense of good humor that was so hard to take. Judy Hickey took a bus the same direction and Tom often saw them talking together as he turned the Lilac Bus and drove off home.

None of them knew where his home was, that was certain. Long ago he had developed a gift for not answering direct questions so skillfully that people thought they had been given some kind of answer but didn't ask again. When Nancy Morris had asked him how much he paid a week for his flat, he said it was hard to work out, and that was that from Miss Morris. Rupert once asked him on which side of the city did he live, and Tom had said that he was sure Rupert must know the trends in what people wanted. He often thought that it was interesting looking at people in cinema queues, for example, and wondering where they lived; he supposed that if he were working in an auctioneer's like Rupert, he'd think it even more interesting. Rupert agreed and had talked cheerfully about the unexpected ambitions of a lot of the people who came into his office. He never again asked Tom where he lived, and he didn't sound as if he had been rebuffed.

Dee Burke had told him that her brother was living in sin and wasn't it monstrous that boys could get away with it and girls still couldn't really. She had asked him suddenly, "Maybe you live in sin too. Do you?"

"I don't know," he had said. "I'm very confused about sin; they never explained it properly at our school. What about yours?" Dee had said gloomily that they never stopped explaining it at her school and they were all so sick of it by the time they left, they had hardly the energy to commit any, which might have been the aim all along. But she still didn't find out what his lifestyle was. And down in Rathdoon he was spoken of as the one Fitzgerald boy that didn't join the family firm, the only one who didn't want to build an empire. He did something arty up in Dublin. But in any gathering of three, if his name came up, there would be three different theories on what he did. It gave the lie to the obsession with gossip that small towns were meant to have automatically, Tom thought. There was Dee with her older chap, Rupert with his boyfriend, Kev with his gambling debts or whatever it was, and no one back home knew a thing about any of them—or about Tom. In Rathdoon only one person knew how Tom lived and why: his mother.

Nobody would guess that in a million years. His mother tutted with the best, sighed over his clothes and bus—genuine sighs. She really would have preferred a nice inconspicuous bus and more conservative clothes: nice neutral colors, stone-colored trousers and brown jackets like her other sons wore. Suits, white shirts, restrained ties for Mass on Sunday. When his father railed about the young generation in general and That Boy in particular, Tom's mother was gentle in her reproach. Anyone looking on might have thought she agreed with her husband. Who could have known that Tom was her lifeline?

She was a handsome woman, Peg Fitzgerald. Fifty-two, very well groomed; you never saw a hair out of place on Mrs. Fitzgerald. She wore knitted suits, in lilacs or dark green, and a good brooch to tone in with whatever color it was. In summer she wore lighter linen suits, but they were the same colors and she had looked the same for years. She had three perms a year in the big town, and she had a shampoo and set every Friday morning of her life with little Sheila O'Reilly, the niece of the parish priest. Sheila didn't do much business in Rathdoon, but she never seemed to mind. She was always cheerful and if there were no heads of hair to deal with she did knitting instead and made a little out of that as a sideline. She wished there were more regular customers like Mrs. Fitzgerald, who wanted their hair done the same way at the same time every week.

Mrs. Fitzgerald was in the shop every day. The craft shop side of it had been her idea and was very successful. Any time a tour bus stopped there was a heavy electronic buzzing of tills in the Fitzgerald Craft Center. There were shawls, lengths of tweed, pottery—a very wide range to suit all tastes. It was also the place where the whole of Rathdoon bought birthday presents for each other. Peg had difficulty persuading the family that it was a good idea, but now they looked at her with a new respect. She was a firm believer, too, that things should be kept in the family. When the boys married it was understood that their wives would work there. In fact, one potential daughter-in-law broke off the engagement because she said all she would get from the marriage contract was to be an unpaid shopworker instead of the bank official that she was. Tom had thought that showed some spirit, but the rest of the family—including the jilted brother—all combined in thinking they had a lucky escape if that was going to be her attitude.

From the outset Tom had said he wouldn't work in the shop; there had been no fight about it, only scorn. He had said reasonably that he thought it was better for his three brothers and two sisters if they *knew* from the word go that he would not be joining them. Then they could make their own plans without any question marks hanging over him. He decided this as long ago as his school days. But they had thought it was like being an engine driver and took no notice. What he would like to do was go to Dublin and live. Just live, not necessarily *do* anything, until he found something he'd like to do, and then maybe America or Paris or Greece. If you didn't have high living standards and want a comfortable house and a lot of possessions and rich food, you could live very cheaply. They had thought it was a phase.

He had got a lot of honors in his Leaving, much more than the brothers who were well on their way to being merchant princes: expanding to other towns, opening new branches, developing their mother's much-mocked idea of a craft shop in other centers all over the West. Tom was pronounced brighter than any of them by the masters who had taught all the Fitzgeralds, but he was adamant and very firm for an eighteen-year-old. He had all these bits of paper to prove he was educated, now could he get on with his own life? He thanked his father as warmly as he could for the grudging offer of university fees, but still it was no. All he wanted was to be left alone. He wouldn't go to the bad, he would come home regularly if they liked so that they could see him and satisfy themselves that he was still normal. He would hitch. He would sign on for the dole each week, and *no,* that would not be an almighty disgrace in Dublin. Who would see him or know him for God's sake, and *no,* it was not unfair, that's what people did nowadays: the rich paid taxes and there was at least bread and a roof for those who weren't rich. We didn't let them die in the streets today, stepping over them saying wasn't it a pity they didn't have the get up and go to find a good job and earn their living. *No,* he did not intend to stay on national assistance forever. And *yes,* he was very grateful for the offer of a place in the family firm, but we only had one life and that was not how he was going to spend his.

And wasn't it lucky that this is what he had decided to do? What on earth would have happened if he hadn't been around?

It had been very easy to live cheaply in Dublin. For a while he lived with a young couple who gave him a bed and some food; they didn't have all that much themselves. He taught their children every evening, two nice bright little boys. He went over everything they had done at school and helped them with their homework. But he didn't really like it because he felt they should be out playing instead of doing more and yet more. They knew enough, he kept telling their worried young parents, they're fine: don't pack their heads with facts and more and more. The parents didn't understand. Surely the best thing was to get a good start, to be in there with a better chance than the others? But they were only ten and nine, it was *years* before they would need to be in there fighting the others for places and points and positions. No, the pale mother and father hadn't got on in their lives because they had nobody to guide them; they weren't going to let the same thing happen to the children. He left them amicably. He worked as a gardener for an old lady and slept in her garden shed for a year without her knowing. She never knew in the end, and he had moved his camp bed and primus stove long before the funeral, so nobody ever knew.

He worked in a nightclub as a sort of bouncer. He was slim and not the typical bouncer material, but he had a look in his eye that was as important as muscle. His boss, who was one of the sharpest men in Dublin, was anxious to keep him on, promote him even, but it wasn't the life Tom wanted. He left again amicably, and before he left he asked the sharp boss what was good about him. He'd like to know just for his own record. The boss said he owed him no explanation if he was leaving, but okay, Tom had a look in his eye that said he would go the distance. People didn't mess with him. Tom liked this reference just as he had liked the old lady saying he was a loving sort of gardener, and the nine-year-old boy saying that he made Latin so much more interesting than they did at school, because there was none of this treating it as a language—more as a puzzle really. But these were not written references. Each new job had to be found on charm or effort; each time he had to go in cold.

He had a summer in Greece driving a minibus, not unlike the Lilac Bus, over mountainy roads, taking holidaymakers to and from airport and hotels. He had a summer in America working at a children's camp with seventy discontented youngsters who would all rather have been at home. He had a winter in Amsterdam working in a souvenir shop. He had a funny three months in London working in market surveys—going up to people on the street with a clipboard and asking them questions. He had a different kind of three months in London working as a hospital orderly; he found it harrowing, and his respect for nurses went way, way up. He had been on the point of telling Celia about those months several times, but he never told stories about what he had done—it led to questions and questions often needed answers.

He didn't think of himself as a drifter, and yet for nine years, since he had left school, he had done nothing with any purpose or any permanence. Still, he wouldn't have missed any of it, not even those strange days in the hospital pushing frightened elderly people on trolleys through crowds, all speaking different languages, all the nationalities under the sun working in the hospital and coming in as patients. And now it meant that he could look after Phil, for he had no job to give up, no real lifestyle to interrupt.

Phil was the nicest in his family, there was no doubt about it. They all agreed on that, just as they all agreed that Tom was the oddest and the most difficult. Phil was the nearest to him in age: she was almost a year to the day older than he was. All the six Fitzgeralds arrived within seven years, and then the young Peg stopped producing a new baby every season. There were pictures of them all when they were toddlers, and Tom always thought it looked like a nursery school rather than one family. But his mother had always said it was great to get it all over at once. You had a period when they all seemed to be unmanageable and then suddenly they had all grown up. Anyway, Phil had always been his special friend, and in the great sixteen- and seventeen-year-old arguments about Tom not joining the firm, Phil had been very supportive. She had been in the big town seventeen miles from Rathdoon learning shorthand and typing at the time, it had been agreed that she should work in the office rather than the shop. But she used to come home at weekends during her commercial course and encourage Tom to live his own life. She had a big round face, Phil had, and she was always laughing. Years ago he remembered her dancing with Red Kennedy and getting a lecture that the Kennedys were perfectly nice, not a thing wrong with them, but she should set her sights a little higher. Phil had said indignantly that she wasn't setting her sights at Red Kennedy or at anyone, she was just dancing with him, but there had still been a lot of head shaking.

Phil was what they called a fine girl in Rathdoon; Mrs. Fitzgerald used to say that she'd slim down when the time came. Hadn't Anna, the eldest of the family, had a lot of puppy fat too? But Mrs. Fitzgerald always thought that there was some kind of law which said that a girl needed to be nice and slim and attractive when she was thinking of choosing a husband and settling down. It was just the way things were. But Phil didn't notice some magical trick of nature: she remained plump and round-faced and never developed the hollow cheeks and small waist which were generally agreed to have been important when her sister Anna attracted and married the very suitable Dominic, whose family made tweeds.

Tom had never thought she was too fat; he had told her that several times when he came home for the weekend. He said she must be losing her marbles to think she was a fatty, and cracked to think that she had no friends because of this.

"Who are my friends then? List them," she had cried.

Tom couldn't, but he said he couldn't list any friends of his family, for God's sake, he was away, he didn't live here. She *must* have friends. No, she claimed, she didn't. That was when meaning to be helpful he had suggested this singles type of holiday. Everyone went on their own, there were no loving couples to start out with but hopefully plenty of them on the way back. Phil had read the brochure eagerly and decided that she should go on it.

"Don't tell anyone it's a singles special," her mother had advised. "It looks a little pathetic. Say it's an ordinary holiday in Spain."

Tom never knew quite what happened, but it wasn't a success. Phil said that Spain was all right, and the weather had been fair, but nothing else. Later, much later, he heard that all the girls except Phil had been topless on the beaches, that almost everyone on the group charter had enjoyed a close physical relationship with one or more other people on the same group charter—again, everyone except Phil— and that there was no question of meeting people and dancing with them and talking to them and getting to know them. This was apparently a much more swinging type of holiday than some singles outings, and swinging meant going to bed with people, people who were total strangers.

But Tom didn't know all this at the time. Phil had come back quiet and noncommunicative. He noticed shortly after this that she seemed to have lost weight, but he didn't say anything, because he had been the one to tell her that weight wasn't important. If he admired her now, she would believe that he had only been kind before. Phil didn't go to the dance anymore and she didn't go out to the sea with a crowd of girls like she used to. But to be honest, he didn't notice these things at the time; it was only afterward he remembered it all.

Phil had come to Dublin on one of the day excursions by train from the town. It was a bit of a killer: the train left at 9 A.M., you were in Dublin at noon, and then the train back was at 6 P.M. So it was some concentrated shopping before they all fell back with sore feet and bulging parcels to go home again that night. Phil always rang Tom if she went on one of these marathons, and he came to meet her at the station in his minibus, which was a dirty beige in those days.

She looked very pale, and said that she had been having really terrible pains like a knife on the train, so bad that the people in her carriage said she should go to a hospital or a doctor, since she had been crying out with the sharpness of them. Tom

224

looked concerned and just at that moment she bent over again, doubled up with pain and letting out a long low scream, so his mind was made up. He drove her to the out-patients of a hospital. He was quiet and firm. He got her seen before anyone by saying it was an emergency. As her brother, he signed the permission to operate for a burst appendix and he was there when she woke up to tell her that it had all been fine, and it was over and all she had to do now was to rest. Her troubled face smiled at him sadly. Their mother came up the next day with a suitcase of things that Phil would need, a lot of reassurance, sighs of how good God was to let it all happen when Tom was there to take charge, and messages of love, boxes of chocolates, bottles of lavender water from the rest of the family.

She was recovering quite well, Tom thought. Well, her strength was coming back quickly and he was very startled when one of the nurses said she would like to talk to him about his sister. Privately. She had made a report to the people who should know already, like the matron and the surgeon who had operated, but this was now something that must be taken further, through Miss Fitzgerald's own doctor perhaps.

He was alarmed. The nurse spoke reprovingly, as if poor Phil had been caught stealing in the wards. What was it? Well, the nurse had noticed she spent a long time at the lavatory, and she had asked her about constipation or diarrhea. Apparently neither, but she was still in there for a considerable time, so the nurse had listened at the door. Tom felt his heart beating: what horror was he going to be told?

It was what the nurse had suspected. Vomiting, retching. Two or three times a day.

"What's causing it?" Tom cried. He had no idea what the tone of shock was all about. Why wasn't he being told this by a doctor?

"She's doing it herself," the nurse said. "Eating chocolates, biscuits, banana, slices of bread and butter. You should have seen the papers and the empty boxes. And then vomiting it all up."

"But why on earth would she do that?"

"It's called bulimia; it's like anorexia nervosa —you know, where people starve themselves to death if they can. It's a form of it. They binge and gorge and then they make themselves sick to get rid of the food they've eaten."

"Phil does this?"

"Yes, she's been doing it for some time."

"And did this cause her appendix to burst?"

"Oh, no, not at all, that was something totally unconnected. But maybe lucky in a way. Because at least now you know and the family will know and help her try to fight it."

"Can't you just tell her to stop? Can't we all tell her it's . . . it's revolting—it's so senseless."

"Oh, no, that's not the way, that's not what they'll say at all when she goes in."

"Goes in where?"

"To a psychiatric hospital. It's a mental condition, you know, it's got nothing to do with us."

226

The nurse wasn't quite correct. It did have a little to do with them because Phil was admitted to the psychiatric wing of that same hospital and there was a medical side to her treatment as well as all the therapy and group discussions on the psychiatric side. She had been very relieved at the beginning to know that other people did the same thing. She thought she was the only person in the world who had ever done it, and she felt a great burden of guilt taken off her shoulders. She never felt guilty about the self-induced vomiting: she said it was the easiest thing in the world. If you just put your finger in the right place down your throat it happened automatically. But she did feel guilty about stuffing herself with the food. Especially eating in a lavatory—that was the thing she felt shameful about. She wasn't ready at all to talk about why she did it. Tom was told that she would undoubtedly do it again and again before she was cured. Before she came back to reality and accepted that she was perfectly fine as she was. The help and support of a family at a time like this was crucial. If Phil was to see that she was a person of high esteem in her own family, that would go a very long way toward helping her have a good image of herself again. The family, yes. But Lord God, the Fitzgerald family. At this time.

Poor Phil couldn't have picked a worse time to call on them, Tom thought grimly. It was the very period that the newspapers were full of the case about the armed raid on the post office in Cork

227

and the subsequent conviction and sentencing of Teddy Fitzgerald, their cousin, who had worked in the business with the family. That had been a heavy cross. Then there was the infidelity of Dominic, the highly suitable husband of Anna, the eldest. There had been many a tale of a relationship and finally the birth of a child that Dominic grudgingly acknowledged as his, even though it was born not to his wife but to one of the most unsuitable women in the west of Ireland, tinkers who had settled down—and according to Mrs. Peg Fitzgerald the only thing worse than a tinker on the road was a tinker who had settled down. So there was that disgrace. There had been a few other things, too, none of them as shocking but all of them adding up to a general family anxiety. It was the wrong time to hear that a member of the family was now entering on to a long period of psychiatric treatment and would need their support.

Mrs. Fitzgerald made her point of view absolutely clear. There would be no talk about Phil whatsoever. This was final. Phil had recovered from her burst appendix, she had been convalescing, she had been visiting friends, she would come back shortly. Meanwhile they would get a temporary girl for the office. Mrs. Fitzgerald would go to Dublin once a month to give this support that the hospital said it needed, Tom would go to see her as often as he could, and that was it. It would not be discussed; they had quite enough problems already without adding this one.

And what would it do to Phil's chances of getting a husband if it was widely known she had been in a mental institution? No more arguments.

Tom was sure that this was not what the doctors meant by family support: hushing it all up, making it into a greater shame than Phil already felt it was. He was certain that his mother's monthly visits—full of assurances that nobody knew, no one suspected, people had been fooled and hoodwinked, cover stories had been invented—were all the worst thing for his sister, who would listen with stricken face and apologize for all the trouble she had caused. Sometimes his mother would reach out awkwardly and take Phil's hand.

"We love you . . . um . . . very much. You are much loved, Phil." Then she would draw her hand back, embarrassed. She had been told by the psychiatrist that this was a good line to emphasize, but she recited it as if it were learned by heart. They were not a demonstrative family, they had never hugged or kissed each other. It was hard for his mother to reach out and say that to Phil—and bewildering for Phil to hear it, just before her mother gathered her gloves and handbag and started to leave.

He went to see Phil every day, every single day, and he telephoned her on each Saturday and Sunday. His mother said that she would telephone except that there was nothing to say, but Tom found things. After all, he knew her much better: they had been meeting each other constantly, and he was able to pick from a variety of things to say.

He never felt as if he were talking to someone who wasn't well. He didn't talk down to her, he would never apologize profusely if he hadn't been able to ring or visit, just briefly. He wouldn't let on that he thought his presence was essential to her. He treated her as if she were as sane as he was.

They talked about childhood a lot. Tom remembered his as happy enough, too much talk about the business, a bit too much of covering over and not letting the neighbors know this or that, and keeping our business to ourselves. Phil remembered it quite differently. She remembered that they were always laughing, and that they had all been sitting around the table together talking to each other, though Tom said they couldn't have been. There would have to have been either their mother or their father in the shop. Phil remembered them going on great outings to the sea and picnics; Tom said he honestly could only remember one. Phil said they used to play games like I Spy and the Minister's Cat, and Sardines, where one person had to hide and when you found them you squeezed in like a sardine beside them. Tom said that was only at parties. But they didn't fight over the memories; they talked them over like an old film that you'd seen years ago and everyone could remember bits of, but nobody could remember all of.

They talked about boyfriends and girlfriends and sex. Tom wasn't surprised to hear that she was a virgin, and she wasn't surprised to hear that he was not. They talked easily and without guilt, sometimes for hours in the day room or in the garden, sometimes just for short times because Phil was silent and withdrawn, or because Tom had to work. He was working in an auction showroom these days, helping to carry furniture in and out, put lot numbers on things and write them up in a catalogue. He had been thinking of moving on, but the hours suited him and it was near the hospital, so he could come and go easily. One of the other patients asked if Tom was her boyfriend. She had laughed uneasily and said she never had a boyfriend. The other girl had shrugged and said she was probably as well off: they were a barrelful of trouble, that's all they were. She hadn't assumed for a moment that Phil *couldn't* have a boyfriend. It made Phil feel a lot more cheerful. She asked Tom what kind of girls he liked, and he said unusual ones, not people who talked about houses and engagement rings and the future. He had a very nice girlfriend once, but unfortunately she met a really dull guy and he offered her all this other business—security, respectability—and she came and told Tom straight out she was going to take it. Phil had been very sympathetic.

"You never told us any of this," she said.

"True, but you never told us that you half fancied Billy Burns, even though he was a married man," he said, laughing.

"You dragged that out of me." She laughed too. He thought it was all too slow, she *must* be better now.

231

He said this more than once to the psychiatrist, and was depressed to hear that Phil was still not happy, still not at ease with herself and sure of her place in the world. They all thanked Tom for coming and said he was invaluable. Not only in his own visits but in the lifeline he offered back to Rathdoon. She never minded his going back home at weekends. In fact, she liked it because it brought her closer to the family and because he always brought back news of them all and, better still, a cheerful letter from her mother.

Every Saturday morning he forced his mother to write her a letter. He literally sat there while she wrote. He wouldn't accept that she had nothing to write about, and he refused to let her wriggle out of it.

"Do you think I'd be doing this, do you think I'd sit here every Saturday morning unless it was important?" he had shouted. "She is desperate to know that we are fond of her, and that her place is here; she won't be *able* to come back unless she knows this."

"But of course it's here; naturally we want her back. For heaven's sake, Tom, you're making a big drama out of it all."

"It is a big drama. Phil is in a psychiatric hospital and mainly because we can't let her know that she is important here."

"Your father and I think that's all mumbo jumbo. She was never made to feel anything but important; we treated her with great respect; people loved having her in the office. She was always so cheerful, and she knew everyone's names: wasn't she the life and soul of that place?"

"Write it. Write it down on paper," he would order.

"I'd feel stupid saying that to Phil. It's silly, it's treating her as if she's not all there. She'll know I'm only acting."

"But you said you meant it, a minute ago."

"Yes, of course I mean it, but it's not something you say, not something you write down."

"Since you're not there to say it, you have to write it. Since you won't let her come home and be treated in the town where you'd only be seventeen miles away, where you could see her every day, then you're going to have to write it. Otherwise how is she to know, how in God's earth can she *know* that she's important here?"

"It's not that I won't let her come back here. It's for her own good, to keep things quiet, to keep our business to ourselves." He had heard it so often, maybe he would hear it forever. Perhaps Phil would never get better.

He was in the middle of yet another Saturday confrontation when Celia Ryan came in. He was surprised to see her, and in a way relieved. His mother had been very hard to pin down today. She had escaped him in the morning by saying she was needed in the shop, and it was only when he brought her a cup of coffee and a writing pad that he could get her to listen. She had been going through one of her Phil-must-pull-her-self-together phases. Tom felt a mad urge to ask

Celia to sit down and explain to his mother her own firsthand knowledge of anorexia and bulimia, mentioning casually that Phil was in a psychiatric ward with the latter. His mother would probably fall senseless to the ground if he were to tell the family disgrace to Mrs. Ryan's daughter. The temptation had only been a flicker.

Celia wanted a loan of his tape recorder, of all things, and a blank cassette. She wanted to record something. She seemed flustered. She didn't tell him what she wanted it for, but then he rarely told people anything, whether they asked him or not, so he couldn't fault her there. She said she'd give it to him on the bus.

"Terrible time she has with that mother of hers," Mrs. Fitzgerald said.

Tom nodded. He thought he didn't have a great time with his own mother, but it was not in him to say it; he just wanted the letter to give to Phil on Monday.

"She'll probably marry Bart Kennedy, and they can keep an eye on the place that way," Tom said.

"Bart Kennedy? Not at all. Sure, nobody will marry Bart Kennedy, he's not the type that marries." Mrs. Fitzgerald was positive.

"Bart, a fairy? Go on out of that."

"No, I don't mean that or anything like it. He's just not the kind of man who marries, you must see that. Maybe men don't notice these things: women do. Red Kennedy, now, he'll be married within the year, I'd say; I hear he's courting. But Bart—not at all."

"I thought that's what she came home for," Tom said.

"She comes home to stop that place going down the drain, that's all."

"Really?" Tom felt pleased. He didn't know why, but he felt a sense of relief.

He went into the pub that night and discovered why she had wanted the tape recorder. It seemed a bit sneaky somehow. Like taking advantage of the poor woman who was slobbering and messing around behind her own bar. Even more humiliating was the thought that Mrs. Ryan's daughter was recording the tuneless singing.

"She doesn't know, she really doesn't know," Celia said as an explanation when he had asked her was it fair. He imagined Celia trying to tell her mother about the excesses of the night before and Mrs. Ryan brushing it away with that businesslike cheerful manner she had when sober. It wasn't the kind of thing anyone else would say to her, so she would be bound to believe that Celia was making it up at worst or at the very least exaggerating it.

"I'll come around tomorrow and pick up the pieces," he said. She smiled back at him, a warm grateful smile. He looked at Bart Kennedy. Bart was pulling pints and laughing with the lads—he and Celia didn't have eyes for each other at all. Tom must have been mad to have thought it in the first place.

There were no pieces to pick up next day. Celia's mother had taken it very well. She was sitting in the back room while Celia and Bart dealt with the Sunday lunchtime trade.

"She's coming to Dublin. I thought it would be easier. I'd be able to get to see her."

"When?"

"Tomorrow. I won't come back on the bus tonight. I'll wait and go with her. I've a great friend, a nurse in Dublin—she'll work for me tomorrow even though it's meant to be her day off."

"Does she live in your harem of nurses?"

"Emer? Not at all: she's a respectable married woman with a family."

"Would you work if you were married?"

"Bloody sure, I would. Catch me giving up a job to cook meals and clean a house for a man. Anyway, everyone has to nowadays. How would you have any life at all if you didn't? And nursing's fine, I'd hate to lose it."

"How long will it be . . . ?" He nodded toward the back room, where Mrs. Ryan sat waiting in a chair.

"I don't know. It depends on her—you know, if she wants to.

"Doesn't it depend on her family, too, and support?"

"Well, there's only me; she can't have the beauties in Australia and Detroit and England, so she'll have to make do with me."

"My sister Phil isn't well, she's got the same problem," he said suddenly.

236

"I never knew Phil had a drink problem." She said it without censure or shock.

"No, not that, I meant she has the same problem: she only has me in Dublin. She's got an anorexic thing, you know, but she does eat and makes herself vomit."

"She's a better chance with that; so many of the anorexics die, it's desperate to see them, little wizened monkeys, and they think that this is the best way to be. But bulimia is very stressful, poor Phil. Isn't that very bad luck."

He looked at her gratefully. "Will they be any help, the ones who've gone away?"

"I shouldn't think so. Will yours?"

"No. I'm beginning to realize it now. I kept thinking I could change them, but it's all head in the sand, pretend it isn't happening, don't tell anyone."

"In time, in their time maybe. Not yours." She was very gentle.

"Well, they'll have to make do with us then," he said, "your half-mad ma and my half-mad sister."

"Aren't they lucky they've got us," said Celia Ryan, and laughed like a peal of bells.

"I'll miss you going back on the bus tonight," he said.

"Well, maybe you might come and console me when I've got my mother in. And if it would be any help, I could come and see Phil with you—if you'd like it, that is?"

"I'd like it a lot," said Tom Fitzgerald.

DUBLIN 4

DINNER IN DONNYBROOK

She drew the dinner table six times and it always came out the same. If you put the host at one end and the hostess at the other it didn't work out. She would sit with her back to the window and have a man on either side of her. Fine so far. Dermot would sit opposite her with a woman on either side of him. Fine again, but what about the two places in between? Whatever way you did it you would have to have man sitting beside man, and woman beside woman.

She shook her head, puzzled. It was like those problems they had always done at school; if you have three missionaries and three cannibals on an island and the boat can only hold two . . . Not that it mattered, of course, and anybody who knew how much time she had spent working it out would say she should spend a week in St. Patrick's, but still it was very irritating. There must be a way.

"There is," said her daughter, Anna. She had telephoned Anna to talk about something else but brought the conversation around to the perplexing dinner table. "At a party for eight, host and hostess can't sit opposite each other. You sit opposite the most important lady . . . and put Dad on that lady's left." Anna had gone on talking about other things, not realizing that her mother was now drawing the dinner table again, with Dermot sitting facing the sideboard and the most important lady sitting at the other end of the table facing herself.

"Are you all right, Mother?" Anna asked. Anna used to call her "Mum," but now she said "Mother." She said it in a slightly joky tone as if she had been saying Your Ladyship, it was as if the word Mother were equally unsuitable.

"I'm fine, dear," said Carmel. It irritated her when people asked was she all right. She never asked anyone else were they all right, even when they sounded most odd or distrait. Everyone felt they could patronize her, and pat her on the head. Even her own daughter.

"Oh, good, you sounded a bit vague as if you'd gone off somewhere. Anyway, as I said, we're off to the cottage at the weekend so you'll have to tell me how the great entertaining went. I'm glad you and Dad are having people around. It's good to see you stirring yourself to do something."

Carmel wondered again why Dermot could still be "Dad" and not "Father," and why it was good to be stirring herself. Why should things be stirred? Particularly, why should people be stirred? They should be left to simmer or cool down or even grow a crust on top of them if they wanted to. She said none of this to her eldest daughter.

"Oh, no, dear, the dinner party isn't this weekend. It's in a month's time. . . . I was just thinking ahead."

Anna burst out laughing. "Mother, you *are* full of surprises. A month ahead! Not even James would insist on that much planning. Anyway, we'll have plenty of time to talk about it before then." She made it sound like basketwork in an occupational therapy ward. Carmel hid her annoyance and hoped they would have a nice weekend. The weather forecast was good, and especially in the southwest.

She thought that Anna and James were quite insane to drive two hundred and nine miles on a Friday afternoon and the same distance again on Sunday. She could see no point in having a house and garden out in Sandycove and never getting to spend a weekend there. The cottage in Kerry had been an albatross around their necks as far as Carmel could see. She never believed that they could enjoy the five-hour drive. "Four hours thirty-five minutes, Grandmama, if you know the shortcuts . . . James always made her feel even more foolish with his Grandmama; she felt like a grand duchess. But still Anna never complained, she spoke of it eagerly: "Oh, Mother, it's so great, we get there around nine-thirty and light a fire, take out the steaks, open the wine, kiddies half asleep already, pop them into bed . . . it's so free . . . the country . . . our own place . . . you can't believe it."

Anna had heard the weather forecast too. "Yes,

243

I am glad, because we're having a huge lunch there on Sunday and it will be so much nicer if we can have them all out of doors."

A huge lunch, down at that cottage, in the wilds of Kerry, miles from her kitchen, her deep freeze, her dishwasher. No wonder Anna must think her pathetic worrying about seating people at a dinner party a whole month away. But, of course, Anna didn't have the same kind of worries. Anna would never let herself get into a situation where she would have those kind of worries.

Carmel drew the table plan again. She wrote in the names of the guests carefully. At one end of the table with her back to the window she wrote Carmel, and at the opposite end she wrote out Ruth O'Donnell, Most Important Lady. She filled in the other names and wrote things under them too. Dermot, Loving Husband. Sheila, Wise Friend. Ethel, Upper Class Friend. Martin, Kind Husband of Wise Friend. David, Pompous Husband of Upper Class Friend. And then on the right-hand side of Ruth O'Donnell she wrote, slowly and carefully, Joe, Life-Saver. She sat and looked at the plan for a long time. It stopped being a drawing of a rectangle with little squares around it holding names and descriptions. It became a table with glasses and flowers and good china and shining silver. She could almost smell the food and hear the conversation. She learned it off by heart, the order they sat in, just like she had learned the Great Lakes or the towns of Cavan when she was a child, by rote with her eyes tightly closed, relating not to things as they were but as they were written down.

Then she took all the bits of paper and put them into the firegrate. There were still some warm embers and some bits of red from last night's fire, but she didn't trust them to burn. She took out half a firelighter and set a match to it. And there in the room where she would give the party in a month's time, she sat and watched the flames burn the lists and the table plans. They burned away until there were only powdery ashes left on top of yesterday's.

"I think Carmel Murray is losing her marbles," said Ethel at breakfast.

David grunted. He was reading his own letters and he did not want to be distracted by Ethel's chat.

"No seriously, listen to this . . ." Ethel went back to the start of the letter.

"In a moment, Ethel . . ."

"No, you'll just leap up and go off, I want you to hear."

He looked at her and knew he might as well give in. Ethel got her way in everything, and it made for an easy life to accept this.

"Carmel has lost her marbles? Go on from there."

"Well, she must have. She's written to us. Written to ask us to dinner . . . next *month* . . . can you believe it?"

"Well, that's nice of her," said David vaguely.

"I suppose we can get out of it. What's the fuss, what's so mad about that? People do ask each other to dinner. They do it all the time."

He knew he was courting trouble to try to be smart-alecky with Ethel. He was right; it had been a mistake.

"I know people do it all the time, dear," she said. "But Carmel Murray has never done it before. Poor Carmel that we have to be nice to because Dermot's a good sort . . . that's why it's unusual. And did you ever hear of anything so strange? A letter when she only lives five minutes away, when she may have heard of the telephone."

"Yes, yes. It is odd. I do agree. You must do what you wish, say we're away, say it's a pity . . . some other time. What?"

"She'll know we're not away. That's what's so odd, it's on the day of Ruth O'Donnell's exhibition, she'll know that we won't be out of town for that."

"How do you know it's that day?"

"Because she says so in the letter . . . she says that she's asked Ruth as well. Now do you see why I think she's losing her marbles?"

Ethel looked flushed and triumphant, having proved her point. She sat imperiously at the breakfast table wearing her silk breakfast kimono and waited for the apology from her husband. It came.

"She's inviting Ruth. . . . Oh, my God. Now I see what you mean."

Sheila hated being disturbed at school. It made the nuns so edgy and uneasy to call someone to the telephone. They hadn't moved into the modern age in terms of communications; their telephone was still in a cold and drafty little booth in the main entrance hall, inconvenient for everyone. She was alarmed when she heard that her husband wanted her.

"Martin, what is it, what's happened?" she said.

"Nothing. Nothing, relax."

"What do you mean, nothing? What is it?"

"Stop fussing, Sheila, it's nothing."

"You brought me the whole way down here from third years for nothing? Sister Delia is looking after them as a great favor. What *is* it, Martin? Are the children—?"

"Look, I thought you ought to know, we've had a very odd letter from Carmel."

"A what . . . from Carmel?"

"A letter. Yes, I know it's sort of out of character, I thought maybe something might be wrong and you'd need to know"

"Yes, well, what did she say? What's the matter with her?"

"Nothing, that's the problem. She's inviting us to dinner."

"To dinner?"

"Yes, it's sort of funny, isn't it? As if she wasn't well or something. I thought you should know in case she got in touch with you."

"Did you really drag me all the way down here,

the third form is at the top of the school you know, I thought it had burned down! God, wait till I come home to you. I'll murder you."

"The dinner's in a month's time, and she says she's invited Ruth O'Donnell."

"Oh, Jesus Christ."

Henry shouted out to Joe, "Hey, that letter's come from Ireland. She must have fixed the date, poor old bat."

Joe came in and opened it.

"Yeah, in a month's time. She says it's all going according to plan. She sent the ticket and the money."

"She's all right, isn't she?" Henry sounded approving.

"Oh, she's really fine, and I owe her, I owe her in a big way. I'll make it work."

"Well, if you can't, I don't know who could," Henry said admiringly, and Joe smiled back as he fetched the coffee percolator.

"I think Mother's coming out of herself a bit more, darling," Anna said to James as they negotiated the early evening traffic.

"Good. It's no wonder this country's going to the dogs. Look at the buildup of traffic here and it's not even four o'clock. I mean, half of them must be taking the whole afternoon off. Never mind, we'll lose them in a few minutes. What were you saying about Grandmama?"

"She's talking of having a dinner party, you

248

know, with a proper dining table, and a seating plan. It all sounds good."

"I've always said that she's not nearly so sleepy and dozy as you and Bernadette make out. I find plenty of things to talk to her about."

"No, you don't, you just talk at her. She sits enthralled because you're so interesting, but it's not a real conversation."

James didn't agree. "You're wrong, she tells me things. No, I can't remember anything immediately. That's silly, looking for examples. But I do get on well with her . . . she just needs a bit of flattery, a few cheerful things. 'You look very dishy, Grandmama,' and she blossoms. She doesn't like people telling her she's silly."

Anna thought for a while.

"I suppose people do tell her she's silly. Yes, you're right. I always say 'Don't be silly, Mother,' but I don't mean it. It's just that she fusses so much, and I think that if I say she's not to be silly, then it's sort of reassuring to her. I'll be very supportive about her poor old dinner party. I'll give her a tactful hand here and there."

James patted her knee.

"You're marvelous, sweetheart. And talking about parties, tell me what you've arranged for Sunday."

Anna settled back happily in her seat and told him about all the good things that were foil wrapped, vacuum packed and airtight in the huge cardboard box which they had loaded carefully into the boot of the car.

Bernadette said, "That's great, Mummy. Great. I'm sure it will be marvelous."

"I just thought you'd like to know," Carmel said.

"Well, of course I'm thrilled, Mummy. Is it tonight, or when?"

"Oh, no, dear, it's a dinner party. It's not for a month."

"A *month!* Mummy, are you all right?"

"Yes, dear, perfectly."

"Oh. Well. I mean, is there anything . . . do you want me to come and help you plan it, or anything?"

"No, no, it's all planned."

"Or serve it? You know, keep you calm and stop you fussing on the night?"

"No, no, dear, thank you, but I won't fuss at all."

"Well, that's great, Mummy, and is Daddy pleased that you're sort of getting into entertaining and everything?"

"It's not exactly getting into entertaining . . . it's just one dinner party."

"You know what I mean. Is Daddy thrilled?"

"I haven't told him yet."

"Mummy, are you sure you're all right, you're not getting upset or anything like . .

"Like what, dear?"

"Like that time when you *did* get upset."

"Oh no, dear, of course I'm not. That was when I had the trouble with my sleep patterns, they got out of kilter. . . . No, that's all totally cured, thank God, now. You know that, Bernadette dear. I sleep like a log these nights. No, no, that's not come back at all, thank heavens."

Bernadette sounded troubled.

"No, well, good. You have to look after yourself, Mummy. You know the way you fuss about silly things, I don't want you fussing about this party—"

"You don't understand, child, I'm looking forward to it."

"Good, oh, and we'll come and see you soon, it's been ages."

"Whenever you can, dear. Ring first though, I'll be out a lot in the next few weeks."

"Will you, Mummy? Where?"

"Here and there, dear. Anyway, it will be great to see you. How's Frank?"

"He's fine, Mummy. Take care of yourself, won't you?"

"Yes, Bernadette. Thank you, dear."

Dermot thought that Carmel was a hundred miles away that morning. Twice he had said that he might be late and not to worry if he dropped into the golf club on the way home. He had to have a few chats and that was the best place to have them. Twice she had nodded amiably and distantly as if she hadn't really heard or understood.

"Will you be all right? What are you going to do today?" he had asked, uncharacteristically.

She had smiled. "Funny you should ask that. I was just thinking that I hadn't anything to do all day so I was going to stroll downtown and look at the shops. I was thinking that it was almost a sinful thing to do . . . just idling away the day."

Dermot had smiled back. "You're entitled to be that sinful, enjoy yourself. And as I said, if I'm late I won't want anything to eat. We might go and have a steak . . . you know. Don't fuss, don't go to any trouble."

"No, that's fine," she had said.

As he sat in the traffic on Morehampton Road listening to the fool on Radio Eireann telling him exactly what he knew, that Morehampton Road was blocked solid, Dermot had a vague sense of unease about Carmel. But he shook himself and decided to put it out of his mind.

"I'm becoming quite neurotic," he told himself. "If she does hound me about my movements and tell me detail by detail the trivia of her day I become annoyed. Now I'm uneasy because she doesn't. Impossible to please me." He decided that everyone was being too bright on the radio and turned to the BBC where they were more solemn and in keeping with a man's thoughts in the morning as he drove in to his office.

Ruth O'Donnell hadn't got her invitation because she was away. She had gone to a farmhouse in Wales for a complete rest. She could have gone to an Irish farmhouse, but she wanted to be sure that she didn't meet anyone she knew. It wouldn't be a complete rest if she met people. She wanted to be absolutely on her own.

Carmel waited until the end of the *Gay Byrne* show. During *The Living Word* she put on her coat and took out her shopping basket on wheels. She never liked to miss Gay; once she had been able to give him a small cooker for a one-parent family. She hadn't spoken to him himself but the girl on the show had been very nice, and they had sent a nice girl to collect it, or else she was from the organization that had asked for it. It had never been made quite clear. Carmel had sent in one or two entries for the mystery voice competition, too, but she had never been called on to guess it. She didn't like to leave the house before *The Living Word.* It seemed rude to God, to walk out just when the few short minutes of religion were on.

She knew she should really listen to programs like *Day by Day,* which followed it, they would make her informed, but somehow she always felt her mind wandering and she never quite understood why people got so hot under the collar about things. Once she had said to Sheila that it would be nice to have someone sitting beside you to tell you what was going on in life, and Sheila told her to shut up, otherwise everyone would say they had learned nothing after all those years with the Loreto nuns. She thought that Sheila had been upset that day but she couldn't be sure.

It was bright and sunny out, a nice autumn day.

She pushed her tartan shopping bag on wheels in front of her, remembering when it had been a pram that she pushed. She used to know many more people in those days. She was always stopping and talking to people, wasn't she? Or was that memory playing tricks, like thinking that the summers were always hot when she was young and that they had spent their whole time on Killiney beach? That wasn't true, her younger brother Charlie said that they only went twice or three times a summer; perhaps the other memory wasn't true either. Perhaps she didn't stop at the bottom of Eglinton Road when she pointed out to the girls where the buses went to sleep in the bus home, perhaps there had been nobody much around then either.

She looked at the prices of wine in the off-license and wrote down the names of some of them so that she could make her list and selection later on. She then spent a happy hour looking at books in the big book shop. She copied down recipe after recipe in her little jotter. From time to time she got a look from one of the assistants, but she looked respectable and was causing no trouble so nobody said anything. Seared in her mind was a remark that Ethel had once made about a house where she had dined. "The woman has no imagination. I can't understand why you ask people round for prawn cocktail and roast beef. . . . I mean, why not tell them to eat at home and come round later for drinks?" Carmel loved prawn cocktail, and had little glass dishes which it would look very well in. They used to have trifle in them when she was young. She had kept them after things had been divided up between herself and Charlie, but she had never used them. They stood gathering dust, eight of them, at the back of the cupboard in the scullery. She would make another kind of starter, not prawn cocktail, and she would use those selfsame glasses for it, whatever it was. She rejected grapefruit segments and worked it out methodically. You couldn't have pâté, that would have to be on a plate, or soup, that couldn't be in a glass, or any kind of fish, of course. . . . No, it had to be something cold you ate with a spoon.

She would find it eventually, she had all day, she had twenty-nine more days—there was no rush. She must not get fussed. She found it. Orange Vinaigrette. Ethel couldn't say that that was unimaginative. You cut up oranges and black olives and onions and fresh mint . . . sounded terrific, you poured a vinaigrette sauce over it . . . It would be perfect. Carmel smiled happily. She knew that she was doing the right thing. All she had to do was go at it slowly.

She would go home now and rest; tomorrow she would come out and find a main course, and then a dessert. She had work to do at home too. Joe had said that if he was going to come and help her he would need cooperation. She mustn't have turned into a dowdy middle-aged old frump, she must look smart and glamorous and well turned-out. She had thirty afternoons to organize that.

Sheila dropped in on her way home from school. She seemed relieved to find Carmel there, and there was a look of worry on her face.

"I was a little alarmed. Martin told me you had sent us a letter."

"It was only an invitation." Carmel smiled. "Come on in and we'll have a coffee. I was in the middle of tidying out some cupboards. I've a lot of clothes that should go to the Vincent de Paul . . . but you know what always happens, you're ashamed to give them the way they are, so you get them cleaned first. Then when they come back from the cleaners they're better than anything else you have in the press so you never give them at all." Carmel laughed happily as they went into the kitchen, and she put on the kettle.

"It just seemed so funny to write, when I talk to you nearly every day."

"Did it? Oh, I don't know, I'm such a bad hostess I thought you have to write things down as invitations or people didn't believe you. I suppose that's why I wrote. I'd have told you anyway."

"But you didn't tell me yesterday."

"No, I must have forgotten."

"There's nothing wrong, is there, Carmel? You *are* all right?"

Carmel had her back to Sheila. She deliberately relaxed her shoulders and refused to clench her fists. Nobody was going to see just how annoyed she became when people asked her in that concerned tone whether she was all right.

256

"Sure I am, why wouldn't I be, a lady of leisure? It's you who must be exhausted coping with all that noise and those demons all day. I think you should be canonized."

"Tell me about the dinner party," Sheila said.

"Oh, it's not for a month yet," Carmel laughed.

"I know." Sheila's patience seemed strained. "I know it's not for a month, but you actually put pen to paper and wrote, so I thought it was a big thing."

"No, no, just eight of us. I said it in the letter."

"Yes, Martin told me. I wasn't at home when it arrived."

"He rang you? Oh, isn't he good? There was no need to. I mean, you could have told me any time."

"Yes, and you could have told *me* any time." Sheila looked worried.

"Yes, of course. Heavens, we are both making a production of it! When you think how many parties Ethel goes to, and indeed gives—"

"Yes, well, Ethel is Ethel."

"And you, I mean you and Martin often have people around, don't you? I often hear you say you had people in.

"Yes, but that's very casual."

"Oh, this will be too. Mainly people we all know well."

"But Ruth—Ruth O'Donnell—we don't know her all that well, and honestly, do you know, I think that's the night that her exhibition opens—in fact I'm sure of it."

"Yes, I know it is, I said that in the letter. Didn't Martin tell you? So I know we'll all be going to it. But it's at four o'clock . . . it will be well over by six, and even if people go to have a drink afterward . . . well, they're not invited here until eight, for half past."

"Yes, but don't you think on the night of her own exhibition she might want to go out with her own friends?"

"But we're her friends, in a way."

"Not really, are we? I mean, are you? She doesn't normally come here?"

"No, I don't think she's ever been here. I thought it would be nice for her . . . and she doesn't live far away, in that new block of flats, so she won't have far to go to change."

Sheila put down her mug of coffee.

"I don't think it's a good idea. We don't know her. Why ask someone we don't know very well to a dinner? Let's just have the six of us . . . it would be more friendly."

"No, I've asked her anyway, and I can't think what you say that for. You're the one who tells me to go out and meet more people."

"I didn't tell you to go out and invite well-known artists to dinner," muttered Sheila.

"Don't lecture me," Carmel said with a laugh, and Sheila had to admit to herself that Carmel did look more cheerful and like herself than she had in the last while. She looked a bit more like the Carmel of the old days.

"All right, I won't. Let me see your cupboard

cleaning. Maybe you could give something to me instead of the Vincent de Paul. I could do with it. A teacher doesn't get paid much, God help us, when you consider how we put our lives at risk."

"How's Martin feeling?"

"Oh, he's fine. He's great, you know, he never complains. I'm sure he's fed up but he never complains." Martin had been made redundant two years ago when two firms had merged. He had got a golden handshake. He was still only fifty-two and he expected to get another job, then he expected to write a book. Everybody else thought he was writing a book, but Sheila never lied to Carmel. To Carmel she admitted that Martin was doing the vacuuming and the shopping. They pretended that Sheila loved being back in the classroom. Not many people knew how much she hated it. Her children didn't know, not even Martin really knew. Carmel sometimes suspected, but Carmel was a longtime friend. It didn't matter what she knew. It was just a bit worrying sometimes the things she did. Like inviting that woman to dinner. Was there a possibility that Carmel's nerves were bad again? She sounded so well, and she looked fine. But it *was* the act of a madwoman.

"Hey, you are doing a thorough job. You've taken everything out. Which is the good pile and which is the bad pile?"

"I don't know, they all seem the same. They're like mouse clothes, aren't they? Do you remember

259

when we went to pantomimes years and years ago? People were dressed in mouse outfits and rat outfits . . . that's what these are like!"

"Carmel, you are preposterous! Of course your clothes aren't like that, they're smashing. Have you two of these blue cardigans?"

"I think I've three of them. Whenever I go to a shop I can never think of anything to buy except gray skirts and blue cardigans. Have one of each."

"I mean it. Quite, quite preposterous."

Carmel smiled happily. Other people said "Don't be silly"; Sheila said she was preposterous. It was much, much nicer.

"Well?" Martin wanted to know.

"I *think* she's all right. It's hard to know."

"You mean it was a joke about the invitation?"

"No, she means it. She's having the party, she just doesn't want to talk about it."

"Then she's not all right."

"I know, but she *seems* normal. She gave me a skirt and a cardigan."

"That makes her normal?"

"No, you know what I mean. She was talking about ordinary things. She hadn't gone off on any flight of fancy or anything."

"So did you talk her out of it?" Martin wanted to know.

"I couldn't; she wouldn't talk about it at all. I *told* you."

"Oh, great," he sighed. "That's all we need. You're her friend, for Christ's sake."

"Martin, I've had a bad day. Not just a bit of a bad day—every single bit of it was bad. I don't want to talk about it anymore. I did my best to talk to Carmel. She wouldn't talk back, that's all. Can't you leave me alone!"

"Yes, I know I should have had a drink ready and the fire lighting and tried to soothe away your cares . . . like a proper housewife. I'm sorry I'm bad at it. You don't have to tell me."

"Jesus, Martin, if this is the night you've picked to do a wretched 'I'm not a good provider' act, then you've picked the wrong night. Will you shut up and sit down. I love you, I don't want you to fart around pandering to me just because *my* outfit didn't close down . . . do you hear me?"

He was contrite.

"I'm sorry. I really am. I'm just worried, that's all."

"So am I."

"Do you think she knows about Ruth? Do you think she heard anything?"

"How could she have heard anything? Who does she meet? Where does she go? Unless it was on the *Gay Byrne Hour* or in the *Evening Press Diary*, she'd not have heard."

"What are we going to do?"

"I haven't a clue."

"I'm sorry I'm late," called David. "The traffic

261

was bloody terrible. There's no point in taking a car in these days, I've said it over and over."

"So have I. The number ten would take you to your door."

"I can't travel on the number ten. It never comes, or it's full when it does."

"Anyway, why buy a big car and not show it off?"

"What?" David sounded bad-tempered in the hall.

"Nothing. You said you're sorry you're late, get a move on then, if you want to change or wash or anything."

"For what?" David sounded even crosser. "Oh, God, I'd forgotten. Do we have to? Can't we—?"

"We *do* have to and we *can't* ring and say we're tied up. We accepted two weeks ago."

"It's all very well for you." David was pounding up the stairs crossly. "You have nothing to do all day but get yourself ready . . . titivate . . . titivate."

"Thank you," Ethel said icily.

She sat at the dressing table in their bedroom. The door to the bathroom was open and he could see the thick colored towels piled up on the chest of drawers. He knew he would feel much better when he had a bath, he knew it was unfair to blame her.

"I'm sorry," he said.

He kissed her at the dressing table. She smelled whiskey.

"Do they serve cocktails in traffic jams?" she asked.

He laughed. "You've caught me out. I dropped into the club." He looked contrite.

"Which is, of course, on the route home." She was still cold.

"No, of course it wasn't, but I took the lower road. Oh, hell, I only had two, but do you know who was there? You'll never guess what happened."

She was interested. He rarely told tales of interest from the outer world; she had to prod and pry and ferret to find out anything that might be happening. She followed him into the bathroom. He flung off his coat and struggled with his shirt.

"I met Dermot, Dermot Murray."

"Oh, yes?" She was as sharp as a hawk now, pique forgotten. "What did he say?"

"Well, it's amazing, it's quite amazing."

"Yes? Yes?"

"He was sitting talking to some fellows, I don't know who they were. I've seen one of them, perfectly respectable, in the property business, I think, out the Northside. Anyway, he was in that corner place with them."

"Yes . . . what did he say?"

"Wait, wait, I'm telling you." David had run the bath as he was speaking. The water gushed with powerful pressure from each tap, the room had steamed up in under a minute.

"I said to him, 'How are you, Dermot?'"

David stood in his underpants tantalizing his wife by the meticulous way he was repeating the trivia of the conversation. She decided not to be drawn.

"I'll sit on the loo here and when you feel like telling me, do."

He pulled the shower curtains around him when he got into the bath. This was a modesty that had grown somewhere around the same time as his paunch. When they had been younger they had often bathed together, and had always bathed in front of each other.

"No, it's really strange," came the voice from inside the curtain. "I said, 'Thanks very much for that invitation,' and he said, 'What invitation?' and I got such a shock I started to play the fool. You know. I said, 'Come on now. You can't welch on us now, an invite's an invite.' "

"What did he say then?"

"He said, 'You have me on the wrong foot, David. I don't actually know what you mean.' He said it so straight, I felt a bit foolish. I just got out of it. I said that I had probably made a mistake, or that you hadn't looked at the letter properly."

"Thank you very much again," said Ethel.

"I had to say something. Anyway he said, 'Letter, what letter?' I was right into it then. I said, 'Oh, it's some mistake. I thought we'd got a letter from you and Carmel inviting us to dinner. I must have got it wrong.' He said it wasn't very likely that she'd have invited people without telling him. Maybe it was a surprise party."

"Boy, some surprise if it is!" said Ethel.

"That's what I thought, so I said the date. I said it's on the eighth. He said, 'Well, I never. Maybe it's all a birthday treat and I'm not meant to know.' But he looked worried. He said 'the eighth' again, as if it were familiar. Then he said, 'Not the eighth?' And I said, nervously you know, 'I'm sure I got it wrong.' "

"He doesn't know. She's doing it without telling him. She's asking us all around there for some kind of terrible drama. That's what it's all about." Ethel's face looked stricken rather than excited. It should be an exciting thing . . . a public row, a scandal. But not with Carmel Murray. Poor Carmel, she was too vulnerable.

David got out of the bath and dried himself vigorously in one of the big yellow towels.

"He really doesn't know she's giving the party, the poor devil. Isn't that a dreadful thing? Thank God I said something, even though I felt I had walked into it. At least it will give him a bit of time to know what action to take."

"But she can't know about Ruth, she can't possibly know." Ethel was thoughtful.

"Somebody may have sent her a poison pen letter—you know, 'I think you ought to know . . .' " David was still toweling himself dry.

"You'll rub the skin off your back. Come on, get dressed. She can't know. If she knew would she in a million years ask her to dinner?"

Joe and Henry were cooking for a party. They

often did home catering; it was very easy money. They made the canapés while they watched television, and put everything in the freezer. They got lots of free perks like plastic wrap and foil from the hotel where Henry worked, and the use of a car from the tourist guide service where Joe worked.

"Why won't the old bat let you do the cooking for her if she's so nervous? You could run up a dinner in two hours."

"No, that's part of it. She has to be able to do it all herself."

"What does she look like? All sad and mopey, is she?"

"I don't know," said Joe. "I haven't seen her for twenty years. She may have changed a lot since then."

"Hallo, Carmel, is that you?"

"Of course it is, love, who else would it be?"

"Carmel, I'm at the club. I told you, I've had to have a few chats, I told you."

"I know you told me."

"So I won't be home, or I wasn't coming home. Have you had your supper?"

"Supper?"

"Carmel, it's eight o'clock. I'm ringing you from the club to ask you a simple question: Have you or have you not had your supper?"

"I had some soup, Dermot, but there's steak here, and cauliflower. . . . I can cook whatever you like."

"Did you write to David?"

"*What?* It's very hard to hear you. There's a lot of noise behind you."

"Forget it. I'll come home."

"Oh, good. Would you like me to?"

He had hung up.

All the way home he said to himself it was impossible. She couldn't have decided to hold a dinner party without telling him, and if she had, if by some mind-blowing horror she had decided to invite all their friends around to witness a scene of marital bliss . . . how could she have chosen the eighth of October?

It was Ruth's birthday, her thirtieth birthday. He had persuaded her to hold her exhibition that day, to show everyone that she had arrived. Ruth had said that she wanted no public exhibitions, no showing the world anything, unless he could stand beside her. She didn't want to go on hiding and pretending. When the reporters were sent to interview her she didn't want to have to laugh anymore and parry questions about why she had never married. She felt foolish telling people that her art was her life. It sounded so hollow, so second best and so phony. She wanted to tell them that she loved and was loved. It was this that gave her strength to paint.

She had agreed reluctantly. The gallery had been found with no trouble. People were anxious to hang the work of Ruth O'Donnell. The work was ready. She was drained. She said she wanted time away, far away, from him. She would not spend the days planning how to walk out of his life, she assured him of that, and he believed her. She just wanted to be free, to rest, and not to hide. He believed that too. He promised he wouldn't telephone her, nor write. That would be the same as being with him, she said. There was no point in a separation if you spent hours writing a letter and waiting for the post.

She was coming back on the first, a full week before it opened, in time to see everything hung. She had only left yesterday. It wasn't possible that coincidence should be so cruel as to mar this night for him by having a weeping Carmel on his hands. Because, by God, if she had arranged a dinner party for the eighth she was going to unarrange it fast. That was why he had left those two auctioneers sitting like eejits in the club. This had to be sorted out immediately.

"I think Mummy's a bit lonely," Bernadette said to Frank.

"We're all lonely. It's the lot of men and women to go through life alone, thinking they are with friends, but only brushing off people."

"I mean it," Bernadette said. "She's very good to us, Frank. She pretends she doesn't mind about us living together but she does, underneath."

"Nonsense. Just so long as we don't do anything too public in front of all those friends of hers, she's as right as rain."

"All what friends of hers? There are no friends."

"There must be. Posh house there in the heart of society . . . of course she has friends. Didn't you tell me tonight that she's organizing dinner parties months in advance?"

"That's what I don't like."

"God, there's no pleasing you! You're like a gnat; say out what you want and I'll debate whether we'll do it or not. Do you want us to kidnap her and keep her in the bathroom here tied by a dressing-gown cord for the rest of her life?"

"No," she laughed.

"What do you want, Ber?"

"I wondered if we might drop in tonight, on our way to the party. Please."

"Aw, God," he said.

"Just for a little bit," she begged.

"We'll be there all night," he said.

"We won't. We'll just get off the bus, run in and have a few words, and then run off again."

"That's worse than not going at all."

"No, it would ease my mind."

"Ten minutes then, right?"

"Half an hour, right?"

"Twenty minutes."

"Done."

"Don't say anything to the O'Briens about it, will you?" Ethel said when they were in the car.

"What would I say? I'm not a one for gossip, I never talk about people. You're the one who likes to tell and be told."

David had his eyes on the road but he knew

269

his wife's profile was stern. "No, I'll say nothing to anyone. God, do you think we should do something or say something? We can't sit back and let it all happen."

"What can we do that would help, heavens above? You sound like Superman or the archangel Gabriel stepping in. What can we do?"

"I suppose we could say to Carmel that it's not a good idea, that she might like to think again."

"It's amazing how you manage to hold down a job, let alone run your own business," said Ethel acerbically.

"It's all due to the loyal little woman behind me. She had faith in me when no one else had," he said in a mock country-and-western accent.

"Well, if ever I meet the woman behind you I can tell you one thing, I'll not invite her to dinner with all our friends," said Ethel, and they drove on to the O'Briens in silence.

Frank and Bernadette were just leaving when Dermot's car drew up.

"Maybe he'd give us a lift," said Frank optimistically.

"I think that's a bit too sunny a view. I wouldn't ask him," said Bernadette. "How are you, Dad?"

"I see it's the annual visit," Dermot said.

"Hi, Mr. Murray," said Frank.

"Hallo, er . . ." said Dermot desperately, stumbling over his name.

Bernadette's fist clenched in her pocket. "We

were just in having a chat with Mummy. We're off to a party."

"Don't let me delay you," Dermot said.

"Oh, Daddy, you can be very rude," Bernadette said. "Why can't you be nice and easygoing, and—"

"I don't know," Dermot said. "It must be something to do with having to go out and earn a living and take on responsibilities."

"We work too, Daddy."

"Huh," said Dermot.

"Nice to have talked with you, Mr. Murray," said Frank in an affected American accent.

"Sorry," Dermot said. "I'm in a bad mood. You do work, both of you. I'm just worried about something. Come back into the house and I'll give you a drink."

"That's mighty white of you, sir," said Frank.

"No, Dad, we've got to be off. We just looked in to see was Mummy all right."

"And she is, isn't she?" Dermot sounded alarmed.

"Oh, yes," Bernadette said, a little too quickly. "She's fine."

"I heard your voices. Did you meet them in the drive?" Carmel asked.

It had always irritated Dermot that she called the small distance to the gate a "drive": it was eleven steps from the hall door to the gate if you took giant steps, and the most you could make out of it was twenty little ones.

271

"Yes. What did they want?"

"Oh, Dermot, they just called in, it was nice of them."

"They said they came to see were you all right. Why did they do that?"

"That's what people do, dear, when they call to see other people."

She looked cheerful and calm. There was no resigned martyred air about her. She wasn't making little jokes that were not funny. She had no hint of tears.

"Will we have a proper meal at the table or would you like a snack by the television?" she asked. "The phone was so crackly and with the sound of people behind I couldn't hear whether you had a meal or you hadn't. You kept asking me had I . . ."

"Sit down, love," he said.

"Yes, I will in a minute, but what would you—"

"Sit down now, Carmel. I want to talk to you, not to your back drifting out the door."

"All right, Dermot, all right. Now, will this do?"

"Have you or have you not invited a whole lot of people here on the eighth of October?"

"Certainly not."

"You haven't?" The relief was overwhelming. It spilled all over his face. "I'm sorry, love. There was a silly misunderstanding."

"No. I just asked our friends and decided we'd have a nice evening and cook a nice dinner. You know you often said—"

"What do you mean—?"

"You've often said that we should have people around more, and somehow I didn't used to feel able for it, but I decided you were right, so I just asked a few people . . . for dinner."

"When? When?"

"Oh, ages away. The eighth as you said, the eighth of October. Just a simple dinner."

"Who have you asked?"

"Just friends. Sheila and Martin, and David and Ethel, and—"

"You've invited them all here on the eighth?"

"Yes. And I've asked that nice Ruth O'Donnell, you know, the artist."

"Carmel. What are you—?"

"You remember her, we met her lots of times, and you told me how good she was. We haven't seen her for ages, but I did say when I wrote to her that there would be lots of people she'd know. I mean, David even knows her professionally. His company gave her a grant once, I read . . ."

"Yes . . ."

"And she'll know Sheila, because I think she came to her school to give a lecture."

"Why didn't you ask me—tell me?"

"But, Dermot, you're always telling me to do things on my own, use my own initiative. I did for once. I sent out all the invitations . . . and now that doesn't please you either."

"But I think you've picked the wrong night. I think that's the night she's having her opening. I thought I told you—"

273

"Yes, you did, I remember. You said she was only thirty and how well she'd done. I remember the date."

"God."

"So I thought it would be nice for her to have somewhere to go after it. I read in the papers that she isn't married and she doesn't even have a 'situation' like our Bernadette, so I thought what would be nicer than for her to have somewhere to go on the night."

"Yes."

"So that's what I said in my letter to her, that it would be a nice rounding off for the evening."

"How did you know where she lives?" His voice was a gasp.

"I looked it up in the telephone directory, silly!"

"You might have sent it to the wrong person—"

"But she told us she lived in the new flats. Remember? I'm not such a featherbrain after all, am I?"

"Sheila, can I have a quick word with you before you go into the school?"

"God, you frightened the life out of me, Dermot Murray. I thought you were a guard."

"Look, have you a minute? Can we get back into your car?"

"Half the sixth form already think you're propositioning me! What is it, Dermot? Tell me here."

"No, it's nothing to tell. I want to ask you, ask you something."

Sheila's heart was leaden.

"Ask on, but make it quick. That bell rings and I'm like a bolt from the blue in the door."

"Does Carmel know about Ruth?"

"I beg your pardon?"

"You heard me."

"I didn't. I did *not* hear you. Begin again."

"Does Carmel know about Ruth and me?"

"Ruth? Ruth O'Donnell?"

"Sheila, stop playing around. I know you know, you know I know you know. All I want to know is does Carmel know?"

"You're assuming a great many things. What is there to know? What should I have known? Stop standing there like a guessing game."

"Sheila, please, it's important."

"It must be. Why else are you up here in a convent? I haven't an idea what you're talking about."

"Think, think quickly. I know you're being a good friend and an old school chum. But think what's for the best. I don't just mean the best for me, I mean the best for everyone."

"What am I to think about?"

"Look, I've known you for years, Sheila, I'm not a shit, now, am I? I'm a reasonable human being. Would I be up here at this hour of the morning if I were a real bum?"

Every day that Sheila had paused at her car for one moment to search for an exercise book, to write

275

a shopping list, to listen to the last bars of some song on the radio . . . the bell had shrilled across her consciousness. Why did it not do it today?

"I can't help you, Dermot," she said. "I don't know anything, I really don't. I don't talk about anything, I don't listen to anything. I'm no help."

He believed her. Not that she didn't know about Ruth. He knew she knew about Ruth. But he believed her when she said she couldn't help him. She didn't know whether Carmel knew or not. She was as much in the dark as he was.

"What am I going to do?" he asked her.

And then the bell shrilled.

"I just telephoned to ask you more about this party you're giving," Ethel said.

"I explained it all in the letter," said Carmel. "You will be able to come? You see, I know how busy you all are so I trapped you by choosing the night of Ruth's exhibition."

"Yes, of course we'll come. You don't have to trap us. Looking forward to it . . . I was wondering whether it was a surprise—a birthday surprise for Dermot or anything. David met him in the club, and I hope he didn't let anything slip."

"No, it's not Dermot's birthday. It may well be Ruth's—I think hers is in October—but no, it doesn't matter at all. I did tell Dermot I was thinking of having a party, but you know what men are, they never listen. Their minds are elsewhere. Probably just as well that we don't know where they are half the time, don't you think?"

Ethel had the uneasy feeling that Carmel was laughing at her. Nonsense, of course, but there was that kind of a feel about the way she spoke.

"Oh, Dermot, I can't tell you where she is. She said the whole point was that you and she were having a separation, wasn't it?"

"Look, I'll go down on my knees to you."

Dermot had never liked Ruth's younger sister. A know-all, a moralizer, and worst of all a contemporary of his daughter Anna's when they were at UCD.

"No, I swore I would reveal nothing. Ruth only told me just in case there was any real crisis, about the gallery, you know."

"There's a very big crisis. I can't tell you how big."

"Honestly, Dermot, be fair. Play it by the rules. Just leave her alone, can't you? It's only a couple of weeks."

"Listen here, smarty pants." Dermot had lost any veneer of manners by now. "Go into Ruth's flat, where there will be a letter with a Dublin 4 postmark addressed to her. Open it and read it. If you think then that it's serious enough perhaps you could ring your sister and ask her to ring me. That's all." He stood up to leave the travel agency where she worked.

"Wait. It's not some awful sordid thing . . . some scandal, is it?" The girl's lip wrinkled with disgust.

"It's only a dinner invitation, but she might want to ring me about it."

He nearly took the door off the hinges as he left.

Dermot telephoned his office.

"Oh, there you are, Mr. Murray," the girl on the switch said with relief. "It's not like you to be late. I didn't know what to do with your calls. We've had—"

"I'm not feeling well today, Margaret. Please ask Miss O'Neill to put someone else on the Foreign Exchange and move her own things to my desk."

"But Mr. Murray—"

"I'll call back later, Margaret. The important thing is that Miss O'Neill sits at my desk. Put any calls for me through to her, she will know how to deal with them."

"When will you—?"

"As I said, I'll call back later, Margaret. The bank is not going to grind to a halt just because for once the manager isn't well."

He hung up and regretted it immediately. The child on the switch didn't care whether the bank ground to a halt or not. Probably hoped it would, if the truth was known. Why had he been so snappy? She was bound to gossip about it too. If only he had just taken thirty more seconds to be soothing and reassuring then it would have passed unnoticed in the minutiae of the day . . . poor Mr. Murray's not well, must have that bug, oh well, Miss O'Neill's looking after his work . . . and that would be that. Now the girl on the switch would be full of indignation . . . bit my nose off, snapped at me over nothing, all I was doing was asking, what do I bloody care where he is, what he does, he can take a running jump at himself.

Why couldn't he have had the patience to exchange just two more conventional remarks? He had been so patient, so very patient about everything so far. Why couldn't he have kept his temper this morning? He frowned at his reflection in the car mirror when he got back into the driving seat. He didn't like the middle-aged tense man that looked back at him. In his mind's eye he didn't see himself that way; in his mind's eye he saw himself as Ruth's man, her strong support, the one she ran to when she was exhausted with her work, when she was full of doubts. To the little girl on the switch back at the bank, he was probably middle-aged Mr. Murray, and if she knew about Ruth (which she might well in this village that they called a city), then she would think he was pathetic with his bit on the side, or a louse cheating on his wife.

Dermot didn't feel like driving anywhere. He got out of the car again and walked until he reached the canal. It was a nice crisp morning. Other people were still in their cars choking with fumes. These must be big executives, the top men, if they could come in to work as late as ten to ten, or was that right? If they were top men maybe they should have been at their desks since seven-thirty? Maybe they were the kind of men who had inherited a family business and who didn't have to work hard because they were the bosses' sons. Funny how you saw different sides of society when you stepped off your own little treadmill for a bit.

Two women passed him on the canal path, bright laughing women in headscarfs. One was carrying a huge plastic bag and the other a large stuffed pillowcase; they were on their way to the launderette. They were the kind of women that Carmel would describe as nice poor things. Yet they weren't nearly as poor as poor Carmel. They were carting their families' washing off without a look of resentment about them. Carmel might be bending over the controls of a washing machine in her own kitchen but more likely she would just sit and stare out into the back garden. He had looked at her in off-guard moments over the last few months and this was how she was when in repose. Her face was empty as if she had left it and gone somewhere else.

He had hoped she would find interests, but he realized more and more that this was a vain hope. She had no interests. She had nothing whatsoever that would lift her out of that sad pose. When Anna and James had had the first baby, Dermot thought that this would absorb Carmel's time, a grandchild out in Sandycove. He was certain she would be out there every second day, or encouraging Anna to leave the child in Donnybrook while she went about her business. But Dermot hadn't understood about modern young mothers like Anna. Cilian first, and then Orla, had just become part of her own life as if they were adults. They were constantly being strapped and unstrapped into car seats. They moved with a battery of educational toys, they were quite self-sufficient wherever they went. Doting grandmothers did not come into the picture at all.

And then, of course, that strap Bernadette shacked up with that Frank; "my flat mate," no less, she called him. She hadn't been much help or support for her mother, had she? Dermot muttered to himself about her. A lot of use it had been paying for her at the College of Art, quite happy to help friends out, to step in and sell things for someone who was stuck.

And friends? Carmel was a great one for talking about the Girls. Where were the girls now when they were needed? That Sheila, the schoolmistress rushing into the convent this morning as if her life depended on it. Great friend she'd be if anyone needed one: "I don't talk, I don't listen, I don't know things . . ." marvelous! And who else was there? There was Ethel . . . she and Carmel had got on quite well at one stage. But there as well as anywhere else Carmel hadn't been able to cope. She had talked and talked about not returning David and Ethel's hospitality, and not accepting any more of it. Why hadn't she just said "Come around to supper," the way Ruth did, the way anyone did . . . anyone except Carmel.

It was fooling himself really to think she would be happier without him, fooling himself to say she

281

wouldn't really notice if he left. She would not be able to cope. She couldn't even muster the politics of solidarity and hate, like that woman they had heard of in Ballsbridge, the wife of the man in the public relations agency. She had been so outraged when he left that she had aligned dozens of women on her side. You could hardly mention the man's name now without hearing a sibilant hiss, so blackened had it become. No, Carmel would do nothing like that.

Dermot stopped suddenly. Carmel would do nothing. And that was why he could never leave her. She would do nothing at all. For the rest of his life he would come home, tell lies, make up excuses, invent conferences, be telephoned by mythical clients who had to be seen after hours. And Ruth would do nothing. Ruth would not make a scene, demand that he choose between them, Ruth would confront nobody, insist on no showdowns. This had been the way things were for two whole years . . . everyone secure in the knowledge that nobody else would do anything; Ruth knowing she would never have to make her mind up about him fully, Carmel knowing that she would never lose him utterly and he knowing that he need never be forced to say "I'll take this one" or "I'll take that."

He laughed wryly to himself. It was most people's idea of a married man's dream: an unquestioning wife and an unquestioning mistress. But it was a bad dream, he could write a book on what a bad dream it was. You were happy in neither place, you were guilty in both places. The very fact that nobody was making any move made it all the more insoluble. If Carmel had threatened and pleaded, perhaps, if Ruth had issued ultimatums, perhaps. *Perhaps* it might have been better. But nothing ever happened. Until now. Until Ruth had been invited to dinner.

Carmel *must* know, he said to himself for the five hundredth time. She *must* know. And yet the memory of last night had been like a vivid movie running through over and over.

"Tell me, why have you decided to ask Ruth O'Donnell, whom we hardly know, whom you only met twice, to dinner? Carmel, what are you playing at?"

"I'm not playing at anything except being a better homemaker. She's nice. Everyone says so."

"But why? Tell me, what made you think of a dinner? Why a month away?"

"To give me time to prepare, to get ready. I'm not like all these marvelous women you admire so much, who can have the entire golf game around for a six-course meal with no notice. I like to take my time."

She had looked at him with a round innocent face. She had prattled on about Sheila having called in, about Anna and James driving off to the cottage, about how she wished she could get the Christmas presents months ahead in September when the shops were nice and empty.

Four times he asked her in a roundabout way,

four times she had answered him with a level look. She just liked the idea of having people to dinner; why was he finding fault with it? And he never answered that question, not even with a lie.

They went to Mass at eleven o'clock in Donnybrook church and bought the papers outside.

"Do you need anything from the shops?" Dermot asked. "Ice cream? A pudding?"

"No, I'm on a diet, but you get some if you like," she said pleasantly. He had looked at her face as she prayed; he had watched her come back from Communion with her head down. She never asked him why he didn't go to Communion; she never asked him anything.

Anna and James were happy. It had been a glorious day and they had had their lunch out in the open. Twelve of them had sat and looked out over the bay and said that this was the life and they must all be mad to live in Dublin. Anna had arranged that a local woman make fresh soda bread and they had had this with their pâté. Everyone had raved about it. Cilian and Orla played at a distance with the three visiting children. Some of their friends had been staying at a hotel, others had rented a cottage. They all looked with open envy at the ease and comfort which James and Anna had built for themselves. This was balm to Anna and James. They stood and waved in the evening as the last guests drove off, they had cups of tea to get rid of the sleepiness the white wine had spread, and they looked at the clock. James had an iron rule: on the road back at seven. This meant an hour to wash up and tidy and pack the children and themselves—plenty of time.

They moved around the cottage gathering the bagful of educational toys. They plunged their twelve plates, twelve glasses, twelve forks and twelve knives into the hot soapy water. A rubbish sack was carefully tied up, and put in the boot as well. There was no collection in this part of heaven, they laughed to each other. Cilian and Orla, sleepy from the day in the sun, were strapped in, the cassette of James Last was at the ready and they faced the road across the country.

They spent much of it congratulating each other on the cottage. Although they would never have admitted it, even to each other, there were times when they thought it was becoming a bit much for them. But on a day like today when they could see the admiration and the jealousy of the people who sat around in the sunshine, then it was all worth it a hundred times over. They forgot the weekends they had arrived to find pipes burst, roof leaking, ants walking the kitchen floor in their thousands, mice making nests in the window boxes . . . all that was as nothing. The strings of the Last orchestra thudded and swept in the background.

James said, "Do you know that your father's having an affair with Ruth O'Donnell, the artist?"

"Dad? Don't be ridiculous."

"He is, though, I heard it before. I heard it from someone who met them in London, of all places. Wouldn't you think you'd be safe having it away in London, ten million people, but no, spotted *in flagrante.*"

Anna looked around almost automatically to see if the children were asleep. If their grandfather's adultery was going to be discussed it would not be *devant* these *enfants* she thought.

"I don't believe a word of it."

"Honestly, sweetheart, Frances and Tim were talking about it this afternoon. They didn't like to mention it in front of you."

"So that's what you were wittering on about. I thought it was business."

"No, they tell me they see him often coming out of Ruth's apartment block, you know."

"The new one . . . yes . . . heavens above."

"Are you upset? Are you upset that I told you?"

"I don't believe it, not *Dad.* I mean, he fancies her maybe and goes in and has the odd little drink. But not an affair, not sleeping with her, not Dad."

"Um."

"Well, don't you agree?"

"I don't know, I only tell you what I hear."

"You think it's possible that Dad would have a real affair?"

"That's what is said."

"But why would she? I mean, she's young and

well known and got her own life . . . she could have anyone or no one if she wanted. What on earth would she want with Dad?"

"Who knows? People want extraordinary people."

"Yes."

"You are upset. I shouldn't have told you like that, straight out. It's just . . . well, it was on my mind."

"I'm not upset. I don't know why. I suppose when I was young, like everyone I was always terrified if they had a row that they were going to part. But they didn't, nobody ever did. Things just go along drifting. That's what happened to marriages in those days."

"And in *these* days, it would appear."

"What do you mean?"

"Well, they say that your papa and Ms. O'Donnell have been constant companions for two to three years."

"Never!"

"Apparently."

"Imagine at Christmas, and the year before and the year before . . . all the family parties . . . and all the time. . . . I don't believe it."

"Do you think Grandmama knows?"

"I'm certain she doesn't. Poor Mother. How odd, I don't know why I'm not crying and thinking it's the end of everything. I suppose I just haven't accepted it."

"I don't know why I told you." James looked worried. "It's only making you sad, but it seemed

287

a big secret to keep from you. . . . We don't have secrets."

"No."

"And you're so practical, I thought you'd want to know about it in case there's anything you wanted to do."

"Like what, frighten her off? Please leave my daddy alone?"

"No, but you do know her sister, don't you? Deirdre?"

"Yes, Deirdre O'Donnell, she was in college with me. God."

"So there we are."

"There we are all right. Are you shocked?"

"I'm a bit stunned, like you. I can't see my father-in-law in the role, but I think I'm mainly sorry for poor Grandmama. I thought that's what you'd feel most."

"No. Mother will survive. She's very rarely living in the real world anyway. She seems a bit stoned to me a lot of the time. I wouldn't be surprised if that doctor has her on Valium most of the time. That's why he's such a success with all that generation, he just prescribes it by the ton. Takes the edge off life, that's his motto."

"Yes, well, it looks as if your mother's going to need her supply."

"Yes, but in a way, why should she? I mean, if it's been going on for years, nothing's going to change."

"I suppose not. Check the mileage, will you, I'm turning in here for petrol."

Anna got out the little leather-covered book and wrote in *11878* under mileage, *Tralee* under place, and then sat with her pencil poised until she could fill in the remaining two columns, gallons and price.

"I'm not going to spend a month going in and out playing cat and mouse with them. I'm not going to do it," Sheila said on Sunday evening. She had the dining-room table covered with books that she was marking for tomorrow's class.

"I suppose you could just be there, you know, if she needed you, that would be a help," said Martin. He was doing the crossword while Sheila corrected her exercises.

"That's not the point. It's unforgivable being drawn into other people's rows and scenes and disasters. I'll never forgive him for accosting me like that and forcing me to take sides and attitudes. People shouldn't drag you into their un-happinesses, it's not fair." She looked very cross and bit on the end of her pencil in annoyance. "No, stop being tolerant and forgiving, Martin. It's a fact. We never drag people into our marriage, now do we?"

"No," said Martin thoughtfully. "But then we're very lucky we don't have any problems in our marriage."

"No," said Sheila sharply, going back to the exercise books. She had resolved long ago that if she was going to be the breadwinner, she wasn't going to complain and ruin it all by being a martyr. The only thing that made the whole bloody business worthwhile was that Martin had no idea how tired she was and how much she hated going into that school each day. She thought of Carmel for a moment, and a great wave of impatience flooded over her. Carmel could get up at any time she liked, she had nothing more pressing in her day than to decide which clothes she should send to the St. Vincent de Paul. Carmel's children were married. Well, Bernadette was as good as married. They weren't pounding home with huge appetites for meals which had to be prepared and shopped for. Sheila tried to give the appearance of being in charge of the kitchen so that Martin's sons should not think him a sissy. They still said "thanks, Mum" when they found their clean clothes in their bedrooms, though as often as not it was their father who had done them.

In a way Carmel had only herself to blame if she was miserable and wretched over all this business about Ruth O'Donnell. Carmel was a lady of leisure with too much time to think about the too little she had to do. Then with a jolt Sheila remembered that it was she and Martin and Dermot who were wretched. Carmel had been very cheerful, and was in fact busy organizing a dinner party and smartening up her wardrobe. Not at all what this wronged wife would have been expected to do.

Ethel and David had people in to bridge on Sunday night. They always had what they called a cur-few on Sunday nights, and everyone had to have played the last card by eleven-thirty.

When the cars had driven off and they were emptying the ashtrays, opening the windows, and taking out the dirty glasses to the dishwasher, Ethel said, "I have the most awful feeling, like doom, as if something dreadful is going to happen. Do you know that feeling?"

"Every day going into work, and it's always accurate," said David.

"Don't be trivial, you love your work, and why wouldn't you? People fussing over you, fuss fuss fuss all day. No, I have a sense of foreboding and I can't think what's causing it."

"Maybe you feel guilty about something," David said.

"It's that kind of feeling, that sort of heavy feeling in the chest, but I've nothing to be guilty about."

"I think it's the bank manager's bit of skirt. I honestly think that's what's making us all so uneasy. I feel a bit edgy myself."

"But we've known about it for ages."
"Yes, but the poor sad wife must have only just found out."

Ethel stood looking at a plate of peanuts thoughtfully. Eventually she tipped them into the pedal bin. "I'd only eat them," she said as an explanation, "and they're more fattening than large g's and t's. I suppose that is what's making us nervous. It's such a mad thing to do. Such a very

291

men-in-white-coats mad thing to do. Ask the woman to dinner and have a public scene."

"She won't go, of course," said David.

"No, but the fact that poor Carmel actually asked her is so mad. That's what's upsetting. Who knows what she'll do next, walk down Grafton Street in her knickers?"

Deirdre O'Donnell had no trouble in getting the porter to give her a key to her sister's flat. She said that Ruth wanted her to post on some things.

She wandered around, luxuriating in being alone among someone else's possessions. Now you could look and stare and ponder to your heart's content. Everyone else in the block had their sitting rooms carefully draped and framed. They looked like the rooms in a doll's house from outside. But Ruth's sitting room was bare, it was in fact her studio, and what other people regarded as the master bedroom and decked with fitted cupboards and thick carpets, Ruth used as a secondary studio and office. The small spare bedroom was her bedsitting room; a sofa that turned into a bed sat neatly in its sofa role, and in the kitchen the saucepans sat shining in a row.

For an artist her sister was very neat, Deirdre thought. Spinsterish, she had once believed—that was before she knew about the regular visits of Anna Murray's father. *Father.* A bank manager. Maybe she should go to him to authorize an overdraft. Seriously, that's not a bad idea at all.

On the mat there were a dozen envelopes. Some

were obviously brochures or advertisements. Then she saw the letter in the neat round handwriting. She eased it out carefully. It might be full of terrible, intimate things . . . things that Ruth would not want her to have read. She must steam the envelope; she could stick it all back with glue if it really was too yucky and Ruth would get into a temper.

Dear Ruth,

I don't know whether you remember me or not, but we met a couple of times with David and Ethel O'Connor and you also know my friend Sheila Healy, who says you gave a wonderful lecture at her school. Anyway, we are great admirers of yours and so looking forward to your exhibition on October 8th.

I'm going to try to steal you for that night to come to dinner with us. This is why I'm writing to you so far in advance, I am sure you will get many invitations nearer the time, but I want to be first in with mine. We will have the O'Connors and the Healys as well, so you will be among friends.

Please let me know soon if you can come. I'm one of these middle-aged fussy sort of women who spend ages getting things organized not like you and your friends. I'm sure you can combine about three lives successfully, but I'll be setting and resetting the table for days before you come, and then I'll pretend it all happened of its own accord. It will give us all a great deal of plea-

sure if you say yes, and I know Dermot, my husband would be thrilled. He has bought three of your paintings for our home. I hope you will like the way we have had them hung. So looking forward to seeing you.

Yours cordially,
Carmel Murray

Poor old cow, thought Deirdre, probably something wrong with her glands. She must know about Ruthie, half the country does. I don't think there's anything for old Dermot to get his knickers in a twist about, but I'd better ring her just in case.

Because Deirdre O'Donnell was essentially a frugal person she saw no reason why she shouldn't make the call from Ruth's own telephone. After all, it was Ruth's romance. It was Ruth's fellow's wife who had gone off her head . . . why not let Ruth pay for the call?

The farmer's wife knocked on her door and said there was a telephone call from Dublin.

"Your sister said you mustn't get alarmed. She says there is no problem."

Ruth got up. She had been lying on the bed over the covers, reading. It was very luxurious somehow to do that, like going to the pictures in the afternoon.

"Ruthie?"

"What's happened?"

"Nothing, I told the old dame that. Nothing. Listen, Romeo asked me to contact you . . ."

"I told you I didn't want any messages. *Any.*"

"I told him that. He said that his wife has gone off her head, and she's written to you."

"Oh, no."

"It's all right, she hasn't called you the whore of Babylon. She's inviting you to dinner actually, the night your exhibition opens."

"She's what?"

"Do you want me to read it to you? 'Dear Ruth, I don't know whether you remember me or not . . .'"

"Stop, stop. Is this serious?"

"Yes, but there's no abuse in it. Honestly, it's all full of admiration."

"Oh, Lord. What does Dermot say?"

"He wants to get in touch with you about it. I told him to leave you alone, but he said—"

"Did he say that she knows?"

"Ruthie . . . of course she knows. What are you talking about? She must know."

"Dermot always said she didn't, or that if it came into her head she put it out again."

"You must be mad. Do you think you're invisible or something, Ruthie? The two of you go everywhere together."

"But if she knows, what's she inviting me to dinner for?"

"Well, that's the point, that's what lover boy was so much in a tizz about."

"What does he think?"

"I don't know. I suppose he thinks that she's

gone over the top, poor old thing. Do you want me to read it to you?"

"Yes, I suppose you'd better. If I've got to ring Dermot about it I'd better know what she says."

"Right. 'I don't know whether you remember me—' "

"Hey, Deirdre. This must be costing you a fortune."

"No, it's costing you a fortune . . . the wages of sin, you know."

"Oh, go on, read it."

Carmel planned her week carefully. It was nice to have so many things to do, it reminded her of being young again, when every day was so full and there seemed to be no waiting about. She would have to choose the main course and the dessert too. That would take two mornings in the bookshop reading the recipes. She was going to have a facial twice a week . . . oh, over on the North side of the city where she wouldn't be known . . . she would take the bus. She was going to spend two mornings shopping for her shoes. She had the dress already; the very good black dress which she had bought when Anna was twenty-one, five years ago. She had worn it that evening . . . the first time . . . that first time when she had discovered about Dermot and the other girl . . . the time she had got so upset. She had never worn it again. But this time she would wear it and it would look magnificent. She would be much thinner . . . she was going to lose a stone this month. Her hair would be much more attractive . . . that man in Grafton Street who had done Ethel's hair was going to put highlights in for her a week before the party. She had telephoned and asked him what would be the best time. She had even told him she was a middle-aged lady, not a dollybird. "I like coiffing mature ladies," he had said.

Coiffing. It had sounded vaguely suggestive.

And there were so many other things to do. Window cleaners to come in. That firm which came and shampooed your carpet in the house. And her notebook to fill in.

She had written down anything anyone said about successful entertaining, like that thing Ethel had mentioned about the prawn cocktails and the roast beef.

She remembered Anna once talking about a house she had visited. "They had fresh flowers in the bathroom, Mother, in the bathroom!" That had been included in the notebook. She had read an interview with a famous hostess who had said that the whole secret of successful entertaining was to have plenty of highly polished glass and thick damask napkins on the table. That was noted, beside the advice about having a lot of salts, peppers, and butterdishes so that people didn't have to keep passing them from one end of the table to the other.

Happier than she had been for a long time and armed with a list of the better cookery books, she

297

started off for Donnybrook. At the hall door she met Anna.

"Oh dear! Why didn't you let me know you were coming, dear? I'm just off," she said, regretfully but firmly pulling the door behind her.

"Hey, that's very welcoming," Anna said, surprised. "I bring your only grandchildren to visit you and that's what we get shown . . . the door."

"Hallo, Cilian . . . hallo, Orla." She waved at them through the window.

Cilian struggled with his harness. "Grandmama, Grandmama," he called.

"Ah, look, he wants to come to you," Anna said.

"I'm sorry, darling, Granny's got to go out. Hallo, Orla, blow Granny a kiss."

"You might just ask us in for a cup of coffee." Anna sounded huffed. "We drove all the way in from Sandycove to see you."

"Oh, I am sorry." Carmel was on her way to the gate.

"But where are you going to, Mother?"

"I'm going out, dear, I have things to do. Will you still be in town this afternoon? Bring them in then and we'll have afternoon tea. Wouldn't that be nice?"

"Yes, but Mother, I wanted to have a little chat . . ."

"Grand. We'll have a little chat this afternoon."

She was gone. Walking purposefully off toward the main road and the good brisk invigorating stretch toward the shops.

298

Anna looked after her, bewildered. Normally Mother was almost pathetically grateful for a visit, and fussed and ran about like an overgrown puppy. Here she was, striding off with no explanation. She looked after her, and Mother, as if she felt her eyes, turned and waved before she went around the corner. It was funny how people looked much younger when they moved quickly. Mother didn't look bad at all in her navy jacket and her check skirt. She didn't look fifty or fifty-one or whatever she was. Sometimes when she sat in that chair looking out into the back garden she looked seventy. Poor Mother, wasn't Dad awful to be fooling around with a young girl? Ruth O'Donnell, too . . . but James was wrong, it couldn't be sex . . . it was just the thrill of the thing, the illicit excitement. Dad in bed with a girl? It was hard enough to imagine Dad being in bed with Mother years ago, but now . . . these days . . . Dad was so old he wouldn't even be interested in it, would he? And suppose he was, who in their right mind would go to bed with Dad?

Anna shrugged and got back into the car.

"Wasted journey," she said to the children, who set up a simultaneous squawk of disappointment.

"Private call, Mr. Murray, will you take it here or—?"

"That's all right, put me through."

He knew it was Ruth from the way she spoke.

299

She had a way of saying "private call" that was almost lascivious.

"Dermot, can you talk?"

"Go ahead."

"In other words, you can't."

"Not yet."

"I got a call from Deirdre."

"So she told you the situation."

"She read me the letter. It sounded as if she doesn't have a clue."

"Yes, well, that's what I've always been saying."

Dermot Murray's secretary felt she had tortured him enough.

"Excuse me," she murmured and left the room.

"So what will I do?"

"Listen, darling love, when are you coming back?"

"In ten days, two weeks."

"I love you."

"You're alone now, presumably."

"No, I'm in the board room, and the board all agree. They love you too."

She giggled. "Dermot, what will I do, will I write and say I'm tied up?"

"It means a lot to her, it means a great, great deal. She's so lively and happy since she thought of the party, you have no idea, it stops that deadness. When I see her like this I can really imagine her living a life, a normal life of her own."

"So, what do you want?"

"Could you accept?"

"Say I'd love to, and then sort of opt out at the last moment?"

Dermot paused. "Yes . . . and, well, maybe in the end, if you could come, could go to the dinner. Could you?"

"*What?*"

"Well, it wouldn't mean all that much to you . . . to us. We have so much, and there you are, a brilliant young girl with your life before you and all that."

"You can't seriously expect me to come into your house as a guest, and say how nice, how delicious, you must give me the recipe for that boiled cabbage."

"Ruth, please."

"No, no please about it, you're sick, that's what you are. I couldn't possibly do it. I wouldn't dream of doing it to another woman, go in triumphantly and sit down with a lot of people who are in the secret. It's monstrous!"

"You don't understand—"

"I don't like what I do understand. Why are you going along with it?"

Her voice was upset; the pips went.

"We can't talk on the phone, let me come to see you."

"*No.* I wanted to be alone. You set all this up as a trick, didn't you? Admit it."

"I swear to God I didn't, I swear I only heard about it on Friday. I might never have heard if I hadn't met David in the club. I don't think she was going to tell me."

301

"You mean you were going to come home and find everyone there?"

"I don't know. I don't know."

"But she must have known that I would have told you. She must have known that."

"She doesn't *know* about you and me! I keep telling you!"

"Deirdre says that's lunacy . . . half of Dublin knows."

"Deirdre doesn't know anything—anyway, Carmel never meets half of Dublin."

"Oh, God, I knew you couldn't let me have this time without spoiling it. I knew you'd have to do something to mess it up for me."

"That is so unfair. I don't even know where you are. I won't talk to you again until you come back. I just wanted you to know what happened. If I hadn't told you, you'd have said I was being devious, wouldn't you? Well, wouldn't you?"

She softened. "I know."

"So if you could do one thing for me, just one. Write a note and say that you are away in the country, that the letter was forwarded to you, and that you'd love to come. Can you do that?"

"No, Dermot, I am not a puppet, I will not be manipulated into awful, sordid, cruel scenes like that. I will not do it."

"Just say you'll come, accept, people are always accepting things they don't go to in the end. Accept, and when you come back you and I will talk, and then you'll do whatever you like."

"And you won't steamroll me into doing what I don't want to do?"

"No, Ruth my love, I will not."

"And if I write this hypocritical note saying yes, you really think this is for the best . . . ?"

"I do."

"For all of us, for her and for me, as well as for you?"

He paused. "Yes. Seriously I do. For her, because she can go on planning her party and it will make her, well, busy and active again, and that's what we want. We want her to have a life of her own."

"And how will it help *me* to accept?"

"Well, you can stop worrying about it. Once you've written a letter saying yes, then a decision is made. You can unmake it any time, but you don't have to dither."

"And how will it help you?"

"Then I can see her absorbed in something, and that's a hell of a lot more positive than seeing her sitting staring out the window and wondering what the future has in store."

"What does the future have in store?"

"It has you coming home to me soon. It has your exhibition and all *that* means."

"I wish I didn't love you."

"I'm very glad you do."

"A ridiculous married bank manager, hundreds of years older than me, knowing nothing about painting—"

"I know, I know." He sounded soothing. He was

happy now; once Ruth got on to the groove of how unsuitable he was, he felt safe.

"I must be quite mad."

"You are, you are. Very," he said.

"I'll write the letter, but I won't go."

"Good girl," he said.

Dear Mrs. Murray,

What a nice surprise to get your letter.

I didn't even think you'd remember that we had met. It's very nice of you to say such flattering things about my work and I am most grateful for your dinner invitation on the night of the exhibition.

I am writing this from Wales, where I am spending a quiet holiday. (My post is forwarded to me, so that's how I got your letter.) I should be very happy to accept. I look forward to renewing my friendship with you, your husband, and your other friends.

Sincerely,
Ruth O'Donnell

Carmel held the letter tightly in her hand after she'd read it. Relief flooded her face. She had been almost certain that Ruth O'Donnell would accept, but there had been the slight fear that she might ruin the whole plan. Now everything was all right. Everything was on target.

That night Dermot told her that she was looking very well, very healthy-looking. Carmel smiled, pleased. "I've been walking a lot lately, I find it

304

does me good." That was true, she did walk and it did make her feel as if it were doing good. But she didn't tell him about the facial she had had—the second this week. The beautician had been giving her a rejuvenating mask. And she didn't tell him that she had now settled on veal with Marsala for the main course, and pears baked in wine for the dessert.

She didn't tell him that she had got a letter that day from Ruth O'Donnell.

Bernadette and Anna had lunch together. Anna had a salad and a coffee; Bernadette had a huge lump of French bread and cheese, and drank a pint of Guinness.

"Only point in having lunch in a pub, really, having a pint," she said.

Anna swallowed her disapproval. They had met to discuss what they should do about Mother and Dad, if anything. There was no point in beginning by criticizing each other.

"Are you sure . . . it's not just gossip?"

"No, a lot of people know, apparently we're the last to know."

"Well, that stands to reason," Bernadette said logically, "people aren't going to discuss our father's little peccadillos in company where we are sitting there listening."

"Now, should we say anything?"

"What could we say? Do you mean ask Dad, Is it true?"

Anna thought. "Yes, we could do that, I suppose, and sort of say that we think it's dreadful and that it must come to an end."

Bernadette pealed with laughter.

"Anna, you are marvelous, you're just like a dowager duchess. 'I think, Father, this is quite dreadful. It must come to an end. Back to Mother. Quick quick. As you were.'" She rocked with amusement at the thought of it. Anna did not rock at all.

"Why is that funny? What do *you* suggest?"

"I'm sorry, I shouldn't laugh. What *do* I suggest? I don't know. I suppose we could ask him does he intend to go off with Ruth and leave Mother, because that's the only thing we have a *right* to know really. I mean, if he does, she'll crack up."

"Yes," Anna agreed. "That's the point. He must be made to see that he can't do that to her."

"He may want to do it, but he must realize that's what's going to happen, and I suppose he should be given the facts about how much he can rely on you and on me . . . to pick up the bits."

"Well, he can't expect us to look after—"

"No, he probably doesn't expect anything. . . . I think he should be put in the picture, that's all."

Anna was surprised to see her younger sister being so firm. She always thought of Bernadette as a bit eejity, but she was being very crisp today.

"Well, Frank and I are thinking of going to Australia in the New Year."

"To Australia, like Uncle Charlie? *He* didn't make a fortune."

"That's not the point. There's a crafts cooperative we are interested in. It's not definite yet, but I don't want Mummy to be one of my reasons for going or staying. I mean, I'll write home every week and all . . . but I don't want to go not knowing whether she'll end up in a mental ward or whether she'll be all right."

"Yes . . . yes." Anna felt left behind.

"And *you're* not really going to move in and look after her, are you, Anna? You've got your own life . . . Dad should be told this . . . just so that he knows the options."

"Yes. But isn't it all a bit harsh . . . a bit final? Mightn't we be sort of taking too much for granted."

"Yes, that's the point. It was you who said we must meet and discuss what to do. I think that's the only thing to do if we do anything, let him know just how far he can rely on us so that there's no misunderstanding."

"Yes, well, I don't know, maybe we should say nothing. . . . Mother's probably better able to look after herself than we realize.

"And you were saying that she actually seems more lively these days."

"Yes, and she looks better, her skin looks less sort of muddy . . . and she's lost a bit of weight, I think."

"She always seems very cheerful when I call in or ring."

"Yes. When you think how awful it was that time her nerves did get bad."

"Oh, years ago, when I was still at college?"

"Yes, it was awful, she used to go and see this psychiatrist and cry all the time."

"What did they do with her, how did they cure her?"

"Oh, Bernadette, you know psychiatrists, they don't do anything or cure anyone . . . they just listen and say yes, yes—or so I hear."

"Why do people go on going to them then?"

"Who knows? I suppose the world's a bit short on people who will listen and say yes, yes."

"But she did get better, she stopped crying and everything."

"I told you, it works, all this yes-yessing."

"And we'll say nothing for the moment."

"I think not, don't you?"

Joe arrived a week before the party. He telephoned one morning and said he was in town.

"Did I send you enough money?" Carmel sounded anxious.

"Darling, you sent me too much money. How are you, Carmel, am I going to come and see you?"

"No, I'll come and see you. I don't want you coming here until the night."

"Where will we go?"

"Let me see . . . I'll go into the hotel. . . . We can have tea or coffee sent up, can't we?"

"Yeah, it's costing a fortune, the hotel. I wonder, Are you putting too much money out on all this, Carmel? There might have been another way."

"I have the money . . . I've always had money, that was never a problem. I'm so grateful to you for coming over, Joe, I'll never be able to thank you. I wish your friend had come too."

"No, a job's a job. Henry understands. . . . It would have messed things up if he'd come here. He says you're as mad as a coot but he wishes you luck."

She laughed happily. "Oh, good, he's on our side. I'll come down to the hotel this afternoon. What room are you? I'll just slip along and get into the lift."

"Oh, Mrs. M., you sound as if you're accustomed to this kind of racy life," Joe laughed. He was pleased that Carmel was so cheerful, he had been afraid that it might be a very glum Carmel. A sort of doom-laden Lady Macbeth. This sounded a lot more jolly. He sat back in his bed and lit a cigarette. It was really the most extraordinary business.

"How nice of you to call, Ethel. No, I'm fine . . . and you? Good. And David? Great. Oh, what a pity, no, I'm just off out as a matter of fact. Yes, it is a long time, isn't it? But never mind, we'll see you next week, won't we? The eighth. Oh good, good. No, not a thing, thank you, no, no, it's all under control. But very nice of you to think of it, Ethel. . . . What? Oh yes, everyone's coming

. . . but it's only a small gathering, heavens, compared to all the ones you go to. Yes, that nice Ruth O'Donnell—I had such a sweet letter from her, Wales is where she was. She's looking forward to seeing you all again, she said. Was there anything else, Ethel? I'm in a bit of a rush. Right, see you both then, love to David. Bye."

"Yes, Aunt Sheila, I'm on my own. I've plenty of time to talk. She seems in great form to me, very perky. And looking very well, I think she looks better now than I've seen her looking for a long time . . . good, yes, I thought I wasn't imagining it. No, of course I don't mind you talking frankly. I mean, I know you're her oldest friend, for heaven's sake. No, honestly Aunt Sheila, I'm telling you the truth, I haven't noticed anything odd about Mother recently. . . . She's in very good form. . . . Yes, well she doesn't have much time for me, either. No, I'm not actually sure what she *is* doing, but whatever little things they are seem to keep her occupied. The way I look at it, isn't she far better this way, all cheerful and mysterious, than she was the time she got upset and her nerves were bad? Do you remember she sat there all day and we all found it a terrible drag to talk to her? She had no interest in anyone."

Anna said to James, "You know that friend of Mother's, the one we call Aunt Sheila, who went back to teaching, remember? She was on the phone whinging and whining and says that she thinks Mother's behaving oddly. How oddly, I ask, and she can't explain. Apparently Mother is too cheerful. Did you ever?"

"Poor Grandmama," said James. "It's bad if she's gloomy, it's bad if she's cheerful. She can't win."

"You look a million dollars. . . You're *not* an old hag . . . you're smashing." Joe was full of admiration.

"I had a make-up lesson. You know the kind of thing the women's magazines advise you to do if your husband's unfaithful. 'Is your make-up old-fashioned?' they ask, and recommend you try out the new shades."

They both laughed, and she looked at him carefully and nodded with approval.

"You look well, Joe, really well. I'm different, I'm just painted up a bit, that's why I appear to be okay, but you're really great . . . You look like a boy."

"An old boy," Joe laughed. "Oh, a very old boy . . . I'll be forty-five soon. That's not a boy these days!"

"You look still in your thirties and you look terrific."

Joe was pleased that her admiration was genuine. "Do you know what I did for us, I went out to that supermarket up in Baggot Street. . . . Lord, has the place all changed . . . and I got us a bottle of fizz, on me. I decided that if we're going to do this mad thing we'll celebrate it in style."

"Do you think we should wait until it's done?" Carmel was unwilling to celebrate yet.

"Hell no, if we say we'll do it, then it will be done." He opened the bottle with a practiced hand and poured into the tooth mugs. "Of course, I still think you're as daft as a brush."

"Why? To get what I want? To try to get what I want?"

"No." He raised his glass to her. "Cheers, good luck. No, that's not daft. To want it is daft."

"Cheers," she said, raising her glass. "Ninety calories for four fluid ounces . . . how many in this glass?"

"I think we could say bang goes one hundred eighty calories there."

They laughed like old times.

"We've done nothing but fight since you came back. It's the last thing on God's earth that I want to do."

"We haven't been fighting," Ruth said wearily. "I keep asking one question and you keep asking it back. I keep saying why do I have to go to this dinner and you keep saying why not. It's not so much a fight, it's a cul-de-sac."

Dermot sighed. "I keep telling you that we're buying time, that's all it is . . . buying peace of mind and opportunities. . . . All of these things we want, and we can get them if you just come to the house and behave nice and naturally and let everybody tell you how wonderful you are for one evening. I know, I know, you don't want to, but it doesn't seem too hard a thing to me."

She got up and walked around her kitchen. "And it seems amazing to me that you don't see how hard it is to do. To go and talk to her, and to smile . . . and eat the food she's been slaving over, and go to the lavatory in your bathroom, and leave my coat on your bed, your marriage bed . . . really, Dermot."

"If I've told you once there are single beds I've told you twenty times. This time you'll be able to see for yourself."

"It's almost as if you felt like a big man, having us both there—"

"Christ, God, if you knew how that is not true. I'll feel nervous and uneasy and anxious . . . and I'll feel a cheat and a deceiver. Do you think I want to draw all that on myself?"

"Please, Dermot—"

"Please, Ruth, please . . . I never asked you anything like this before and I swear I'll never ask you again."

"Oh, for all I know it could become a weekly affair, maybe I'll be invited to move in . . . put a third bed in the room."

"Don't be coarse."

"Isn't it bad enough to deceive her without rubbing her nose in it?"

"Ruth, I love you, don't you know?"

"I think you do, but it's like believing in God—sometimes it's very difficult to remember why you ever did."

"Aren't you having even numbers, Mother? I thought you were asking me once about how to seat eight at a table."

It was the day before the party. Anna had dropped in to check up on Mother. Bernadette was right, Mother had never looked better, slimmer and with color in her cheeks, or could that possibly be a blusher? And what smart shoes! Mother said she had bought them for tomorrow and she was running them in. They were super, they cost about twice as much as Anna would have paid for a pair of shoes and ten times what she thought Mother would have paid.

"No, just seven . . . I suppose I did think of getting an extra man, but people say that it's very old-fashioned nowadays making up the numbers. Ethel says that more dinners have been ruined by people struggling to make the sexes equal."

"Oh yes . . . I quite agree, really dreary men being dragged in, there are more really dreary men than dreary women around, I always think."

"So do I, but maybe we're prejudiced!" Mother laughed, and Anna laughed too. Mother was fine, what was all the fuss about? In order to let Mother think she was interested in the famous dinner, she asked brightly, "Who's coming then, Mother? Aunt Sheila and Uncle Martin, I suppose . . ."

"Yes, and Ethel and David . . . and Ruth O'Donnell, that nice young artist."

Anna dropped her handbag.

314

"Who?"

"Oh, you must know her, the painting in the hall, and this one. And the one on the stairs. Ruth O'Donnell . . . her exhibition opens tomorrow, and we're all going to it and then coming back here for dinner."

Bernadette wasn't in, but Anna told the whole thing to Frank and had a glass of parsnip wine to restore her.

"Are there bits of parsnip in it?" she asked suspiciously.

"No, it's all fermented, it's all we have," Frank said ungraciously.

Anna told the whole story, interspersed with explanations of how her heart had nearly stopped and she hadn't known what to say, to think, to do. Frank listened blankly.

"Isn't she a fifteen-carat bitch," Anna said in the end.

"Your mother?" Frank asked, puzzled.

"No, the woman. Ruth O'Donnell. Isn't she a smug, self-satisfied little bitch? It's not enough for her to have her own exhibition, which half the country seems to be going to; it's not enough for her to have poor Dad like a little lap poodle running after her . . . she has to get him to get Mother to ask her to a dinner party and make a public humiliation of her in front of all Mother's friends."

Frank looked unmoved.

"Well, isn't it appalling," she snapped.

He shrugged. "To me there are two ways of looking at it, and both of them are from your Ma's point of view. Either she knows, in which case she knows what she's doing, or she doesn't know, in which case nobody's about to announce it to her over the soup, so either way *she's* all right."

Anna didn't like the way Frank had emphasized the word *she*. If he meant that Mother was all right, who wasn't? Could it be Anna, sharp and shrill and getting into a tizz? She drained her parsnip wine and left.

"For God's sake, stay out of it," James said. "Don't ring all those fearful old women up. Let it go its own way. You'll hear soon enough if something disastrous happens."

"But they're my own mother and father, James. It's not as if they were just neighbors. You have to care about your own mother and father."

"Your own daughter and son seem to be yelling for you in the kitchen," he said.

She flounced out. James came out after her and gave her a kiss. She smiled and felt better. "That's soppy," said Cilian and they all laughed.

Radio Eireann rang and asked if Ruth would go on the *Day by Day* program. She said she would call them back.

"Should I?" she asked Dermot.

"Definitely," he said. "Absolutely. Go straight out."

Thank God, he thought, at least that will take

her mind off Carmel and the dinner. This time tomorrow it would all be over, he told himself. This time tomorrow he would sit down and take stock of his life. He had all the information that anyone could ever gather about early retirement plans . . . or he could ask for a transfer.

Ruth had often said she would like to live out of Dublin, but of course in a small place it wouldn't be acceptable. Anyway, no point in thinking about all that now; the main thing was that Carmel was quite capable of living a life of her own now . . . might even get herself a job like her friend Sheila. That was something that could be suggested—not by him, of course. Oh God, if she only knew how he wanted her to be happy, he didn't want to hurt her, or betray her, he just wanted her to have her own life.

"Your wife on the line, Mr. Murray."

He jumped physically. "What? What?"

"Shall I put her through?"

"Of course."

Carmel never rang him at the bank; what could have happened?

"Hallo, Dermot, I'm awfully sorry for bothering you, were you in the middle of someone's bank account?"

"No, of course not. What is it, Carmel?"

"Do you remember Joe Daly?"

"What? Who?"

"I was asking you did you remember Joe Daly, he used to write for the paper here, then he went off to London. Remember?"

"Vaguely, I think. Why?"

"Well, I met him quite by chance today, and he's been doing interviews with Ruth O'Donnell, he knows her quite well it turns out. Anyway, I thought I'd ask him tonight, isn't that a good idea?"

"Joe who?"

"Daly, do you remember, a mousy little man . . . we knew him ages ago before we were married."

"Oh, he's our age . . . right, whatever you say. If you think he's nice, then do. Whatever you like, dear. Will he fit in with everyone else?"

"Yes, I think so, but I wanted to check."

"Sure, sure, ask him, ask him."

Thank God, he thought, thank God, a mousy little failed journalist to talk about things that none of them were tied up in. There was a God in heaven, the night might not be so dreadful after all. He was about to dial Ruth when he realized she was probably on her way to the studio.

"Can you record *Day by Day,* please, on the machine over there," he said to Miss O'Neill. "There's going to be an item on banking I'd like to hear later." He watched as she put on the cassette, checked her watch and set the radio tape recorder to begin at eleven.

Joe rang her at noon.

"Can I come up now?" he asked.

"Be very careful, look like a tradesman," she said.

318

"That's not hard," he said.

She looked around the house. It was perfect. There were flowers in the bathroom, lovely dahlias and chrysanthemums, all in dark reds, they looked great with the pink soaps and pink towels. The bedroom where they were going to leave their coats was magnificent, with the two thick Kilkenny Design bedspreads freshly cleaned. The kitchen had flowers in it, too, orange dahlias and rust chrysanthemums; she had bought tea towels just in that color. Really, it was such fun showing off. She didn't know why she hadn't done it ages ago.

He came in very quickly. She looked left and right, but the houses weren't near enough for anyone to see.

"Come in and tell me everything," she said.

"It's worked . . . so far."

She poured a coffee for him.

"Won't it spoil the beautiful kitchen?" he teased.

"I have five hours to tidy it up," she laughed.

"So, I'll tell you from the start. I arrived at her flat, your man was in there, I could hear his voice. They were arguing."

"What about?" Carmel was interested.

"I couldn't hear. Anyway, I waited, I went down to the courtyard place. I sat on the wall and waited, he left in an hour. I pressed her bell. I told her who I was, that I had an interest in a gallery in London, that I didn't want to set up huge business meetings and press her in the week of her exhibition but I was very interested in seeing whether it was the kind of thing we could bring to London."

"Did she ask why you were at the door?"

"Yes. I said I'd looked her up in the phone book . . . she thought that was very enterprising."

"It is," laughed Carmel. "Nobody ever thinks of it."

"Anyway, I told her I was staying at the hotel, but that if she liked we could talk now. She laughed and said why not now, and let me in."

"And . . . ?"

"And it's very nice, all done up as a studio, not a love nest at all . . . hardly any comfort, nothing like this." He looked around the smart kitchen and through the open door into the dining room with its dark polished wood. "So we had a long talk, all about her work. She showed me what she was doing, showing, we went through the catalogue. I explained what I could do. . . Jesus, if you'd heard the way I dropped the names of galleries and people in London—I even impressed myself. I promised nothing. I said I'd act as a middleman. I even sent myself up a bit and said I saw myself as a Mister Fixit. . . . She liked that and she laughed a lot—"

"Yes," said Carmel before he could say it. "I know, I know, I've heard. She's very nice. Go on."

"Yes, well. I think I played it well. I must have. When I was leaving I said that we must keep in touch, that I could be here for a week and perhaps she would like to have a lunch one day. She said that would be nice, and I said the next day and we picked the place you said. . . . I said I'd heard it was good."

"Was it?" asked Carmel with interest.

"It was and so it should be, it cost you an arm and a leg. I kept the receipt for you."

"Joe, I don't need receipts."

"I know, but it is *astronomical.* "

"Was it the right place?"

"Yes, we sat on and on. She doesn't drink much but they kept bringing pots of coffee. . . . Nobody rushed us . . . it was very relaxed and we broadened the conversation. . . . She told me about how she began and how this nun at the school she went to had great faith in her even when her parents didn't really believe she had talent."

Joe paused. "I kept leaning heavily on the notion that I was just passing through, not a permanent fixture. She was quite anxious to talk, actually, I don't need much congratulation."

"So she did tell you . . ."

"Yes, I sort of squeezed it out of her bit by bit— not with crude questions like, 'Why isn't a girl like you married?' More about Dublin being full of gossip and disapproval. . . . I told her I'd never be able to live here nowadays because of my own life. She said no, it wasn't too bad . . . things had changed, but people did let others go their own way. I argued that with her, and then she had to get down to specifics. She had a false start, then she said she didn't want to be unburdening her whole life story to a total stranger.

"I said that total strangers were the only people you could possibly unburden things to. They passed like ships in the night. Sometimes it happened that you got a bit of advice from a passing ship but even if you didn't, what the hell, the ship had passed on . . . it wasn't hanging around embarrassing you every time you saw it."

"And?"

"And she told me . . . she told me about her married man."

"Was it anything like the truth? I mean, did she describe things the way things are?"

"Very like the way you told me. She met him when she was doing a job for the bank. He had taken her out to lunch, she had been lonely, he had understood. . . . her father had died recently. Her mother was dead years ago. The married man was very sympathetic."

"I'm sure," said Carmel.

"They met a lot and he was so interested in her work and so encouraging—and he believed in her—and the reason she liked him so much . . ."

"Yes . . . ?" Carmel leaned forward.

"He didn't want to hurt people or do people down. He never wanted her to score over other people. He wanted her to be content in herself and with her work. . . . She liked that most about him."

Joe paused. "So I put it to her that he must have a bit of the louse in him to maintain two ménages, he must be a bit of a crud to have it both ways . . . you know, not disturbing his own lifestyle . . ."

"What did she say?"

"She thought not, she thought he was a victim of circumstances. His wife hadn't been well, she had been—sorry, Carmel—the phrase she used was 'suffering from her nerves.' "

"Fine, fine," said Carmel.

"Then I talked about Henry a bit, I didn't want her to think that she was confiding too much, you know . . . people turn against people when they tell them too much."

"Yes, I know," Carmel agreed.

"So anyway, it went on from there . . . could she guide me around Dublin a bit? We had lunch at the National Gallery . . . we went in and out of the place that's giving her the exhibition, we went—oh, God knows where. . . . I kept her occupied during the days, and I faded out a bit at night because I knew she'd be meeting your man after work. On Wednesday she asked me would I like to meet him. I said no."

"Wednesday," Carmel said softly to herself.

"Yes. I said no way did I want to get involved in people's private lives. That was the night she told me that she had been invited here and she was worried sick, she couldn't think why—she said she didn't want to come and hurt you."

"No. No, indeed," said Carmel.

"So she said she didn't know how to get out

of it, the Man wouldn't hear of her refusing. I said the married man wanted to get a kick out of seeing you both together. She went quite white over it all. 'He wouldn't want that,' she said. 'I don't know, it gives some fellows a real charge,' I said, 'seeing the two women there and knowing they've screwed both of them.' "

"Really?" Carmel said.

Joe laughed. "That's what she said too. Anyway, it upset her. And she said he wasn't like that. Well then, he shouldn't force you to come to the dinner, I said. It's being a real voyeur, isn't it, having the both of you there?"

Joe paused for a gulp of his coffee.

"Then I said, 'I wouldn't be surprised if he forced the wife to ask you to dinner, after all. Why would the wife ask you? If she doesn't know about you and him it's an odd thing she should suddenly decide to pick you of all the people in Dublin and if she *does* know it's even odder.' She said that's what she'd been thinking herself. She's just an ordinary woman you know, Carmel, just an ordinary female with a slow brain ticking through and working things out. . . . She's no Mata Hari."

"I know," said Carmel.

"So I said then, and the others are his friends really, maybe they're all in on it, they know about you and him, don't they?" Joe leaned over. "So that was part one over, she really believed he was setting her up, she was so convinced. I don't know what kind of an evening they had that night, but it didn't last long. He was out of there in an hour."

"Yes, he was home very bad-tempered and very early on Wednesday," Carmel said, smiling.

"So Thursday I ring her and say come on, I'll buy you lunch and no gloomy chat, because isn't it a small world, I've just run into my old friends the Murrays and ha ha isn't Dublin a village? I now know who the mystery bank manager is, it's Dermot Murray. I didn't know he knew you. . . . She's amazed.

" 'Oho,' I say, 'can't keep a secret in this town. No, really, isn't it a scream, I knew brother Charlie years ago, long before he went to Australia or anything, and I remember Carmel, and Carmel was walking out with Dermot Murray, a lowly bank clerk then . . .' Oh, she's all upset, she can't believe it, it's too much. I say stop all that fussing and fretting, I'll buy you a big lunch. I keep saying it's a scream."

Carmel smiled.

"I arrive and collect her. She's been crying, she's so ashamed, she wouldn't have dreamed of telling me all those intimate things if there was a chance I'd have known anyone . . . but I was a stranger in town and outside, someone who went away years ago. I kept laughing, the odds against it must be millions to one, forget it, anyway, wasn't it all for the best? Because now that I knew that it was Carmel and Dermot I could say definitely that they weren't the kind of people who would be involved in anything sordid. Everyone had spoken very well of Dermot, and poor Carmel had always been very nice.

"Poor Carmel," Carmel said, smiling still.

"You asked me to play it for all I could," Joe said.

"I know. Go on."

"It took a lot of coaxing to get her back where she was. I reminded her of all the indiscretions I had told her, about being gay, about Henry. I told her that nobody in Ireland knew that about me, that we each knew secrets about the other. We shook hands over lunch. I felt a real shit."

"Joe, go on."

"She left more cheerful. I rang her yesterday morning and asked could I come by for coffee. I told her that I had heard at the hotel a man talking to a friend. I described David perfectly . . . he's not hard to describe from what you told me."

"There's only one David," said Carmel.

"Yes, well she identified him, and oh, I wove a long tale. It could have been something else entirely, but it did sound as if it could have been Dermot he was talking about. . . . I kept pretending that it might have been imagination, but she saw it wasn't. She knew that if I had heard him talking like that it must be Dermot, and Dermot must indeed have told David that she was coming to the party and wasn't it all very risqué."

Joe looked at Carmel. "She cried a lot, she cried and cried. I felt very sorry for her."

"I cried a lot. I cried for four months the first time, the time he went off with that Sophie."

"But she has nobody to comfort her."

"I had nobody to comfort me."

"You had a psychiatrist."

"Great help."

"He cured you, didn't he?"

"No, he didn't, he asked me to ask myself was my marriage with Dermot so important that I should save it at all costs. What the hell does he know about marriage and importance, and all costs? What else is there for me but to be married to Dermot? There *is* nothing else. It's not a choice between this and something else, it's this or nothing."

"You're fine, you could live on your own. You don't need him. I can't see what you want him around for. He hasn't been any good to you for years, he hasn't been kind or a friend. You haven't wanted any of the things he wanted. Why didn't you let him go then, or indeed now?"

"You don't understand. It's different for . . . er . . . gays, it's not the same."

"Hell, it's not the same, of course it's not the same. I love Henry, Henry loves me. One day one of us will stop loving the other. Hopefully we'll split and go our own ways . . . but the worst is to stay together bitching."

"But your world, it's so different . . . so totally different . . . I couldn't do that."

"Well, you didn't. And you've won."

"I have, haven't I?"

"Yes . . . it's all fixed up. I told her this morning that I'd be here for moral support if she wanted to come. She said no, she didn't want to make a fool of herself in front of everyone. She'll tell you tonight at the exhibition that she can't come after all. She says she'll do it gently, she knows you are just as much a pawn as she is."

"Good, good."

"And she's not going to tell him at all. She's going to leave him stew, let him think what he likes."

"Suppose he runs after her, suppose he won't let her go?"

"I think she'll make it clear to him. Anyway, she's already set up some other friends to go out with. She says she's sorry for you because you're a timid sort of person and you'd been planning this for a month. . . . She's afraid that the whole thing will be a damp squib."

"That's very nice of her."

"It is, actually, Carmel, she's a very nice person."

"So you keep saying, but I'm a very nice person. I'm an extremely nice person, and very few people ever realize that."

"I realize it. I've always realized it," Joe said.

"Yes," Carmel said.

"I'd have done this for no money, you were always good to me."

"I sent you money because I have it, you don't. It seemed only fair that your week should be subsidized."

"You were always a brick, Carmel. Always. I'd have had no life if it weren't for you."

There was a silence. In the gleaming kitchen

they sat and remembered the other kitchen, the kitchen where Carmel's brother Charlie and Joe had stood scarlet-faced in front of Carmel's father. Words that had never been used in that house were used that evening. Threats of ruin were made. Joe would be prosecuted, he would spend years and years in jail, the whole world would know about his unnatural habits, his vile seduction of innocent schoolboys . . . an act so shameful not even the animal kingdom would tolerate it, and Charlie might grow up warped as a result. Joe's father, who worked as the gardener, would be sacked, and the man would never work again. He would be informed this night of his son's activities.

It was then that Carmel had found her voice. She was five years older than Charlie; she was twenty-two. She had been a quiet girl, her father had not even noticed her in the kitchen so great had been his rage.

"It was Charlie's fault, Dad," she had said in a level voice. "Charlie's been queer for two years. He's had relationships with a lot of boys, I can tell you their names." There had been a silence which seemed to last for an hour. "I don't like unfairness. Joe Daly has done nothing that Charlie didn't encourage. Why should his father be sacked, why should he be disgraced, why should Charlie get away with it, Dad, because Mr. Daly is a gardener and you're a company director?"

It was unanswerable.

Charlie went to Australia shortly afterward. Mr.

Daly was never told, and Joe Daly got a little assistance from Charlie's father indirectly, so that he could go to a technical school and do English and commerce and bookkeeping. During that time he wrote the odd article for evening papers, and Carmel had seen him casually around Dublin. He had sent her a wedding present when she married Dermot two years after the distressing events in the kitchen. It was a beautiful cut glass vase, nicer than anything she had got from any of her father's friends, or any of Dermot's side. It would be on the dining table tonight, with late summer roses in it.

"So will I leave you to rest and think over it all?" Joe said.

"I *wish* you thought I'd done the right thing," she said.

"You know what I think. I think you should have given him away. I really do. There are other lives."

"Not for fifty-year-old women there aren't."

"I know what you mean, but there are. Anyway, there you go."

"Why are you so fed up with me?"

"Carmel, I'm not fed up with you. I owed you, I'd do anything for you anytime, I told you that and I meant it. You asked me one favor. You've paid me handsomely for it. I've done it, but I don't have to approve of it."

"Oh, Joe, I thought you'd understand."

"You see, it's the total reverse of all that happened, years ago. Then you did something brave just—well—just so that the right thing should be done."

"But this is the right thing! She's young, she'll find somebody else, a proper person, not a married man . . . not somebody else's husband."

"No, you see, this time you've arranged it so that the truth is hidden, lost. She thinks that Dermot is setting her up, she thinks he's having a laugh at her, that he wanted her to come to the party as some kind of macho thing. Dermot thinks that she's let him down, promised to go through with it and then thrown him over unexpectedly. Neither believes that the other is actually honest."

Carmel stood up. "I know it's complicated. That psychiatrist said to me, you know, the first time, that there's no such thing as absolute right and absolute wrong. He also said that we can't control other people's lives, we must only take responsibility for our own. I decided what I wanted to do with mine, and I did it. That's the way I see it. I don't see it as meddling or playing God or anything."

Joe stood up too. "No, whatever else it is, I don't think it's playing God," he said.

He slipped quietly out of the house, making sure that he wasn't observed, because he wasn't meant to be a great friend of Carmel's—he was only a casual friend whom they had met luckily again, and his last job was to make sure that the dinner party was great fun.

FLAT IN RINGSEND

They said you should get the evening papers at lunchtime and as soon as you got a smell of a flat that would suit you were to rush out and sit on the step at the head of the queue. You shouldn't take any notice of the words "After six o'clock." If you got there at six o'clock and the ad had sounded any way reasonable then you'd find a line trailing down the road. Finding a good flat in Dublin at a price you could afford was like finding gold in the gold rush.

The other way was by personal contact; if you knew someone who knew someone who was leaving a place—that often worked. But if you had only just arrived in Dublin there was no chance of any personal contact, nobody to tell you that their bed-sit would be vacant at the end of the month. No, it was a matter of staying in a hostel and searching.

Jo had been to Dublin a dozen times when she was a child; she had been up for a match, or for a school outing, or the time that Da was in the Chest Hospital and everyone had been crying in case he wouldn't get better. Most of her friends had been up to Dublin much more often; they talked about places they had gone to in a familiar

332

way, and assumed that she knew what they were talking about.

"You *must* know the Dandelion Market. Let me see, you come out of the Zhivago and you go in a straight line to your right, keep going and you pass O'Donoghue's and the whole of Stephen's Green, and you don't turn right down Grafton Street. Now do you know where it is?"

After so much effort explaining things to her, Jo said she did. Jo was always anxious to please other people, and she felt that she only annoyed them by not knowing what they were talking about. But Dublin was a very big blank spot. She really felt she was stepping into the unknown when she got on the train to go and work there. She didn't ask herself why she was going in the first place. It had been assumed by everyone that she would go. Who would stay in a one-horse town, the back of beyonds, the end of the world, the sticks, this dead-and-alive place? That's all she had heard for years. At school they were all going to get out, escape, see some life, get some living in, have a real kind of existence, and some of the others in her class had gone as far as Ennis or Limerick, often to stay with cousins. A few had gone to England, where an elder sister or an aunt would see them settled in. But out of Jo's year none of them were going to Dublin. Jo's family must have been the only one in the place who didn't have relations in Glasnevin or Dundrum. She was heading off on her own.

There had been a lot of jokes about her going

to work in the post office. There'd be no trouble in getting a stamp to write a letter home; what's more, there'd be no excuse if she didn't. She could sneak the odd phone call, too, which would be fine, but they didn't have a phone at home. Maybe she could send a ten-page telegram if she needed to say anything in a hurry. They assumed that she would know the whole business of the high and the mighty in Dublin the way Miss Hayes knew everyone's business from the post office at home. People said that she'd find it very easy to get to know people, there was nowhere like a post office for making friends, it was the center of everything.

She knew she wouldn't be working in the GPO, but whenever she thought of herself in Dublin it was in the middle of the General Post Office chatting up all the people as they came in, knowing every single person who came to buy stamps or collect the children's allowances. She imagined herself living somewhere nearby, maybe over Clery's or on the corner of O'Connell Bridge so that she could look at the Liffey from her bedroom.

She had never expected the miles and miles of streets where nobody knew anyone, the endless bus journeys, the having to get up two hours before she was meant to be at work in case she got lost or the bus was canceled. "Not much time for a social life," she wrote home. "I'm so exhausted when I get back to the hostel I just go to bed and fall asleep."

Jo's mother thought that it would be great altogether if she stayed permanently in the hostel. It was run by nuns, and she could come to no harm. Her father said that he hoped they kept the place warm; nuns were notorious for freezing everyone else to death just because they wore thermal underwear. Jo's sisters who worked in the hotel as waitresses said she must be off her head to have stayed a whole week in a hostel; her brother who worked in the creamery said he was sorry she didn't have a flat, it would be somewhere to stay whenever he went to Dublin; her brother who worked in the garage said that Jo would have been better off to stay where she was—what would she get in Dublin—only discontented—and she'd end up like that O'Hara girl, neither one thing nor the other, happy neither in Dublin nor at home. It had to be said that he had fancied the O'Hara girl for a long time, and it was a great irritation to him that she wouldn't settle down and be like a normal woman.

But Jo didn't know that they were all thinking about her and discussing her, as she answered the advertisement for the flat in Ringsend. It said "OWN ROOM, OWN TELEVISION, SHARE KITCHEN, BATHROOM." It was very near her post office and seemed too good to be true. Please, St. Jude, please. May it be nice, may they like me, may it not be too dear.

There wasn't a queue for this one because it wasn't so much "FLAT TO LET," more "THIRD GIRL WANTED." The fact that it had said "own television" made Jo wonder whether it might be in too high a class for her, but the house did not look any way overpowering. An ordinary red-bricked terraced house with a basement. Her father had warned her against basements; they were full of damp, he said, but then her father had a bad chest and saw damp everywhere. But the flat was not in the basement, it was upstairs. And a cheerful-looking girl with a college scarf, obviously a failed applicant, was coming down the stairs.

"Desperate place," she said to Jo. "They're both awful. Common as dirt."

"Oh," said Jo and went on climbing.

"Hallo," said the girl with "Nessa" printed on her T-shirt.

"God, did you see that toffee-nosed bitch going out? I can't stand that kind, I can't stand them."

"What did she do?" asked Jo.

"Do? She didn't have to *do* anything. She just poked around and wrinkled her lip and sort of giggled and then said 'Is this it?' in a real Foxrock accent. 'Oh dear, oh dear.' Stupid old cow, we wouldn't have had her in here if we were starving and needed her to buy us a crust, would we, Pauline?"

Pauline had a psychedelic shirt on; it almost hurt the eyes, but was only marginally brighter than her hair. Pauline was a punk, Jo noted with amazement. She had seen some of them on O'Connell Street, but hadn't met one close up to talk to.

"No, stupid old bore. She was such a bore.

336

She'd have bored us to death. Years later our bodies would have been found here and the verdict would have been death by boredom."

Jo laughed. It was such a wild thought to think of all that pink hair lying on the floor dead because it hadn't been able to stand the tones of the flatmate. "I'm Jo, I work in the post office and I rang." Nessa said they were just about to have a mug of tea. She produced three mugs; one had NESSA and one had PAULINE and the other one had OTHER written on it. "We'll get your name put on if you come to stay," she said generously.

Nessa worked for the bus company, and Pauline worked in a big firm nearby. They had got the flat three months ago and Nessa's sister had had the third room, but now she was getting married very quickly, very quickly indeed, and so the room was empty. They explained the cost, they showed her the geyser for having a bath and they showed her the cupboard in the kitchen, each shelf with a name on it, Nessa, Pauline, and Maura.

"Maura's name will go, and we'll paint in yours if you come to stay," Nessa said again reassuringly.

"You've no sitting room," Jo said.

"No, we did it in three bed-sits," said Nessa.

"Makes much more sense," said Pauline.

"What's the point of a sitting room?" asked Nessa.

"I mean, who'd sit in it?" asked Pauline.

"And we've got two chairs in our own rooms," Nessa said proudly.

"And each of us has our own telly," said Pauline happily.

That was the point that Jo wanted to discuss. "Yes, you didn't say how much that costs. Is there a rental?"

Nessa's big happy face spread into a grin. "No, that's the real perk. You see, Maura's Steve, well, my brother-in-law as he now is, I hope, my brother-in-law Steve worked in the business and he was able to get us tellys for a song."

"So you bought them outright, did you?" Jo was enthralled.

"Bought in a manner of speaking," Pauline said. "Accepted them outright."

"Yeah, it was his way of saying thank you, his way of paying the rent . . . in a manner of speaking," Nessa said.

"But did he stay here too?"

"He was Maura's boyfriend. He stayed most of the time."

"Oh," said Jo. There was a silence.

"Well?" Nessa said accusingly. "If you've anything to say, you should say it now."

"I suppose I was wondering, did he not get in everyone's way? I mean, if a fourth person was staying in the flat, was it fair on the others?"

"Why do you think we organized it all into bed-sits?" Pauline asked. "Means we can all do what we like when we like, not trampling on other people. Right?"

"Right," Nessa said.

"Right," Jo said, doubtfully.

338

"So, what do you think?" Nessa asked Pauline. "I think Jo would be okay if she wants to come, do you?"

"Yeah, sure, I think she'd be fine, if she'd like it here," said Pauline.

"Thank you," said Jo, blushing a bit.

"Is there anything else you'd like to ask? I think we've covered everything. There's a phone with a coin box in the hall downstairs. There's three nurses in the flat below, but they don't take any messages for us so we don't take any for them. The rent on the first of the month, plus five quid each and I get a few basics."

"Will you come, then?" asked Nessa.

"Please. I'd like to very much, can I come on Sunday night?"

They gave her a key, took her rent money, poured another cup of tea and said that it was great to have fixed it all up so quickly. Nessa said that Jo was such a short name it would be dead easy to paint it onto the shelf in the kitchen, the shelf in the bathroom, and her mug.

"She wanted to paint the names on the doors, too, but I wouldn't let her," said Pauline.

"Pauline thought it looked too much like a nursery," said Nessa regretfully.

"Yes, and also I wanted to leave a bit of variety in life. If our names are on the doors then we'll never get any surprise visitors during the night—I always like a bit of the unexpected!"

Jo laughed too. She hoped they were joking.

She assured her mother in the letter that the flat was very near Haddington Road, she told her father how far it was from the damp basement, and she put in the bits about the television in each bedroom to make her sisters jealous. They had said she was an eejit to go to Dublin; the best Dublin people all came to County Glare on their holidays. She should stay at home and meet them there rather than going up and trying to find them in their own place.

They were having tea in the hostel on Sunday when Jo said goodbye. She struggled with her two cases to the bus stop.

"Your friends aren't going to arrange to collect you?" sister said.

"They haven't a car, sister."

"I see. Often, though, young people come to help a friend. I hope they are kind people, your friends."

"Very, sister."

"That's good. Well, God bless you, child, and remember that this is a very wicked city, a lot of very wicked people in it."

"Yes, sister, I'll keep my eye out for them."

It took her a long time to get to the flat.

She had to change buses twice, and was nearly exhausted when she got there. She had to come down again for the second case, and dragged the two into the room that had been pointed out as hers. It was smaller than it had looked on Friday, yet it could hardly have shrunk. The bedclothes were folded there, two blankets, two pillows and a quilt. Lord, she forgot about sheets; she'd assumed they were included. And God, she supposed there'd be no towel either, wasn't she an eejit not to have asked.

She hoped they wouldn't notice, and she'd be able to buy some tomorrow—or she hoped she would, as she only had an hour for lunch. She'd ask one of the girls in the post office, and she had her savings for just this kind of emergency.

She hung up her clothes in the poky little wardrobe, and put out her ornaments on the window sill and her shoes in a neat line on the floor. She put her cases under the bed and sat down feeling very flat.

Back home they'd be going to the pictures or to a dance at eight o'clock on a Sunday night. In the hostel some of the girls would watch television in the lounge, others would have gone to the pictures together and go for chips on the way home, throwing the papers into the litter bin on the corner of the street where the hostel was, since sister didn't like the smell of chips coming into the building.

Nobody was sitting alone on a bed with nothing to do. She could go out and take the bus into town and go to the pictures alone, but didn't that seem ridiculous when she had her own television. Her very own. She could change the channel whenever she wanted to; she wouldn't have to ask anyone.

She was about to go out to the sitting room to see was there a Sunday paper, when she remembered there was no sitting room. She didn't want to open the doors of their rooms in case they might come in and think she was prying. She wondered where they were. Was Nessa out with a boyfriend? She hadn't mentioned one, but then, girls in Dublin didn't tell you immediately if they had a fellow or not. Perhaps Pauline was at a punk disco. She couldn't believe that anyone would actually employ Pauline with that hair and let her meet the public, but maybe she was kept hidden away. Perhaps they'd come home about eleven o'clock (well, they had to get up for work in the morning); perhaps they all had cocoa or drinking chocolate in the sitting room—well, in the kitchen, to end the day. She'd tell them how well she'd settled in. In the meantime she would sit back and watch her own television set.

Jo fell asleep after half an hour. She had been very tired. She dreamed that Nessa and Pauline had come in. Pauline had decided to wash the pink out of her hair and share a room with Nessa. They were going to turn Pauline's room into a sitting room, where they would sit and talk and plan. She woke suddenly when she heard giggling. It was Pauline and a man's voice, and they had gone into the kitchen.

Jo shook herself. She must have been asleep for three hours; she had a crick in her neck and the television was flickering. She stood up and turned it off, combed her hair and was about to go out and welcome the homecomers when she hesitated. If Pauline had invited a boy home, presumably she was going to take him to bed with her. Perhaps the last thing she might need now was her new flatmate coming out looking for company. They were laughing in the kitchen, she could hear them, then she heard the electric kettle hiss and whistle. Well, she could always pretend that she had been going to make herself a cup of tea.

Nervously, she opened the door and went into the kitchen. Pauline was with a young man who wore a heavy leather jacket with a lot of studs on it.

"Hallo, Pauline, I was just going to get myself a cup of tea," Jo said apologetically.

"Sure," Pauline said. She was not unfriendly, she didn't look annoyed, but she made no effort to introduce her friend.

The kettle was still hot, so Jo found a mug with VISITOR on it and put in a tea bag. "Nessa's going to paint my name on a mug," she said to the man in the jacket, just for something to say. "Oh, good," he said. He shrugged and asked Pauline, "Who's Nessa?"

"Lives over there," Pauline said, indicating the direction of Nessa's room.

"I'm the third girl," Jo said desperately. "Third in what?" he said, genuinely bewildered. Pauline had fixed the tray of tea and biscuits and gas moving toward the door.

"Night," she said, companionably enough.

"Good night, Pauline, good night . . . er . . ." Jo said.

She took the cup of tea into her own room. She turned up the television slightly in case she heard the sound of anything next door. She hoped she hadn't annoyed Pauline. She couldn't see what she had done that might annoy her, and anyway she had seemed cheerful enough when she was taking this boy off to—well, to her room. Jo sighed and got into bed.

Next morning she was coming out of the bathroom when she met Nessa.

"It's just *J* and *O*, two letters, isn't it?" Nessa asked.

"Oh yes, that's right, thank you very much, Nessa."

"Right. I didn't want to do it and then find you had an *E* on it."

"No, no, it's short for Josephine."

"Right on." Nessa was off.

"What time are you coming home tonight?" Jo asked.

"Oh, I don't think I'll have them done tonight," Nessa said.

"I didn't mean that, I just wondered what you were doing for your tea . . . supper. You know?"

"No idea," said Nessa cheerfully.

"Oh," said Jo. "Sorry."

Jacinta, who worked beside her, asked her how the flat was.

"It's great altogether," Jo said.

"Dead right to get out of that hostel, you'd have no life in a hostel," Jacinta said wisely.

"No, no indeed."

"God, I wish I didn't live at home," Jacinta said. "It's not natural for people to live in their own homes, there should be a law about it. They have laws over stupid things like not importing live fowl, as if anyone would want to, but they have no laws about the things that people really need."

"Yes," said Jo dutifully.

"Anyway, you'll have the high life from now on. You country ones have all the luck."

"I suppose we do," Jo agreed doubtfully.

If she had stayed in the hostel they might have been playing twenty-five in the lounge now, or someone might have bought a new record. They would look at the evening paper, sigh over the price of flats, wonder whether to go the pictures and complain about the food. There would be talk and endless tea or bottles of cola from the machine. There would not be four walls as there were now.

She had bought a hamburger on the way home and eaten it. She washed her tights, she put the new sheets on the bed and hung her new towel up in the bathroom on the third hook. The other hooks had N and P on them. She took out her writing pad but remembered that she had written home on Friday just after she had found the flat. There was nothing new to tell. The evening yawned ahead of her. And then there would be Tuesday and Wednesday and Thursday. . . . Tears came into her eyes and fell down on to her lap as she sat on the end of her bed. She must be absolutely awful to have no friends and nowhere to go and nothing to do. Other people of eighteen had great times. She used to have great times when she was seventeen, at school and planning to be eighteen. Look at her now, sitting alone. Even her flatmates didn't want to have anything to do with her. She cried and cried. Then she got a headache so she took two aspirins and climbed into bed. It's bloody fantastic being grown up, she thought, as she switched off the light at nine o'clock.

There was a *J* on her towel rack, her name was on the bathroom shelf that belonged to her, and her empty kitchen shelf had a "Jo" on it also. She examined the other two shelves. Nessa had cornflakes and a packet of sugar and a lot of tins of soup on her shelf. Pauline had a biscuit tin and about a dozen tins of grapefruit segments on hers.

The kitchen was nice and tidy. Nessa had said the first day that they never left any washing up to be done and that if you used the frying pan you had to scrub it then, not let it steep until the morning. It had all seemed great fun when she was talking about it then, because Jo had envisaged midnight feasts, and all three of them laughing and having parties. That's what people *did*,

346

for heaven's sake. She must have just got in with two recluses, that was her problem.

Pauline came into the kitchen yawning, and opened a tin of grapefruit segments. "I think I'd never wake up if I didn't have these," she said. "I have half a tin and two biscuits for my breakfast every day, and then I'm ready for anything."

Jo was pleased to be spoken to. "Is your friend here?" she said, trying to be modern and racy.

"Which friend?" Pauline yawned and began to spoon the grapefruit out of the tin into a bowl.

"You know, your friend—the other night?"

"Nessa?" Pauline looked at her blankly. "Do you mean Nessa?"

"No, the fellow, the fellow with the jacket with the studs. I met him here in the kitchen."

"Oh, yes. Shane."

"Shane. That was his name."

"Yeah, what about him, what were you saying?"

"I was asking was he here?"

"Here? Now? Why should he be here?" Pauline pushed her pink hair out of her eyes and looked at her watch. "Jesus Christ, it's only twenty to eight in the morning. Why would he be here?" She looked wildly around the kitchen as if the man with the studded leather jacket was going to appear from behind the gas cooker. Jo felt the conversation was going wrong.

"I just asked sociably if he was still here, that was all."

"But why on earth would he be still here? I went

out with him on Sunday night. *Sunday*. It's Tuesday morning now, isn't it? Why would he be here?" Pauline looked confused and worried, and Jo wished she had never spoken.

"I just thought he was your boyfriend—"

"No, he's not, but if he was, I tell you I wouldn't have him here at twenty to eight in the morning talking! I don't know how anyone can talk in the mornings. It beats me."

Jo drank her tea silently.

"See you," said Pauline eventually, when she had finished her biscuits and grapefruit and crashed into the bathroom.

Jo thanked Nessa for putting up the names. Nessa was pleased. "I like doing that, it gives me a sense of order in the world. It defines things; that makes me feel better."

"Sure," said Jo. She was just about to ask Nessa what she was doing that evening when she remembered yesterday's rebuff. She decided to phrase it differently this time.

"Are you off out with your friends this evening?" she said timidly.

"I might be, I might not, it's always hard to know in the morning, isn't it?"

"Yes, it is," said Jo untruthfully. It was becoming increasingly easy to know in the morning, she thought. The answer was coming up loud and clear when she asked herself what she was going to do in the evening. The answer was Nothing.

"Well, I'm off now. Good-bye," she said to Nessa.

Nessa looked up and smiled. "Bye bye," she said vaguely, as if Jo had been the postman or the man delivering milk on the street.

On Thursday night Jo went downstairs to answer the phone. It was for one of the nurses on the ground floor, as it always was. Hesitantly she knocked on their door. The big blond nurse thanked her, and as Jo was going up the stairs again she heard the girl say, "No, it was one of the people in the flats upstairs. There's three flats upstairs and we all share the same phone."

That was it! That was what she hadn't realized. She wasn't in a flat with two other girls, she was in a flat by herself. Why hadn't that dawned on her? She was in a proper bedsitter all of her own, she just shared kitchen and bathroom facilities, as they would put it in an ad. That's what had been wrong. She had thought that she was meant to be part of a jolly all-girls-together. That's why she had been so depressed. She went over the whole conversation with Nessa the first day; she remembered what they had said about doing it up as bedsitters but not telling the landlord anything, it never did to tell landlords anything, just keep paying the rent and keep out of his way.

There was quite a bounce in her step now. I'm on my own in Dublin, she thought. I have my own place, I'm going out to find a life for myself now. She didn't have to worry about Pauline's morals anymore now. If Pauline wanted to bring home a rough-looking person with studs on his jacket, that was Pauline's business. She just lived in the flat next door. That's what Pauline had meant when she had said Nessa lived next door. And that's why Nessa went in for all this labeling and naming things. No wonder they had been slightly surprised when she kept asking them what they were doing in the evening; they must have thought she was mad.

Happy for the first time since Sunday, Jo did herself up. She put on eyeshadow and mascara, she put some color in her cheeks and wore her big earrings. She didn't know where she was going, but she decided that she would go out cheerfully now. She looked around her room and liked it much better. She would get some posters for the walls, she would even ask her mother if she could take some of the ornaments from home. The kitchen shelves at home were chock-a-block with ornaments; her mother would be glad to give some of them a new home. Humming happily, she set off.

She felt terrific as she swung along with her shoulderbag. She pitied her sisters, who were only finishing the late shift now at the hotel. She pitied the girls who still had to stay in a hostel, who hadn't been able to go out and find a place of their own. She felt sorry for Jacinta, who had to stay at home and whose mother and father interrogated her about where she went and what she did. She pitied people who had to share television sets. What if you wanted to look at one thing and they wanted to look at something else? How did you decide? She was so full of good spirits that she nearly walked past the pub where the notice said: "Tonight—the Great Gaels."

Imagine, the Great Gaels were there in person. In a pub. Cover charge £1. If she paid a pound she would see them close up. Up to now she had only seen them on television.

They had been at the Fleadh in Ennis once about four years ago, before they were famous. She had seen an advertisement, all right, saying that they would be in this pub, and now here she was outside it. Jo's heart beat fast. Was it a thing you could do on your own, go into a concert in a pub? Probably it was a thing people went to in groups; she might look odd. Maybe there'd be no place for just one person to sit. Maybe it would only be tables for groups.

But a great surge of courage came flooding over her. She was a young woman who lived in a flat on her own in Dublin, she had her own place and by the Lord, if she could do that, she could certainly go into a pub and hear the Great Gaels on her own. She pushed the door.

A man sat at the desk inside and gave her a cloakroom ticket and took her pound.

"Where do I go?" she almost whispered.

"For what?" he asked.

"You know, where exactly do I go?" she asked. It seemed like an ordinary pub to her, no stage, maybe the Great Gaels were upstairs.

The man assumed she was looking for the Ladies. "I think it's over there near the other door, yes, there it is beside the Gents." He pointed across the room.

Flushing a dark red she thanked him. In case he was still looking at her she thought she had better go to the Ladies. In the cloakroom she looked at her face. It had looked fine at home, back in her flat. In here it looked a bit dull, no character, no color. She put on much more makeup in the dim light and came out to find out where the concert would be held.

She saw two women sitting together. They looked safe enough to ask. They told her with an air of surprise that it would be in the pub, but not for about an hour.

"What do we do until then?" she asked.

They laughed. "I suppose you could consider having a drink—it is a pub after all," said one of them. They went back to their conversation. She felt very silly. She didn't want to leave and come back in case there was no readmittance. She wished she had brought a paper or a book. Everyone else seemed to be talking.

She sat for what seemed like a very long time. Twice the waiter asked her would she be having another drink as he cleaned around her glass of orange, which she was eking out. She didn't want to waste too much money; a pound already coming in was enough to spend.

Then people arrived and started to fix up microphones, and the crowd was bigger suddenly and she was squeezed toward the end of the seat, and she saw the Great Gaels having pints up at the bar just as if they were ordinary customers. Wasn't Dublin fantastic? You could go into a pub and sit and have a drink in the same place as the Great Gaels. They'd never believe her at home.

The lead singer of the Great Gaels was tapping the microphone and testing it by saying, *"a haon, a dhó a thrí."* Everyone laughed and settled down with full drinks.

"Come on, now, attention please, we don't want anyone with an empty glass now getting up and disturbing us," he said.

"Divil a fear of that," someone shouted.

"All right, look around you. If you see anyone who might be fidgety, fill up their glass for them."

Two men beside Jo looked at her glass disapprovingly. "What have you in there, miss?" one said.

"Orange, but it's fine, I won't get up and disturb them," she said, hating to be the center of attention.

"Large gin and orange for the lady," one man said.

"Oh, no," called Jo. "It's not gin—"

"Sorry. Large vodka and orange for the lady," he corrected.

"Right," said the waiter, eyeing her disapprovingly, Jo felt.

When it came she had her purse out.

"Nonsense, I bought you a drink," said the man.

"Oh, but you can't do that," she said.

He paid what seemed like a fortune for it; Jo looked into the glass nervously.

"It was very expensive, wasn't it?" she said.

"Well, that's the luck of the draw, you might have been a beer drinker." He smiled at her. He was very old, over thirty, and his friend was about the same.

Jo wished they hadn't bought the drink. She wasn't used to accepting drinks. Should she offer to buy the next round? Would they accept, or would they, worse still, buy her another? Perhaps she should just accept this one and move a bit away from them. But wasn't that awfully rude? Anyway, now with the Great Gaels about to begin, she wouldn't have to talk to them.

"Thank you very much indeed," she said, putting the orange into the large vodka. "That's very nice of you, and most generous."

"Not at all," said the man with the open-neck shirt.

"It'sh a pleashure," said the other man.

Then she realized that they were both very drunk.

The Great Gaels had started, but Jo couldn't enjoy them. She felt this should have been a great night, only twenty feet away from Ireland's most popular singers, in a nice, warm pub, and a free drink in her hand, what more could a girl want? But to her great embarrassment the man with the open-neck shirt had settled himself so that his arm was along the back of the seat behind her, and from time to time it would drop

354

round her shoulder. His friend was beating his feet to the music with such energy that a lot of his pint had already spilled on the floor.

Jo hoped fervently that they wouldn't make a scene, and that if they did nobody would think that they were with her. She had a horror of drunks ever since the time that her Uncle Jim had taken up the leg of lamb and thrown it into the fire because somebody crossed him when they had all been invited to a meal. The evening had broken up in a shambles and as they went home her father had spoken about drink being a good servant but a cruel master. Her father had said that Uncle Jim was two people, one drunk and one sober, and they were as unlike as you could find. Her father said that it was a mercy that Uncle Jim's weakness hadn't been noticeable in any of the rest of the family, and her mother had been very upset and said they had all thought Jim was cured.

Sometimes her sisters told her terrible things people had done in the hotel when they were drunk. Drunkenness was something frightening and unknown. And now she had managed to land herself in a corner with a drunk's arm around her.

The Great Gaels played encore after encore, and they only stopped at closing time. Jo had now received another large vodka and orange from the friend of the open-shirted man, and when she had tried to refuse, he had said, "You took one from Gerry what's wrong with my drink?"

She had been so alarmed by his attitude, she had rushed to drink it.

The Great Gaels were selling copies of their latest record, and autographing it as well. She would have loved to have bought it in some ways, to remind herself that she had been right beside them, but then it would have reminded her of Gerry and Christy, and the huge vodkas which were making her legs feel funny, and the awful fact that the evening was not over yet.

"I tried to buy you a drink to say thank you for all you bought me, but the bar man told me it's after closing time," she said nervously.

"It is now?" said Gerry. "Isn't that a bit of bad news."

"Imagine, the girl didn't get a chance to buy us a drink," said Christy.

"That's unfortunate," said Gerry.

"Most unfortunate," said Christy.

"Maybe I could meet you another night and buy you one?" She looked anxiously from one to another. "Would that be all right?"

"That would be quite all right, it would be excellent," said Gerry.

"But what would be more excellent," said Christy, "would be if you invited us home for a cup of coffee."

"Maybe the girl lives with her Mam and Dad," said Gerry.

"No, I live on my own," said Jo proudly and then could have bitten off her tongue.

"Well, now," Gerry brightened. "That would be a nice way to round off the evening."

"I don't have any more drink, though, I wouldn't have any beer—"

"That's all right, we have a little something to put in the coffee." Gerry was struggling into his coat.

"Are you far from here?" Christy was asking.

"Only about ten minutes' walk." Her voice was hardly above a whisper. Now that she had let them know that the coast was clear, she could think of not one way of stopping them. "It's a longish ten minutes, though," she said.

"That'll clear our heads, a nice walk," said Christy.

"Just what we need," said Gerry.

Would they rape her? she wondered. Would they assume that this was why she was inviting them back—so that she could have sexual intercourse with both of them? Probably. And then if she resisted they would say she was only leading them on and insist on having their way with her. Was she stark staring mad? She cleared her throat.

"It's only coffee, mind, that's all," she said in a schoolmistressy way.

"Sure, that's fine, that's what you said," Christy said. "I have a naggin of whiskey in my pocket. I told you."

They walked down the road. Jo was miserable. How had she got herself into this? She knew that she *could* turn to them in the brightly lit street and say, "I'm sorry, I've changed my mind, I have to

357

be up early tomorrow morning." She *could* say, "Oh, heavens, I forgot, my mother is coming tonight, I totally forgot, she wouldn't like me bringing people in when she's asleep." She *could* say that the landlord didn't let them have visitors. But she felt that it needed greater courage to say any of them than to plod on to whatever was going to happen.

Gerry and Christy were happy, they did little dance steps to some of the songs they sang, and made her join in a chorus of the last song the Great Gaels had sung. People looked at them on the street and smiled. Jo had never felt so wretched in her whole life.

At the door she asked them to hush. And they did in an exaggerated way, putting their fingers on their lips and saying "shush" to each other. She let them in and they went upstairs. Please, please God, may Nessa and Pauline not be in the kitchen. They never are any other night, let them not be there tonight.

They were both there. Nessa in a dressing gown, Pauline in a great black waterproof cape; she was coloring her hair apparently, and didn't want bits of the gold to fall on her clothes.

Jo smiled a stiff "good evening" and tried to manipulate the two men past the door.

"More lovely girls, more lovely girls," said Gerry delightedly. "You said you lived by yourself."

"I do," snapped Jo. "These are the girls from next door, we share a kitchen."

358

"I see," Pauline said in a huffed tone. "Down-graded."

Jo wasn't going to explain. If only she could get the two drunks into her own bed-sitter.

"What are you doing, is that a fancy-dress?" Christy asked Pauline.

"No, it's not a fancy-dress, wise guy, it's my nightdress—I always go to bed in a black sou'wester," Pauline said and everyone except Jo screeched with laughter.

"I was just going to make us some coffee," said Jo sharply, taking down three mugs with VISITOR painted on them. Gerry thought the mugs were the funniest thing he had ever seen.

"Why do you put visitor on them?" he asked Jo.

"I have no idea," Jo said. "Ask Nessa."

"So that you'll remember you're visitors and won't move in," Nessa said. They all found this very funny too.

"If you'd like to go into my bedroom—my flat, I mean—I'll follow with the coffees," Jo said.

"It's great fun here," said Christy and produced his small bottle from his hip pocket.

Nessa and Pauline got their mugs immediately. In no time they were all friends. Christy took out a bit of paper and wrote Christy and Gerry and they stuck the names to their mugs—so that they would feel part of the gang, he said. Jo felt the vodka and the heat and the stress had been too much for her. Unsteadily she got to her feet and staggered to the bathroom. She felt so weak af-

359

terward that she couldn't face the kitchen again. She went to the misery of her bed, and oblivion.

She felt terrible in the morning. She couldn't understand why people like Uncle Jim had wanted to drink. Drinking made other people ridiculous and made you feel sick, how could anyone like it? She remembered slowly, like a slow-motion film, the events of the night before and her cheeks reddened with shame. They would probably ask her to leave. Imagine coming home with two drunks, and then abandoning them in the kitchen while she had gone away to be sick. God knows who they were, those two men, Gerry and Christy. They might have been burglars even. . . . Jo sat up in bed. Or suppose when she had disappeared . . . suppose they had attacked Nessa and Pauline?

She leapt out of bed, uncaring about her headache and her stomach cramps, and burst out of her door. The kitchen was its usual tidy self: all the mugs washed and hanging back on their hooks. Trembling, she opened the doors of their bedrooms. Pauline's room was the same as ever— huge posters on the wall and a big long clothes rail, like you'd see in a shop that sold dresses, where Pauline hung all her gear. Nessa's room was neat as a pin, candlewick bedspread, chest of drawers, with photographs neatly arranged; little hanging bookshelf with about twenty paperbacks on it. No sign of rape or struggle in either room.

Jo looked at her watch; she was going to be late for work, the others had obviously gone ages ago.

360

But why had they left her no note? No explanation? Or a note asking her for an explanation?

Jo staggered to work, to the wrath that met her as she was forty minutes late. Jacinta said to her at one stage that she looked pretty ropy.

"Pretty ropy is exactly how I feel. I think I'm having my first hangover."

"Well for you," said Jacinta jealously. "I never get a chance to do anything that might give me even a small hangover."

She was dreading going home. Over and over she rehearsed her apologies. She would put it down to the drink. Or would that be worse? Would they find her even more awful if they thought she was so drunk last night she didn't know what she was doing? Would she say she had been introduced to them by a friend, so she thought they were respectable and when she found out they weren't it was too late? What would she say? Just that she was sorry.

Neither of them were there. She waited for ages but they didn't come in. She wrote out a note and left it on the kitchen table. "I'm very very sorry about last night. Please wake me when you come in and I will try to give you an explanation. Jo."

But nobody woke her, and when she did wake it was Saturday morning. Her note was still on the table. They hadn't bothered to wake her. She was so despicable they didn't even want to discuss it.

She made her morning cup of tea and stole back to bed. It was lunchtime before she realized that neither of them was in the flat. They mustn't have come home.

Jo had never felt so uneasy in her life. There must be a perfectly reasonable explanation. After all, there had been no arrangement to tell any of the others their movements. She had realized this on Thursday night. They all lived separate lives. But what could have happened that they had disappeared? Jo told herself that she was being ridiculous. Nessa lived in Waterford, or her family did, so she had probably gone home for the weekend. Pauline was from the country, too, somewhere. Well, she had to be, otherwise she wouldn't be in a flat. She'd probably gone home too.

It was just a coincidence that they had gone the same weekend. And just a coincidence that they had gone after the visit of the two drunks.

Jo stood up and sat down again. Of course they had to be at home with their families. What else was she imagining? Go on, spell it out, what do you fear, she said to herself, that those two innocent-looking eejits who had a bit too much to drink kidnapped two big strong girls like Pauline and Nessa? Come on! Yes, it was ridiculous, it was ludicrous. What did they do, hold them at gunpoint while they tidied up the flat and then pack them into a van and bear them off?

Jo had often been told she had a vivid imagination. This was an occasion when she could have done without it. But it wouldn't go away. She couldn't pull a curtain over the worries, the pictures that kept coming up of Christy hitting Nessa and of Gerry strangling Pauline, and all through her mind went the refrain, "There must be something wrong, otherwise they would have left me a note."

It was her fourth Saturday in Dublin. The first one she had spent unpacking her case and getting used to the hostel; the second one had been spent looking at flats which were too expensive and too far from work, and which had already been taken by other people; the third Saturday she had spent congratulating herself on having found Nessa and Pauline; and now on this, the fourth Saturday, Nessa and Pauline had most likely been brutally murdered and ravaged by two drunks that she had brought back to the flat. How could she explain it to anyone? "Well, you see, it was like this, sergeant. I had two double vodkas in the pub bought by these men, and then when we came home—oh yes, sergeant, I brought them home with me, why not? Well, when we came home they poured whisky into our coffees and before I knew where I was I had passed out in a stupor and when I woke up my flatmates were gone, and they never came back. They were never seen again."

Jo cried and cried. They *must* have gone home for the weekend. People did. She had read a big article in the paper not long ago about these fellows making a fortune driving people home in a minibus; apparently lots of country girls missed the fun at home at weekends. They must have gone off in a minibus. Please, please St. Jude, may they have gone in a minibus. If they went in a minibus, St. Jude, I'll never do anything bad for the rest of my life. More than that. More. If they're definitely safe and they went off yesterday in a minibus, St. Jude, I'll tell everyone about you. I'll put a notice in the two evening papers—and the three daily papers, too, if it weren't too dear. She would bring St. Jude's name into casual conversation with people and say that he was a great man in a crisis. She wouldn't actually describe the whole crisis in detail, of course. Oh, dear Lord, speak, speak, should she go to the guards? Should she report it or was she making the most ludicrous fuss over nothing? Would Pauline and Nessa be furious if the guards contacted their homes? God, suppose they'd gone off with fellows or something? Imagine, if the guards were calling on their families? She'd have the whole country alerted for nothing.

But if she didn't get the guards, suppose something had happened because of those drunk men she'd invited into the house, yes, she, Josephine Margaret Assumpta O'Brien had invited two drunk men into a house, not a week after that nun in the hostel had said that Dublin was a very wicked city, and now her two flatmates, innocent girls who had done nothing to entice these men in, were missing, with no trace of them whatsoever.

She had nothing to eat for the day. She walked around hugging herself, stopping when she heard the slightest sound in case it might be a key in the lock. When it was getting dark she remembered how they had written their names on bits of paper: they could have taken them away with them, but they might be in the rubbish bin. Yes, there they were, Christy and Gerry, scrawled on paper with bits of tape attached to it. Jo took them out with a fork in case they might still have fingerprints on them. She put them on the kitchen table and said a decade of the rosary beside them.

Outside people passed in the street going about the business of a Saturday night. Was it only last Saturday that she had gone to the pictures with Josie and Helen, those two nice girls in the hostel? Why hadn't she stayed there? It had been awful since she left, it had been frightening and worrying and getting worse every day until . . . until *this*.

There was nobody she could talk to. Suppose she phoned her sister in the hotel, Dymphna would be furious with her; the immediate reaction would be, come-home-at-once, what-are-you-doing-by-yourself-up-in-Dublin, everyone-knew-you-couldn't-cope. And it was a temptation to run away. What time was the evening train to Limerick? Or tomorrow morning? But she didn't want to go home, and she didn't want to talk to Dymphna and she couldn't explain the whole thing on the phone downstairs in the hall in case the people in the flat below heard—the people in the flat below! *That* was it!

She was halfway down the stairs when she paused. Suppose everything were all right, and suppose St. Jude had got them on a minibus, wouldn't Nessa and Pauline be furious if she had gone in and alarmed the three nurses downstairs? They had said that they kept themselves very much to themselves; the nurses were all right but it didn't do to get too involved with them. Yes, well, going in and telling them that you suspected Nessa and Pauline had been abducted and mal-treated was certainly getting involved.

She went back up the stairs. Was there anything that the nurses could do to help that she couldn't do? Answer: No.

Just at that moment the big blond nurse that she had spoken to came out. "Hey, I was just going to go up to you lot above."

"Oh, really, what's wrong?" Jo said.

"Nothing's wrong, nothing at all. We're having a party tonight, though, and we just wanted to say if any of you lot wanted to come, it starts at—well, when the pubs close."

"That's very nice of you. I don't think—"

"Well, all we wanted to say is, there may be a bit of noise, but you're very welcome. If you could bring a bottle it would be a help."

"A bottle?" asked Jo.

"Well, you don't have to, but a drop of wine would be a help." The nurse was about to walk past her up the stairs.

"Where are you going?" Jo asked, alarmed.

"I've just told you, to ask the others, the ones in the other flats, if they'd like to come."

"They're not there, they're not at home, they're gone away."

"Oh, well, all for the best, I suppose." The girl shrugged.

"I've got my meat and my manners now, can't say they weren't asked."

"Listen," Jo said urgently, "what's your name?"

"Phyllis," she said.

"Phyllis, listen to me, do the girls up here go away a lot?"

"What?"

"I mean, I'm new here, do they go home for the weekends or anything?"

"Search me. I hardly know them at all. I think the punk one's a bit odd, a half-wit, between ourselves."

"But do they go away at weekends, or what? Please, it's important."

"Honestly, I'd never notice, I'm on nights a lot of the time, I don't know where I am or whether people are coming or going. Sorry."

"Would the others know, in your flat?"

"I don't think so, why? Is anything wrong?"

"No, I expect not. It's just, well, I wasn't expecting them to go off and they, sort of, have. I was just wondering whether . . . you know, if everything's all right."

"Why wouldn't it be?"

"It's just that they were with some rather, well, unreliable people on Thursday, and—"

"They're lucky they were only with unreliable people on Thursday, I'm with unreliable people all the time! Maureen was meant to have hired

367

the glasses and she didn't, so we had to buy paper cups, which cost a fortune."

Jo started to go back upstairs.

"See you later then. What's your name?"

"Jo O'Brien."

"Okay, come on down when you hear the sounds."

"Thank you."

At twelve o'clock she was wider awake than she had ever been in the middle of the day; she thought she might as well go down as stay where she was. The noise was almost in the room with her. There was no question of sleep. She put on her black dress and her big earrings, then she took them off. Suppose her flatmates were in danger or dead? What was she doing dressing up and going to a party? It somehow wasn't so bad going to a party without dressing up. She put on her gray skirt and her dark gray sweater, and went downstairs.

She arrived at the same time as four others who had been beating on the hall door. Jo opened it and let them in.

"Which are you?" said one of the men.

"I'm from upstairs, really," Jo said.

"Right," said the man, "let's you and I go back upstairs. See you later," he laughed to the others.

"No, no, you can't do that, stop it," Jo shouted.

"It was a joke, silly," he said.

"She thought you meant it!" The others fell about laughing. Then the door of the downstairs flat opened and a blast of heat and noise came out. There were about forty people crammed into the rooms. Jo took one look and was about to scamper upstairs again, but it was too late and the door had banged behind her. Someone handed her a glass of warm wine. She saw Phyllis in the middle of it all, her blond hair tied in a top knot and wearing a very dazzling dress with bootlace straps. Jo felt foolish and shabby: she was jammed into a group of bright-faced, laughing people and she felt as gray as her jumper and skirt.

"Are you a nurse too?" a boy asked her.

"No, I work in the post office."

"Well, can you do anything about the telephones? Do you know there isn't a telephone between here and—"

"I don't give a damn about telephones," she said and pushed away from him. Nessa and Pauline were dead, battered by drunks, and here she was talking about telephones to some fool.

"I was only making conversation—piss off," he shouted at her, hurt.

Nobody heard him in the din.

"Which are your flatmates?" Jo asked Phyllis.

"The one in the kitchen, Maureen, and the one dancing with the man in the aran sweater, that's Mary."

"Thanks," said Jo. She went into the kitchen.

"Maureen," she said. The girl at the cooker looked up with an agonized face. "I wanted to ask you—"

"Burned to a crisp, both of them. Both of them burned to a bloody crisp."

"What?" said Jo.

"Two trays of sausages. 'Just put them in the oven, stop fussing,' Mary says. I put them in the oven. And now look, burned black. Jesus, do you know how much sausages are a pound, and there were five pounds altogether. I told her we should have fried them. Stink the place out, frying them, she said. Well, what will this do, I ask you?"

"Do you know the girls upstairs?" Jo persisted.

"No, but Phyllis said she asked them, they're not making trouble, are they? That's all we need."

"No, I'm one of them, that's not the problem."

"Thank God. What will I do with this?"

"Throw it out dish and all, I'd say, you'll never clean it."

"Yes, you're right. God, what a fiasco. What a mess."

"Listen, do you know the girls, the other ones, Nessa and Pauline?"

"Just to see. Why?"

"Do you know where they are?"

"What? Of course I don't. If they're here they're in the other room, I suppose, waiting to be fed, thinking there's some hot food. I'll *kill* Mary, I'll literally *kill* her, you know."

"Do they normally go away for the weekend?"

"God, love, I don't know whether they go up to the moon and back for the weekend. How would I know? There's one of them with a head like a lighthouse and another who goes round with that dynatape thing putting names on anything that stands still . . . bells and doors and things. I think they're all right. We never have many dealings with them. That's the best way in a house of flats, I always say."

Jo left it there. It seemed unlikely that Mary would know any more, and she decided to leave her happily with the man in the aran sweater until she was given the bad news about the sausages.

A hand caught her and suddenly she was dancing herself. The man was tall and had a nice smile.

"Where are you from, Limerick?"

"Not far out," she said, laughing. Then dread seized her again. What was she doing dancing with this stranger and chatting him up like she might have done at a dance at home? "I'm sorry," she said to him, "I'm sorry, I have to go. I've got something awful on my mind, I can't stay."

At that moment the window in the kitchen was broken by a big stone, and glass shattered everywhere. There were screams from the garden and shouts.

"I'm getting the guards, this looks like a bad fight," said the tall boy and like a flash he was out in the hall. Jo heard him speaking on the phone. In the kitchen people were shouting to each other to move carefully. A huge lump of glass lay precariously on top of a cupboard: it could fall any moment.

"Is anybody hurt? Stop screaming, is anybody cut?" Jo recognized Phyllis and felt a small amount of relief flood back into her. At least they were nurses; maybe a lot of them were. They'd be able to cope better than ordinary people. People had run out the front door and an almighty row was going on in the garden. Two men with cut heads were shouting that they only threw the stone in self-defense, people had started firing things at them from the window first; one of them was bleeding over his eye. They only picked up the stone to stop the barrage coming at them.

The guards were there very quickly, four of them. Suddenly everything was different; what had looked like a party began to look like something shameful. The room that had been full of smoke and drink and music and people dancing and people talking about nothing was now a room full of broken glass and upturned chairs and people shouting trying to explain what had happened, and people trying to comfort others, or get their coats and leave. Neighbors had come to protest and to stare: it was all different.

It didn't take long to work it out: the two men in the garden were crashers. They had tried to come in the front door and been refused admittance; they had then gone around to see if there was a back entrance. That was when the first one had been attacked with a hot weapon which had both burned and cut his face. Investigating the attack, the other one had been wounded in exactly the same way. (The weapons were, of course, Mary's burnt sausages.) They thought that everybody in the party was firing things at them so they threw one stone before leaving.

Notebooks were being put away. Phyllis said that one of the men needed a stitch, and she would go to the hospital with him, taking Mary as well, since Mary's arm had been cut by flying glass. The party was over. The guards said that too much noise was being made for a built-up area and, since two of the hostesses were disappearing to the hospital, there didn't seem to be any point in guests staying on in a flat which was now full of icy winds because of the window. Some of the men helped to pick the last bit of broken glass out, and a sheet of tin was found in the boot of somebody's car. It was a sorry end. The guards were leaving; one of them saw Jo sitting on the stairs.

"Are you all right for a lift home?" he asked.

Jo shook her head. "I don't need one. I live upstairs."

"You look a bit shook, are you all right?"

She nodded wordlessly.

"What a night, not much of a Saturday night in Dublin for a little country girl, is it?"

He was trying to cheer her up. It didn't work.

"Well, I'll be off, you go off, too, and get some sleep, you need it by the look of you."

She nodded again.

"You are all right, you're not in shock or anything? It's all over, it was only a broken window," he said soothingly. "There'll be worse than that before the night's over."

"Oh, God," she said.

373

"Hey, Sean," he called, "this one's going to faint, I think, give me a hand."

She came to as they were getting her in the door of the flat. She had had the key in her hand and it had fallen when she fell.

"Which is her room?" Sean said.

"How would I know?" said the one who was carrying her. "Here's the kitchen, get her in there."

She saw the names on the table.

"Don't touch those, they're evidence," she said. "Please don't touch them."

They decided they'd better all have a cup of tea.

"It's television, that's what it is," Mickey said.

"It's that and eating too much rich food late at night," said Sean.

"But how can you be sure they're all right?" Jo wasn't convinced.

"Because we're normal human beings," said Sean.

Jo flushed. "So am I. I'm normal, too, that's why I'm worried. I'm just concerned and worried about them. Stop making horrible jokes about my eating rich food and having nightmares. I haven't eaten anything, I'm so worried, and that is exactly why I didn't come to the Garda station because I knew that's the kind of reception I'd get."

She burst into tears and put her head down on the table.

"Mind the evidence," Sean giggled.

Mickey frowned at him. "Leave her alone, she

is worried. Listen here, those two will be back tomorrow night right as rain. Nobody abducts people like that, honestly. Nobody says please wash up all the mugs and tidy up your rooms and come on up the Dublin mountains to be abducted, now do they?" He smiled at her encouragingly.

"I suppose they wouldn't."

"And you are kind to be concerned, and we'll say no more about it tonight now because you're exhausted. Go to sleep and have a lie in tomorrow. Those two rossies will be home tomorrow night and you'll think you were mad crying your heart out over them. Do you hear me?"

"But I'm so stupid, I'm so hopeless. I can't cope with Dublin, I really can't. I thought I'd have a great time when I got a flat, but it's all so different, and so lonely, so terribly lonely, and when it isn't lonely it's like a nightmare—"

"Now, stop that," Mickey said firmly. "Stop it at once. You never talk about anyone but yourself, I this, I that. You're constantly wondering what people are thinking about you. They're not thinking about you at all."

"But I—"

"There you go again. I, I, I. You think that there's some kind of gallery of people watching you, sitting there as if they were at the pictures, watching you leave the house each day, all your movements, saying, is she having a good time, is she being a success in Dublin? Nobody gives one damn. Why don't you start thinking about other people?"

375

"But I am thinking about other people, I'm thinking about Nessa and Pauline—"

"Oh, no, you're not, you're only thinking about what *you* did to them, whether *you're* responsible for their kidnapping and disappearance, or whether they'll think *you're* silly."

Jo looked at him.

"So, lecture over. Go to sleep." He stood up. So did Sean.

"You're probably right," she said.

"He's always right, known for it," said Sean.

"Thank you very much indeed, it is a bit lonely at first, you get self-centered."

"I know, I felt a bit the same last year."

"Sligo?"

"Galway."

"Thank you very much again."

"Good-bye, Jo."

"Good-bye, Guard, thank you."

"Mickey," he said.

"Mickey," she said.

"And Sean," Sean said.

"And Sean," Jo said.

"And maybe some night you might come out with me," said Mickey.

"Or me, indeed?" said Sean.

"I saw her first, didn't I?" said Mickey.

"You did," said Jo. "Indeed you did."

"I'll wait a bit until the two lassies are back and installed, but I've a night off on Monday."

"You're sure they'll come back?"

"Maybe if I called for you about eight on Monday? How's that?"

"That's grand," said Jo. "That's grand altogether."

DECISION IN BELFIELD

She had been reading the Problem Pages for years. One or two of them always said things about having done grievous wrong in the eyes of God and now the only thing to do was to Make Restitution. Most of them said that your parents would be very understanding—you must go straightaway and tell them. You will be surprised, the Problem Pages said, at how much tolerance and understanding there will be, and how much support there is to be found at home.

Not in Pat's home. There would be no support there, no understanding. Pat's mother wasn't going to smile like people did in movies and say maybe it was all for the best and it would be nice to have another baby around the place, that she had missed the patter of tiny bootees. And Pat's father wasn't going to put his arm around her shoulder and take her for a long supportive walk on Dun Laoghaire pier. Pat knew all this very well, even though the Problem Pages told her she was wrong. But she knew it from personal experience. She knew that Mum and Dad would not be a bundle of support and two big rocks of strength. Because they hadn't been any of that five years ago when her elder sister Cathy had been pregnant.

There was no reason why their attitude should have changed as time went by.

Cathy had actually finished college when her little drama broke on the family. She had been twenty-two years old, earning her own living and in most ways living her own life. Cathy had believed the Problem Pages, she thought that Mum wouldn't go through the roof. Cathy had thought that there were ways you could talk to Mum and Dad like ordinary people. She had been wrong. Pat remembered as if it were yesterday the weekend of the announcement. It seemed to have gone on all weekend, Cathy saying she didn't want to marry Ian and Dad saying Ian must be brought around to the house this minute; Mum saying this was the result of trusting people to behave like adults and like responsible people; Cathy looking frightened and bewildered. She had said over and over that she thought people would be pleased.

Pat had been sixteen, and she had been shocked to the core. She had never heard words used like the words that were used that weekend. Dad had even apologized for some of the things he had called Cathy, and Mum had never stopped crying. Cathy had come and sat on her bed on the Sunday evening. "It's not the end of the world," she had said.

"Oh, but it is," Pat had said, almost afraid to look at Cathy in case she saw under her waist the whole dreadful shame that was going to cause such trouble.

"It's just that I can't see myself spending the rest of my life with Ian," Cathy had said. "We'd be ridiculous together, we wouldn't last a year. It's such a terrible way to start a marriage with anyone."

"But don't you love him?" Pat had asked. The only possible reason you could do the things that Cathy must have done with Ian to get herself to this stage must have been love.

"Oh, yes, in a way, I love him, but I'll love other people and so will he."

Pat had not understood, she had been no help. She had said useless things like maybe it wasn't really positive, the test, and maybe Ian might like to get married if Cathy explained it properly. Cathy had taken the whole thing very badly; she had refused to accept that Mum and Dad might have any right on their side. "They're so liberal, they *say* they're so liberal," she had scoffed. "They keep saying they're in favor of getting divorce introduced and they want contraceptives, and they want censorship abolished, but they refuse to face facts. They want me to marry a man knowing it will ruin my life and ruin his life, and probably wreck the baby's life as well. What kind of liberal view is that?"

"I think they believe that it would be the best start for the . . . er . . . the child," Pat had said uncertainly.

"Great start . . . forcing two people who should love the child most into a marriage they're not prepared for in a country which doesn't see fit to set up any system to help when the marriage breaks down."

"But you can't have people going into marriages knowing they can get out of them." Pat was very familiar with the argument from fourth-year debating clubs at school.

"Well, you certainly can't go into a marriage, a doubtful marriage, knowing you can't get out of it," Cathy had said.

She had gone to London five days later. Everyone else had been told that she was doing this wonderful new postgraduate course. It was a special qualification in EEC law; it was obviously the absolutely necessary qualification of the future. Mum had said that with all the changes that were going to come about from Brussels and Strasbourg and everything, Cathy was doing the right thing. Pat had known that Cathy would not come back. She knew that the family had broken up, and broken much more permanently than when Ethna had gone to be a nun. Ethna hadn't really left at all, even though she was in Australia: Cathy was only an hour away but she had gone forever.

Ethna had never been told why Cathy had gone to England. At Christmas the long letter with the small slanted writing had wanted to know all about the course that Cathy was doing and what her address was and what holidays she would get for the Christmas festivities. Nobody wrote and told Ethna that Cathy hadn't come home for Christmas. Perhaps Cathy had written, but it was certainly never mentioned in the weekly letters which came and went—every week a green Irish air letter on the hall table begun by Mum, where Dad and Pat added bits; and every week, but slightly out of synch, a blue air letter from Australia with details of Sister this who had done that and Sister that who had done this. And all of the time nothing from Cathy.

At about the time that Cathy's baby should be born Pat had asked Mum for the address. "I wanted to write and see if there was anything we could do."

"Oh, there's nothing any of *us* could do," Mum had said bitterly. "If there had been anything then we would have been glad to do it, but no, we knew nothing, your sister knew everything. So she knew best and went off on her own. No, I don't think there's anything *we* could do. I don't think it would be welcomed."

"But, Mum, it's your grandchild. Your own grandchild." Pat had been almost seventeen and full of outrage.

"Yes, and Ian's mother, Mrs. Kennedy, it's her first grandchild too. But are either of us being allowed the privilege of having a grandchild, and a baby we all want, and a christening, and a fuss, and the birthright of any child? No, no, a lot of claptrap about not wanting to settle down and not wanting to be tied down. I wonder does Miss Cathy ever ask herself where she would be if I had felt that way?" Mum had got very pink in the face about it.

"I'm sure she's very grateful to you, Mum."

"Oh, I'm sure she is, very sure. Yes, she must be. Fine life she'd have had if *she'd* have had been given away to an adoption society the moment she saw the light of day because I couldn't be tied down."

"But you were married already, Mum, and you did have Ethna."

"That's not the *point*" Mum had roared. And suddenly Pat had realized what had been said.

"Is Cathy giving the baby away, she can't be giving the baby away, can she?"

"I'm not permitted to know what she's doing. We're not in her confidence, your father and I, but I *assume* that's what she's doing. If she can't be 'tied down' to a perfectly reasonable, nice boy like Ian Kennedy, then it's very unlikely that she can be tied down to an illegitimate baby which she would have to rear on her own."

Pat had gone to the firm of solicitors where Ian Kennedy worked with his father. He was a nice, red-haired boy, about the friendliest of all Cathy's boyfriends; it was a pity she hadn't married him.

"I came to talk to you about Cathy," she had said.

"Yeah, great, how is she?" he had asked.

"I think she's fine." Pat had been nonplussed.

"Good, give her my love when you write, will you?"

"I don't have her address, and Mum is being difficult. You know, not being able to lay her hands on it."

"Oh, I don't know where she is now," Ian had said.

"Doesn't she keep in touch?" Pat had been shocked again.

"No, she said she didn't want to. Said she wanted to be free."

"But . . . ?"

"But what?"

"Doesn't she keep you informed . . . let you know . . . ?"

"Know what?"

Pat had paused. Now, it had been definitely said, definitely, about six months ago, that Ian had been told of her decision to go to England on account of the pregnancy. Yes, Ian had even been in the house. He had said to Dad that he was very happy indeed to acknowledge that he was responsible for the child, and to marry Cathy if she would have him. Pat knew that he had said he wanted to support the child, and to see it when it was born; he couldn't have forgotten about all that, could he?

"I'm sorry for being silly," Pat had said. "I'm the baby of the family and nobody tells me anything."

"Yes?" Ian had smiled kindly.

"But I thought she'd be having the, er, baby, now and I wanted to know how she was. . . . That's why I'm here."

"But didn't she tell you? She must have told you?" Ian's face was lined with concern.

"What? Told me what?"

"It was a false alarm—she wasn't pregnant at all."

"I don't believe you."

"Of course! Hey, you must know this. She wrote and told everyone just after she went to London."

"It's not true—"

"Of course it's true. She wrote and told us all. It was a very early test she had here, not a proper one."

"So why didn't she come back?"

"What?"

"If it was a false alarm why didn't she come back to her job and home and to you and everything?"

"Oh, Pat, you *know* all this . . . she was a bit peeved with your Mum and Dad. She thought there'd be more solidarity, I think. And she was very pissed off with me."

"Why was she pissed off with you? You said you'd marry her."

"But that's not what she wanted, she wanted . . . oh, I don't know . . . anyway, it wasn't necessary."

"So why isn't she back?"

"As I said, we all let her down. She was annoyed. She wrote, when she told me about the false alarm bit, and said she didn't feel like coming back. She must have written to your family too. Of course she did."

"She didn't," Pat had said definitely.

"But whyever not? Why didn't she put them out of their agony?"

"*Their* agony?"

"You know what I mean. It's an expression."

"She never wrote."

"Oh, Pat, nonsense, of course she did. Maybe they didn't tell you. You said yourself they kept things from you."

"They don't know it was a false alarm, I know that much."

She had said good-bye to Ian, and had promised she wouldn't make a lot of trouble for everyone, she'd be a good little girl.

"You're a real *enfant terrible*, you know. You're much too grown-up and pretty to be playing that Saint Trinian's kind of thing."

She had put out her tongue at him, and they had both laughed.

Mum had said she didn't want to discuss Cathy. Cathy had found nothing to discuss with her, why should she spend time talking about Cathy?

"But Ian says he heard from her as soon as she went. It was all a false alarm, she never had a baby, she was never pregnant at all. Aren't you pleased now, isn't that good news, Mum?" Pat had pleaded with her.

"That's as may be," Mum had said.

Just as she was dropping off to sleep that night,

Pat had thought of something that made her sit up again, wide awake.

Now she knew why Mum hadn't been pleased. Cathy must have had an abortion. That's why there was no baby, that's why Cathy had not come back. But why hadn't she told Ian? Or Mum? And mainly why hadn't she come back?

"Do you think the other nuns read Ethna's letters?" Pat had asked a few days later when the green aerogram was being sealed up and sent off.

"Very unlikely," Dad had said.

"It's not the dark ages. They don't censor their correspondence," Mum had said.

"Anyway, she can be fairly critical of some of the other nuns; she gives that Sister Kevin a hard time," Dad had said. "I don't expect she'd do that if they read her outgoing letters anyway."

Pat thought that it was nice that Dad read Ethna's letters so carefully that he knew which sister was which.

Pat had written to Ethna; first of all a probing letter. "I'm getting older and a bit, though not much, wiser. One of the things that upsets me is the cloak of silence that hangs over Cathy, and where she is in England and what she's doing and what the situation is. Could you tell me what the situation is as far as you know it and then I'll take it from there . . ."

She had a letter from Ethna, not on an aerogram but in an envelope. On the outside of the envelope

387

it said, "The Stamps You Wanted." That satisfied any curiosity Mum and Dad might have had. Inside it was very short.

"I really think you are making a mystery about nothing. Poor Cathy has been punished quite enough, she thought that she was indeed going to have a child. And since she was not at all willing or ready to marry the father then it is merciful that this was not so. She is happy in London, where she is doing social work. She has hardened her heart to Mother and Father, which is a great pity, but in time I am sure she will feel ready to open up doors of friendship again. She doesn't write to me, apart from that one letter which told me all these things; since nobody has ever mentioned anything to me about it in letters from home, I have never mentioned anything either. I pray for her, and I pray for all of you. Life is so short, it seems sad that any of it should be spent in feeling a grievance and a hurt when a hand held out would brush all the unhappiness away."

Great help, Pat had thought at the time; punished enough, hardened her heart, brush all the unhappiness away; nun's phrases, and not a word of blame about Mum and Dad, who were always writing letters to the paper protesting about letting South African rugby teams into the country. They were always talking about itinerants, and they had raised money for refugees. Why were they so hardhearted about Cathy?

Pat had decided that she was not going to allow Cathy to disappear without trace as if some terrible crime or shame had settled on the family and people hoped that by ignoring it things would return to normal. She had tackled them at supper the night she had got Ethna's letter.

"This family is becoming a bit like nine green bottles," she had said.

"What on earth do you mean?" Dad had smiled.

"First Ethna goes off to the other side of the world, and then we are four. Then six months ago Cathy disappears without trace and now we are three. Will I go off somewhere too?"

Dad had kept smiling, but he looked puzzled. He stood up to fetch the coffee percolator. He looked tired and a bit beaten. Not the cheerful doctor, always in a smart suit, always optimistic, always seeing the best for patients and neighbors alike. He wore his cardigan at home, and Mum wore an old jumper that was torn under the arms. They looked shabby and a bit disheveled as they sat in the big dining room with its good furniture and its expensive cut-glass decanters. Pat felt that somehow they didn't make any effort when it was only just her. She was sure they had been far more elegant and lively when Ethna was at home and when Cathy was there.

"Are you just waiting for me to go off and that will be the hat trick?"

"What is this, Pat, what silly game are you playing?" Mum had not been very amused.

"No, I mean it, Mum. It's not much of a family, is it?"

"Don't speak to your mother like that." Dad had been surprised and hurt. He had thought that talking about green bottles was going to be a joke; now it had turned into a row.

"It's not normal. People marry and have children, they don't have them just to export them off as fast as possible."

Mum had been very annoyed indeed. "Ethna was twenty-one when she left. She had wanted to join this order for two years. Do you think we wanted Ethna to go to that outlandish place? Or to be a nun at all? Don't be so ridiculous, and have some thought for other people before you start your hurtful accusations."

"No, I know that's Ethna, but then Cathy's gone. This house used to be full of people, now it's just us. And soon I suppose you'll want me to go. Would you prefer if I tried to get into UCC or Galway or maybe England rather than Belfield, then you wouldn't have to have me around the place and you could be all on your own?" She stood up, tears in her eyes.

"Apologize this minute to your mother, this minute, do you hear me!"

"Why to Mum? I'm saying it to both of you."

She was about to leave the room when Mum had said wearily, "Come back, Pat. Come back and I'll talk to you about Cathy."

"You owe her no explanation, Peggy, none, not after the way she's spoken to you." Dad's face had been red with disappointment.

"Sit down, Pat. Please." Grudgingly and shrugging, Pat had sat down.

"I'm not going to fight with you. I'm going to agree with you. It's not much of a family, it certainly isn't. When your father and I got married this is not what we had in mind at all."

"Now, Peg; now, Peg," Dad had said warningly.

"No, the girl is right to question what's happened. We question it ourselves, for God's sake. Not at all what we had in mind. I suppose we had in mind the practice getting bigger and going well. It has. That's all fine, that side of it. And we had in mind our friends and all the people we like being around, and that's gone well. And our health has been fine. But mainly what we had in mind was the three of you. That's what people do have in mind actually, Pat, that's what they have in mind most of the day and night when they have children. From the time that Ethna was here we've had you three in mind more than anything else."

Pat had given a very slight shrug. It was a disclaimer. It was meant to say, you don't have to tell me all this. I know you tried. As a shrug it worked. Mum had known what she meant.

"I know you think I'm just saying this to be nice to you, or maybe perhaps that we started out with good intentions and lost them on the way. But it wasn't like that. I think some of my best times, and yours, Hugh, were when Ethna was about six or seven, and Cathy was five, and you, Pat, were

391

a baby. Three little girls totally dependent on us, all lighting up with enthusiasm—"

"Sure, Mum. Yes. Sure."

"No, give me a very short minute for the sentimental sugary bit, because it didn't last long. Then, you were all so bright. This was another joy, some of our friends had problems. Well, we didn't call them problems but so and so's child couldn't read until he was seven, or someone couldn't settle at school, or another wouldn't manage to get on with the teachers, or failed the third Honors in her leaving. Not you three, from Ethna on we knew, top of the class, exams no real problem. Do you remember Ethna's conferring?"

"Yes . . . I got the day off school."

"And she looked so bright . . . that's a funny word, but she did, you know, clear eyes and alert face, compared to a lot of the others. I thought, ours is very bright, there's so much before her when she gets this ridiculous nunnish thing out of her system—"

"But I thought you approved?"

"We had to approve in the end." Dad had spoken for the first time. "Of course we didn't approve. Use your head, Pat, suppose you had brought up a lovely girl like Ethna, as bright as a button as Mum says, who has just got a first class honors degree in history and who wants to go with a crowd of half-educated women to a school in the outback of somewhere because she read a book about the damn place and she met a recruiting team!"

"But you never said. I don't remember—"

"You don't remember. How old were you-twelve, thirteen? What discussions could we have had with you about it that would have helped anything except add to the argument?"

Mum had interrupted. "We didn't even discuss it with Cathy because we didn't want gangs forming and pressure being put on Ethna. We just talked to her."

"And what did you want her to do?" Pat had wanted to know.

"I'd have liked her to do an M.A. and then a doctorate. She was very, very good. I spoke to some of the people in there, they said she had the makings of a scholar, and I'd have liked her to have had a good lively life here, instead of putting up with Sister Kevin's tantrums in a jungle." Dad had sounded very defeated when he said that, as if remembering the whole battle and how it was lost.

"Yes, that's what I'd have liked too. I'd have liked her to go on living here, it was so near and handy, and got a small car and had friends and gone off to the West for weekends. And then married someone in her own field, some professor, and got a house nearby and I could have seen the whole thing over again with her children, growing up and learning to walk . . ."

"It's a fairly normal, reasonable wish, isn't it?" Dad had asked defensively. "Rather than see a whole life, a whole education, and talent, thrown away."

393

"She's happy though, she says she is," Mum had said.

"I suppose her letters to us are about as near the truth as ours are to her," Dad had said. And there was a silence as they thought about the implications of that.

"So Cathy . . . ?" Pat had spoken softly, hoping that the mood hadn't been broken, that she could still get her mother to talk.

"Cathy," Mum had said.

"Cathy was no trouble either. Everyone else told us of all their sleepless nights over their terrible teenage children. We never had any." Dad smiled at Pat as if he was thanking her. She felt a twinge of guilt.

"And Cathy did have her friends around much more than Ethna, and they used to laugh, and they were full of life. Do you remember the summer they did the whole garden, Hugh?"

Dad had laughed. "All I had to do was provide one of those big cans of beer at the end of the day. They dug and they weeded and they cut hedges and grass."

"It never looked back since," Mum had said. "It used to be a wilderness and they tamed it."

"All for a few cans of beer," Dad had said. They stopped talking for a moment. Pat said nothing.

"So Cathy was going to be the one who might be with us, when Ethna went. It wasn't a transfer of love. I suppose it was changing the plans or hopes. And she was so enthusiastic, about everything."

"We felt we were qualifying with her, she was so entertaining about it all—the lectures, the course, the solicitors' exams down in the Four Courts, the apprenticeship—it was all so alive," Dad had said.

"And she seemed to get on so well with Ian. I kept thinking, she's only twenty-two, she's far too young to settle down, but then of course I told myself I was only twenty-two when I married. Then on the other hand, I didn't have a career to decide about. Then I went back to the first hand and said, since Ian and Cathy were both solicitors and Ian's father had a firm, well then, surely if they did have a couple of children and she wanted to work part-time it couldn't be too hard to arrange."

Dad had interrupted. "This is what your mother meant about you children always being in our minds. We had Cathy married to Ian in our minds long before they even kissed each other."

"But why couldn't you accept Cathy's decision like you did for Ethna? You didn't want Ethna to go off and be a nun but when she did you sort of acknowledged it."

"Yes," Mum had said. "Yes, it made her so happy and it was her life. Much as I wanted to I couldn't control it anymore . . . she had to do what she wanted."

"So why couldn't Cathy do what she wanted?"

"That was different."

"But why, Mum, why? It's not as if you and

Dad were prudes or anything, it's not as if your friends would cut you off, or as if you'd be ashamed to lift your heads. Why can't Cathy bring her baby home?"

"It's different," Dad had said.

"I can't think why, I really can't. Nobody minds. Ian doesn't mind. I talked to him. He's very casual about Cathy— 'send her my love' he said. Ethna won't mind. I wrote to her about it, but, but—"

"You wrote to Ethna?" Mum had said, surprised.

"Yes, to try to clear things up."

"And did it?"

"No, not at all."

"What did you want cleared up?" Dad had asked.

"Whether Cathy is having a baby or is not. Something very basic and simple like that, which most normal families would know."

Dad had looked at Mum, and she had said, "Tell her."

"The answer is . . . that we don't know." "You don't *know?*"

"No. That's the truth." Mum had continued, "We were very shocked by Cathy's attitude. She was very harshly critical of us, and the way we lived, and thought that our attitudes were hypocritical, you know, to preach some kind of broadmindedness and then not to follow it.

"But we didn't see it like that. You see, it was nothing to do with acceptance or reputations, we thought Cathy was being silly and making extravagant gestures, turning herself into a Protest just for the sake of it. 'Look at me, I'm too modern to do like anyone else, give my child a name and a home and a background, no, I'm far too sophisticated for that!' We didn't like it, Pat, it was too studenty.

"There's no need to go over all that was said, you probably heard most of it, but to cut a long story short we have only heard from Cathy once since she went to London. I always imply—well, let's be honest, I always tell people lies and say that we've heard from her, but she wrote only once two weeks after she left."

"Did she say . . . ?"

"She said that it had been a false alarm, that her dates had been wrong, that she was only a shorter time overdue than she thought and that everything was fine."

There was a silence.

"And did you believe her, Mum?"

"No."

"Did you, Dad?"

"No. I didn't."

"It was too far for there to be a mistake?"

"Well, she said she had left a specimen in Holles Street and they had said it was positive. They don't make mistakes."

"But she says they did."

"No, she's forgotten she told us that bit, I think."

"Oh."

"So we know no more than you do," Mum had said, spreading out her hands helplessly.

"But why do you say everything's all right . . . ?"

"Because it will be one way or another, sometime, and we don't want Cathy to have to walk back into a whole lot of complications. Keep it simple, is our motto."

"So what do you believe if you don't believe what Cathy said?"

"Well, what do you think?"

"No, what do you think?"

"Pat, either she had a termination or she is in fact having the child, and as you so rightly pointed out to me, if she is having the baby it's due this month."

"And we don't know?"

"We don't know."

"We don't even know where she is?"

"No."

Then Mum had started to cry, and she cried with her arms down on the table and her head on top of them. Right into the dishes and the food. And Dad had stood up and come over and patted her awkwardly on one side and Pat had patted her awkwardly on the other.

"It's all right, Peg," Dad had said, over and over.

"It's all right, Mum," Pat had said, over and over.

It had been a hard thing to sit your Leaving Certificate not knowing where your sister was, whether she was alive or dead, and not knowing if you were an aunt or not. But Pat had gone on and done it; she had got all her Honors and plenty of points. Peggy and Hugh's third daughter was on her way to University College, Dublin, registering as a student in Belfield.

Cathy wrote home that year just before Christmas. She said she had seen enough of other people's miseries in her caseload in London to make her realize that most of life's troubles were caused by families. She would like to say very sincerely that she had been entirely to blame for any little fracas they had had. She asked forgiveness and if they liked she would love to come home for Christmas, but since she had been so difficult and stayed out of touch for so long, over a year, she could well understand if they said no. She gave her address for them to reply. It was in Hackney. Mum and Dad had sent a telegram five minutes after the letter arrived. The telegram had read, "Welcome home, darling Cathy, to the silliest parents and the happiest Christmas ever."

Cathy had also written to Pat.

"You may well wonder what the Prodigal thinks she's up to, and I don't want to put your nose out of joint. I'll tell you everything you want to know, if you want to know anything, when I see you, and if you have no time for me I'll understand that too. It was utterly selfish of me to go away and leave you as a teenager, in your last year at school, to cope with all the trauma and drama.

But when there's a crisis people only think of themselves, or I did anyway. I hope the reunion won't be a damp squib. I haven't kept in touch with most of my friends, so can I ask you to fill the house a bit with people so that we don't become too hothouse and raise our family expectations too high? I'll stop asking and taking soon and start giving, I promise.

Pat had thought this was very sensible. She asked her college friends in on the evening that Cathy came back. Mum had gone to the airport to meet her and by the time Pat had come home conversation was quite normal. In fact, so normal it was almost frightening. It was as if Cathy had never gone away, as if no mystery hung over the events of the past year. Cathy had said that Pat looked smashing, and that students must be dressing better than in her day, and there wasn't time for much more conversation because they had to get the mulled wine ready, which involved a lot of conversation about what you did to mull it, and how to ensure you didn't boil the alcohol out of it. Pat had been startled to see that they were all laughing quite naturally in the kitchen when Dad had said he should test each batch they made, just in case the flavoring needed adjusting. "You haven't changed, Dad," Cathy had laughed, and nobody made any flicker of an eyelid as the moment passed and Cathy's long absence had now sunk into the collective memory. It could be mentioned without being questioned.

It had been like that all that Christmas, and

nothing seemed more natural at the end of the holiday than for Cathy to say that she would be coming back for good as soon as she had found a replacement for herself. She was going to work in Ian's office; they had a vacancy in a couple of months. Pat had been puzzled when she saw Cathy and Ian Kennedy strolling around the wintry wilderness of garden, plucking at bushes and pointing out what should be done with hard, frozen-looking flower beds. What was going on inside that red head of Ian Kennedy's? Did he not wonder whether Cathy had given birth to his child in London all by herself in a hospital with no friends to come and visit her? Did he not worry about his child, their child, being given to an adoption society and never knowing what it should have known?

Did Ian Kennedy wonder whether Cathy had gone long, long ago to a doctor in England in order to organize a termination of pregnancy and then overnight in one of those nursing homes everyone knew about, where simple minor surgery under anesthetic would ensure that Cathy and Ian's child didn't ever come into being? Surely he wasn't so foolish as to think that a girl could be pregnant, disappear for over a year, and have some vague belief that the pregnancy was all a false alarm.

People were really behaving more and more peculiarly, Pat decided. The older they got the vaguer they became. Ethna's letters now had nice bland welcoming bits about Cathy in them. Had she forgotten all that earlier stuff about punishment, and hardening her heart, and praying for her? Once people got any way settled they seemed to lose touch with reality and built themselves a comfortable little world, like a Wendy House, entirely of their own creation.

She had told this to Rory a few times, and he had tried to understand it. But Rory thought that her whole life was a fraud, and that anyone who owned any kind of private house was already out of touch with society. Rory was in her economics tutorial, by far the most brilliant student of his year, a great thorn in a lot of university flesh. Rory had economic arguments for revolution which could not be faulted. Rory agreed with Pat that the whole Cathy business was very unreal. Rory said he loved Pat, and Pat was very sure that she loved Rory.

"It's a mistake to get too involved with anyone your first year in college," Cathy had said. "It ties you down, you should have the freedom to roam around and see who you like and who you don't. You should get to know a lot of people, not just sticking together two by two as if you were the animals going into the ark." Pat didn't like this remark. It was too reminiscent of Cathy saying she couldn't be tied down to marry Ian. It also implied a criticism of Rory. And that was not allowed.

There was nothing that Mum and Dad could

find fault with in Rory; they wanted to, but they couldn't actually put a finger on anything. He certainly didn't distract her from her work; in fact he insisted that she work harder than she was prepared to. He said her essays weren't sufficiently researched; he lent her books, he came with her to the library and sat opposite her. It was easier to do the damn stuff than to find excuses. He didn't keep her out at all-night parties. He had explained to Mum and Dad that he didn't drink much so there wouldn't be any danger of drunken driving late at night in his little beat-up car. When they went away to conferences or student festivals in Cork or Galway, Rory always managed to drop the one phrase which would reassure Mum and Dad about the set-up. "I'll leave Pat at the girls' house first and then she can settle in and I'll go off and find where they're putting the lads up." Some trivial little remark which would prevent Mum and Dad from wondering what exactly the score was.

The score was exactly as Rory described it for a long time.

"I suppose you think it's silly not to," Pat had said.

"Silly, no. Wasteful, yes," Rory had said. "It's up to you entirely what you would like to do. I don't ever believe in putting on the pressure. Too much of what's wrong is wrong because people felt forced to do things for approval. But I think you're wrong. It would give us both so much pleasure and it would hurt exactly nobody. We aren't

403

betraying anyone, we can be sure that we aren't irresponsibly conceiving a child we don't want. So wasteful is all I think I'd say it was."

She adored Rory, his intensity and his boyish enthusiasms. She went to the family planning clinic. She knew the doctor who was on duty that day. It was a friend of her father's. "Glad to see you, that's a good sensible girl," the friend of Dad's had said. No explanations asked for, no curiosity, no condemnation. It was all so simple. Why hadn't Cathy done this? They had clinics, even in her time.

Cathy was still a mystery. There she was, living at home so calmly. If anyone ever asked about the Common Market legal course she was meant to have done, she would shake her head and say that she hadn't done it after all, she had worked for the council in East London. Mum had been right in her way to have kept things simple, to have rocked no boats. Cathy came back and stepped in more or less where she had got out. It was just that time, all those months that remained as inexplicable. What had she been doing, what had she been thinking? She was so placid now, sometimes going out to the theater with Ian, sometimes with other people. Holidaying with two girls in the Greek islands, sitting with Mum and Dad sometimes in the evenings looking at television.

Pat had insisted on Rory discussing it. "Is it natural for them not to mention it? Is it normal? I mean, there she is at home, and nobody ever once refers to the fact that she left home pregnant and

404

stayed away from home for fourteen months and came back and everything is as you were."

"Um." Rory was reading.

"But why, why do they say nothing? It's like not noticing someone is naked or not referring to someone being in a car crash or in jail. It's not real."

"Um. I know," he said.

"But they don't seem to want to know, it's only me, it's only me that wants to know."

"Well, why don't you ask her then?" Rory said.

"Cathy, did you have any problems with the Pill, you know, have you had to change brands or anything?"

Cathy looked up from the papers she was studying. She was sitting at the big desk in her bedroom, which she had converted into a kind of study.

"No, I was never on the Pill, so it didn't occur."

"Never on the Pill, at all?"

"No."

"How amazing."

"Pat, you are twenty, going on twenty-one. You aren't actually a wise old sociologist commenting on the funny things society does." Cathy laughed good-naturedly as she spoke.

"Yes, but . . . not ever?"

"Not ever. If I *had* been, that little incident which you may remember would never have happened."

"Yes, well, after the little incident . . . ?"

Pat felt she was treading on a minefield. She had to remain lighthearted and casual.

"Oh, after the little incident, I didn't—how shall I put it—well, I didn't actually need the services of a contraceptive."

"Not ever?"

"No, not ever." Cathy smiled, relaxed and calm as if they had been talking about the replanting of the herbaceous border.

"Oh."

"So I'm not much help. But you could go to the family planning clinic, tell them if it doesn't suit you. They'll change it."

"Yes, good idea. Cathy?"

"Yes?"

"Remember that time . . . the little incident. . . . What happened?"

"How do you mean, what happened?"

"I mean, did you go through with it? Did you have the baby?"

"Did I what?"

"Did you have the baby? In London?"

"Hey, what is this? A joke?"

"No, seriously. I wish you'd tell me. I hate us all pretending, it's so artificial."

"Tell you what?"

"When you went off to London, did you actually have the baby?"

"No, of course I didn't, are you feeling all right? What an extraordinary question to ask. Have a baby? Where is it, then, if I had it, was I meant to have left it in a telephone box?"

"Well, what did you do? Did you have an abortion?"

"Seriously, is this some kind of game? Of course I didn't. What on earth are you saying?"

"But you *were* pregnant."

"No, I thought I was. I wasn't."

"You were, Dad knows, he said so when you were gone."

"Oh no, he can't have, I wrote telling them it was a false alarm."

"He didn't believe you."

"Listen, don't start stirring up a lot of trouble over nothing. It was nothing. Why all this interrogation?"

"Is that what put you off the whole thing, fellows and making love?" Pat asked. "They say people can get very depressed."

"I *didn't* have an abortion, and I wasn't very heavily into fellows and making love, and I haven't gone off fellows."

"That's all you'll say."

"Jesus Lord, what is this, Pat, one of Rory's revolutionary tribunals? You've asked me about ten questions. I've answered all of them honestly— which is rather good of me since *none* of them are any of your business."

"I'm sorry."

"No, you're not, you want some awful group where everyone sits and tells the most god-awful, self-centered, boring details of what they did and what they thought and what they felt and what they did then, and what they thought then and what they felt then. . . . Honestly, I can't stand that kind of thing. Even Woody Allen laughs at it, for heaven's sake. It's not going to solve the world's problems."

"What is?"

"I don't know, but a lot of people's are solved by playing down dramas rather than creating them."

"And is that what you're doing?"

"I'm refusing to invent them, refusing to make myself into a tragedy queen."

"I'm sorry I spoke."

"I'm not, but I'm glad you've stopped." Cathy grinned.

Pat gave a watery grin back.

"So you see, she's *got* to be lying. Somewhere along the line she told a lie." Pat frowned as she ticked the items off on her fingers.

"There are times you can be very boring, Pat," said Rory.

She was hurt and upset. "You're often analyzing what people say and why society forces us to tell lies and role-play. Why is it boring when I do it?"

"Because it's repetitive and it's slapdash."

"How do you mean?"

"Well, you haven't even included all the possibilities, have you?"

"I *have.* Either she was not pregnant, or she was and she had either a baby or an abortion."

"She could have had a miscarriage, you clown."

All that had been a year ago. Pat remembered the conversation word for word. They had been all at the turning points of things somehow. The very next day, the day following the interrogation, Cathy said that she and Ian were going to get married. The news coincided with a letter from Ethna. She was leaving the order. And everyone might remember that she had spoken quite a lot of Father Fergus. Well, Fergus was in Rome at the moment and the laicization process was well under way. She and Fergus would be married in Rome during the summer. Then they would come home, possibly try to get a teaching job. It shouldn't be hard. Both of them had a lot of qualifications and a lot of experience.

"It's all working out as you want, isn't it, Mum?" Pat had said.

"It's what all you girls want that's important, you know that," Mum had said; she was laughing at herself a little, and she tried to take the triumphant look off her face.

That time had been a turning point for Pat too. Rory had told her about the South American woman, Cellina. Pat had liked Cellina; she had helped her to organize a solidarity campaign for fellow students back home, and she had introduced her to Rory. She had been pleased when Rory had liked Cellina. She had never seen exactly how much he had liked Cellina until he told her.

She had stopped taking the Pill. To use Cathy's marvelous, old-fashioned phrase, she felt she didn't need the services of a contraceptive. She did a lot of work on her thesis, and she did a great deal of work at home too. A family wedding for Cathy, with the Kennedys screaming their delight as loudly as Mum and Dad. Then there was the trip to Rome. Why not? If Ethna was doing something as huge as this they must all be there, and they were. Mother had Ethna back, and she had Cathy back.

But she was about to lose Pat. Temporarily perhaps, who could tell? Rory had come back from Bonn where he and Cellina had been living. He had come home alone. They had met a lot during the two weeks he was back. It seemed silly and wasteful not to go to bed with him. They were giving each other a lot of pleasure and they weren't hurting anyone, since Cellina would never know. And were they betraying anyone? The word betrayal is such a subjective one.

But now Rory had gone back to Bonn, and Holles Street, which is never wrong over such things, had said Positive. And Pat had learned enough over the years not to believe the Problem Pages. It would be best if she went to London, on her own. Connected with work. And the possibility of getting into the London School of Economics—yes, that would be a good one. She had often spoken of the LSE. Mum and Dad would be interested in that as a project.

And as long as she wrote regularly and seemed happy, that was the main thing.

410

MURMURS IN MONTROSE

Seven people woke up that morning and remembered that this was the day Gerry Moore came out of the nursing home. He wouldn't be cured, of course. You were never cured if you were an alcoholic. Four of them shrugged and thought perhaps he wasn't really an alcoholic—these things were so exaggerated nowadays. There was a time when a man took a drop too much, but now it was all endogynous, and in the glands, and in the bloodstream, and there were allergies and addictions that had never existed before. Two people knew very well that he was an alcoholic, and the remaining one, waking up that morning, looking forward to his release, had never believed for one moment that there was anything the matter with Gerry. He had gone into that home for a good rest, and that's all there was to it.

Gerry's mother was seventy-three, and there had never been any scandal in her life before and there wasn't going to be any. She had reared five boys on her own. Three of them were abroad now, all of them making a good living; only two were in Ireland, and of those Gerry was easily her favorite. A big innocent bear of a man without a screed of harm in him. He worked too hard, that was the problem; and in his job, Gerry had told her often, the best place to meet clients was in pubs. A grown man couldn't sit like a baby in a pub, drinking a pint of orange juice! Naturally a man had to drink with the people he talked to. They wouldn't trust him otherwise. His health had broken down from all the antisocial hours, that's what he had told her. He had to go into the nursing home for six weeks for a total rest. No one was to come to see him. He would be out in the first week of May, he had said. Now it was the beginning of May and he'd be home, as right as rain. That's if anyone could be as right as rain in the house his precious Emma ran for him. Stop. She mustn't say a word against Emma, everyone thought Emma was the greatest thing since sliced bread. Keep your own counsel about Emma. Even her son Jack had said that Emma was a walking saint. Jack! Who never noticed anyone . . .

Jack Moore woke up that morning with a leaden feeling in his chest. He couldn't identify it for a while. He went through the things that might cause it. No, he had no row going on with Mr. Power in the showrooms; no, he had no great bag of washing to take down to the launderette. No, there had been no bill from the garage for his car— and then he remembered. Gerry came home today. Insisted on taking a bus home in his own time, no, he didn't want anyone to collect him, didn't want to look like a wheelchair case. Anyway, he had to start taking control of his own life again. Jack knew that the visit to the nursing home was going to be a big talking point, a drama, a bit of glamour, just like losing his driving license had been. Gerry had held them spellbound with his story of the young guard asking him to blow into the bag. The jokes that Gerry had made had cracked a smile even in the Gardai. It hadn't done any good in the end, of course, he had been put off the roads for a year. Emma had taken twenty-five driving lessons in ten days: she had passed her test. She drove the car, remembering to take the keys out of it when she was going to leave both the car and Gerry at home. Emma was a saint, a pure saint. He hoped her children appreciated her.

Paul and Helen Moore woke up and remembered that this was the day that Daddy came home. They were a lot more silent at breakfast than usual. Their mother had to remind them of the good news. When they got back from school their Dad would be sitting at home as cured from his disease as he could hope to be. Their faces were solemn. But they should be cheerful, their mother told them, everything was going to be fine now. Dad had gone of his own choice into a place where they gave him tests and rest and therapy. Now he knew that drinking alcohol for him was like drinking poison, and he wouldn't do it. Paul Moore was fourteen. He had been going to go and play in his friend Andy's house after school, but that

413

wouldn't be a good idea now. Not if a cured father was coming back. He never asked his friends to play in their house. Well. It was only one day. Helen Moore was twelve; she wished that her mother didn't go on about things so much, with that kind of false, bright smile. It was better really to be like Father Vincent, who said that the Lord arranged things the way the Lord knew best. Father Vincent believed that the Lord thought it was best for Dad to be drunk most of the time. Or that's what it seemed that Father Vincent thought. He was never too definite about anything.

Father Vincent woke wishing that Gerry Moore had a face that was easier to read. He had been to see him six times during his cure. Gerry had ended up the most cheerful patient in the nursing home; he had nurses, nuns, and other patients agog with his stories of the people he had photographed; the adventures, the mistakes corrected just in time, the disasters miraculously averted. Alone with the priest, he had put on a serious face the way other people put on a raincoat, temporarily, not regarding it as anything to be worn in real life. Yes, Gerry had understood the nature of his illness, and wasn't it bad luck—a hell of a lot of other fellows could drink what he drank and get off scot free. But he would have to give it up. Heigh ho. But then the priest had heard him tell stories about photographing film stars on location, and meeting famous people face to face. Nowhere did he seem to remember that he hadn't done a book for four years, nor a proper commission for two. He had spent most of his time drinking with that friend of his from the TV station, the fellow who was apparently able to get his work finished by twelve noon and spend the rest of the day in Madigan's. A hard man, poor Gerry used to call him. Des the hard man. Father Vincent hoped that Des-the-hard-man would be some help when Gerry got out of all this. But he doubted it. Des didn't look like a pillar for anyone to lean on.

Des Kelly woke up at five o'clock as he always did. He slipped out of the bed so as not to wake Clare; he had become quite an expert at it over the years. He kept his clothes in a cupboard on the stairs so that he could dress in the bathroom without disturbing her. In half an hour he was washed, dressed, and had eaten his cornflakes; he took his coffee into his study and lit the first cigarette of the day. God, it was great that Gerry was being let out of that place at last, the poor divil would be glad to be out. He'd been up once to see him and he'd known half the crowd in the sitting room, or half-known them. Gerry wasn't well that day, so he'd scribbled a note to say he'd called. He'd felt so helpless, since his automatic response had been to leave a bottle of whiskey. Still, it was all over now, and no harm done. Pumped all the poison out of him they had, told him to lay off it for a bit longer, then go easy on it. Or that's what Des supposed they told him, that made sense anyway. If you got as reached by the stuff as poor old Gerry had been getting there over the last few months, it was wiser to call a halt for a bit. What he couldn't stand was all this sanctimonious claptrap about it being an illness. There was no fitter man in Dublin than Gerry Moore. He had been a bit unfortunate. But now he had time to take stock and get his career together, well, he'd be back on top in no time. That's if know-all Emma, you-name-it-I'm-a-specialist-in-it Emma, didn't take control of him and crush any bit of life that was left in him right out of him. Gerry would need to watch it: with a friend like that creeping Jesus Father Vincent, with a coffin-face of a brother like Jack and with know-all Emma for a wife, poor Gerry needed a couple of real friends. One of the few things he and Clare ever saw eye to eye about these days was what a mystery it was that a grand fellow like Gerry Moore had married that Emma. Des sighed at the puzzle of it all and opened his file; he always got his best work done at this time of the morning.

Emma woke up late. She had hardly slept during the night but had fallen into one of those heavy sleeps at dawn. She was sorry now that she hadn't got up at six o'clock when she was so restless; the extra three hours weren't worth it. She tumbled out of bed and went to the hand basin. She gave herself what her mother had called a lick and a promise. She smiled at the way she had accepted

416

the phrase for so long and never questioned it until today. Today of all days she was up late and examining her face in the mirror musing over what old childhood sayings might mean. She pulled on her pale blue sweater and jeans and ran downstairs. Paul and Helen looked at her as reproachfully as if she had handed them over to Dr. Barnardo's.

"We had to get our own breakfast," said Helen.

"You'll be late for work," said Paul.

"The place looks awful for Daddy coming home," said Helen.

With her lip well bitten in to stop her shouting at them, Emma managed a sort of smile. They had managed to spill water, cold and hot, all over the kitchen. God almighty, it's not that hard to fill an electric kettle and then to pour hot water into cups of instant coffee, is it? She didn't say it, she didn't ask the rhetorical question which would result in shrugging and counter-accusation. They had trailed coffee powder, buttered the sink as well as their bread, there was a line of crumbs from the toaster . . . calm, calm.

"Right, if you've had your breakfast, you head off, and we'll have a celebration supper tonight. Isn't it marvelous?" She looked brightly from one to another.

"Why didn't you get up in time, Mummy, if it's such a marvelous day?" Helen asked. Emma felt that she would like to slap her hard.

"I was awake most of the night and I fell into

417

one of those heavy sleeps just a short time ago. Come on now, hoosh, you should be gone."

"Will the celebration supper last long? Can I go over to Andy's afterward?"

"Yes!" snapped Emma. "When supper's over you can do what you like."

"Is Father Vincent coming to supper?" Helen asked.

"Heavens, no. I mean, who would have asked him, why do you think he might be here?" Emma sounded alarmed.

"Because he's often here when there's a crisis, isn't he?"

"But this isn't a crisis. This is the end of the crisis, Daddy is cured, I tell you, cured. All the awful things about his disease are gone, there's no need for Father Vincent to come and be helpful."

"You don't like Father Vincent much, do you?" said Helen.

"Of course I do, I like him very much, I don't know where you got that idea. It's just that he's not needed tonight." Emma was wiping and cleaning and scooping things into the sink as she spoke.

"Would you say you like Father Vincent less or more than you like Dad's friend Mr. Kelly?"

Emma put her hands on her hips. "Right, is there anything else you'd like to do before you go to school? Play I Spy? Maybe we could have a few games of charades as well or get out the Monopoly? Will you get yourselves—"

They laughed and ran off. She ate the crusts of their toast rinsed the cups and plates and ran from the kitchen into the sitting room. The children had been right, it was a mess. She took a deep breath and made a big decision. One hour would make all the difference. Please God, may she get someone who was understanding and nice, someone who realized that she wasn't a shirker.

"Hallo? Can you put me through to—" No, suddenly she hung up. It was bad enough having one in the family who let people down: she had never missed a day since she had got the secretarial job in Montrose, she was damned if she was going to miss even an hour today. She swept up the worst of the untidiness, shoving newspapers and magazines into the cupboard, gathering any remaining cups or glasses from last night. Gerry wasn't one to notice what a place looked like.

She threw out the worst of the flowers and changed the water in the vase; then she took out her Welcome Home card and wrote "from all of us with love." She propped it up beside the flowers, ran out pulling the door, leapt on her bicycle and headed for Montrose. Because she was a little later than usual there was more traffic, but she didn't mind, she thought of it as a contest. She would fight the cars and the traffic lights and the bits that were uphill. She would think about nice things, like how she had lost a stone and a half in two months, how she could fit into jeans again, how someone had really and truly thought

419

she was a young woman, not the forty-year-old mother of teenagers. She thought of the great suntan she would get in the summer; she thought that she might get highlights in her hair if it weren't too dear. She thought of everything in the world except her husband Gerry Moore.

Gerry Moore was going to be a great loss in the nursing home. The nurses all told him that and so did the patients. The doctor had his last chat with him that morning and said that in many ways he had been one of the most successful patients who had ever done the program because he had refused to let it depress him.

"You've been in such good form all the time, Gerry, you've actually helped other people. I must admit at the start I was less than convinced. I thought you were just marking time to get out and get at the stuff again."

"Wouldn't I have to be half mad to do that?" Gerry said. The doctor said nothing.

"I know, I know, a lot of the lads you get in here are half mad. But not me. Honestly, I know what I'm doing now. I just have to change my lifestyle, that's all. It can be done. I once had a lifestyle, a grand lifestyle, without drink. I'll have one again."

"You'll be in here lecturing to us yet," the doctor laughed.

Gerry had a dozen people to say good-bye to; he promised he'd come back to see them. "They all say that," people said, yet people believed that

Gerry Moore would, he had that sort of way with him.

Nurse Dillon said she was surprised that a man like Mr. Moore with so many friends of his own didn't want anyone to come and collect him. Gerry had put his arm around her shoulder as she walked him to the door.

"Listen here to me, I'm thinner, I'm much more handsome, I'm a sane man, not a madman. I'm a great fellow now compared to the way I was when I walked in—so don't you think I should go home my own route and let the world have a look at me?"

She waved at him all the way to the end of the avenue. He was a gorgeous man, Mr. Moore, and actually he was right, he did look fabulous now. You'd never think he was an old man of forty-five.

"Mind yourself as you go your own route," she called.

His own route. Now, where would that have taken him in the old days? Stop remembering, stop glorifying . . . a taste was only a taste, it wasn't anything special. He knew that. Stop glamourizing it all. These pubs, the ones he might have dropped into, they weren't welcoming corners where friends called him to join their circles; some of them were sordid and depressing. If ever he had got talking to anyone it had been a sour depressed man who might have looked at him with suspicion. It was only when he got back nearer home

421

that he would find people he knew in pubs. Friends. Stop glorifying it. It had *not* been a constant chorus of "There's Gerry, the very man, come on over here, Gerry, what'll you have?" No, it hadn't been like that. People had avoided him, for God's sake, in the last months. He knew that, he had faced it. People he had known for years. Boy, was it going to come as a shock to them when they saw him with his big glass of slimline tonic and a dash of angostura bitters, the nondrinkers' cocktail. Ho, they'd be surprised, never thought old Gerry Moore had it in him to change his life.

Gerry walked to the bus stop. He had a small overnight case. He hadn't needed much in the hospital, just his dressing gown and pajamas and a wash bag, really, a couple of books and that was it. Why had his suitcases always been so heavy in the old days? Oh, of course, booze in case he would ever be caught short, and gear for work. No more attention to booze ever again, but a lot of attention to work. He was looking forward to spending a good month sorting himself out and seeing where he was, then another month sending out mail shots offering specialized work. By midsummer he should be back where he had been, only better. A bus came and he got into it. Happily, he reached into his pocket and got out the money Emma had brought him. He hadn't wanted money but of course he had been admitted to that nursing home penniless; she had given him money for tipping and taxis or whatever he needed. He hated taking her money, he hated that more than anything.

He got off the bus in the city center. Other people were walking about normally, it seemed to him; they had no problems and big decisions. They looked vacantly into windows of shops, or screwed their eyes up against the sunlight to see whether the traffic lights were green or red. A few early tourists strolled, everyone else seemed to bustle a bit. He looked at them wonderingly; most of them would have no problems handling a few glasses of spirits, a few pints, a bottle of wine with their meal, yet a lot of them wouldn't even bother to. He saw with annoyance a couple of Pioneer Pins pass by; that total abstinence in order to make reparation to the Sacred Heart always annoyed him deeply. Nine tenths of these fellows didn't know what they were giving up. It was as if he said that he'd give up mangoes or passion fruit, something he'd never tasted. The Lord couldn't be all that pleased with such a sacrifice; the Lord, if he was there at all, must know that these Pioneers were a crowd of hypocritical show-offs. Easy, easy. Stop thinking about drink as some wonderful happiness creator. Don't imagine that a drink suddenly turns the world into an attractive technicolor. The world's fine now, isn't it? He didn't want a drink this moment, did he? No. Well then, what was the problem?

He caught the number ten with agility just as it was about to pull out. There right in front of him was Clare Kelly. "The lovely Clare . . . well, aren't I steeped?" he said with a mock gallant manner that played to the rest of the bus.

Clare was embarrassed and irritated to have run into him. Gerry could see that. She was a distant, cold sort of woman, he had always thought. Full of sarcasm and the witty answer. Gave poor Des a bloody awful time at home. Des had nothing to say to her these days, he had often told that to Gerry. He had said that he and Clare didn't actually talk, have real conversations; there was always a state of war, where one or the other was winning. Nobody could remember when the war had been declared but it was there, in private as well as in public, putting each other down. Not that there was much in public these days. Clare didn't have much time for her husband's friends. Des preferred it that way. Let her have her meetings and her own life, let her laugh and sneer with her own friends, mock and make little of people. That suited him fine. Gerry had been very sorry for Des, the best of fellows. No matter what things went wrong in his own life at least Emma didn't mock him.

Clare had moved over to make room for him. "You're looking marvelous," she said.

"Why wouldn't I, with all it cost?" he said, laughing. "Can I get your ticket? Two to—are you going home or are you off to reform the world somewhere?" He paused as the conductor waited.

"Home," she laughed at him. "You haven't

changed Gerry, they didn't knock the spirit out of you."

"No, only the spirits," he laughed happily, and handed her her ticket like you would give it to a child. "Here, take this in case we have a fight before we get home and you and I separate."

"Are you on your way home now from—you know?"

"Yes, just released. They gave me back my own clothes, a few quid to keep me going and the names and addresses of people who might take on an ex-con." He laughed, but stopped when he noticed that Clare wasn't laughing at all.

"Wouldn't you think Emma . . . ? It's awful to have you coming out on your own, like this."

"I wanted to. Emma said she'd come in the car after work, your Des said he'd come for me in a taxi, Brother Jack, the ray of sunshine, said he'd arrive and escort me home after work, Father Vincent said he would come with a pair of wings and a halo and spirit me home, but I wanted to come home on my own. You could understand that, couldn't you?"

"Oh, yes," said Clare, managing to get some lofty superiority into the two words.

"Well, how's everything been, out in the real world?"

"Quiet, a bit quieter without you." She didn't smile as she said it. She said it as though he were a dangerous influence, someone who had been upsetting people. There was ill-concealed regret that he was back in circulation. He smiled at her pleasantly as if he hadn't understood her tone. He had to be very calm, no point in becoming touchy, no seeing insults, fancying slights, imagining hostilities; no running away to hide because people were embarrassed about his treatment; no rushing out to console himself because the world didn't understand. Nice and easy.

"Ah, if that's the case we'll have to liven it up a bit. A quiet world is no use to God, man, or the devil, as they say." He left the subject and drew her attention to some demolition work they could see from the bus. "Hey, that reminds me," he said cheerfully, "did you hear the one about the Irish brickie who came in to this site looking for a job . . ."

Clare Kelly looked at him as he told the story. He looked slimmer and his eyes were clear. He was quite a handsome man in a way. Of course it had been years since she had seen him sober, so that made a difference. She wondered, as she had wondered many times, what people saw in him; he had no brain whatsoever. In between his ears he had sawdust.

She smiled politely at the end of the story, but it didn't matter to Gerry because the bus conductor and three people nearby had laughed loudly. And he was really telling the joke to them as much as to Clare.

He was pleased to see the flowers. That was very nice of Emma. He put his little case down in the sitting room and moved automatically to the cup-

426

board under the music center to pour himself a drink. He had his hand on the door when he remembered. God, how strong the old habits were. How ridiculous that in all those weeks in the hospital he never found himself automatically reaching for some alcohol, but now here at home. ... He remembered that nice young Nurse Dillon saying to him that he would find it hard to make the normal movements at home because he would be so accustomed to connecting them with drink. She had said that some people invented totally new things to do, like drinking Bovril when they came in to the house. Bovril? He had wrinkled his nose. Or Marmite, or any unfamiliar beverage, like hot chocolate. She had been very nice, that Nurse Dillon, regarded the whole thing as a bit of bad luck like getting measles; she had even given him a small Bovril last night and said that he might laugh, but it could well come in handy. He had said that he was such a strong character he would go to the drinks cupboard and pour the bottles down the sink. Nurse Dillon said that he might find his wife had already done that for him.

Gerry opened the doors. Inside there were six large bottles of red lemonade, six of slimline tonic, six of Coca-Cola. There was a bottle of lime cordial and a dozen cans of tomato juice. He blinked at them. It was a little high-handed of Emma to have poured away all his alcohol without so much as a by-your-leave. He felt a flush of annoyance creep up his neck. In fact it was bloody high-handed of her. What did all this business about trusting him, and relying on him, and not pressuring him, mean if she had poured his drink away? There had been the remains of a case of wine, and two bottles of whiskey there. Money to buy things didn't grow on trees.

Very, very upset he went out to the kitchen and put his hands on the sink deliberately to relax himself. He looked at the plug hole. Without a word of consultation she had poured about twenty pounds' worth of drink down there. Then his eye fell on a box in the corner of the kitchen, with a piece of writing paper taped to it. "Gerry. I took these out of the sitting room cupboard to make room for the other lot. Tell me where you want them put. E." His eyes filled with tears. He wiped his face with the back of his hand and sniffed as he struck the match to light the gas to boil the kettle to make his cup of Bovril.

Mrs. Moore had rung once or twice during the day, but there had been no reply. That Emma and her precious job. What was she, except a glorified typist? Just because she was in Montrose, just because she had sat at the same table as Gay Byrne in the coffee shop, and walked down a corridor with Mike Murphy, just because she had given Valerie McGovern a lift and had a long chat with Jim O'Neill from Radio Two, did that make her special? Oh, no, it didn't, just a clerk is all she was. And a clerk with a heart of stone. The girl had no feeling in her. Wouldn't any normal person have taken the day off to welcome her husband back from six weeks in hospital? But not Emma. The poor lad had to come back to an empty house.

"Ah, there you are, Gerry, how are you, are you feeling all right now, did you have a good rest?"

"Like a fighting cock, Mother, grand, grand altogether."

"And did they give you medicines, injections, did they look after you properly? I can't think why you didn't go to Vincent's. Isn't it beside you? And you have the Voluntary Health."

"Oh, I know, Mother, but they don't have the course there. I had the whole course, you know, and thank God it seems to have worked. But of course, you never know. You're never really sure."

"What do you mean you're not sure, you're all right! Didn't they have you in there for six weeks? Gerry? Do you hear me? If you don't feel all right, you should see someone else. Someone we know."

"No, Mother, I'm fine, really fine."

"So what did they tell you to do, rest more?"

"No, the contrary in fact, keep busy, keep active, tire myself out even."

"But wasn't that what had you in there, because you were tired out?"

"Don't you know as well as I do what had me in there? It was the drink."

His mother was silent.

"But it's all right now, I know what I was doing to myself and it's all over."

"A lot of nonsense they talk. Don't let them get you involved in their courses, Gerry. You're fine, there's nothing the matter with you, you can have a drink as well as the next man."

"You're not helping me, Mother, I know you mean well, but those are not the facts."

"Facts, facts . . . don't bother with *your* facts, with *their* facts up in that place. The fact is that your father drank as much as he liked every evening of his life and he lived to be seventy, Lord have mercy on him. He would have lived to be far more if he hadn't had that stroke."

"I know, Mother, I know, and you're very good to be so concerned, but believe me, I know best. I've been listening to them for six weeks. I can't touch drink anymore. It's labeled poison as far as I'm concerned. It's sad, but there it is."

"Oh, we'll see, we'll see. A lot of modern rubbish. Emma was explaining it to me. A lot of nonsense. People had more to do with their time when I was young than to be reading and writing these pamphlets about not eating butter and not smoking and not drinking. Wasn't life fine in the old days before all these new worries came to plague us, tell me, wasn't it?"

"It was, Mother, it was," said Gerry wearily.

It *had* been fine for a while. When Gerry and Emma got married he had a good career. There was a lot of money to be made from advertising in the sixties: one day it had been a bottle and an elegant glass, another it had been a consultation about photographing new banks, the sites, and personnel, the buildings. He had known all the agencies, there was no shortage of work. Emma had been so enthusiastic about his work— she had said it was much more vibrant and alive than her own. She had taught bookkeeping and accountancy for beginners in a technical school. She never called it a career; she had been delighted to leave it when Paul was expected, and she had never seemed to want to go back when Helen was off to school and out of the way, and that was a good seven years ago. Now that the bottom had fallen out of the market in advertising and there were no good photographic jobs left, Emma wasn't able to get back into teaching either. They didn't want people who had opted out for fifteen years, why should they? That's why she was up in the television station doing typing, and thinking herself lucky to get the job.

They had said in the nursing home it wasn't very helpful to look back too much on the past; it made you feel sorry for yourself, or wistful. Or else you began to realize what had happened was inevitable, and that wasn't a good idea either. You started to think you had no responsibility for your actions. So let's not think of the past, the old days when life was fine. He made the Bovril and took it, sniffing it suspiciously, into the sitting room. Hard not to think of the old days. A picture of their wedding in the silver frame, laughing and slim, both of them. His own father and both Emma's parents, now dead, smiled out more formally. His mother had looked confident, as if she knew she would be a long-liver.

Then the pictures of Paul and Helen, the series he had done; they looked magnificent, people said, on an alcove wall, a record of the seventies children growing up, turning into people before your eyes. But they had stopped turning into people photographically about five years ago. The children seemed stuck in a time warp of his making.

He looked back at the wedding picture and again he felt the prickling in his nose and eyes that he had felt when he read Emma's note in the kitchen. Poor girl, she was only a girl, she was only thirty-nine years old and she had been keeping four people for two years on a typist's salary. That's really what it boiled down to. Of course, there had been the old check coming in for him, the royalties from some of those coffee-table books; a little here for a print he'd taken from stock for someone's calendar, a little there for a permission to reprint. But he had cashed those checks and spent them himself. Emma had kept the family. God, he would make it up to her, he really would. He would make up every penny and every hour of worry and anxiety. He wiped his eyes again, he must be big and strong. Gerry Moore was home again, he was going to take over his family once more.

Emma hadn't liked to make a phone call while the office was quiet. It was too important a call, she couldn't suddenly hang up if she felt that people were listening to her. Anxiously she watched the clock, knowing that he must be home by now, wishing that she had done more to make the place welcoming, mentally ticking off the shopping she had done at lunchtime; she was going to make them a celebratory meal. She hoped he wasn't regretting his decision to come home alone; going back to an empty house, to a changed lifestyle after six weeks in a hospital, it wasn't such a good idea. To her great delight the office filled up with people and she was able to turn her back and call home.

"Hallo?" His voice sounded a little tentative and even snuffly, as if he had a cold.

"You're very welcome home, love," she said.

"You're great, Emma," he said.

"No, I'm not, but I'll be home in an hour and a half and I can't wait to see you. It's grand you're back."

"The place is great. Thank you for the flowers and the card."

"Wait till you see what we're going to have tonight—you'll think you're in a first-class hotel."

"I'm cured, you know that."

"Of course I do. You're very strong and you've got a terrific life ahead of you, we all have."

His voice definitely sounded as if he had a cold, but maybe he was crying—she wouldn't mention it in case it was crying and it upset him that she noticed.

"The kids will be in any minute, you'll have plenty of company."

"I'm fine, I'm fine. You're very good to ring. I thought you couldn't make calls there." She had told him that the organization expressly forbade private calls in or out. She had said this to stop him ringing when he was drunk.

"Oh, I sneaked one because today is special," she said.

"I'll soon have you out of that place, never fear," he said.

She remembered suddenly how much he hated her being the breadwinner.

"That's great," she said. "See you very soon." She hung up. He sounded grand. Please, please God may it be all right. There was a man at work who hadn't touched a drop in twenty years, he told her. A lovely man, great fun, very successful, and yet he said he was a desperate tearaway when he was a young fellow. Maybe Gerry would be like him. She must believe. She must have faith in him. Otherwise the cure wouldn't work.

Paul came home first. He shuffled a bit when he saw his father sitting reading the *Evening Press* in the big armchair. It wasn't just six weeks since he had seen such a scene, it was much longer; Dad hadn't been around much for ages.

He put down his books on the table.

"You're back, isn't that great?" he said.

Gerry stood up and went and put both hands on his son's shoulders. "Paul, will you forgive me?" he asked, looking straight into the boy's eyes.

Paul squirmed, and flushed. He had never been so embarrassed. What was Dad saying these awful corny lines for? It was worse than some awful old film on the television. Would he forgive him? It was yucky.

"Sure, Dad," he said, wriggling away from the hands. "Did you get the bus home?"

"No, seriously, I have been very anxious to say this to you for a few weeks, and I'm glad to have a chance before there's anyone else here."

"Dad, it doesn't matter. Aren't you fine now, isn't that all that counts?"

"No, of course it isn't. There's no point in having a son unless you can talk to him. I just want to say that for too long this house hasn't been my responsibility. I was like someone who ran away, but I'm back, and it will all be like it was when you were a baby and don't remember . . . but this time you're grown up."

"Yes," said Paul, bewildered.

"And if I make rules and regulations about homework and helping in the house, I'm not going to expect you to take them meekly. You can say to me, what kind of sod are you to be ordering us about, where were you when I needed you? I'll listen to you, Paul, and I'll answer. Together we'll make this a proper family."

"I wouldn't say things like that. I'm glad you're

home, Dad, and that it's cured, the illness bit, honestly."

"Good boy." His father took out a handkerchief and blew his nose. "You're a very good boy. Thank you."

Paul's heart sank. Poor old Dad wasn't in good shape at all, maybe his mind had gone in that place, talking all this sentimental crap, and tears in his eyes. Oh, shit, now he couldn't ask to go over to Andy's house. It would cause a major upheaval and maybe his father would burst into tears. God, wasn't it depressing.

Helen went into the presbytery on her way home in order to speak to Father Vincent.

"Is anything wrong?" The priest immediately assumed the worst.

"No, Mummy keeps saying there's no crisis, so it must all be fine, but I came to ask if you'd call in tonight on some excuse. If you could make up some reason why you had to call—"

"No, child, your father's coming home tonight, I don't want to intrude on the family, you'll all want to be together. Not tonight, I'll call in again sometime, maybe in a day or two."

"I think it would be better if you came in now, at the beginning, honestly."

The priest was anxious to do the best thing but didn't know what it was. "Tell me, Helen, what would I say, what would I do? Why would I be a help? If you could explain that to me then I would, of course."

Helen was thoughtful for a moment. "It's hard to say, Father Vincent, but I'm thinking of other times. Things were never so bad when you were there, they used to put on a bit of manners in front of you, you know, Mummy and Daddy, they wouldn't be fighting and saying awful things to each other."

"Yes, but I don't think—"

"It mightn't have looked great to you, but if you weren't there, Daddy would be drinking much more and saying awful things and Mummy would be shouting at him not to upset us."

The child looked very upset; Father Vincent spoke quickly. "I know, I know, and a lot of homes that sort of thing happens in. Don't think yours is the only one where a voice is raised, let me assure you. But you're forgetting one thing, Helen, your father is cured. Thank God he took this cure himself. It was very hard and the hardest bit was having to admit that he couldn't handle drink. He now has admitted this and he's fine, he's really fine. I've been to see him, you know, up in the home. I know he didn't want you children going there, but he's a new man, in fact he's the old man, his old self, and there won't be a thing to worry about."

"But he's still Daddy."

"Yes, but he's Daddy without drink. He's in grand form, you'll be delighted with him. No, I won't come in tonight, Helen, but I'll give a ring over the weekend and maybe call around for a few minutes."

Helen looked mutinous. "I thought priests were meant to help the community. That's what you always say when you come up to the school to talk to us."

"I am helping, by not poking my nose in. Believe me, I'm older than you are."

"That's the thing people say when they've no other argument," Helen said.

Emma cycled down the road and saw Helen moodily kicking a stone.

"Are you only coming home now?" she asked, annoyed that Helen hadn't been back to welcome Gerry earlier.

"I called in to see Father Vincent on the way," said Helen.

"What about?" Emma was alarmed.

"Private business, you're not to ask people what goes on between them and their confessor, it's the secrecy of the confessional."

"Sorry," said Emma. "He's not coming around here tonight by any awful chance, is he?"

Helen looked at her mother with a puzzled look. "No, he's not actually."

"Good, I want us to be on our own today. You run ahead and say hello to your father, I'll be in in a moment."

Unwillingly Helen walked on; as she turned in the gate she saw her mother take out a comb and mirror and pat her hair. How silly Mummy could be at times. What was she combing her hair for now? There was nobody at home to see her. You'd

438

think she'd have combed it when she was at work where she might meet people who'd be looking at her.

Gerry gave Helen a hug that nearly squeezed the breath out of her.

"You're very grown up, you know, a real teen-ager," he said.

"Oh, Dad, it isn't that long since you've seen me, it's only a few weeks. You sound like an old sailor coming back from months abroad."

"That's what I feel like, that's exactly the way I feel—how clever of you to spot it," he said.

Helen and Paul exchanged fairly alarmed glances. Then they heard Mum's bicycle clanking against the garage wall and everyone looked at the back door. She burst in through the scullery and into the kitchen. She looked flushed from riding the bicycle; she had a huge bag of groceries which she had taken from the basket. In her jeans and shirt she looked very young, Gerry thought.

They hugged each other in the kitchen, rocking backward and forward as if the children were not there, as if Gerry weren't holding a second mug of Bovril in his hand and as if Emma weren't holding the shopping in hers.

"Thank God, thank God," Gerry kept saying.

"You're back, you're back again," Emma said over and over.

Solemn-eyed, their children looked at them from the door into the hall. Their faces seemed to say that this was almost as bad as what they had been through before.

The telephone rang as they were having supper. Emma, her mouth full of prawns, said she'd get it.

"It's probably your mother, she said she'd ring."

"She has," said Gerry.

It was Jack. He had been kept late at the shop. Mr. Power had decided at the last moment that all the furniture in the showrooms should be shifted around so that the cleaners could get at the place from a different angle. Emma spent two and a half minutes listening to a diatribe against Mr. Power; she grunted and murmured soothingly. Then the tone of Jack's voice changed, it became conspiratorial.

"Is he home?" he whispered.

"Yes, thank God, he came home this afternoon. Looks as fit as a fiddle. We'll all have to go up there and be pampered, I tell you." She laughed and sounded lighthearted, hoping Jack would catch her mood.

"And is there—is there any sign of—?"

"Oh yes, very cheerful, and he sends you his good wishes—we're just having a welcome-home supper for him actually." Would Jack take this heavy hint, was there the remotest chance that he might realize he had rung at a mealtime?

"Is he listening to you, there in the room?"

"Yes, that's right."

"Well, I obviously can't talk now. I'll ring later, when he's asleep maybe."

"Why don't you ring in the morning, Jack, say, late morning. Saturday's a good day, we'll all be around then, and you could have a word with Gerry himself. Right?"

"I'm not sure if I'll be able to ring in the late morning."

"Well, sometime tomorrow." She looked back at Gerry and affectionately they both raised their eyes to the ceiling. "If only you'd get a phone, we could ring you. I hate you having to find the coins always for calls."

"There's no point in paying the rental for a telephone, and they charge you any figure that comes into their heads, I tell you, for the number of calls. No, I'm better to use the coin box, it's not far away. It's just that there's often a lot of kids around on a Saturday."

"Well, whenever you can, Jack."

"You're marvelous with him, marvelous. Not many women would be able to cope like you."

"That's right," she laughed. He was such a lonely figure she didn't like to choke him off too quickly. "And how are you keeping yourself?" she asked.

Jack told her at length: he told her that he had a bad neck which resulted from a draft that came through a door which Mr. Power insisted on being open. He told her that people weren't buying as much furniture as they used to, and that this craze for going to auctions and stripping things down

441

was ruining the trade. She motioned to Paul, who was nearest to her, to pass her plate. She was annoyed with Jack's timing and his insensitivity, but if she hung up she would feel guilty and she wanted to be able to relax tonight of all nights without another problem crowding her mind.

She looked over at the table as she let Jack ramble on; they all seemed to be getting on all right. Gerry looked great, he had lost weight too. The two of them were much more like their wedding photograph than they had ever been. His jaw was leaner, his eyes were bright, he was being endlessly patient with the kids, too, which was a lot more difficult than it sounded. Helen in particular was as prickly as a hedgehog, and Paul was restless. Jack seemed to be coming to an end. He would ring tomorrow and talk to Gerry, he hoped Gerry appreciated all that she did for him, going out and earning a living, keeping the family together. If only he had had sense long ago and not put so much at risk. "But it's all fine now," Emma said wearily. Jack agreed doubtfully and hung up.

"Was he repenting of my wicked life?" asked Gerry.

"A bit," Emma laughed. Gerry laughed, and after a moment the children laughed too. It was the nearest to normal living they had known for about four years.

Gerry spent Saturday in his study. It was a four-bedroom house and when they had bought it they had decided at once that the master bedroom should be his study. Other men rented offices, so it made sense that the big bedroom with the good light should be where Gerry worked. The little bathroom attached to the bedroom was turned into a darkroom. Once it had been a miracle of organization: a huge old-fashioned chest of drawers, a lovely piece of furniture, held all his up-to-date filing system. As efficient as any steel filing cabinet, only a hundred times more attractive. The lighting was good, the walls were hung with pictures; some of a single object, like his famous picture of a diamond; some were pictures that told a success story. Gerry receiving an award here, Gerry sharing a joke there. Then there was the huge, bulging desk, full recently of bills or handouts, or refusals or rubbish, making a mockery of the filing.

He had sighed when he saw it, but Emma had been beside him.

"Tell me what you want except a couple of black plastic sacks to get rid of the rubbish," she had said.

"And a bottle of Paddy to get rid of the pain of looking at it," he had said.

"You poor old divil, it's not that bad, is it?" she said lightly.

"No," he said, "I'm only being dramatic. I'll need a dozen plastic bags."

"Don't throw everything out," she said, alarmed.

"I'll throw a lot out, love. I have to start again from scratch, you know that."

"You did it once, you'll do it again," she said and went downstairs.

Gerry made himself four big, sweeping categories: Real Rubbish; Browsing Through Later Rubbish; For the Filing Cabinet; and Contacts for the New Life.

Almost everything seemed to fit into those; he was pleased with himself and even hummed as the marathon sorting work went on.

Emma heard him as she made the beds and she paused and remembered. Remembered what it used to be like; a cheerful, confident Gerry, whistling and humming in his study, then running lightly down the stairs and into his car, off to another job. In those days there was a big pad beside the phone where she put down the time the person called, their name, their business. She had always sounded so efficient and helpful; clients had often asked was she Mr. Moore's partner and she would laugh and say "a very permanent partner"—they had found that entertaining. For months, years, the phone had hardly rung for Gerry, except a call from Des Kelly or a complaint from his brother Jack, or a list of complaints about something from his mother. Should she dare to believe that things were ever going to be normal again? Was it tempting fate to believe that he might really stay off the drink and build his business up? She didn't know. She had nobody to ask, really. She couldn't go to Al-Anon and discuss it with other wives and families, because that somehow wasn't fair. It would be different if Gerry had joined Alcoholics Anonymous; then she would be able to join something that went hand in hand with it, but no. Gerry didn't want to go to some room every week and hear a lot of bores standing up and saying, "I'm Tadgh, I'm an alcoholic." No, the course was the modern way of dealing with things and he had done that and been cured.

She sighed; why was she blaming him? He had done it his way and he had done it. For six weeks in that home he had become stronger and more determined. For two days now at home he was managing. She must stop fearing and suspecting and dreading, dreading things like the first phone call from Des Kelly, the first row, the first disappointment. Would he have the strength to go on being sunny after all these?

Gerry had tucked three bags of Real Rubbish into the garage, all neatly tied at the neck. He insisted that Emma come up and admire what he had done. The room still looked very much of a shambles to her, but he seemed to see some order in it, so she enthused. He had found three checks as well—out of date, but they could be redated. They totaled over £200. He was very pleased with himself for finding them and said that it called for a dinner out.

"Are you sure they weren't reissued already? One's three years old." Emma wished she hadn't said it. It sounded grudging. She spoke on quickly.

"If they have been, so what? You're quite right, where will we go?"

He suggested a restaurant which was also a pub. She kept the smile on her face unchanged. There was going to be a lot of this kind of thing, she'd better learn to get used to it. Just because Gerry Moore had to cut alcohol out of his life, it seemed a vain hope that the rest of Ireland would decide to stop selling it, serving it, and advertising it.

"I'd love that," she said enthusiastically. "I'll wash my hair in honor of it."

Des Kelly rang a bit later.

"How are you, old son?" he asked.

"Ready for the Olympics," Gerry said proudly.

"Do they include a few jars of orange juice, or is that more than flesh and blood could stand?"

"Oh, this flesh and blood can stand anything, but not tonight—I'm taking Emma out to a slap-up meal to say thank you."

"Thank you?"

"For holding the fort and all while I was above in the place."

"Oh, yes, of course, of course."

"But tomorrow, Des, as usual. Twelve-thirty?"

"Great stuff. Are you sure you won't—"

"I'm sure, I'm sure. Tell me about yourself—what have you been doing?"

Des told him about a script which he had sweated blood on which was refused by a jumped-up person who knew nothing, and he told him about one that had gone well and got a few nice write-ups in the paper.

446

"Oh, yeah, I remember that, that was before I went in," Gerry said.

"Was it? Maybe it was. The time gets confused. Well, what else? The same as usual. I've missed you, old son, I really have. There's not much of a laugh around. I tried leaving Madigan's and I went to McCloskey's and I went down to the Baggot Street area for a bit, Waterloo House, Searson's, Mooney's, but there was no one to talk to. I'm glad you're out."

"So am I."

"Were they desperate to you in there?"

"Not at all, they were fine, it was up to me. If I didn't want to go along with any of it I didn't have to."

"Well, that's good."

"And you can relax, I'm not going to be producing leaflets at you and telling you that you should cut it down a bit." Gerry laughed as he said it. Des laughed, too, with some relief.

"Thanks be to God. See you tomorrow, old son, and enjoy the second-honeymoon night out."

Gerry wished that he had found checks for two thousand, not two hundred, then he would have taken Emma on a second honeymoon. Maybe when he got himself set up again he'd be able to do that. He'd think about it. It would be great to be out with a villa hired for two weeks in one of these places like Lanzarotte. There was a fellow in the nursing home who had bought a house there with a whole group of other Irish people, like a little complex of them out there. They made

447

their own fun, they brought out a ton of duty-free—well, forget that side of it, but there were marvelous beaches and great weather even in winter. He went back to his sorting. It was the section on contacts that was giving him most trouble. A lot of agencies seemed to have changed, merged with others, or gone out of business. A lot of new names. A lot of bad blood with some of the old names—work promised and not done, work done but not accepted. Jesus, it might be easier starting afresh in another country. Australia? This place was a village, what one knew at lunchtime everyone else knew at tea time. Still, nobody had said it was going to be easy.

Gerry was in very low form by the time it came to dress up for going out. The children were out of the house: Paul was with Andy as usual and Helen had gone to a tennis lesson. She had asked that morning at breakfast if the household budget would cover tennis lessons. She didn't really mind if it didn't, and she wasn't going to be a strain on people, but if the money was there she would like to join the group. Gerry had insisted she join, and said that he would get her a new racquet if she showed any promise. She had departed in high spirits and would stay and have tea with one of her friends who lived near the courts.

Emma was fixing her newly washed hair; she sat in a slip at the dressing table and watched Gerry come in. At first she had thought he might want them to go to bed. They hadn't made love last night, just lay side by side holding hands until he drifted off to sleep. This seemed like a good time. But no, that was the last thing on his mind, so she was glad he hadn't really attended to her slightly flirtatious remarks. It didn't seem so much of a rejection if he hadn't heard what she had said. His brow looked dark.

"It will be nice to go out, I'm really looking forward to it."

"Don't rub it in. I *know* you haven't been out for a long time," he said.

She bit back the aggrieved retort. "What will you have, do you think?" she said, searching desperately for some uncontroversial side to it all.

"How the hell do I know until I see the menu? I don't have radar eyes. I'm not inspired by the Holy Ghost to know what's going to be served."

She laughed. She felt like throwing the brush and every single thing on the dressing table at him. She felt like telling him what to do with his dinner invitation—an invitation she would have to pay for anyway until those out-of-date checks were cleared—if they ever were. She felt like saying the house had been a peaceful and better place while he was in the nursing home. But she managed to say, "I know. Deep down I'm just a glutton, I expect. Don't mind me."

He was shaving at the small hand basin in their bedroom. His eyes caught hers and he smiled. "You're too good for me."

"No, I'm not, I'm what you deserve," she said lightly.

In the car he took her hand.

"Sorry," he said.

"Don't mind about it," she said.

"The night just seemed hard ahead of us, no wine with the dinner and all."

"I know," she said sympathetically.

"But you're to have wine, you must, otherwise the whole thing's a nonsense."

"You know I don't mind one way or the other. You know I can easily have a Perrier water."

"Part of the fact of being cured is not to mind other people. It was just that I got a bit low there, inside, in the house, I don't know. I'm fine now."

"Of course you are, and I'll certainly have a glass or two if it doesn't annoy you." She put the key into the ignition and drove off.

Technically he was allowed to drive again now, but he hadn't reapplied, or whatever you were meant to do. And in the last few months he wouldn't have been able to drive. She had offered him the keys as they came to the car and he had shaken his head.

In the bar, as they looked at their menus, they met a couple they hadn't seen for a while. Emma saw the wife nudge her husband and point over at them. After what looked a careful scrutiny he came over.

"Gerry Moore, I haven't seen you looking so respectable for years. And Emma . . ." They greeted him with little jokes and little laughs; both

450

of them patted their flatter stomachs while the man said they must have been at a health farm, they looked so well. Emma said she owed hers to her bicycle and Gerry said that, alas, he owed his to laying off the booze. It was like the first hurdle in an obstacle race. Emma knew from the whispers between the couple that there would be many more. The news would get around, people would come to inspect, to see if it was true. Gerry Moore, that poor old soak, back to his former self, you never saw anything like it, doesn't touch a drop now, made a fortune last year, back on top as a photographer, you never saw anything like him and the wife. Please. Please, God. Please let it happen.

Father Vincent called around on Saturday night and knocked for a long time at the door. The car was gone, Emma's bicycle was there, and there was no reply. He assumed they must all be out at some family gathering. But that child had seemed so white and worried, he hoped that Gerry hadn't broken out immediately and been taken back into the home. He debated with himself for a long time about whether to leave a note or not. In the end he decided against it. Suppose poor Gerry had broken out and been taken back in, it would be a sick sort of thing to leave a welcome home card. Father Vincent wished, as he often did, that he had second sight.

Paul came home from Andy's and turned on the television. Helen came in shortly afterward;

they sat with peanut-butter sandwiches and glasses of milk and watched happily. They heard voices, and a key turn in the lock.

"Oh, Lord," said Paul, "I'd forgotten *he* was back, pick up the glass, Helen, give me those plates. We're meant to be running a tidy ship here!" Helen laughed at the imitation of her father's voice, but she looked out into the hall anxiously to make sure that Daddy wasn't drunk.

It was very expensive having Gerry home. Emma realized this, but couldn't quite think why. She realized that he wasn't spending any money on drink; apart from that one Saturday night out they didn't entertain people. Gerry bought no clothes or household things. Why then was her money not stretching as far as it used to? A lot of it might be on stationery and stamps. Gerry was as good as his word about writing to people with ideas—just bright, cheery letters which said, without having to spell it out, I'm back, I'm cured, and I'm still a great photographer. Then he liked to cook new things, things that he wouldn't associate with alcohol. Together they had spent a great deal of money on curry ingredients, but then he had tired of it, and said it wasn't worth all the trouble—they could slip out and buy a good curry if they needed one. She didn't grudge it, but she had been so used to accounting for every penny carefully, putting this little bit there toward the electricity, this toward the gas, and that toward the phone. She didn't know what she was going to do when the next bills came in. And talking of bills, what the phone bill was going to be like made her feel weak around the legs.

Gerry had been talking to somebody in Limerick for nearly fifteen minutes one night, and he mentioned calls to Manchester and London. She had said nothing; she just prayed that the rewards and results of all these phone calls might be felt by the time the telephone bill came in.

Gerry's mother thought that he wasn't himself at all since he came out of that place. He had gone up to see her and the visit was not a success. She had bought a naggin of whiskey for him specially. It was in the glass-fronted cupboard there beside the china dogs. Ah, go on, surely one wouldn't do him any harm.

"No, Mother. That's the whole point. I've got something wrong with my insides, it turns to poison in me. I told you this. Emma explained—"

"Huh, Emma. High-brow talk. Allergy addiction. I'm sick of it."

"Yes, Mother, so am I"—Gerry's patience was ebbing— "but it happens to be true."

"Look, have just the one and we'll quit fighting," his mother had said.

"It would be easy for me to say Thank you, Mother, to hold it here in my fist and when you weren't looking to throw it away. But I can't do that. I can't bloody do it. Can you have the wit of a half-wit and understand that?"

"There's no need to shout at me, I've quite

enough to put up with," his mother had said, and then she had started to cry.

"Listen, Mother, give me the bottle you so kindly bought for me. I'll give it to Father Vincent for his sale of work, he can use it on the tombola or something. Then it won't be wasted."

"I will not. If I bought whiskey it will be there to offer to someone who has the manners to take it."

No other subject managed to bring them onto the same plane. Gerry left, and hoped that nobody who lived on earth had such a poor relationship with a parent as he had. That was the day that he went home and found Paul fighting with Emma in the kitchen. They hadn't heard him come in.

"But *why*, if you could tell me *why* I might do it. He's not an invalid, he's not soft in the head, so why does he want to play happy families sitting down to supper together every night? If I go over to Andy's after supper it's too late, then the evening's spoiled."

"Ask Andy here."

"No fear."

Gerry came in and looked at them, first one and then another.

"Please spend the evening with your friend tonight, Paul. Emma, can I have a word with you in my study when you're ready?"

He walked on upstairs. He heard Helen, giggling nervously.

"That's just the voice that Reverend Mother

454

uses when she's going to expel someone," she said, stifling her laughs.

"The boy is right. I am not soft in the head. I get weary of all these family meals, if you must know."

"I thought with my being out all day and you getting back into a routine—"

"You thought, you thought, you thought—what else is it in this house except what you think?"

She looked at him in disbelief.

"I mean it, Emma, morning, noon, and night . . ."

Two large tears fell down her face and two more were on the way down like raindrops on a window. She didn't even brush them aside; she didn't try to deny it, to reason with him, or to agree with him. She just looked beaten.

"Well, say something, Emma. If you don't agree with me say something."

"What is there to say?" she sobbed. "I love you so much and everything I do seems to hurt you. God Almighty, how can I do what will please you? I'm obviously doing all the wrong things."

He put his arms around her and stroked her hair. "Stop, stop," he said. She cried into his chest.

"You're very good. I'm really a shit, a terrible shit." She made a muffled denial into his shirt.

"And I love you, too, and need you . . ."

She looked up at him with a tear-stained face. "Do you?"

"Of course," he said.

Downstairs, Helen said, "They've gone into the bedroom, isn't that odd?"

Paul said, "He can't be going to expel her then."

Helen said, "What do you think they're doing?"

Paul laughed knowingly. "I'll give you one guess," he said.

Helen was horrified. "They can't be. They're much too old."

Paul said, "Why else have they closed the door?"

"God, that's awful, that's all we need."

Father Vincent called just then. Helen was so embarrassed when she recognized his shape through the door that she ran back for Paul.

"I can't tell him what we think," she said. "You couldn't tell a priest something like that."

Paul let him in. "Mum and Dad are upstairs at the moment, having a bit of a lie down. If you don't mind, Father, I won't disturb them."

"Of course, of course." Father Vincent looked confused. "But can I get you a cup of tea, coffee?" The priest said he didn't want to be any trouble.

"A drink?"

"No, no, heavens, no."

"We have drink. Dad insists it be kept there for visitors."

Father Vincent stayed for about ten minutes with no drink and hardly any conversation. When he was at the porch again, he looked timidly at the stairs. "If your father has taken a turn for the worse and your mother wants any help, she only has to call on me." Paul said that he didn't think Mother wanted any help just now, and when the door was safely closed he and Helen rolled around the sitting room floor laughing at the idea of leading Father Vincent upstairs, knocking on the bedroom door and calling out that Father Vincent wanted to know if Mother wanted any help or could manage on her own.

Gerry and Emma lay in their big bed and Gerry said, "It's been so long, I was afraid to, I was afraid, in case. . . ." Emma said, "You were lovely, as you were always lovely." She lay counting the days since her last period; she was safe, she had to be safe. The very notion of becoming pregnant, now, was too much to contemplate. She had stopped taking the Pill two years ago. It was said to have some side effects and women were warned not to stay on it forever. And what on earth had been the point of taking the Pill when there was simply no risk of becoming pregnant?

Jack was sorry that Gerry was back. It sort of put a stop to his Monday visits. He used to visit Gerry at the nursing home on a Sunday, and then took the bus to their house on a Monday night after work to report on what he saw, what he said, what was said back to him, and what he thought. The first couple of times they had been eager to know what he reported because they still hadn't got used to life without Gerry. Then, after that, it had become a little ritual. Emma used to cook a nice meal, and then they would all wash up. Jack would sit down in the comfort of a nice big sitting room, not his own cramped little bed-sitter. They used to watch television, while Emma sometimes did mending; the television set was turned low so as not to disturb the two children, who did homework. All through April and May Jack had been involved in their life. There was no excuse for him to come anymore.

He had liked those evenings sitting there with Emma; she had been so nice and interested in everything he had been doing at work. It was so cozy. Gerry must have been a madman, stark staring mad to throw away all his money and his good living and spend time drinking with a crowd of eejits. You wouldn't mind a man who had nothing at home, but a man who had Emma. It was past understanding.

It seemed a very long summer for everyone. Father Vincent spent a lot of time wondering what he had done to offend the Moores; every time he went there those two young children, who had seemed nice and normal at one stage, were exceedingly silly with giggles. Gerry wanted to hear no inspiring tales of how others triumphed, he had said curtly, and Emma was too busy to say more than the time of day. She had taken some home typing and had rung him once to inquire whether there was any parish work to be done on a professional basis. He had said they would always be glad of some voluntary help, but she had said

458

sorry, that she was not yet in a position to be able to offer that.

Mrs. Moore thought that Gerry had become short-tempered and intolerant. Her grandchildren never came near her, and that Emma seemed to be too busy even to talk to her on the telephone.

Paul fell in love with Andy's sister, but Andy's whole family, sister and all, went to Greece for a month. If Paul had two hundred pounds he could have gone out to visit them. His Dad had said he could bloody earn it if he wanted it, and his Mum had said he must be a selfish little rat to think that money like that was available for a holiday for him.

Helen was very bored and very worried. She had become very ugly suddenly, she thought, after years of looking quite reasonable; now, when it was important, she had become revolting looking. In books people's mothers helped them when this kind of thing happened, lent them make-up and bought them dresses. In real life her Mum told her to stop sniveling, there would be time enough for that later.

Des felt the summer was long too. He had nothing but admiration for Gerry—he sat there with the best of them, bought his round like any man, but it wasn't the same. Des could never relax like he had, he couldn't get it out of his head that he was waiting for Gerry to start, to catch up on the rest of them. It was restless drinking with him. God damn it, Gerry was very extreme; when he was going on that batter he was a fierce drinker, got them barred from several places, but now that he'd had a fright, instead of taking it nice and easy like any normal person and just watching it, here he was like a bloody Pioneer, sitting there with a glass of lime and soda or whatever he drank nowadays.

Gerry found the summer slow. He found the replies to his letters even slower, and the offers of any work were the slowest of all. How could the whole photography world have collapsed without his noticing it? There must be people getting work; he saw their pictures in the advertisements, on the television, in the magazines. "Maybe," Emma had said, "maybe you should show them what you can do *now*, rather than old portfolios, maybe you should get a collection for another book together?" But did Emma have a clue of any sort how long it took to put a book together? You didn't go out with a camera and snap one hundred fifty things and mark them pages one to one hundred and fifty. There was a theme, there was an interest, there was a commission: a lot of the pictures had been done and paid for already in somebody else's time. Oh, it was all so slow getting back, and it had seemed so very fast, the fall down the ladder. Or was he just being melodramatic?

Emma realized one day during that endless summer that she had no friend. Not no friends but not even one friend. There was nobody she could talk to about Gerry. There never had been.

Her mother had thought he was a little too flash for her and her father had wondered about security. But no matter who had asked her to marry them her mother would have seen flashness and her father suspected insecurity all around him. She never talked to her sister about anything except her sister's five children, all of whom seemed to be doing spectacularly well in exams at any given season of the year. She couldn't talk to her mother-in-law, she certainly couldn't talk to that Des Kelly, who always looked at her as if she were a particularly dangerous kind of snake. Poor Jack was so kind and anxious to help, but really the man was so limited, he couldn't have a serious conversation about Gerry's future to save his life. She had formed an unreasonable dislike of Father Vincent, who used to be quite a friend of theirs ten years ago. He had always been quick with liberal attitudes and a broad spectrum but that was not what she needed now. She needed specific advice. It was now four months since Gerry had come home from that nursing home; he had not earned one penny from his trade of photography. To complain about that seemed untimely and ungracious because after all, the man had not touched one drop of alcohol either. There was no point in going to the nursing home and asking the doctors. They had asked her to be cooperative and not to boss him around. She thought that she was doing that part of it. But Lord God, how long would it go on? Already the small debts were building up—

paradoxically more frightening than when he had been drinking and the bill from the off-license would arrive. Those drink bills had a terrifying unreality about them. Today's bills, high telephone charges, photography equipment, printing costs, expensive cuts of meat, they had a ring of permanency. And what Emma wanted to know was how long to go on. How long did the ego have to be flattered, the image of self restored? How soon, in other words, could she tell him that there was a job going in a photography studio in town, a very down-market photography job for the great Gerry Moore, but she knew the man who ran it needed an assistant? Did she dare yet tell Gerry, suggest it to him, say that it would be a good idea for a year or two and he could build up his contacts after work? No, it must be too soon, otherwise why would she feel sick at the stomach even thinking about it?

That September they went to a wedding. They didn't know the people well and in fact they were rather surprised at the invitation. When they got there and discovered that they were among four hundred people it became clear that the net had been spread fairly wide. It was a lavish do and there was no effort spared to see that the guests had a good time.

"Isn't it marvelous to give two kids a send-off like this—they'll remember it all their life," Gerry had said. Something about the way he spoke made Emma look up sharply from her plate of smoked salmon. She stared at his glass. He was drinking champagne. She felt the blood go out of her face.

"It's only a little champagne for a wedding," he said. "Please. Please, Emma, don't give me a lecture, don't start to tell me it's the beginning of the end."

"Gerry," she gasped at him.

"Look, it's a wedding. I don't know people, I'm not relaxed, I'm not able to talk to them. Just three or four glasses and that's it. It's all *right* tomorrow it's back to the everyday business of drying out."

"I beg you—" she said. He had held his glass out to a passing waiter.

"What do you beg me?" His voice had turned hard and the edge of it, the cutting edge, had a sneer as well. "What could you possibly beg from me, you who have everything?"

His voice was loud now and people were beginning to look at them. Emma felt the kind of dread and panic that she used to know as a child when she was at the carnival. She hated the carnival each year—the bumpers, the chairoplane, and the ghost train. Most of all she hated the helter-skelter, and this is what it felt like now. Fast and furious and not knowing what lay ahead.

"Could we go home, do you think?" she asked faintly.

"It's only beginning," he said.

"Please, Gerry, I'll give you anything."

"Will you give me champagne, and fun and a bit of a laugh? No, you'll give me a lecture and a flood of tears and then if I'm very good a piece of shepherd's pie."

"No."

"What, no shepherd's pie? Oh, that settles it, I'll have to stay here."

She whispered, "But the whole life, the plans . . . the plans. Gerry, you've been so good, God Almighty, five months and not a drop. If you were going to have a drink, why here, why at this place, why not with friends?"

"I haven't any friends," he said.

"Neither have I," she said seriously. "I was thinking that not long ago."

"So." He kissed her on the cheek. "I'll go and find us some."

He was sick three times during the night, retching and heaving into the hand basin in their room. Next morning she brought him a pot of tea and a packet of aspirins, half a grapefruit and the *Irish Times*. He took them all weakly. There was a picture of the wedding they had been at, of the young couple. They looked smiling and happy. Emma sat down on the bed and began to pour tea.

"Hey, it's after nine, aren't you going to work?" he asked.

"Not today. I'm taking the day off."

"Won't they fire you? Recession and all that?"

"I don't think so. Not for one day."

"That's the problem hiring married women, isn't it, they have to stay at home and look after their babies?"

"Gerry."

"You told them you'd no babies, but still here you are staying at home looking after one."

"Stop it, have your tea."

His shoulders were shaking. His head was in his hands. "Oh, God, I'm sorry, poor poor Emma, I'm sorry. I'm so ashamed."

"Stop now, drink your tea."

"What did I do?"

"We won't talk about it now while you feel so rotten. Come on."

"I must know."

"No worse than before, you know."

"What?"

"Oh, it's hard to describe, general carry-on, a bit of singing. A bit of telling them that you had had the cure and you could cope with drink now; a servant, not a master—"

"Jesus."

They were silent, both of them.

"Go to work, Emma, please."

"No. It's all right, I tell you."

"Why are you staying at home?"

"To look after you," she said simply.

"To do sentry duty," he said sadly.

"No, of course not. It's your decision, you know that well. I can't be a jailer. I don't want to be."

He took her hand. "I'm very, very sorry."

"It doesn't matter."

"It does. I just want you to get inside my head. Everything was so drab and hard and relentless.

Same old thing. Dear Johnny, I don't know whether you remember my work. Dear Freddie. Dear Everybody."

"Shush, stop."

"No, thanks, I'll have a Perrier water, no, thanks, I don't drink, no, seriously, I'd prefer a soft drink, nothing anywhere, nothing, nothing. Do you blame me for trying to color it up a bit, just once, with somebody else's champagne? Do you? Do you?"

"No, I don't. I didn't realize it was so gray for you. Is it all the time?"

"All the bloody time, all day, every day."

She went downstairs then and sat in the kitchen. She sat at the kitchen table and decided that she would leave him. Not now, of course, not today, not even this year. She would wait until Helen's fourteenth birthday perhaps, in June. Paul would be sixteen, nearly seventeen then. They would be well able to decide for themselves what to do. She made herself a cup of instant coffee and stirred it thoughtfully. The trouble about most people leaving home is that they do it on impulse. She wouldn't do that. She'd give herself plenty of time and do it right. She would find a job first, a good job. It was a pity about RTE, but it was too close, too near, in every sense. She could rise there and get on if she had only herself to think of. But no, of course not, she had to get away. Maybe London, or some other part of Dublin anyway, not on her own doorstep. It would cause too much excitement.

She heard him upstairs brushing his teeth. She knew that he would go out for a drink this morning. There was no way she could play sentry. Suppose he said he wanted to go out and buy something; she could offer to get it for him, but he would think up a job that he could only do himself.

There were maybe another thirty-five or forty years to go. She couldn't spend them with her heart all tied up in a ball like a clenched fist. She could not spend those years half-waking, half-sleeping in an armchair, wondering how they would bring him in. And even more frightening was sitting watching and waiting in case he broke out, the watching and waiting of the last five months. She would be blamed, of course—selfish, heartless, no sense of her duty. Could you believe that anyone would do it? Emma believed that quite a lot of people could do it, and would if the occasion presented itself, or if the situation was as bad at home as hers was.

She heard Gerry come downstairs.

"I brought down the tray," he said like a child expecting to be praised.

"Oh, that's grand, thanks." She took it from him. He hadn't touched the grapefruit, nor the tea.

"Look, I'm fine. Why don't you go into work? Seriously, Emma, you'd only be half an hour late."

"Well, I might, if you're sure—"

"No, I'm in great shape now," he said.

"What are you going to do this morning, follow up some of those letters?"

"Yes, yes." He was impatient.

"I might go in." She stood up. His face was pure relief.

"Do. You'd feel better. I know you and your funny ways."

"Listen before I go. There's a job going in Paddy's business, only an assistant at the moment, but if you were interested he said that he'd be delighted for you to come in, for a year or two, say, until you got yourself straight." She looked at him hopefully.

He looked back restlessly. He didn't know that so much of his future and hers rested on the reply he gave.

"An assistant? A dogsbody to Paddy, Paddy of all people. Jesus, he must be mad to suggest it. He only suggested it so that he could crow. I wouldn't touch it with a barge pole."

"Right. I just thought you should know."

"Oh, I'm not saying a word against you, it's that eejit Paddy."

"Well, take it easy."

"You're very good to me, not giving out, not telling me what an utter fool I made of myself, of both of us."

"There's no point."

"I'll make it up to you. Listen, I have to go into town for a couple of things this morning, is there anything you—?"

She shook her head wordlessly and went to the

garage to take out her bicycle. She wheeled it to the gate and looked back and waved. It didn't matter that people would blame her. They blamed her already. A man doesn't drink like that unless there's something very wrong with his marriage. In a way her leaving would give Gerry more dignity. People would say that the poor divil must have had a lot to put up with over the years.